A YEAR WITH
GRACE

Published under licence by Brown Dog Books and
The Self-Publishing Partnership Ltd, 10b Greenway Farm, Bath Rd, Wick, nr. Bath BS30 5RL

www.selfpublishingpartnership.co.uk

ISBN printed book: 978-1-83952-472-1
ISBN e-book: 978-1-83952-473-8

Cover design by Kevin Rylands
Internal design by Andrew Easton

Printed and bound in the UK
This book is printed on FSC certified paper

FSC

MIX
Paper from
responsible sources
www.fsc.org FSC® C013604

A YEAR WITH
GRACE

LEWIS HUNT

BROWN DOG BOOKS

This intimate tale of tangled emotions is based upon real lives. Set in the green heart of Yorkshire's East Riding, it is a tale of hope and optimism in the face of adversity.

We all have secrets. Harry's secrets are hidden so deeply that he does not even know what they are. It would take someone or something special to enable him to unravel the conundrum of his life. Grace, though delicate, is special.

For a while, their lives are in tandem. Harry brings happiness and stability into a young girl's life: or is it the other way round?

For my boys.

AT THE HOCKNEY EXHIBITION LAST YEAR

The white-haired couple stood like two snowdrops in a wood before the huge painting. Their heads bobbed like delicate blooms in a breeze as their eyes struggled to take in the dimensions of the work before them. They had known of this exhibition for years, but it had taken them until now to gather the courage to confront it.

In truth, the couple had been at first just a little affronted and confused: many of the paintings were far brasher and brighter than their own memories of this countryside kept so assiduously over the years. But soon they had managed to assimilate and accept the painter's own interpretation and style – he was, after all, considered by many to be the country's greatest living artist – so that the art was soon able to work its evocative magic upon their awakening senses.

They had moved carefully and patiently through the exhibition, silent but appreciative of each other's presence. She had settled her elegant, though slightly stiffened, figure patiently beside him as his eyes and emotions had lingered longingly for some time over the composition of 'The Road Across the Wolds', but then they had moved methodically onwards to complete their scrutiny of the exhibition.

At last, they had reached the largest painting: a monumental work made up, in fact, by fifty smaller canvasses. And, though they had not realised it before, it had always been this particular picture that they had been longing to see.

It held their gaze, though his eyes were soon drifting past the dominant *tree and through the woodland to the spaces beyond, as if the horizon had always held more promise. Despite the crudity of some brushstrokes, her eyes carefully caressed the limbs and trunks of the trees before her as if something, or even someone, might eventually emerge from behind them. The eager mind behind pale eyes soon examined her memory with equal care as if in hope that she might spot some detail that could have somehow changed the outcome of those times.*

They had no need of speech. The picture said it all. It took them back to that time and that place with the one who was so dear to their memories.

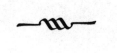

THE LAST WEEK OF
FEBRUARY

Loneliness rested upon the shoulders of the solitary beach walker almost as visibly as his stark blue rucksack. Dropping the bag to the cold paving, he leaned wearily into the promenade railings and sighed deeply. He knew that he had missed his chance.

In February the light changes so quickly.

He had set off in afternoon sunshine so bright that it had hurt his eyes. But then, little more than two hours later, it had dimmed so abruptly that the day had felt almost over. The sea had darkened to blackness and the sky slipped to crepuscular gloom.

Tugging his battered, similarly blue hat more tightly onto his head, he returned his gaze to the seascape before him. The light was not the only thing to have changed so dramatically: the broad swathe of sand and shingle along which he had set out in such brilliant sunshine has been devoured so voraciously by the inrushing tide that only a pale, thin strip remained to separate land from sea. He looked back along the beach as if to recall the warmth of the sunny afternoon and, sadly, of the opportunity lost.

The fascination of the water held his attention for so long that he was suddenly surprised to notice that the beam from Flamborough Lighthouse had begun its arcing path across the waves. He shuddered. In truth the sea scared him. He shook his head, glad not to be one of those whose livelihood depended upon spending the night out there.

A glance at his watch warned that he had little time to prepare for his arranged meeting. His exaggerated dalliance at the seafront had resulted, no doubt, from his anxiety about this meeting. It was looming in his mind more heavily than he cared to admit to himself. But he knew the importance of the meeting and of moving on. So, with one last effort of self-determination he turned his back upon the sea, pulled his bag up onto his shoulders and headed landward into a wind that smelt of rain. Before he had reached his own street, the first cold drops were already falling.

The rain had pattered with increasing relentlessness against the bathroom window while he had stripped to the waist and stood there before a sink full of hot, steamy water. As he had wiped away the condensation, a stranger's face had emerged to stare back. It had been so long since he had contemplated his own reflection with any seriousness that he had been almost surprised to be confronted with a thick beard that had grown without him really noticing. He had begun his shave with hope that the man emerging from beneath the unruly growth might in some way be more assured, but as he stepped out into the street twenty minutes later he was as anxious as ever.

Heavy rain still slanted through the bare branches of the trees lining each side of Scarborough Avenue. He felt into his pocket for the tiny scrap of paper upon which he had written the address of his assignation, already knowing it perfectly well, but checking anyway.

Bede House.

Looking up he could see that it was the house with the tower: he had guessed all along that it would have been that one. The paper scrap had soon become sodden, so he stuffed it back into his pocket and walked to the door. Then, pushing in the button of an old, brass bellpush and listening to its chimes echoing within, he looked up to a small window above the door. It seemed to stare down like an all-seeing eye, and he began to feel uncertain. He contemplated flight until, suddenly, the door was opened to flood the steps with light. And to his surprise it was the girl herself who had opened the door. She appeared calm and assured, taking no notice of his own erratic movements as he pulled his hood back to reveal his naked, freshly shaven face.

'Hello. What's your name?'

'Harry,' he told her instantly before recoiling at the ineptitude of stating his surname.

'You look wet, Harry. You had better come in.'

The hall was clean, well-polished and rather bare. Besides a plain table there was a stand holding a small collection of old walking sticks and on the wall a single painting. It was of a middle-aged man, formally dressed and unsmiling. Drops of water from Harry's saturated duffle coat were dripping onto the polished floor, making him feel like a wet nuisance with no right to be there. But the girl was disappearing through to another room, so he quickly followed.

The next room was large, though equally sparse in its furnishing and lack of ornamentation. The girl motioned him towards one of the two leather settees that faced each other there.

'Would you like tea?'

He nodded in response, not really knowing whether he wanted tea or not, but simply succumbing to her pleasant invitation. As soon as the girl had left he removed his coat and folded it inwards to contain the dampness before placing it on the floor so that it did not mark the settee. He began to relax, just enough to notice the Persian rug that lay between the two settees. Its colours were quiet, but the design and weave were, even to his inexpert eyes, exquisite. Just as the sea had done earlier, he allowed the subtle shades and patterns of the rug to absorb his attention completely until the girl returned to sit opposite.

'Maude is bringing tea,' she informed him. Then she just sat and smiled. Harry smiled back. The situation was calling out for light, sophisticated conversation, but all he could manage was a nervous smile. He began to feel that he had made a mistake in coming. It crossed his mind that he had made some pretty big mistakes in the recent past and he did not feel well equipped to deal with another. His eyes and mind searched around for some easy means of escape, though none was immediately apparent. Instead, he finally managed to speak.

'Listen. My name is David ... well, it's Harry as well! That's my surname ... I'm David Harry ... Mr Harry ...'

He stopped. The girl was still looking and smiling, but he could tell that she had stopped listening. She was just looking and smiling. There was no intensity or threat to her stare, however. There was something not quite right about it, but it was an agreeable smile nonetheless and he began to relax. He smiled back, which seemed to encourage her.

'It's my birthday on Friday!' she announced.

'Oh, really? How old will you be?'

'I'll be sixteen ... Maude says I'm only four! ... It's a trick!' she added, suppressing a laugh.

Harry thought that perhaps she had meant riddle rather than trick, but he guessed the root of it anyway. He had a friend from childhood in the same situation, who had been full of quirkiness; like having one green eye and one brown one. He checked the girl's eyes quickly. They were both the same colour: such a startlingly pale blue that he was surprised that he had not noticed them earlier.

'Now let me see,' he mused, returning to the riddle, ' ... what date is it on Friday?'

'Oh, you know it! You know it! Tell me what it is!' she laughed.

'Now let me see ...' he repeated, twisting his face in contorted concentration and making her wait. He was enjoying the game, enjoying the control. The thought surprised him, though really it should not have.

'I think it could be ... though it's only a guess ... it might possibly be ... that your birthday is on ... February the twenty-ninth!'

The girl was rocking back in delight, her laughter falling gently and happily upon Harry's ears so that for the while he felt almost like his old self. But then, abruptly, an old woman came into the room carrying a heavily laden tray. The tray was silver. She was dressed in black. She looked like a waitress, a very old waitress. Harry got to his feet.

'Hello, I'm David Harry. I've come about the position ...'

But Maude, he guessed it must have been her, did not respond. She placed the tray on a small table beside the settee and straightway withdrew from the room without a single word, leaving Harry once more hesitant and uncertain. The girl came to his rescue.

'I can pour,' she said, lifting the teapot. Her hold was awkward and somewhat shaky, however, so Harry soon took over.

'I like to pour,' he insisted. 'Would you like to do the milk?'

'Is she a servant? Perhaps she's your grandmother.'

'No. I don't think so. She might be ... she's Maude.'

'And you are?'

'Grace.'

There were biscuits on the tray, and an envelope as well. Harry ignored the envelope until they had both munched a couple of biscuits and the tea had cooled enough to be drunk. Then he picked it up. The front was addressed to 'Whomever it might concern'. Harry assumed that it meant him, so he soon tore open the expensive-looking stationery. The note inside made a brief apology before inviting the recipient to return to the house between 6.00 and 7.00 pm on any day of the next week to speak to Mrs Hall. There was no telephone number.

For some reason, the letter seriously spooked Harry, and his building confidence was instantly smashed down by a rush of insecurity. He began to sweat. He looked at his watch, which showed him that it was only a minute or two before six. Should he stay or should he go? The writer of the letter would be returning soon. She was bound to see the cups on the tray. He edged to the front of his seat, wondering which way to jump. These days, even such small decisions filled him with indecision and helplessness.

'For God's sake don't get worked up about nothing!' he screamed inside his own head. But it was not working. He was losing control. The girl was still smiling at him. She seemed unaware of his inner turmoil. He managed a smile back. It relaxed him just a little.

'I'll come back later!' he managed to wrest out with just a semblance of being a mature adult.

'Yes, alright … if you like,' the girl was saying pleasantly.

But Harry had already picked up his wet duffle and was heading for the hallway in some haste. He reached the door and had just grasped the handle when the bell rang. Panic. He jumped back in surprise before recovering to open the door.

It revealed a woman in the still falling rain. A coat was draped over her shoulders in an attempt to shelter the collection of folders that were cradled between her arms. The frown on her forehead deepened as she saw Harry.

'Who are you? What are you doing in my house?'

Several responses came into his mind, though he stood frozen, unable to deliver any one of them. The folders within the woman's arms were in danger of falling. Harry thought to put out his own arms to help, but succeeded only in presenting his own wet duffle coat to the struggling woman. Ignoring his incompetent efforts, she brushed past to deposit the folders upon the hall table where they spread out in a fan as if she had been an expert card dealer. She turned, perhaps angrily, towards the hapless visitor and again demanded to know what he was doing in her house.

For some reason, this request presented itself as far too difficult for Harry to manage. Losing all sense of calm or dignity, it was all he could manage to shout, 'I'll come back later!' over his shoulder as he made his escape out of the house and back into the wet darkness.

Back at the cottage Harry forced himself through a succession of simple tasks: taking off his wet clothes; standing beneath his powerful shower, which always seemed to calm him; and getting dressed again. He was even able to congratulate himself on having a clean, ironed shirt to put on. As he pulled it over his head the smell momentarily reminded him of his mother, though he did not know why.

Then there was nothing left but the grind of his own thoughts. He tortured himself with a re-run of his flight from the house and was at least able to console himself with having not collapsed completely, which was progress of a kind for him.

It was still less than a year since he had collapsed completely and the reminders of the incarcerating depression, into which he had then descended, were never far away. He allowed himself to think about it for a while. He could clearly remember his break-up with Marianne, fragments of their bitter rows. It was still too vivid, but remembering exactly the details of that time of his acute depression was more difficult. He had no more than a few indistinct images of it, like sepia frames from an old movie.

Comfort food was one of Harry's coping strategies. There was an old gas range in the cottage, not quite as posh as an Aga, but functional and warm. He sat beside it as two slices of bread quickly toasted on one of its hobs. A spread of buttered toast soothed him considerably.

Then, even though it was still quite early, Harry retired to his bed. Sleep was another of his coping strategies. As usual, he closed his eyes and began to paint in his mind's eye. It was a seascape with a lighthouse in the background. Soon he slept.

Morning dawned cool and grey, though dry. Harry thought about visiting his good friend, Moses, but decided that it would be better to walk first so that he could clear his thinking before confronting his old friend with his troubles. More toast for breakfast and then he was soon down beside the sea: at his favourite seat, an old, upturned boat hull left forlornly outside the yacht club fence on the clifftop.

Harry had only been to the sea once in all his youth and childhood. It had been a primary school day trip to Clevedon, which he still remembered on account of the terrible sunburn that he had suffered following a very sunny day there without his shirt on. Now that he resided less than a mile from the sea, he was drawn there on most days.

It was unspectacular coastline, but he liked it.

They called it the Holderness: a long stretch of glacial clay stretching down from the chalk hills above Bridlington all the way to Spurn Point on the Humber. Sadly, its soft, clay cliffs lay hopelessly defenceless to the sea's incessant erosion, so that each year a whole swathe of land as wide as a country road fell into the sea to be completely washed away.

'Why, they's whole villages alyin' out there beneath them waves,' Moses had told him more than once.

Harry smiled wryly to himself at the irony. Here he was, trying to establish some semblance of stability in his life, living on land that was, before long, likely to fall from beneath his very feet and into the sea. Too soon, however, his face regained its more accustomed aspect of placid loneliness and his thoughts returned to machinations of his self-perceived failure.

Most of what he knew about his recent depression was, in fact, not from his own memories, but from those of his old friend and mentor, Howard. Apart from doctors and nurses, Old Howard had been the only person who had really talked to him about it. Everyone else had been unwilling or unable to confront the sudden change and deterioration in his behaviour. Harry had always accepted having brought the problems leading to his breakdown upon himself, but he still thought it unfair that so many of his old friends had disappeared so quickly in the time of his greatest need.

Almost thirty years previously he had been Howard's protégé, the young, up-and-coming art teacher, and Old Howard had quietly been there for him ever since, even though they were clearly an 'odd couple' together.

During his months of depression Old Howard had remained sympathetic but challenging, so that finally he had been able to help Harry emerge from his darkness. At first it had been walks: 'You can't sit around here moping all day,' Howard had urged. Then it was Howard's painting expeditions. Howard had always encouraged him with painting: 'Paint what you feel,' he used to tell him. Next Howard had forced his old bike upon him: 'Get some bloody exercise. It'll do you good!' Part of Harry had wanted to tell Old Howard to bugger off and leave him alone, but a better, saner part of his brain had been happy to let the old friend push him up out of the miserable cell of his depression and back towards a more normal life: at least as normal as it could be after losing his wife and his job.

One day Old Howard had said, 'What you need is a holiday!'

He had persuaded Harry that it would even be a favour to him for the protégé to capture the wild spaces of the old man's youth in paintings. 'You can bring it all back to me in paintings. I'm too bloody old to ride a bike anymore, but you can do it for me!'

Although he could have easily countered Old Howard's arguments, Harry had allowed his friend to arrange a stay away in East Yorkshire with someone who the old mentor was sure would look after him 'right and proper!' Old Howard had then put him on a train to York with his bike and instructions on how to reach the friend on the east coast.

Harry looked back upon it as a minor miracle that he had been able to cycle out of the station in the middle of that old but busy city and make his way around the teeming ring road, through the suburbs, and out towards the coast.

Mostly that journey had remained in his mind like a dark dream, cycling in a panic of self-preservation across those miles of tarmac like a chased animal.

He could, strangely, think back with some pleasure to recall just one clear cameo of peacefulness amongst all the cloudy darkness in his memory. It had been as he had reached the summit of the steep climb up onto the Wolds. He could not recall whether it was mental or physical exhaustion that had made him stop during his stricken flight to lay down away from the road, but something had made him stop, lay down his bike and do so. Both his heart and mind had been racing like crazy, but then, slowly, he had been able to calm down and begin to absorb his surroundings. He could remember the depth of the blue above him and the prickle of rough grass into his back. Gradually he had been able to stand and look around across the miles and miles of peaceful emptiness that makes up most of the Wolds. And seeing that great patchwork of yellows, greens and browns stretching out across the rolling hills had been an awakening for him. He remembered wanting to capture it on canvas so that he could send it back to Old Howard.

Moving on, not just from the Wolds that day, but through all the days since, had been difficult, but made possible by Howard's friend, Moses. 'You can use my ol' 'oliday cottage,' Moses had told him in his own frank way. 'Got no bookings right now.'

Looking back over the past six months, Harry could see that Moses had been his saviour: not in an overt way like Old Howard, but in his own plainer manner, like providing simple jobs that he 'needed a 'and with' to force Harry out of physical inertia.

Late summer had passed into autumn and then on to the start of the new year and Harry had remained. There had been nothing to which he wanted to return and so he had stayed.

Some days he had helped Moses with his simple gardening jobs, and though on some days he still did nothing, he gradually made more excursions out into the countryside or along the coast on the old bike. On rare days he even managed to put paint to canvas. His early attempts disappointed him to the point of anger, but gradually they had become something that he considered as almost worthwhile. He still hadn't produced a painting that he thought was worthy of sending to Old Howard, but the aspiration kept him going.

*

'Well, you're a lucky soul, a'lying there and daydreaming!'

Harry looked up to see that it had been an old woman with a springer spaniel passing by who had broken him from his reverie. It sounded as if she had said it with a smile.

'Yes, I guess I am. I was just ...' But woman, smile and the dog were already disappearing down the gulley where the tractor towed the sailing boats down to the sea, and Harry was left to address his remarks simply to himself. However, simple and random as it had been, the brief social exchange had left Harry in better humour: more resolved even. Despite everything, Harry knew that he should return, that evening, to Bede House, as the building with the tower was named. He realised that there were few chances for him to move forward and that this was one he should not miss.

Later, standing in the security of his own shower, Harry had rehearsed in his mind all the steps required for him to confront the woman at Bede House. His planning had worked well so far as walking up the path and ringing the bell, but as the door began to open his courage wavered. In an instant the woman was there, silhouetted against the bright light of the hallway. He hesitated like a child at the dentist, but it was too late to retreat. Then, thankfully, his preparation paid off and, as if from somewhere outside his own body, he heard a quiet but steady voice say, 'Good evening. I hope you will excuse me for having left so abruptly yesterday, but my name is David Harry and I have come about the position.'

Mrs Hall invited him in by way of gesture and he followed her through the hallway and into the same position on the settee that he had taken with the girl. As his eyes sought comfort from the patterns of the Persian rug, he wished that the girl had been there too, but she was not in attendance. Instead, he lifted his gaze away from the intricacies of the rug to meet another pair of equally pale, blue eyes, though this pair offered none of the warmth or welcome that had been present in the girl's.

Harry was relieved that the woman had made no reference to the previous debacle at the front door, but he was slightly startled by her questioning that began without any of the usual preliminaries.

'I presume that you are properly qualified and experienced. You do not appear to have brought anything with you.'

'No. I left all that behind.'

'What? Behind? Behind where? Where are you working now?'

The interview had begun badly and had not improved throughout the twenty minutes or so that followed. At the end he was pleased to have simply survived the ordeal, but he left feeling dissected and exposed.

It had been a relief to escape the house, but on his walk home anger had risen within him. Ignoring lights, he had climbed the stairs to stand in darkness before his bedroom window where he gazed into the darkness outside. It had stopped raining, but the cold moon in the clearing sky offered no release to his shaking anger. After a while, however, it finally subsided. He was able to lay down on the bed. Then, still wearing the 'best clothes' that he had selected for the interview, he pulled the thick quilt over himself and fell asleep even before he had opened his imaginary paint box.

In the cold light of the next morning, he had been able to reflect that the absence of appropriate paperwork, his current state of underemployment, and his general lack of clear intentions had not helped him to present himself as the experienced and capable professional that he had once been. He argued to himself that he had been expecting no more than a gentle conversation and the opportunity to establish mutual understanding, rather than the harsh cross-examination that he had undergone. Though he could not rid himself completely from his feelings of inadequacy and defeat, beneath the shower, Harry was able to console himself with having not completely gone to pieces. It had been, he concluded inside his mind, a chance lost, though, paradoxically, perhaps a step forward too.

'Perhaps it's all for the best,' he muttered, though the reflection in the mirror looked unconvinced and he turned away, unable to cope with the contemplation of his own face any longer. He was poor at consoling himself, so he was likely to spend the rest of the day hiding in the cottage to swirl the meagreness of his performance tormentingly around in his head.

Thankfully, it was not too long that morning before Moses appeared. Moses made a habit of popping up when he was most needed. Harry knew well that without Moses' support it would have been impossible to have come through the previous six months. Moses had welcomed Harry into his bucolic lifestyle and made him feel at least a little useful in helping with everyday tasks and the myriad of little favours he performed for a host of old friends and neighbours. Though Moses liked to chide Harry over his inadequacies – 'If a job's wo'th doin', it's wo'th doin' well,' was his favourite saying – his touch was both gentle and benevolent, like a kindly uncle.

Harry allowed Moses to lead him out to the cottage's vegetable patch, which, Moses had assured him, needed turning over so that there was still time for tomorrow's expected frost to break up the soil nicely. Once they had settled to the rhythm of digging, the old man began, as usual, to warmly ruffle Harry's composure with playful wit.

Grace hesitated at the doorway. Her day had started early and happily. She had opened her presents with Mummy before her mother had left for work and had been still flushed pink with joy and excitement as she had reached the threshold, but there all that happiness had disappeared as she had contemplated another day at her new school. Before she was able to react decisively, however, Maude had arrived to fuss her through the door and out into the new day.

The world before her felt cold and appeared strangely white. As she moved haltingly down the pathway, the sun's first weak rays edged over the top of the roof to fall upon the soft fabric of her smart, new coat and upon the neat posy of white flowers that she carried in her tightly clenched hand. Maude had picked the flowers, just as she had picked them every year on Grace's birthday, and Mummy had suggested that Grace should take the flowers to school to share with her class. Grace stared at the flowers and at the soft faux rabbit fur that edged the cuffs of her new coat. Mummy had carefully told her that it was not real fur but it was just as soft and cuddly as baby rabbits. She put one cuff against her cheek just for comfort, but the tips of the flowers had tickled and, anyway, before she could really savour the touch, Maude was hastening her down the frosty path and off to school. Maude always took her to school, though by now she was trusted to find her own way home.

The walk to school had passed quite dreamily along the avenue of frost-covered trees, but as they reached the entrance to the playground Grace's spirits sank. She did not know why it was called a playground since no-one ever played there; not properly anyway. Ignoring Maude, she picked her way forward between the pools of boisterous students to avoid any contact or friction, but then the shrill of a loud whistle split the air and she was instantly caught up in one of the streams of humanity that were being sucked into the building like coffee grounds being poured into a drain.

And so another day of trial and confusion began for her. She did not like her new school. It was so frightening and unlike her old, little school where she had learned to pass the days safely. Here she faced a whole catalogue of fresh puzzles and problems each day. She had learned to face them simply with a smile. Sometimes she felt like lashing out with claws like a wildcat, but she knew that this would only bring more trouble and anguish in the long run, so she just smiled, knowing that if she smiled long enough then whatever confronted her would sooner or later go away. She cried about it all at home, but Mummy had said that there was no other way and that she would simply have to learn to swim in the mainstream. For Grace, each day felt more like drowning than swimming.

Outside, no-one had noticed the formerly neat posy of snowdrops that had fallen from a startled hand to be trampled under the wave of adolescent feet. Just one single bloom had survived intact to nod in the breeze that whispered across the empty playground. Survived, that is, until the start of break time, when an exuberant foot had soon booted it into oblivion. Such delicate flowers are destined not to last too long.

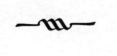

MARCH

The final two days of February had been particularly bleak, which had not seemed completely unhelpful to Harry since he felt that the cold had, to an extent, numbed the sense of melancholy that had fallen across his shoulders since his hapless interview at Bede House.

Now, as if pre-arranged on the calendar, March had drifted in on a wave of softer and milder air. There had even been a hint of sun to encourage Harry out into the garden. He wandered up to the massive, old ash tree that dominated the far end of the garden and was lifted to discover snowdrops nestled in the dark soil between the roots. At first he thought to pick them, but then decided rather to leave them to be beautiful in their own place. Though he was cheered by them, the flowers still stabbed his senses with some remorse that his winter had passed so emptily.

As if to make up for lost time, Harry bent his back into several minor tasks in the garden. As he busied himself with absent-mindedly raking up the midden and wind-blown debris, he forced his mind to remember some moments from the winter past. He could recall sweeping up the leaves then and how he had been filled with the desire to burn them all up, until Moses had cautioned him to leave them so that they could, in time, return their goodness to the soil. He remembered mostly how Moses had kept him busy, whenever possible, with all types of manual work, and he recognised the old man's transparent wisdom. He remembered also complaining to the old man about the cold, though there had been little response since Moses, it seemed, was impervious to whatever the winter threw at him. Nothing, it seemed, could bother Moses' sturdy frame: certainly not rain, nor frost, nor wind off the North Sea that made Harry count the minutes until the next cup of tea took them inside.

After raking, Harry could not think of much to do except clean up the riot of now redundant canes and pots that filled the greenhouse. He leant against the fence to begin his reveries once more, until—

'You haven't got many flowers!' broke the silence.

His mind struggled for a few seconds to break away from his thoughts until his own eyes managed to recognise the familiarity of the pale blue ones that they now beheld.

'You have not got many flowers!' Grace repeated, emphasising each word in order to overcome Harry's apparent inertia and lack of understanding.

'There are snowdrops,' Harry offered finally.

'Can I see them?'

A minute later she was crouched beside Harry to inspect them. Just as he had done, she lifted the heads to look inside the globular, white blooms.

'They're lovely ... but a little bit sad really, aren't they? I had some, but I lost them.'

'Would you like a cup of tea?' Harry asked her cheerily, repaying some of the kindness that she had shown him at their first meeting.

They sat on the bench at the back of the cottage to enjoy the warmth of the tea and the pale sunlight. The conversation was thin, but each of them smiled a lot and they felt comfortable despite the edge of coldness that descended with the lateness of the day. Harry noted the new coat, the gloves and the hat. They looked expensive, though, even to his undiscerning eye, somewhat old fashioned as well.

'You look like you are dressed up for a long walk!'

'I got lost,' she said with a laugh. But it was a hollow laugh and tears appeared in the corners of each pale eye. Soon one ran down her cheek to drop off her chin.

'Don't cry … you're nearly on your own street!'

'Am I?' she smiled through the tears. 'I saw you in the garden.' She laughed again. And then she cried.

'Don't worry … I'll take you home.'

Harry walked the few streets to her house. Grace held onto his hand, which made him smile and he felt somehow warmer inside. Apart from the regular sniffing, Grace remained silent. Harry wished that he had had some tissues in his pocket: he had always carried some at school, but had since fallen out of that habit.

'Here we are,' said Harry as they reached the gate.

'Ah, yes,' she chirped, 'would you like to come in for tea?' The sight of her house appeared to trigger an automatic response of politeness and civility in her, but Harry declined.

'Oh, I almost forgot!' Harry called as she began to move away. 'Put your hands out.'

And he dropped a small bunch of snowy white blooms into her palms. She beamed a smile at him over her shoulder as she made for the front door, which opened before she had reached it, and there was the old woman to shepherd her in without comment.

Harry turned around from the closed door and walked home. It had been an unusual but pleasant encounter and retrospectively he appreciated the unexpected interruption into his day.

Back at the cottage he built up a raging fire in his stove and sat before its spreading warmth. He thought about writing a letter to

Old Howard, but so little had occurred since his previous one and he did not want to explain about the events of the past couple of days. He wished he could have written to Marianne, but he knew that she would not have thanked him for it.

Out of nowhere there was a sudden knocking. At first Harry could not think from just where it was coming. Then he realised that it was from the knocker on his front door: no-one had ever used it before.

At first the door had refused to open: lack of use had left it stiff in its frame. Harry pulled harder and suddenly it released in a quick jerk that wrenched it abruptly from the hand that was just about to use the knocker again. Harry's visitor stepped back in alarm and self-defence.

'I'm so sorry,' he began, before noticing that there was a light to switch on. The glow revealed to him that it was Mrs Hall, the woman from Bede House.

'I'm so sorry,' he repeated. 'No-one ever knocks ...'

'It's quite alright. I'm fine.'

'No, really ... it must have got stuck!'

'It's quite alright,' she reiterated.

'I must have nearly pulled your hand o—'

'Look!' she cried emphatically, without being able to hide her irritation any longer, 'I am fine. There has been no harm done!' Then, as her composure returned, she added, quite formally it appeared to Harry, 'I've come to thank you for returning my daughter ... it was very kind of you. There are so many strangers and dangerous people out there ... one really doesn't know sometimes ... I can't imagine what Maude was doing, letting Grace wander off like that. She's not always easy; Grace, I mean ...'

The litany of staccato statements stopped. It was as if she had already said too much. She turned her troubled eyes on Harry, searching, it seemed to him, for understanding or even pardon. Harry's affronted feelings melted immediately.

'I was pleased to help ... really ... it was a pleasure. She's a nice girl ... I can imagine that she is not easy sometimes ...' It was his turn to say too much.

'How did you come to ...? I mean, how did she find you?'

'Look!' Harry countered, slightly surprised at the aggression that had risen so quickly within himself. 'She just appeared at the fence ... I showed her the snowdrops, that's all ... I didn't know she was lost until she told me. She was upset and we had a cup of tea ... that's all! Anyway,' he countered, 'why wasn't she at school?'

'It's Saturday!'

'Oh, yeah. Of course ...' Harry cringed inwardly, and probably outwardly too. It would have served no real purpose to have explained to the woman how, for him, one day just ran into another. The error, though, had served to dissolve his aggression and confidence. He just stood there in awkwardness and silence.

It was the woman's turn to break the tension. 'Well, thank you so much for your help and kindness,' she offered, extending her hand towards him. He took it and shook it intently. Her hand felt small, though the grip was surprisingly firm. It was like shaking hands with another man: well, perhaps not quite. He watched her walk away until she had disappeared around the corner.

'Yeah, no problems. Any time,' he spilled quietly into the darkness. 'Any time.'

*

Harry finally awoke late into the next morning. For some reason he felt irritable: frustration hung upon his shoulders like a hair shirt. After downing his tea and a plain bowl of cereal he could do little more than simply pace around his kitchen. Then, out of the blue, a small, unexpected seed of inspiration dropped into his mind to penetrate his senses. He determined right away to fetch Old Howard's bike out of the shed: he still called it Howard's bike even though it had unmistakeably been donated to him for perpetuity. Without hesitation or inspection, Harry wheeled the bike out to the road and set off along it at a quite furious pace.

Though late, the morning was misty with what Moses called 'sea rorke': a blanket of air that, quite often in those parts, drifted in from the relative warmth of the overnight sea to condense into fog upon the coldness of the coastal strip. A misty Sunday morning and the road was almost completely empty of traffic so that there were no obstructions to Harry's progress northwards along the coast road towards Bridlington. At Seawick, however, he turned inland in the hope of finding clearer conditions, but, as he pumped his legs to their maximum along the lattice of quiet lanes that lie inland between the sea and the River Hull, there was no noticeable improvement. The opaqueness of the mist served rather to emphasise the emptiness of the road and, as he pounded along within his own cocoon of mist-wrapped privacy, he began to feel quite elated.

Sadly, the elation was short-lived. The intensity of effort became too much for a body that had not enjoyed regular physical exercise over the past year and, almost without warning, Harry was forced to an inelegant halt. Though he recognised the limits of his fitness, Harry was shocked and almost frightened by the way in which chronic fatigue had wrapped itself so suddenly and completely around his gasping lungs. As dizziness took away his balance, he could do no more than roll as gently as he could manage off the cycle and into an inert heap beside the road.

He lay there trying hard not to vomit as a pounding pulse shook through his body and the tiny amount of air still left in his lungs forced its escape in nauseous retches. As he looked helplessly around the wispy outline of an ecclesiastical building to his side seemed to be reaching out its fingers to grab him up. Despite a sense of panic, his only tactic was to lie as still as possible until things returned to something approaching near to normal. The ground was cold on his back, but that seemed to help and gradually he managed to get his breathing under some degree of control to the point where he could gasp out a quiet and unimaginative 'Oh fuck!' Then he succeeded in sitting up.

'So, you're not dead then!' said an old woman who had tottered out from behind the ruins of Keeling Nunnery with her frisky black and white dog. She stood above him like a magpie inspecting carrion.

'No. Just winded.' At least her timing was good, Harry thought to himself. She did not quite have the aura of an angel of mercy, but he was pleased to see humanity in any form at that moment. But the woman turned away as though finding him recovered had taken away all her interest.

'You didn't ought to be doing that sort of thing at your age!' she threw unkindly over her shoulder as she walked off.

'Oh fuck!' came into his mind again, but he choked that back. 'I'll take it steady going home. You don't need to worry.'

'I won't!' came back firmly from the shadows of the mist.

'Steady' was probably an overstatement of Harry's shaky return back to the cottage. It was still misty when he reached his street. Before heading in on the pathway, he turned to regard the indistinct outline of the buildings around him.

'What am I doing here?' he asked himself, though the challenge of his question was easily defeated by the paucity of better options.

Rather than put the bicycle away, Harry sat on his bench slumped against the cottage wall. He hoped that the pounding inside his head would gradually ease as he sat in reverie trying to assess the value of his present existence now that the familiar boundaries of work and a steady relationship had disappeared. In such a state of tiredness and disappointment, he could have easily descended into deep gloom had his melancholy not been interrupted by the tap, tap, tapping of Moses' stick as the old man came up the path. Moses always carried a shoot of hazel with a peculiar 'v' shaped fork at its head: too short to be a staff, but too long to be a walking stick.

'I aren't stoppin',' the old man announced, using the vernacular of East Yorkshire. 'Thought you might like this,' he added, dropping an envelope onto the bench where Harry was sat. 'It were stuck in ya' front door.'

'Come on in. I was just about to brew up,' Harry invited over his shoulder as he led the way into the cottage. Harry paced around the cottage while Moses sat quietly by. After pouring the boiling water onto the leaves in the pot he sat down, but was then up almost straight away to tend again to the tea-making.

'Settle a while, lad,' the old man soothed. 'Let it brew. You're alwus in such a 'aste.' Moses liked his tea well brewed, 'jus' like treacle,' Harry's mum would have said.

'Bin out on yer bike then?' Moses liked to think that nothing much got past his observation.

'Only got as far as them old ruins ... not far and I was done in!'

'Ah well, stick at it, lad. Anythin' worth 'aving is wo'th workin' fo'.' Moses liked to throw out nuggets of advice: Harry did not enjoy them, though he had to admit that most of what the old man had to say was worth listening to.

'Any road, what's in envelope?'

Harry had been thinking to open the envelope himself but had held back just to tease Moses into having to make a request. He then felt bad about treating him in such an unworthy manner when the old man's support clearly deserved better from him. Harry felt Moses' stare upon his face as his own eyes scanned the contents of the letter inside the envelope.

'It's about some part-time tutoring. This woman up Scarborough Avenue wants her daughter tutoring in the evenings.'

'Well, how come she asked you?' Moses asked with mock nonchalance.

'I've been up there already ... sort of made introductions. We had a chat and now it seems she wants me to go round there again.' Harry's motives for being economical with the truth were not clear to himself: perhaps he did not wish to expose any more of his weaknesses to Moses. He put away the envelope and returned towards the tea-making.

'What's she like then?' Moses broke back in.

'What, the woman?' replied Harry while picking up a spoon.

'No, you barmpot! The daughter, the young girl!'

'Well, I hardly know her yet,' Harry pondered with spoon in the air like an orchestral conductor: there was a sudden lightness in his mood that had been missing for a very long time. 'But, yeah ... she smiles a lot. She seems really nice.'

'Nice! Nice! My ol' English teacher told us not to use "nice". She said it were "overused an' quite inadequate". Least, that's what she used to say.' Moses seemed to disappear for a while into his own reminiscing. 'Any road. You fancy this tutorin' then?'

'Yes, I do,' Harry pondered further. 'The money would help too. I can manage on the bit of pension that they give me, but a bit extra would help. Besides, I think I could make a good job of it.'

'Mek a better job of it than you are wi' that tea! You stir it any more an' that spoon'll disappear!'

'At least it will be strong, Moses ... nice and strong,' Harry replied, emphasising the 'nice' just to tease his old friend.

*

Standing before the door of Bede House for a third time gave Harry a semblance of confidence up until the moment the door opened, and the woman was there to confront him. In that instant he could not remember her name, which immediately threw him into a mild panic. He supposed that confusion must have been written all over his face, but if the woman had noticed, she gave no sign of having done so. 'Mr. Harry! Please come in,' she offered straight away.

Harry followed her in to sit in the same seats as on his previous interview. He was tempted to lose his gaze again within the patterns of the rug, but as she rustled her copy of the interview invitation, Harry's mind was jolted into remembering the woman's name: he could picture it written at the bottom of his invitation in neat copperplate: 'Mrs EM Hall' he remembered. He lifted his eyes to regard her. He thought that the name suited her. It did not take a lot of his imagination to be able to picture her there before him in some elegant, aristocratic attire. Her posture was extremely upright and correct, though there were no rich trimmings: just a pair of single pearls, one on each earlobe. Even from a distance it was clearly apparent from their lustre that the pearls were, indeed, the real thing. Harry was pleased with his own little thoughts and their secrecy brought a smile to his lips. But his smile was short-lived as he was suddenly caught in the crossfire of her first question. Luckily, he was just able to work out what it was that she had said.

'Yes,' he replied, 'I had noticed that she was not quite like most girls of her own age ... but that's fine by me. I mean ... I think she is a very nice girl. I like her ... I ...'

'Yes, Mr Harry, she seems to like you too.'

That made Harry sit up. He had not been expecting anything so positive. He gawped at her almost in disbelief. Then he concentrated on keeping his own eyes firmly upon the pair of very pale and blue ones opposite. In that way he was able to avoid sneaking any more sly appraisals of the rest of the woman's appearance. His previous glimpses had already confirmed that she was, physically at least, very attractive. But he did not want to allow his mind to get at all involved with that, nor did he wish to invade her space. He concentrated upon what she was saying.

'What I mean to say is that Grace has special needs. She was, unfortunately, slightly brain-damaged at birth ... Learning is a slow process for her. There are some things that she does not grasp at all ... She responds well to a firm, but friendly approach. I am concerned that she is supported so that she is able to cope with mainstream schooling and thought that tutoring in the evenings would afford her that necessary support.'

It all came out very formally, as if she had been the girl's psychologist reading from a report rather than her mother. Harry had to suppress a nervous laugh. He nodded and coughed into his hand. It had not been too difficult to guess an outline of the girl's background, and he realised, as sanity returned, that it would not have been easy for Mrs Hall to make her revelations.

'That's fine Mrs Hall. I think I have some understanding of your daughter's needs. I am not an out and out specialist in this area, but as a former head of year, I often got involved with children who had extra needs ... and all sorts of problems. You would not believe some of them ... well, perhaps you would ...' Harry's nervousness returned. He realised that he was talking too much, but did not seem able to stop himself. 'Most kids have some problem or other ... I guess we all do ... I've had a few myself recently ...'

'Yes. I know,' she said simply.

The comment struck Harry like a harpoon.

'What? You know! What do you mean "You know"?' he snapped back furiously.

'I do not mean anything particularly by it,' she countered. 'It's just that I telephoned the school you had mentioned in our last meeting. They said ... I mean he said ... the person I spoke to, the deputy head teacher, I believe ... that you had ...' But she was unable to complete her sentence as Harry burst in upon her sophisticated, clipped tones.

'You mean you went to the school behind my back!' he cried accusingly, feeling exposed and betrayed. He realised he was shouting and stabbing his finger in an extremely ugly way, and the intensity of his venom surprised even himself, but he could not stop. 'You had no bloody right!'

'Of course I had a right!' she struck back. Her own voice had become tinged with anger and aggression, but she immediately choked it back, like a mother confronting a child.

'You had no papers ... no references ... or anything. So, I got in touch with your school ... the one you mentioned. Surely I had that right! You could have been anyone. You could have been anything. For all I knew, you could be ...' But, whatever it had been that she was thinking, she left it unsaid. 'That is why I spoke to your ex- colleague.'

Her point was valid. Harry had to admit that to himself. It still felt underhand somehow, but he then felt rather ridiculous standing there in such an aggressive pose. He sat down. 'Well ... what did he have to say?'

'He simply said that you had had ... an emotional crisis.'

'Oh, an emotional crisis! Is that what he said? Did he have any other personal details to deliver? Any other vital secrets to disclose?' Even before he had finished, Harry could recognise the sad edge of self-pity that had crept into his onslaught.

'He said ...' she began before pausing to collect her breath and composure. 'He said that you were, otherwise, one of the nicest and worthiest men he knew ... at least, before your crisis ...'

A second harpoon crashed into Harry's flank. But this time, the sting of raw emotion was that of kindness and generosity. Strange, well maybe not too strange in his circumstance, that he should be stilled and stunned by a compliment. His eyes watered and his voice crumpled to a whisper.

'He said that? He said that about me, did he?'

'I'll fetch some tea.' Mrs Hall used the opportunity to escape from the room and the spectacle of the broken man before her.

The settee accepted Harry into its secure, comfortable hold: it was a friend after all. Harry reflected upon what had just been said. He had worked with Phil Dowd for years but had never known that the deputy had held him in such high regard. He could recall from his memory not being so generous himself about the deputy: 'If the head is the shepherd of the school, then the deputy is the crook on the end of his staff!' he remembered quipping in the staffroom. He would not have guessed that anyone had such a high opinion of him and he wondered why it felt so raw to discover it now.

And, as he grew calmer, he recognised the validity of Mrs Hall's enquiry to his former school. How could she have known how much he liked kids? How could she have guessed that he was a good teacher? How could she have accepted him just like that? He wondered how much chance there was of her accepting him now. Had he managed to snatch disaster from the jaws of reason yet again?

Mrs Hall re-entered the room with her eyes firmly fixed upon the tray she carried. 'Tea's going to be a bit awkward!' Harry thought to himself. But, to his surprise, she settled opposite, after pouring the tea, to question him about his availability and the terms of his engagement. Harry began to try to express his appreciation that she had been willing to employ him despite his unacceptable behaviour, but she waved it away in saying simply that Grace liked him. It all became rather formal again, but Harry was not unhappy about that.

In the end, stood outside, he reflected with some surprise that they had agreed that he should spend two hours of every weekday evening with the girl, but he was not overly concerned since he had no other clear agenda for that time. They had settled upon a trial period of four weeks, which would coincide with the start of the Easter holidays and the end of term. As Harry walked home he whistled into the darkness. He had not whistled for quite a while and the sound was unsure, just like the mix of emotions he felt inside.

*

'Another fine day for the garden.'

According to Moses every day and every type of weather was beneficial for the garden in one way or another. He stood sideways to the door with his fist around the 'v' in the top of his stick in expectance of Harry's reply.

'What about tea first?' Harry offered, looking at the rain and the dark clouds behind him.

The old man's face showed no surprise, though he gave a snort of mock indignation through the thick growth of hair in his nostrils as he followed Harry in to take one of the two wooden carvers that flanked the stove. His large frame fairly filled the chair's generous capacity. He was too active to become fat, though it was evident that he ate well and, even at an age not far short of eighty, he still carried a physical presence in most company.

They drank the tea, comfortable enough in each other's company not to mind the silences. Moses was trying not to show any emotion on his face, but Harry could tell from his deep sighing that his mind was restless. Their relationship appeared rather lopsided to Harry: Moses seemed to put far more into it than he did. He sometimes wondered why Moses had bothered with someone so emotionally frail and lacking in practical abilities. But, despite the deficit, Harry still toyed with him. The rain had stopped and, though he did not like to be rushed, Moses rarely wasted daylight hours. His lingering was a sure sign that he wanted to talk, but Harry gave no sign of knowing this. At last Moses broke the silence.

''Appen you'll have less time for gardening now you've got all this tutoring work,' he said.

'Oh, I dunno. It's only a couple of hours a day,' Harry told him. 'And I have to say, it's a lot better than I thought. Bit easier helping one nice little girl than a classful of ungrateful, yelling, vicious ... kids.' Harry struggled to complete the sentence. The bitterness was sudden and palpable. It hung in the silence and surprised them both. 'Anyway, it's fine,' he added, trying to move on.

'So, she's a nice little lass then, is she?' said Moses, also keen to move on, but unable to resist the opportunity to emphasise Harry's previous overuse of 'nice' again.

'Yes. She is very ... pleasant. She smiles a lot ... she's very innocent ... always polite.'

'Oh aye, innocent?' said Moses with a touch of intrigue.

'Yeah, innocent. You see ... she's not quite like most kids ... brain damaged at birth. It's funny ... she's not stupid. In some ways she's really normal, but it's as if ... as if she doesn't get the whole picture. You can talk to her like an adult about some things, and then, other things, she doesn't get at all. She seems to live in her own world. It's like ... as if she can see all the bits of the jigsaw, but she can't put them together.'

Harry realised that he must have been giving Moses a really muddled picture, but, in truth, he had not been able to work her out for himself during that first week. She had been able to read quite fluently, but if he asked her simple questions about what she had just read it was as if he was asking her to solve a clue from the *Telegraph* crossword. She was an expert at polite, meaningless small talk, but shuddered to a bewildered halt if questioned about what had happened at school that day. He had known children with degrees of autism or Asperger's in the past, but Grace was not like that. She lived in her own world alright, but it was not as if she wanted to be distant or uncommunicative. She just did not appear to know what was going on around her.

'She seems happy in her little world, but she's vulnerable,' was all he could summon up to conclude.

'Well, what's her name then?'

'Grace.'

'So its Grace then, is it?' he said. 'But from a nice family then?'

Harry could tell that Moses' casual manner was forced: he liked to know about new people in his area.

'Well, I wouldn't say "nice",' Harry told him, partly out of lexical revenge and partly because he was not certain whether he really did like them or not. 'I don't really know them yet. Her mother ... single parent ... her mother ...' He hesitated, since he had not yet sorted out his thoughts about her either. 'She's a good-looking woman ... younger than me. She's a bit ... well, powerful is the word that comes to mind. Bit cold I'd say.'

'Powerful, eh? Well, what's her job then?'

'Dunno,' Harry told him. 'Dunno much, do I?'

Moses did not bother to answer and Harry followed him out into the garden.

*

That night the resident owls disturbed Harry from his sleep with their loud screeching. He woke with a start and realised for the first time since the dark days that he had been dreaming: a woman had emerged from the mist; at first he thought it was Marianne and he called out to her; but when she came to him, it was his mother; 'Hello, Davey,' she had said to him; then she had gone and he had awoken.

After breakfast Harry could still recall the dream. He took out some pastel crayons and placed them before him on the table next to sheets of quality paper. He wanted to recreate the shadowy walls of the old Keeling Nunnery and the feel of the morning there. Several colours sat in his fingertips but they remained suspended above the clean page. He just could not bring himself to use any of them. The images of that misty morning remained elusive to his interpretation.

Harry liked to paint and to draw, but, recognised that he was not brilliant or exceptional. Some people had 'oohed' at his pictures in appreciation, but amongst real artists, and he had known a few, his talents could be seen as pretty ordinary. He enjoyed it and sometimes he could come up with something worthwhile, but brilliant he was not.

It was the first time he had brought himself to the point of drawing or painting for many weeks and he was determined to create something. He eventually persuaded himself into action, allowing his fingers to select and use the pastels almost without thinking. How long he had worked was beyond him: it could have been less than twenty minutes, it could have been two hours. But there was no mistaking the image that stared out from the paper when his hands eventually stopped working. It was a face. It was Marianne's face, sombre in greens, blues and browns, lit by yellow lights in her eyes and on her lips.

Looking for meaning beneath the surface of the lines and colours, he did not know which emotions or memories had touched him most. He felt sad and confused. Whatever he felt for her now, whether guilt or anger, humility or longing, he only knew that he still missed her desperately. If only he could have gone back, he thought to himself.

He stared out into the garden. For some reason birds had gathered in the topmost branches of the ash tree, gradually and in small groups until there must have been more than a hundred. From a distance they looked like big, dark leaves. Then, for no apparent reason, they were up and gone, leaving the tree bare again. He supposed that there was some reason for their action and he envied their purpose.

The rest of the day stretched out before him, seemingly endless until he remembered the regular appointment with Grace. Their sessions together were already becoming the highlight of his days.

APRIL

In just two weeks Harry's time with Grace at Bede House had become a bit of a ritual. After ringing the bell, he would be met by Maude and led in silence up the stairs to a bedroom at the back of the house. At precisely five o'clock Maude would push her way into the room with tea and biscuits on a tray. Then, at six, Grace would show him to the door and wave until he reached the gate.

His visits there had already been programmed into the orderly routine of the house. That did not upset him, even though he had never been one to follow routines for their own sake. At the same time, he was becoming a little bothered over the sameness of the sessions: they read together; with some prompting Grace wrote out sentences about her day; with Harry's help she drew pictures; they played dice games; and Harry occasionally persuaded her to think through numerical problems. But really, Harry thought they were just replicating some of the more mundane aspects of regular schoolwork.

Grace read well, though often without any sign of under-standing. She was keen to write, and Harry genuinely enjoyed her stories even if her creativity was not matched by her grammar or spelling accuracy. It seemed, however, that all matters numerical and spatial were pretty much absent from the workings of her mind.

Harry was already running out of ideas to approach these areas with any semblance of originality or freshness. In fact, he had begun to wonder whether his visits were of any real use at all in terms of developing her academic achievement. She was pleasant and polite, and it definitely seemed that she liked him to be there, but, stories apart, she showed no real interest in the activities.

Grace's aim to avoid schoolwork was clear and transparent. With a subtleness that belied her intellectual performance with schoolwork, she would lead him into story telling. At first it was persuading him to talk at length about anything, probably just as a diversionary tactic to get away from the other tasks. But then, without Harry knowing how, it developed into an exploration of the adventures and exploits of an imaginary girl: an imaginary girl who had formed in their mutual understanding with characteristics just like those of Grace. This new, imaginary girl had the name of Sascha. Harry had no idea why Grace chose that name, but Sascha it was. She was just like Grace but, it soon became apparent to him, was freer and cleverer, so that she always managed to escape from the difficult situations that confronted her. Of course, in this way Grace was not only able to think through the difficulties that fell across her path every day but was also able to lift herself to a better and happier place beyond the harsher constraints of reality.

It became standard that, as soon as Maude had left them with the tray and their hands were engaged with tea and biscuits, Grace would lead him into some story. 'What did the girl do when no-one picked her for their netball team?' or 'Why did Sascha cry in the assembly hall?' was typical of the way her stories began. It concerned Harry somewhat at first, but after a while he considered it to be time well spent.

A month in and Harry was beginning to find the routine a little stifling. But then, without planning or warning, events took a change of direction. The room in which they worked was sparsely furnished and without decoration, though there was a generous table placed under the window where the two of them sat. The room was plain apart from its beautiful, arched window, which, although architecturally simple, seemed to fit the room perfectly.

Harry had been looking out through the window one Friday. It overlooked the rear garden, which had been completely laid to lawn. The grass was pale and as yet untouched by the warmth of spring, but on this day the rays of late afternoon sun had broken through flimsy cloud and filtered between the bare branches of the trees to light up the garden in pools of pale lemon light. In that low projection of light, it was possible to trace in shadows the outline of former borders and beds that had been the orderly divisions of a previously more formal garden. Tall, mature trees lined the rear boundary, but their leafless state failed to mask the area beyond, where a tangle of angular tiles and brickwork marked the new housing that had more recently filled in the spaces between the more established streets.

Harry's eyes quickly travelled beyond that bland modernity to the lines of an older, Victorian terrace that marked the coastal edge of the town and, although he could not see it, the sea lay immediately beyond.

'Do you like the beach, Grace?'

'The beach?' she questioned as if she had never heard the word before.

'Yes. Do you like going to the beach?'

'I don't know. Do I?'

'Right. We'll find out then. Get yourself a coat. We're going out for a while.'

'Oh, good.'

The decision to go out had broken a film of tension that was there, but hitherto unrecognised. Within two minutes she was back from Maude with coat, hat and gloves, and they were ready to go. Maude was there, silent and questioning, but Harry ignored her querulous stare and they were soon out onto Scarborough Avenue.

'Which way?' Harry wondered aloud into her upturned face, 'Down past the school? Or along the bridleway?'

'The other one,' she answered quickly and emphatically.

'You mean the bridleway?'

'Yes.'

Grace walked behind him down the narrow pathway that skirted the fields on the edge of town, but when they reached the roadway at the sea front, she stretched out her hand to hold his. Once again, it felt a little uncomfortable for Harry to hold the hand of a girl as old as her, but he did not want to spoil her pleasure so they stayed that way along the promenade, down the steps of the huge, concrete defence walls, and onto the beach. The sea met them with the saltiness of an inshore breeze; Harry could fairly taste it.

Once onto the beach he let go her hand, expecting her to scamper off like every other kid he knew, but she just stood there smiling and looking around. The beach was an ever-changing mix of sand, gravel, pebbles and stones. Luckily, the tide was at its furthest ebb, revealing a wide expanse of glistening strand. Long lines of wooden groins stretched out from the sea wall, dividing the beach up into little, square parcels and keeping it from being washed away. There was no obvious order to the patterns of sand and shingle, at any one time, or from day to day. Often the sea demonstrated its enormous power by changing the patterns, or even the entire shape, of the beach. On one day the beach could be piled up against the north-facing side of the groins, and then, overnight, massive waves could move whole beaches back in the opposite direction. Sometimes there were only stones, and at other times it was completely sandy. On this day there was a mix. Its natural state made it beautiful and absorbing at the same time.

For five minutes or so they just stood and stared, during which time the cloud had thickened to block out the sun and to change the beach's mood with more sober colours. That was the fascination of the beach: it was just sea, strand and sky, but the light could change everything; to Harry it was an endless wonder.

A quick look at Grace's face told Harry that she was already starting to get cold, so he began to drag her along through the roughs and smooths of the beach's surface. He knew that she was not a robust child, though she did, in fact, smile at that moment to defy his thought. Soon they were rummaging through the shingle to pick out interesting shapes and colours. Harry loved the feel of the pebbles and the salt-earth smell as he picked them up.

'Look at this!' he exclaimed, holding up a globule of gleaming, wet, orange-stained quartz between thumb and forefinger to catch what was left of the dimming light. Grace looked and laughed approvingly at that and all the other finds: smooth marbles; sharp flints; flat skimmers; and even a crab's pincher.

'Look at this!' cried Grace in imitation, holding out a small, grey stone in her own hand.

'Oh yes. Great!' he told her, though he could see nothing that made it interesting or attractive apart from her own enthusiasm. 'Let's put it in our collection.' And he dropped it into his pocket along with the others.

'Now, this one is really special,' he told her, displaying a contorted scrap of sandstone through which the sea had worn holes from one side to the other. 'If you can see right through it, then it's a "lucky stone"!'

Then he explained, quite dramatically for him, that this entitled the finders to make a wish.

'Right, when it's up in the air, and before it hits the water, you have to make your wish!'

'Like in fairy tales?' she asked.

'Just like in fairy tales. But you mustn't tell what the wish is ... or it won't come true!'

Grace nodded that she understood. Harry threw the stone long and hard to make sure it reached and splashed into the water. Then they stood to watch the waves move relentlessly in to cover over the spot where the stone had landed. They stood there silently for a while.

'I wished I was clever,' Grace announced into the silence.

'No ... you mustn't say what the wish was! Besides ... there are more important things than being clever,' he told her as gently as he could.

'What are they?' she asked, looking hard into his face.

'Well,' he stalled. 'Being kind and being generous ... being honest ... being ... nice! Things like that are more important.'

Grace held his arm more tightly, leaning into his side for warmth and reassurance. It took him a few moments to feel comfortable with that, but they stayed that way for several minutes until it began to feel much colder. She allowed him time enough to feel good about pleasing her before displaying what he would come to recognise as an uncanny sense of timing. Just as they were about to make their move homeward, a small voice cried out into the emptiness of the deserted beach.

'I'd rather be clever!'

*

Ever since the clock hands had leapt forward to herald British Summer Time, Harry had been in a better and lighter mood. The onset of spring had allowed Moses to fill up Harry's days with tasks in the cottage's or his own garden or in those of Moses' many friends: and Harry had his sessions with Grace to look forward to. It suited him to be busier and there was more purpose to his days. He had even written to Old Howard promising him a sincere intention to capture the serenity of the East Riding onto canvas or paper.

So, on one morning he had somewhat selfishly brought Grace to the lake that sat almost ignored on the edge of the town. At first he had tried, without too much success, to capture the light as it filtered in greens and yellows through the shallow waters beside them. Then a whole gaggle of Brent geese had passed busily by, breaking the mirrored surface into shattered shards and reflecting the black and white of their plumage in kaleidoscopic splendour. Escher, no doubt, would have drawn it into orderly perfection, but for Harry it appeared too difficult so he concentrated instead on the simpler lines of several swans that were drifting placidly on a further stretch of the lake where the waters were less disturbed, on the surface at least.

Grace sat next to him with pencil and paper, reluctant to commit herself to definite lines on the clean page, but happy to sit and talk.

'What will I be in my next life?' she asked him out of the blue.

'What life's that then?'

'The teacher said in school … in some regions we come back as something else,' she expanded.

'You mean religions, not regions. Some religions believe that we come back as something else when we die. It's a bit early to be thinking about it.'

'But what would I be, Harry?'

'Dunno,' he said looking out over the lake. 'You might be a swan.'

'Maude says I'm an ugly duckling.' Grace looked sad.

'Yes, but you know the story don't you …?' Grace looked non-plussed, so Harry continued. 'Well, in the story, the bird thinks she is an ugly duckling, but then, in the end, she discovers that she isn't ugly at all … but a beautiful swan!'

Grace thought about what Harry had said. Gradually her countenance improved. 'If I was a swan, would I be clever?'

'Clever? Dunno … you'd be beautiful,' he told her. She smiled at that and they sat quietly for a long while before Harry repacked his kit into the old, blue rucksack. In fact, she hardly spoke again until they said goodbye at her gate, but she seemed happy.

Back at his cottage, Harry looked down at the watery scene he had replicated on his pad. It wasn't the best work he had ever done, as his fingers were too rusty from lack of practice, but there was a hint of freshness about it that pleased him, and a vibrancy to the flora surrounding his lake that promised warmer days ahead. He was pleased by that thought and a little surprised at having allowed himself to think it: during the past year he had not really thought about times ahead.

The teacher's voice bounced off the walls and hard surfaces of the classroom. His class was quiet and indolent, playing out time until the bell rang for lunch. No one was prepared to commit themselves at this stage to answer his banal questioning. He looked into their eyes for a sign of weakness but found none.

'What about you, Grace?'

'What?' She was startled. Like the others, she had been letting his voice and the questions bounce harmlessly off her.

'I told you last week,' he intoned metronomically. 'You remember ... for your homework ... be prepared to tell me ... what you would choose ... for a reincarnation.'

'I don't know rein ...'

'Come along, Grace. Let's think, shall we? If you were to come back recreated as ... say, an animal of some kind ... what would you choose?'

Silence: Grace; Mr Bale; and the whole class. Then: 'A swan,' she said.

'A swan you say. That's excellent, Grace. Now then, the rest of you ... I know the bell has just rung, but you'll leave when I say so!' his voice tailed off, since the class was already scraping furniture and heading for the door before he had reached mid-sentence. 'Yes. Off you go, Grace ... good girl.'

Grace found her locker to retrieve lunch then ambled her way down the corridor in no rush to go anywhere in particular. A knot of gangling boys slouched along the radiators next to the toilets. One of them got up to affirm his air of superiority.

'Oooh, Grace the swan, the beautiful swan,' he cried clutching his hand to his chest and staggering before her in mock melodrama.

'More like the dead duck!' cackled one of his cronies. They all laughed.

Grace laughed too. Uncertain of what to do next, she stood there smiling at the clowning youth.

'Ey up, Baz ... I reckon she fancies you!' called a crony, beside himself with the perceived magnitude of his own wit.

'Baz 'n' Grace! Baz 'n' Grace!' the 'knot' chanted to the accompaniment of resounding radiators as they banged their heels into the metal. The knot laughed, Grace laughed, but Baz scowled. Being the butt of their humour was too much for his delicate shield of macho bravado.

'I wouldn't touch her with yours!' he leered at his cronies in an effort to regain the initiative. But the knot was enjoying the weakness shown by their bullying leader and they maintained solidarity by increasing the volume of their chant. Baz could see that there was only one means of escape.

'I wouldn't touch you with a manky bog brush, ya' ugly cow!' he pointed at Grace, who knew no other than to keep smiling.

'You're friggin' barmy you are!' he spat at her while jabbing the air in front of her with his malicious finger.

'If you had mad cow disease, we'd never know t' difference!' he continued with increasing anger. The cronies were silent by now.

'Mad ... ugly ... barmy ... manky ...'

And with each word he pushed his finger spitefully into the top of her sternum.

It hurt Grace.

He was about to deliver 'cow!' with a flourish, but before he could draw back the digit to make his final thrust, she grabbed it and sunk her teeth into the meagre flesh. She bit it hard. Too hard.

There was a moment of profound silence, and then a gasp, and then a shrilling scream. The crescendo of agony disappeared down the corridor, followed by the shocked stare of the knot and stream of tiny, red droplets.

Grace did not bother to smile. She simply fled to the girls' toilets. Huddled in the corner of the furthest cubicle she tried to make more sense of the incident just passed. Images whirled around in her mind and *she fought to put them into order. To other people it might appear that the thoughts and emotions of those with more limited intellect would be shallow and uncomplicated, with few dimensions. But Grace was a whole person. She experienced as much pain and worry as anyone else. It was just that she had more difficulty than usual in the interpretation of her feelings into words.*

Harry had no reason to expect other than a routine evening when he approached the door of Bede House, but as he stepped inside Maude handed him a letter. He could detect apprehension in her approach.

'Where's Grace?' he asked, not expecting a reply, but taking the opportunity to tease her mildly. Maude remained silent, of course, but lifted her eyes to indicate either that Grace was upstairs or that something was amiss.

The envelope was blank and unsealed, so Harry took out the letter inside. His name was at the top and that of Elizabeth Hall at the bottom. It told him: that she, Mrs Hall, had been summoned to the school for an urgent appointment with the headteacher; that she was, however, in London and not able to get back in time; that she did not know what to do; and would he go to the school with Grace the next morning?

The handwriting was not dissimilar to the fine copperplate with which his previous letter from her had been completed, but different, less tidy and rather shakily done. Harry was speechless with surprise. He shifted his gaze angrily towards Maude.

'What am I ... look ... why can't she ...? How ...? Oh, I get it. You wrote this didn't you? What? Did she dictate it? How can I ...?'

Maude's expression remained passive. Even if she had been able to understand his incoherent stream of speech, he knew better than to expect any reply.

'I just don't ... It's just not on. I've only known her for four weeks, for goodness sake! What am I, her bloody guardian now or something?'

Grace appeared then at the top of the stairs. The movement caught Harry's eye and he looked up into a tearful and frightened face. Consequently, he looked again at the old woman, who seemed, at that moment, to be very frail; barking out his dissatisfaction and bewilderment to her had been unfair: her silence always made him feel aggressive.

Harry stopped ranting and felt a little ashamed. He held up his hands to them in contrition.

'OK, let's be calm. I'm sure we can sort this out … yes, of course, I'll go.'

*

They sat together like two naughty children outside the office of the headteacher. It was quiet and calm at the front of the school. There were no signs of the labours, the shared laughter, or the restless attrition that took place daily beyond the glass doors of the foyer where they sat. In front of the school there were green spaces of tranquil grass undisturbed by adolescent turmoil, edged with tall trees where only light zephyrs of wind bothered the idyllic calm.

A squirrel danced into one of the spaces. Harry nudged Grace and they watched it together, Harry smiling bravely in the face of their anticipated confrontation and Grace leaning forward, open mouthed in total absorption. They concentrated for that moment on the squirrel.

Out on the grass, which appeared so benevolent and tranquil to the human spectators, but which was so real and dangerous to the squirrel, the object of their attention made a few hurried hops forward and then stopped. Rising up on its hind legs, it turned its head in each direction to detect whether its progress had been noticed. Then, two seconds later it hopped forward again, only to stop and repeat the scouting exercise in its entirety. And so, like some pantomime villain, it progressed across the grass, performing its intricate dance. The squirrel's tail hung out in the light breeze like a flag, like a knight's pennant, lending a fairy tale quality to the rodent's activity.

This distraction outside the window was soon lost from Harry's thoughts to be replaced by a simmering anger at being kept waiting outside the headteacher's office and also, he would have admitted if pushed, at the expectation of being admonished.

'If they think I'm taking any shit from them ...' but his thought was interrupted by the arrival of an immaculately dressed young woman whose voice and appearance just oozed correctness and efficiency: women like that always seem to undermine his confidence.

'They are ready for you now Mr ... Mr ...?' she announced with a smile that dared him to be anything other than perfectly pleasant.

'Mr Harry,' he told her.

'They? They?' he thought to himself, re-gathering his defences.

'Would you like to go through?' asked the secretary rhetorically in tones of over-politeness like dripping honey.

'Come on, Grace, there's nothing to worry about,' he said, more to himself than to her.

They entered the headteacher's office and a dark-suited man behind a desk half rose to his feet before quickly sitting again, as if he had suddenly realised that his trousers were about to fall down. He held a limp hand before him, palm down as a sign of authority.

'Please sit down, Mr ...'

'Harry!' called the secretary over her shoulder and in the process of closing the door.

'Does she not trust me to remember my own name?' Harry thought to himself.

'Perhaps you could get Grace a drink, Mrs Luscombe,' the headteacher called out before she had shut the door completely, and the secretary returned to retrieve Grace from the fray. Harry wondered why the headteacher did not want Grace there, but left it unchallenged for the moment.

'Thank you for coming at such short notice, Mr Harry. I did speak to Mrs Hall by telephone earlier today. She explained her inability to attend. She expressed her hope that you would feel able to deal with our problem.'

He smiled with his mouth only and waited, presumably for Harry to speak, but Harry contrarily kept silent.

'This is Miss Bentham,' the headteacher continued, indicating a teacher sat to the side previously unnoticed by Harry. The other teacher smiled briefly but continued to sit at the side so that they formed a triangle.

'Miss Bentham is Grace's form tutor. She's been keeping ... supporting Grace since she arrived here.'

The woman smiled again and said hello before quickly reassuming her serious pose and expression.

'We've had rather a serious incident,' the headteacher droned before pausing again. He pursed his lips, plaited his fingers together and leaned forward like an obsequious priest awaiting confession, but Harry did not reply.

'I'm afraid that we have received a serious complaint from a parent, a complaint ... a complaint of assault ... by Grace.'

'Assault! What do mean, assault?' Harry fairly leapt from his seat. 'What do you mean?'

At the headteacher's invitation, Miss Bentham gave an 'as

accurate-as-she-knew' account of what had happened in the corridor the previous day. Harry had managed to contain himself until she had completed her account, but by the end his anger was approaching incandescence.'

'Just 'cos she bites the finger of some soddin' bully, some nasty youth with no more guts than to pick on a little girl ... that's ... that's not assault! That's self-defence! That's justice! That's what that is!'

He stood there quivering with anger, blinded by an anger that he hated, but could not contain. His finger was pointing: the irony – he knew he must have looked just like Baz the bully had in the corridor with Grace. Self-disgust spread through him like a hot flush.

The head and Miss Bentham sat open mouthed; 'gob-smacked' the kids would have said.

'I'm sorry. I'm so sorry,' Harry apologised. The words hung in the silence. 'I'm sorry ... I've been unwell recently.' It was the only excuse he could think of to help them past the impasse, but it seemed to be one that they were prepared to accept to a degree. Some colour crept back into their cheeks.

'Look, perhaps we could start again,' Harry countered in the moment of respite. 'I really am sorry. I promise that I'll be calm.'

They talked about Grace and the incident for some time. While he had been successful in getting them to accept his apology, he had lost the moral high ground born of indignation and, subsequently, he felt inadequate in his defence of Grace's actions. Clearly the head felt pressured by parental complaint and wanted to take a firm line with Grace, despite her obvious problems and despite what Harry suspected was a mutual abhorrence of bullies like Baz. But the preceding outburst had left Harry in no position to make adequate protestation, though, thankfully, Miss Bentham came out of her serious-faced shell to quietly preserve a well-reasoned level of fairness in their collective resolutions.

Miss Bentham promised to talk to Grace. Harry promised to talk to Grace and Mrs Hall. And the head agreed to talk to Baz and his, almost certainly over-indulgent, parents. The conclusion, however, was that Grace should be kept at home for the next day. For Harry it was not the best outcome, but one that he was resigned to accept in the light of what had gone on in the head's office.

*

Mrs Hall, however, was far less accepting of the situation when he told her that evening after her return from London.

'Suspended? Grace suspended from school? It's not on, Mr Harry. She's not an animal or even a malicious girl. She wouldn't hurt anyone on purpose. She must have been provoked ... she wouldn't do that ... you should have told them, Mr Harry!'

'I did tell them. And anyway ... YOU should have told them, not me!' he snapped back. He could feel the anger inside rising up again, but he still felt guilty about the way he had handled things in the school; he had not told her about that, so he managed to fight the anger back down. He remembered about the deep breathing and forced himself to stay composed.

'Look, it's only one day ... it's Friday tomorrow ... I'll take Grace out for the day. She won't notice there's anything wrong,' he told Mrs Hall more reasonably.

'That's not the point!' the offended and proud mother fumed.

'No. It's not the point. The point is that I was there, and you bloody weren't! I did my best!'

The ugly anger had surfaced in him again. Mrs Hall made no attempt to conceal a reciprocated antagonism from her face. Tight lipped, with nostrils flared and steely blue eyes boring into Harry's, she squared her shoulders to his verbal assault, and they stood there toe to toe like duellists.

'I ... I couldn't help not being there ... I do everything I can. That's not fair, Mr Harry ... You have no right!' she said with such surprising softness, as if the thought had drained her emotions.

'You have no right!' The phrase reverberated in his head. It was barely a month since the same words had fallen from his own mouth in that same room. He had a strange sensation of standing outside his own body, of staring down on himself. He did not like the angry man standing there, teeth grinding and mind straining viciously. He did not like him at all, but as he watched the rage drained from him.

'No ... I'm sure that wasn't fair ... I'm sorry I said that,' he told her as lightly as he could. 'I'm sure you do everything you can. I'm sure you're a good mother,' he continued, trying to ease the offence he had caused.

Her eyes softened: perhaps there were even tears in the corners. Now that he had removed the resistance to her challenging anger it collapsed, and she was left with only hurt. She left the room.

Not knowing whether to stay or go, Harry finally sat down and stared into the mysteries of the Persian carpet. No doubt it held many secrets, but they were not revealed to him. He was still puzzled by the anger that once again had risen so easily in him and he rubbed his eyes hard with his fingers as he searched in his mind for some understanding.

When he looked up Mrs Hall was standing there again, hands twisted nervously across her chest. He thought she was about to terminate their arrangements, but he was mistaken.

'It would be very helpful if Grace could spend the day with you tomorrow,' she said in a clear, controlled voice.

'Excellent,' Harry told her. 'Tell Maude to have her ready for nine o'clock.'

There did not appear to be anything else to say. Well, there was probably far too much to say. But it was beyond them at that time, so they simply walked to the door. Harry turned on the step to look into Mrs Hall's face. Her mouth formed into a very brief smile, but he was unable to guess at what it hid.

Walking back home down the quiet streets, the words and incidents of the previous thirty minutes tumbled over and over in his mind, but he was not able to sort them into any satisfying pattern: he lacked the rug-maker's skill. The evening felt lonely.

*

Grace hesitated on the first step of the bus. She looked around as if she were on the brink of a new world.

'Go on, girl,' Harry told her. 'Up or down?'

'Up or down,' she repeated. Her head shook and her eyes danced around in complete awe and wonder. There seemed to be no message between her head and feet.

'What? Have you never been on a bus before?' Harry laughed.

She shook her head.

'Stupid,' he said to himself about himself. He should have guessed.

'Well, go up the stairs then,' he told her, and then addressed the driver. 'Two returns for Bridlington, please.'

'Two t' Brid. How old's the lass then?' the driver asked.

'Uh, sixteen … just sixteen.'

'Go on, pay a 'alf for her … she don't look that old.'

'Thanks,' Harry told him, not wishing to reject his generosity, and he followed Grace up onto the top deck, where she had taken a seat at the very front.

She sat looking around as if truly in wonderland. It made Harry feel good to see her so enthralled. He pointed out items of interest along their route beside the windswept coast, and she smiled, though he could tell that whatever he said went straight over her head. It was enough for her that they were sat on the upper deck of a bus, let alone where they might be. It could have been the dullest street or the far side of the moon for all she would have noticed.

When they stepped off the bus she watched it go with longing in her eyes. 'Perhaps we'll get the same one going back,' Harry consoled her.

'Will we?' she smiled.

And then her eyes were off again, bouncing over the seaside images that lay before them.

'Oooh,' she cooed, grabbing his arm, and they set off down the promenade.

It was a clear, blue-skied day, but, as often, there was a fresh wind blowing in over the sea. They had stopped, leaning against the sea wall, to look out to the horizon and the spectacular white cliffs of Flamborough Head. The sea was a mix of blues and greys, and, sadly, a tinge of brown, fringed creamy white at the edge where it curled over in long lines of surf onto the unbroken sands.

The long, curved beach at Bridlington is truly wonderful, though, in honesty, it is not nearly matched by the ragged jumble of grey buildings that falls down from the old town to the sea front. One tall block of flats, in particular, blights the townscape: a remarkable piece of ill planning, which, no doubt, created someone's nest-egg. But Harry and Grace's eyes were only for the sparkling sea as it frothed against the beach.

There were no stones on the beach, though they did manage to collect a pocketful of assorted shells that Grace declared would look good on the windowsill of their workroom.

A man was strenuously digging holes in the sand into which he frequently thrust his hands to retrieve some form of bounty. The woman with him held up a bucket into which he threw his findings.

'What's he doing?' Grace asked Harry.

'Dunno. Why don't you ask him?'

Grace walked up to the bending man, looked back to check with Harry, then bent and twisted herself down until her face was close and aligned to the man's.

'What are you doing?' she asked him from no more than a hand's width away.

'Digging for "wherms", me luv',' he told her.

'What for?' she persisted.

'T' stick on 'ooks, t' catch fishes,' he explained patiently. He straightened up and Grace did likewise. Then he craned his neck over to look in the bucket: Grace mirrored his movements so that their noses almost touched above the bucket. After a poke and a thrust he jerked upright again holding two large 'wherms'.

Grace's head snapped upright as well, but this time she stood a little apart, mouth open and eyes goggling at the two wriggling creatures in his fingers.

'Them's lugwherms,' he informed her solemnly.

'Oooh … I don't like them!' winced Grace.

"Appen you don't, sweetheart. But fishes likes 'em … An' we likes fishes, don't we, Mother?' he concluded, winking conspiratorially at his wife, who smiled warmly upon the little drama before her.

'Do you catch much?' Harry asked him as Grace continued to stare and wince at the dangling lugworms.

'Nay, lad,' he told Harry. 'See, the fishermen in their boats had this idea. Out there, on the bottom, there's big flatfish, flounders. An' the fishermen's nets used to go over the top of 'em an' miss 'em. So, they gets this idea of draggin' big concrete rollers on the bottom of their nets what made them flatfish rise up an' get caught in the nets.'

'And did it work?' Harry asked again.

'Did it "wherk"? It wherked a treat! Trouble was, them rollers destroyed the weed on bottom, an' it never grew back age'n. An' no weed … no fish!' the forager explained. 'But we catch enough, don't we, Mother?'

'We certainly do!' she beamed. And Harry and Grace left them to their happy prodding of the beach.

It was cold, so on occasions Harry pulled Grace into a slow jog across the sand to get her circulation moving. After a while, however, she was beginning to look too cold and he led her round to the more sheltered area of the harbour. Bridlington has a proper working harbour with a mottled assortment of boats, from little pleasure dinghies to large sea-going fishing craft. The waning tide was only just beginning to come in again, so most vessels were left perched off-balance atop the sludge that coats the floor of the harbour. All along the slabbed sides of the quay were nets, lobster pots, fish trays and the rest of the fishing trade's seaweed-smelling paraphernalia. They stopped regularly for Grace to investigate most things as they made their way slowly round the perimeter.

'It's a bit smelly,' she said, though there was no hint of complaint on her rosy-cheeked face.

It dawned upon Harry that he had made no arrangements for food so he trawled the tiny streets, which huddle above the harbour, for something to eat. Grace was inexorably drawn to the brightest and gaudiest of the shops where her eyes poured over pink sticks of rock, phosphorescent sweets and vividly packaged burgers. With unworthy self-righteousness Harry made her settle for fresh seafood sandwiches, which they ate, sat on benches above the harbour.

'You've got to eat these when you come to the seaside,' he told her, trying to justify his prejudice. She ate them with a smile, but without taking much notice of what was inside. The thought of eating crab that had just been taken from the sea beside which they had been walking had enthralled Harry as they had stood outside the shop window, but in the event the sandwiches were rather disappointing.

Guilt, and the fact that thickening cloud had finally hidden the sun completely, persuaded Harry to take Grace's hand and lead her into a cosy café, where they were heartily welcomed by the embrace of thick, warm air, the pervading aroma of slightly stale chip fat and a smiling waitress. A family of four was seated at the table next to the door, parents and two children dressed in clothes appropriate to a much warmer day. Harry smiled and nodded as they entered. The adults both swivelled their eyes towards him, but remained tight lipped, while their son and daughter looked up solemnly from heads bent down to the red gingham tablecloth before them. For just a moment Harry let his mind wonder at what might be at the root of their apparent malaise: no doubt, the kids would be suffering as a result of their parents' tensions.

'What would you like?' he asked, returning his attention to Grace.

'What?' she replied blankly.

'This is a café ... we can have something to eat or drink.'

'Can we?'

'Yes! What would you like?'

'I don't know.'

Harry held his breath, smiled, and then let it out slowly to allow the exasperation to seep away. The waitress re-emerged from a doorway behind the counter and accosted them with a broad, welcoming smile.

'Right, luv. What can I fetch yer?' she asked nudging Harry's shoulder with her ample bosom as she stretched across to wipe remains from the table. 'Gary' was proclaimed in blue across a red heart tattooed on her bicep, but he refrained from asking her the obvious question.

It was rather cold for ice cream, so Harry selected milkshakes for them both: strawberry for Grace and banana for him. The friendly waitress disappeared through the door behind the counter but returned within five minutes to deliver two milkshakes in tall, fluted glasses.

They drank them without talking. Grace's eyes looked large as gobstoppers as she goggled at the family beside them in the café. Soon the pink liquid of the milkshake reduced towards the bottom of her glass and the straw popped out to make a loud slurping noise. Grace paused with lips puckered around the straw while her eyes looked into Harry's for reproach or approval. He gave her a little heartening smile then adjusted his own straw to slurp too. Grace giggled and her amusement encouraged Harry to even louder and bigger slurps.

From the table inside the door, the neighbouring mother and father looked towards them with scowling disapproval. Harry and Grace looked at each other for a second before bursting out into laughter. In an effort to support him, Grace struggled with her straw to make further slurping. Unfortunately, she blew instead of sucked and a spurt of frothing pink shot up from the end of the straw to land in speckles across her face, hands and the table. Harry tried for a moment to look serious, but the laughter inside him burst out in a snort through his nose, allowing Grace, in turn, to squeal with delight at her own misdemeanour.

This was all too much for the father of the family opposite, who without speech ushered them up and out of the salon in haste. He hesitated at the door, swayed and then leaned back in to address Grace.

'Tell that father of yours he's a disgrace!' he snarled at her while keeping his eyes on Harry.

Grace looked quizzically at Harry for a few seconds before turning to watch them go swiftly past the window and up the street.

'Oooh!' said Grace.

'Oooh!' Harry agreed. It was a sure signal to laugh again, but before they could do so, the waitress came out from the kitchen to confront them.

'Where's yon family gone?' she demanded with an anxious nod towards the now vacant table.

'They just left ... I'm sorry ... we were being a bit silly.' Harry really did feel very foolish and glanced toward Grace for reassurance. But when he looked back to the waitress she had already begun to move.

'I don't give a chuff about silly,' she cried. 'They've left without feckin' paying!'

And with that she dived out the door to give pursuit. Harry and Grace were too astounded to move for a while, but then the door began to bang in the breeze and Harry got up to shut it. He looked down the street to check on the progress of the chase, but both family and waitress had disappeared from view, so he sat down again.

Grace simply stared while Harry stroked his chin in indecision. After some minutes she asked him, 'Why did that man call you "my dad"?'

'Dunno. Perhaps he thought I looked like your dad.'

'Do you?'

'Do I what, Grace?'

'Do you look like my dad?'

'That's not what I meant. I meant … I dunno. Do I look like your dad?'

'I don't know,' she said with a faraway look of hurt in her eyes. 'Was he kind?'

'Sorry, Grace … I didn't know your dad … you'll have to ask your mum.'

She said no more on the subject.

'They'll be back soon,' Harry said to himself more than to her.

But they were not back soon. Minutes went by and then half an hour. It felt bizarre to them to be sat in the empty café. Outside the day had turned greyer and the promenade emptier, adding to the mounting surrealism of their circumstance. The suspense was beginning to get to Harry as he sat facing another 'shall I go or shall I stay' situation. He stood up before the ill ease could grow into something worse.

'Well, we can't stay here forever … Come on, Grace. We shall just have to go,' he told her, and she followed him to the door.

There seemed to be no other choice than to just leave. Harry had left money on the table to cover the cost of their drinks then moved to the door. Carefully he twisted over the sign on the glass door so that it read 'closed' and then pulled it to. But just as they turned towards the pavement, the waitress, and a very large police constable, blocked their way. Harry seemed to be making a habit of getting caught in doorways.

'If I could just 'ave a few moments of your time, sir,' the constable requested in the manner of an order. 'Perhaps you could give me a description of the people who sat next to you?'

Harry spread his hands upwards in front of himself as if balancing a great weight. 'Well, dunno really!' he sighed, trying to buy time enough to recall anything significant.

The constable held Harry in his glance with an air of resigned but ill-concealed disenchantment as he continued with his routine of facial acrobatics.

'I know ...' threw in Grace sincerely.

'It's alright, Grace. I'm sure I can manage ...'

'Now then, sir ... If the young lady is able to offer something more definite,' rebuked the constable. 'What is it, miss?' he said, turning his eyes to her in optimistic appraisal.

'They didn't look very happy!' she stated with an emphatic nod.

'Yes, miss, and ...?' asked the constable. His buoyant glance remained upon Grace for long enough to realise that he was going to get no more than the smile that was fixed upon her face before returning it to Harry with increased disillusionment.

'Anythink else, sir?' he offered into the ether.

But there was no response. It was not that Harry wished to be disobliging in any way, only that the melancholic mood of the family had stopped him from bothering to notice them further.

'Eee ... you'd get more sense out of dead 'addock!' sighed the waitress regaining her breath, but none of her former friendliness.

At length, Grace and Harry left them to it.

They were quiet on the return bus journey, since the exasperating episode in the café seemed to have stolen the magic from their day.

'We didn't do anything wrong,' Harry assured Grace, but, nevertheless, it seemed that events had conspired to leave them empty of joy or satisfaction.

'Never mind,' she confided to him later in the trip. 'You tried hard!'

She had a way of stating the obvious that often floored him.

*

Harry felt some relief getting back to the uncomplicated demands of gardening, though working alongside Moses was always demanding enough. According to him the ground needed a thorough, good, deep dig, and that is exactly what they were giving it.

'No substitute for 'ard wo'k if yer wants to grow decent brassicas,' Moses had stated bluntly.

Indeed, Harry had enjoyed those green vegetables through the winter so he had not argued. But, after more than two hours of digging, the labour was beginning to have effect upon the muscles in his back and he used the excuse of making tea to gain some respite. Moses continued with the deep digging until Harry returned to force a mug into his strong, weathered hands.

'I didn't see any "M Farrow" listed on the role of honour when I was down at the school the other day. I did see a "D Farrow", but no "M"!' Harry told him. It was a feeble attempt to make fun when what he really wanted to do was guide the conversation round to his last interlude with the redoubtable Mrs Hall and how he had lost his temper yet again.

'Well, you wouldn't, would you? Since I don't know any "M" Farrow!' Moses told him, turning and walking off to find a seat outside the kitchen door. Harry followed.

'What's that then? You're Mr Farrow aren't you?'

'Well, you know I am, but I aren't no "M" Farrow. I'm "R", "R" for Reginald.'

'What about "Moses" then? That's your name, isn't it?'

'Well, sort of … but that's only a nickname.'

'Oh, I never knew. Everyone calls you Moses.'

'Aye, everyone, ever since I were a lad,' he told Harry.

Harry raised his eyebrows to him as a signal to continue, and, after a slightly self-conscious pause, he did so.

'Well … see … when I was little, no more than seven or eight … we moved. We used to live on 'Ezzle Road, but when me father were made first mate 'e said it were no good living there an' we'd have to move. We came 'ere an' 'e caught the train in to 'Ull an' back as 'e needed. Any road, I didn't like it in me new school … didn't like school altogether, but it were w'oss when I 'ad to go to a new 'un. So, on the second day I ran off an' 'id all day … down by the lake … I'd been there all day 'idin' in rushes while they found me at teatime. Unlucky fo' me, me father were 'ome that night an' I got a real good 'idin', I can tell thee. Next day, the teacher, Mrs Worsley she were called, an' right nice when I got to know 'er … when I comes in the classroom, she announces, "Oh, here he is, little Moses found in the bulrushes!" Well, it stuck … an' there we are … I bin Moses ever since. But, any road, "Moses" were better than what they called me on 'Ezzle Road.'

'And what was that then?'

'Oh, they called me "runt"!'

'Runt?'

'Yeah; on account o' bein' a Farrow.'

'Farrow?' Harry was beginning to sound like an echo.

'Yes … "farrow" is what yer calls a litter o' piglets … So, bein' the youngest, younger than our Daniel, I wus called "runt" … the runt o' the farrow! So, compared to that, livin' wi' Moses as me name hasn't been so bad. An' I were called Moses ever after by everyone, even me own mother. Everyone 'cept me father … he called me Reginald until the day 'e died.'

Harry was about to encourage him on until he noticed that Moses' eyes had focussed onto some point that was way beyond the present moment and he let it pass. They finished their tea in silence and soon got back to the digging.

That evening when Moses was alone, he took out an old biscuit tin full of photographs. He opened the lid and stared for a while as if unwilling to disturb all those old, familiar secrets. Slowly he picked up the first few. The top one was of a young mother, with one child on her lap and another stood beside. She was smiling graciously and happily into the lens, though the two boys gazed uncertainly. The edges of the snap were well worn through frequent handling, but, on this occasion, it was soon discarded and overlooked for a couple of others a little deeper into the pile. He took them out and laid them side by side on the table before him.

The left of these two was very old, sepia brown and even more cracked at the edges. It was of his mother and father and had been taken shortly after their wedding. They looked serious, even stern, but comfortable with each other.

His father was in the one on the right too, stood between two taller and younger men in uniform. Moses could remember the day it had been taken. His father had travelled down to London for the first and only time. 'Your mother sends her regards,' was all he had said, hiding whatever emotions or motives had made her stay behind in East Yorkshire. It had not been too difficult to guess at her reasons since she had been consumed with anxiety from the day, the same day that he and his elder brother, Daniel, had enlisted with the army. His father wore the same serious expression as he did on all photographs: if he had felt any anxiety, he had not shown it; and if he had felt pride in his two sons then he had hidden that too. His father rarely showed any sign of the emotions that lay beneath the surface, and when he did it was invariably anger, though Moses distinctly remembered an awareness of being loved in some way by his father.

He remembered that on this day it had been enough that their father had travelled all that way to see his sons before they had embarked on their journeys into war. He and his brother smiled out from this photograph with barely concealed pride and pleasure. They were strong and confident, and unafraid of any perils that might be waiting for them. They faced war with the romanticism of songs and propaganda, eager to prove their courage and masculinity.

How quickly the romance had faded, Moses remembered. It had been the last time the three of them had stood together.

Moses remembered the years of war and the incredulous, miraculous reunion with his brother towards the very end of it. His brother had, as a fully trained mechanic, travelled to other operations of war than himself with the REME. It had been almost five years to the day after the photograph had been taken until they met again. The years in between had passed excruciatingly slowly for Moses. He had begun the war as part of a decoy force in the eastern Mediterranean, captured within months by an overwhelmingly superior German presence on the island of Kos, and then shipped by rail across Europe until they reached the POW camps in Estonia still clad in their sub-tropical khakis. Being a prisoner in Estonia became his way of life. It seemed as if he would be there forever, until rumours began to circulate of German losses in the war, and they were railed overland again, this time into the heart of the North German Plain.

There, one day soon after arrival, he had walked headlong into his brother. In front of their comrades they had managed to keep 'a stiff upper lip', but alone together they had hugged and wept: wept for joy at seeing each other again, and wept for the fear of all that they had suffered and endured silently in the years apart.

Those few months they had spent together in the camp, Stallag 13, Fallingbostel it was called, had passed happily since they were so pleased to be together, so pleased to be sharing life together despite the hardship. And there was hope. Rumours of an end to war were substantiated by the course of events.

One day, issued with a single loaf and a large German sausage, they had set off with all the other British prisoners on a march across The Luneburger Heide. For some reason Moses had felt safe within the company of his elder brother. They had marched together, shared their bread and sausage until it ran out after a week, and then foraged together as the march dragged on into a month. They were exhausted and starving, but word had gone around that the end was near; they had been marched between the advancing Russians in the east and the Allies in the west, kept as bargaining power for the Germans' own prisoners.

The perceived wisdom of the rumour kept them going, kept everyone going, for those last days. But they were fateful days, cruelly fateful days. Moses shivered involuntarily as he remembered that one particularly fateful day.

It had been a clear day. They had seen the lone aeroplane approaching from a distance, they looked for cover, and then someone raised a hand. The shout went up gleefully, 'It's one of ours!' Men were waving with newfound energy, there was a cheer, and then, for just a moment, silence before the guns spat out their venomous load with roaring spite. 'What the heck, it's one of ours!'

'Yeah, well someone ought to tell that mad fucker!' responded another.

The plane circled, Moses remembered clearly, before flying back towards their column. But it seemed as if the pilot had realised his tragic mistake and on the return there was a waggle of wings rather than a volley of fire. 'Thank Christ for that!' Moses had whispered to his brother, but there had been no reply, only a stare, an endless stare from unmoving eyes in a still body that had taken in the tragedy most fully.

The very next day their column had been rescued by soldiers from the Wiltshire Regiment. Moses had returned home soon after. He was so thin that friends had not recognised him. His mother had wrapped her arms around his bony frame and hugged him until the front of his demob shirt had become wet with tears, but his father had been unable to move from his chair. His parents had already been informed of his brother, Daniel's death, though he had retold the events to his father just as they had happened up to the point where his brother had lain motionless on the lonely heath. He had thought it best not to tell his father of how he had held his older brother in his arms, how he had wept and raged against the unfairness, though in later years he wished he had unburdened it all.

An uncommunicative man at the best of times his father had found it almost impossible to talk to anyone thereafter. He never spoke his elder brother's name again and uttered Moses' real name, Reginald, just once more. Moses could also remember that occasion with harsh clarity too.

It had been just months later, at the event of the general election. He had cycled into Beverley with his father to vote for the first time. He had found it exciting and satisfying to walk into the booth and make his mark without ordering or hindrance from any other. It seemed that his father had enjoyed the experience as well since he broke the silence on their cycle back home.

'Well, there's two more votes for Labour and the working man,' he had said in dignified self-satisfaction.

Moses had remained silent. His friend with whom he had been drinking down the length of Hessle Road on the nights of the previous week had inherited his father's boat; he had urged Moses against the dangers of nationalisation and rallied him to the cause of private enterprise. It had all sounded right and plausible to Moses and he had placed his mark against the name of the conservative candidate with clear conscience. He knew now that he could not say that to his father. His silence, however, had been enough to tell his father everything. Moses remembered the moment with utmost clarity and pain. It had taken only a raised finger from his father to make himself stop and dismount.

'Tell me you haven't,' his father had demanded quietly.

He remembered the awkwardness of his own feet on the hard road, he remembered the silence save the whisper of the long grass beside them, and he could still feel the burn as his father's hand had smacked smartly against the side of his face.

'Your brother died for working men, our Reginald, and you vote for some Tory bastard!' his father had raged. And they had stood there toe to toe for a long while, the younger, bigger man submissive to the older.

Moses knew in his heart that it was the pain of his brother's dying rather than the politics that had made his father act so extremely, but that did nothing to ease the indignation and humiliation that he had felt from the blow. No-one had been there to witness the incident and neither of them ever spoke of it, but he carried the burden of it for the rest of his life. People looked upon him as a solid and dependable man without the usual fears or worries. And he was keen to maintain that image, though sometimes he ached to unburden himself of the secret weaknesses that sheltered beneath the surface.

At length Moses replaced the photographs in the tin. He closed the lid firmly, though not firmly enough to keep in the pain that he took to bed with him.

The evenings still passed slowly for Harry, though, as Easter approached, a new project cropped up for a few evenings to help the hours pass. He had started to paint two eggs, one for Grace and one for Moses. Having selected the two largest chicken's eggs he could find in the supermarket, he had carefully pierced them with a needle, then blown out their insides with his own breath to leave just the empty shells. It had reminded him of childhood when he and his friends used to collect wild birds' eggs. He pondered that in modern days of increased ecological awareness it seems almost unthinkable that people used to spend so much of their time searching out birds' nests and stealing the eggs, but back then Harry and all his friends had done it without a second thought. People used to have books to identify all the different eggs, though Harry and his friends knew the common ones readily enough without extra reference, and could easily tell, for example, the spotted brown freckles on a pale blue blackbird's egg from the black dotted markings on an even bluer thrush's. Harry could still remember the excited expectancy of sliding a hand into an unguarded nest to feel the undiscovered treasures there. Then he thought about the startling blue of thrushes' eggs and knew that it was the same blue that he remembered from the eyes of Grace and her mother.

Harry put those thoughts and the innocent crimes of childhood behind him and set about painting the eggs. In previous years he had painted them for Marianne, of course; one each year, a whole collection depicting various nursery rhymes. He wondered for a while whether she would have kept them.

This time he had chosen 'Hey Diddle Diddle' for Grace and 'The Owl and the Pussycat' for Moses: he had no idea why, but each gave plenty of scope for imagination and he was particularly amused for some reason by his own choice for Moses even though he could not quite work out the meaning of his own joke.

No sooner than he had laid out all the equipment, however, there was a knock to the front door. Not wishing to repeat the uncertain manoeuvre with the sticking door he went out by way of the back door and walked up beside the cottage to the gate. He saw Mrs Hall before she noticed him. She appeared to be composing herself at the doorstep, her eyes were closed in concentration and she appeared to be breathing in slowly and deeply to gain control. It made Harry smile to see her.

'So, you're not that different from me!' he thought to himself.

'Hello there,' he called as softly as he could, though it still made her jump quite violently.

'I am sorry. I didn't mean to make you jump,' he told her honestly.

'It's quite alright. I didn't see you,' she conceded. 'I wondered if I could talk to you about Grace.'

'There's nothing wrong is there?'

'No, no, nothing at all. I just wondered …' she looked a bit lost, so Harry asked her into the cottage. She hesitated before agreeing, but then followed him round to the kitchen.

'Would you like a cup of tea? I was just about to …'

'No, no, I mustn't bother you too much … I really can't stay long.'

But, despite her protestations Harry ushered her into a chair. She really did look anxious about being there, a little like someone trapped. Then she noticed the eggs, the paintbrushes and the coloured inks, and she became quite animated.

'What are you doing?' she exclaimed rather than enquired. Harry explained.

'I'm only just beginning,' he told her defensively, though pleased at her interest. 'That one in the eggcup, that's for Grace. A sort of Easter present.' Then, 'Do you paint?'

'Me? No. I'm hopeless at anything like that ... Numbers! ... That's all I'm good at. But that's so kind that you're painting it for Grace. She'll be just delighted! She really does like you ... I've been really surprised.'

'Surprised?' Harry queried.

'No! I didn't mean it like that ... It's just that she hasn't got on very well with men ... I mean she hasn't had good experiences ... Oh dear, I'm not explaining myself very clearly am I? ... I mean she enjoys being in your company. And ... you're safe ...'

'Safe?'

'Well, I mean a lot more than that ... I'm sure you are a very good tutor. That's what I've come to talk to you about. I was hoping ... that you would be able to do a little extra tutoring over the Easter holiday.'

'Extra tutoring? I'm not sure Grace would benefit from any more extra work than she already has ...' he began to explain before Mrs Hall started in again.

'Well, not necessarily extra tutoring ... perhaps just more days out. Grace so enjoyed your trip to the seaside. I thought ...'

'Oh, you thought, did you?' It was Harry's turn to interrupt and as he did so the anger rose from somewhere in his guts. 'You mean bloody babysitting don't you!'

'Please don't get angry, Mr Harry,' she said so quietly and with such deliberation that it shocked him. It seemed that she had been bracing herself for such a response. She had been expecting him to get angry. The thought hurt Harry. 'Is that what I've become?' he thought to himself. 'An angry, shouting man?'

He felt himself filling with shame, so that his shoulders sank in defeat: he sank into a chair. He closed his eyes and put his hands over his head in despair.

'I'm sorry,' he said, also in a whisper.

'You don't get angry like this with Grace, do you?' she demanded.

'No, no! Of course not. It's just … I really don't know. It's just … no, of course I'd never hurt Grace. Just lately, I don't know, I just get angry sometimes … I'm very sorry … I'm sure it's a very reasonable request …'

'You know I want what's good for Grace … Maude is getting too old now … Grace seems to have such a good time when she's with you. It's just a couple of days after Easter Monday. I have to work … a bit unexpectedly … I'd like to spend more time with her. It's not easy you know!' And all of a sudden, Mrs Hall appeared very vulnerable as well. The storm had passed, though Mrs Hall still looked anxious to leave.

'Yes, it's fine with me,' Harry told her. 'In fact, I'll be pleased to spend a few days with her … I'll just let Moses know.'

'Moses?' she asked.

'Yes, Moses … Moses Farrow … Mr Farrow. He's my friend. I do some gardening for him … with him … You won't tell Grace about the egg will you?'

'No, of course not.' And with that she left.

*

A week later Harry was able to present Grace with a small box. She handled it with great care just as he had asked. 'What is it?' she asked him shyly. Harry simply smiled at her intrigue.

'What's inside it, Harry? Is it a secret?' Harry nodded and Grace held it to her chest as if it was the most precious gift. Harry's eyes watered.

'Aren't you going to open it?' he asked at length. Grace looked agog.

'But … but, won't that spoil the secret?'

Harry laughed, partly to disguise the tears that had formed in his eyes for some reason.

'Go ahead and open it. We can share the secret.' He watched her carefully untie the string from around the box and slowly remove the lid. Grace looked at the egg in wonder. She looked across to Harry and smiled into his eyes, but it was too tender for Harry to bear and he was forced to look away.

'It's just an egg,' he told her in a rush. 'I painted it for you … Look, there's the cat, and the cow jumping over the moon.'

'Did it really?'

'No, of course it didn't.' He should have been expecting that. 'It's just the nursery rhyme.'

'Yes, I know,' she said, screwing up her nose and laughing.

'Mmm …' he told her with a wry smile, realising that she had been taking the rise out him all along. 'You're not as silly as you pretend, are you? Come on, we're going for a long walk.'

'Over the hills and far away?' she teased.

*

There are no real hills in this part of the land, though they did walk quite far for Grace's legs. They had previously walked just by the sea on each excursion, so this time Harry headed into the country lanes instead. He knew them well from the cycling jaunts that he had been taking more regularly again after recovering from the short ride to Keeling Nunnery a month previously.

On this morning the countryside was resplendent in its uniform of green and white. It seemed that all of a sudden every hedgerow was bursting with may blossom to break up the pastures into neat rectangular packages. Harry could hear Moses in his mind complaining that may was supposed to flower in the month of May whence it was named, but that nowadays spring came weeks earlier so that it bloomed in April. Harry smiled at his friend's concern and at the beauty around them. Then he breathed in as deeply as he could to capture as much of the essence of spring as he could: he could fairly taste spring in the air.

Soon they passed by the entrance to 'Honeysuckle Farm' where adults and children were able to walk around and enjoy the animals. He knew that Grace would have loved to stroke the young lambs. Sadly, the farm's entrance was shuttered and silent. 'Closed due to family bereavement,' read a sign. 'Oh, what a shame,' he wondered out loud. 'Moses said something about that the other day, but I wasn't really listening.'

'Moses?' asked Grace.

'Yes, Moses is my friend. We do the gardens together.'

'Moses? ... Is he old?' she pursued.

'Yeah, he is. But you'll like him. You'll have to come around and meet him sometime.'

Grace remained silent, so they walked on.

Harry took a footpath away from the road at the bend in the lane and headed along it through the fields towards Seawick. Two or three fields along the pathway skirted around a farmhouse and its outbuildings. It was clear that the buildings had been abandoned for some time. A thick stem of ivy had begun to take over the brickwork around the old farmhouse door and pigeons strutted indolently across the roof tiles. It was a sad scene considering the dilapidation, but beautiful in its own way. A new blush of green hung upon the shoulders of the hedgerows between the fields, and behind the farmhouse a stand of willows was dusted with the pastel yellow of their catkins. Harry considered it all to be worthy of an artistic attempt. He had become quite a bit fitter over the past month, working with Moses and making regular cycling forays into the countryside, but he needed to remember that Grace found physical exercise to be something of a challenge.

'Let's have our picnic here,' he suggested, sitting down and taking his pad and crayons out of the familiar blue rucksack and putting on the blue canvas hat that he invariably wore on his painting expeditions. Old Howard had told him that these two gifts would add a sense of flamboyance to his appearance. Harry had no wish to appear so, but he would have felt guilty over his indebtedness to Howard if he had not used them. And they were useful.

He asked Grace if she would like to draw, but she shook her head. As usual she was happy to stare around a new environment.

Within twenty minutes his picture was completed and he held it up for appraisal.

'What do you think?' he asked Grace.

'I don't like it,' she told him.

'I thought you liked my pictures.'

'I don't like this place … It's watching me,' she added, staring into the silent farmhouse.

'Don't be silly. Houses can't see! Oh, you are funny sometimes, Grace.'

'Am I?' she asked seriously.

'No, not really. I told you before … I think you are very nice.

And that's important. Come on; let's walk a bit further 'til we picnic – if you don't like it here.'

Grace held his hand as they followed the track out into the open fields. For a while she looked back over her shoulder behind them. Harry pointed out things to her: a hare in the distant furrows; a skein of geese above them, no doubt headed for the lake; and a decrepit scarecrow.

'What's it for?' she asked him about the scarecrow, and he told her that it was to scare away the birds.

'That's not very nice,' she concluded, but there was no edge to her comment, and he could tell that she was relaxed again.

Just before the track met the quiet lane down to Seawick they came across a metal plaque set into the ground. It was inscribed to the memory of six Canadian Air Force men who had perished when their plane came down there during the Second World War. Harry read the text out to Grace.

'Why is it here in the ground?' she queried.

'This is where they died. I expect the people who loved them wanted them to be remembered and so they put the plaque here so that we could read it when we walked by,' he explained.

'How did they know we would be here?' she asked him.

'I don't know, Grace. I really don't know!'

Along the road through Seawick and on to the coast he wondered about those dead airmen. He wondered what sorrow their deaths had caused and whether anyone was still alive to miss them and grieve for them. He wondered if anyone would grieve for him when he died; probably not, he mused to himself.

They ate their picnic sat on the grassy field of one of the many caravan sites that rested precariously along the cliff's edge there. Grace was still quiet but seemed contented enough, so Harry just looked out across the sea and let his thoughts follow their own path too. He wondered if Marianne would grieve for him if he died now.

The pain of their separation came back as sharply as if it had been yesterday. He had put so much of his life and energy into loving her, despite the mistakes, despite, even, the big mistake. And then it had all ended so abruptly. It was not just loneliness that hurt, it was raw grief. They had separated as if she had died. How could he possibly stem the flow of emotion through channels that had been so abruptly severed? The pain was physical, his arms needed to hold her, needed to feel the softness of her skin, the roundness of her arms.

'Are you alright?' Grace broke into his reveries. 'You look sad.'

'I'm fine,' he reassured her automatically. 'I just feel ...' He could not realise the exact words to express his feelings; if he could have done then perhaps he could have better coped with them. 'Yeah, I just feel a bit sad.'

They got up to walk back. It was a bit early to go back, but Harry felt drained of energy. Grace held his hand again. This time he thought it was good for him.

*

Moses came round early on the Saturday morning.

'I aren't stoppin',' he announced. 'I expect you'll need t' look after the lass.'

'No, not today,' Harry told him. 'She's out with her mother somewhere.'

''Appen you'll want to be 'elpin' me in the garden, then?'

''Appen I will,' Harry told him with a smile.

It was rather a pleasure to be working with the old fella after a few days' break. They took their time over the heavier labours as older men tend to do, and there was plenty of opportunity to talk. The conversations were light- hearted, without reference to anything of real consequence. Well, there was just one thing that caught in the tangles of Harry's consciousness: he had been telling Moses about his walk with Grace the previous day.

'It's just there on the edge of the path,' he was exclaiming about the plaque. 'I mean how many people go down that path, anyway!'

'Aye, yer right. Them lads died for the 'onour o' their country, but I wonder who thinks about them now,' Moses responded laconically. 'S'pose memories of the war will die with my generation.'

'Oh, I don't know about that,' Harry countered. 'We ... I mean my own generation ... we heard plenty about the war. People were always talking about it when I was a kid.'

'Aye, well people 'ad a lot to talk of. An' it probably done 'em good t' let it out too. Don't always do good t' keep them things in.'

'Yeah, but my Mum an' her sisters, my aunties, they were always on about the war ... but it was all about music and dancing and American airmen. Sounded a bit ... like ... immoral to me,' he persisted.

'It might o' done t' you, Young David, but you weren't there was you'? Half the country thought they were gunna die before the year were out ... them or the ones what they loved. You shouldn't be too 'asty t' judge 'em.' he told Harry warmly but emphatically.

'Well,' Harry stalled.

'S'right you know. You don't know 'alf the things that people carry round insides.'

'Yeah, guess so,' Harry conceded.

'Well then, lad, since you're now more in empathy like with the older generation, perhaps you wouldn't be mindin' doin' a favour or two for 'em?'

'Come on, Moses. Out with it! What is it? Mowing lawns, trimming hedges, digging boarders?'

'You know, lad, you do surprise me sometimes. There's me thinkin' there's nought but space between yer ears, an' all t' time you're knowing just what needs doin'!' Moses jested. 'An' there might be a bob or two in it for yer, lad!'

Harry assured him that he would be pleased to help. The way Moses had looked after him for the past ten months alone would have seen to that, but also Harry liked the idea of being busy and helping.

'Done deal!' they agreed.

'When do we start?'

'When do we start? We already started, lad. Grab yer walkin' shoes an' we'll be takin' ol' Barbara's dog out a while.'

They were soon out into the same lanes that Harry had trod the day before. The advent of spring had advanced incredibly in just one day, it appeared to him, and the hedgerows and fields were just bursting with fecund vitality. Just before they reached what Moses called 'Old Roland's Place', he pulled Harry and the dog into the opening of a field. They looked across the field to a small woodland, the canopy of which now lay verdant with spring greenery. Moses stood still; the dog obedient at his feet.

'Listen!' he said.

Harry listened.

'I can't hear anything,' he told Moses honestly after a minute of listening intently.

'Exactly, lad. You can't 'ear nothin'! I bin comin' up this lane all me life ... an' this time every year you could 'ear a cuckoo telling you it were springtime. It were one o' those special things! But I ain't 'eared one while two or three years since ... perhaps I never will.'

'Like you said, Moses, nothing stays the same,' Harry agreed.

'But you don't get the enormity of it, lad! Men, and women, been comin' up 'ere and listening to them cuckoos for thousands o' years ... prob'ly since man set foot on this island, an' that's a long time. An' all those years, every single one of 'em, they listened to that magical sign that spring had come fo' another year. It were part o' the magic of spring. But no more!'

And, perhaps for the first time, Harry did get it. He could sense and share Moses' profound concern.

'Yeah, you're right. I'm sorry.'

'Well, I aren't blamin' you! It's all of us. We're jus' lettin' it 'appen. It's not just cuckoos. It's skylarks, and little flycatchers, an' nightingales, an' all of 'em! Don't 'spose you've ever 'eard one o' them nightingales 'ave yer! An' it's swifts, an peewits, an' all the others!'

After which there was silence between them and, Harry felt, across the countryside. There was nothing that Moses or anyone could say on the matter. They just had to let it drop as if it did not exist.

They walked on, still in silence until they were stood before the abandoned farmhouse.

'Oh aye,' Moses confided. 'That were Roland's place. Farmed it since 'e were a lad. First fo' 'is father, then on 'is own ... Lived there all 'is life. That is while 'is wife died on 'im sudden like ... One minute she were feedin' chickens, the next she were gone. So were 'e t' next week! Day after 'er funeral 'e were gone 'imsen. No word t' anyone, just gone.'

'What? Dead?' Harry interjected.

'Alive? Dead? Dunno, just gone. No-one seen 'im since. Though ol' Purvis, that's one of 'is neighbouring farmers, did find one day, the top of a walkin' stick! You know, one o' them posh silver things that gets put on the end o' posh sticks. An' it had got … sort of ash in it, like the stick got burned. So ol' Purvis reckons 'e wus hit by lightnin'! An' the poor ol' bugger was burned up in a snap like that! … Atomised!'

'You mean vaporised!'

'I knows what I means! Any road, atomised or vaporised … e' were gone!'

'Just disappeared into thin air?'

'Aye, jus' disappeared. 'Cept, perhaps, maybe 'is spirit is still out there.' Moses mused with a stare into the distance. 'There's no tellin'. It's a funny thing.'

'That is a funny thing,' Harry thought to himself remembering the previous day there with Grace.

On his next visit to Bede House, Grace surprised Harry with a letter. They were about to start one of their evening sessions when she popped it out onto their shared table.

'Go on! Open it,' she cried excitedly. 'I know who it's from.'

'Do you now? … Let me guess,' he deliberated teasingly.

'No, don't guess,' she implored. 'Just open it!' And she clapped her hands in delight.

Harry did open the letter and kept it close to his face so that his expression was hidden. It was a bit of a surprise, but not one nearly as big as he pretended.

'Well, well, well,' he pondered. Then, 'Well I never … fancy that!'

Next he poked his nose around the side of the letter to pull a face at Grace, who almost exploded with laughter and delight.

'Fancy getting a letter from Mrs Button.'

'No, that's not her name!' she squealed uproariously.

'Mrs Bent Them?'

'No. Stop being silly, Harry,' she told him, reasserting a straight-faced expression. Obviously his joke had worn thin too quickly. Grace became sensible almost without another breath. Harry regarded her as gravely as he could with a mock sad face, to which she responded by pulling an equally sad face and pushing it up towards his. They held their mimes for only a few seconds before breaking into smiles, but good sense had been restored.

'So, you've been writing stories for young children and now you are going to the infants' school to read them to the children themselves?'

'Yes,' beamed Grace.

'And Miss Bentham wants me to come along and help?'

'Yes, yes … Will you, Harry? … Will you?'

'Of course, I will,' he told her quickly to allay her anxiety. 'Wild horses wouldn't keep me away.'

'Why would wild horses want to keep you away?'

*

It felt very strange for Harry to be walking into a working section of a school again. He smelt that unmistakeable odour of paper and shoes and energy, and he felt half a lifetime of memories on his back. All kinds of emotion coursed through him as he stood there trying to take it in: teaching had brought him the highest satisfaction and, yet, the most extreme despair. The feeling of holding a class's attention and respect in the palm of the hand had always been a magical feeling for him, while losing control had invariably created instant panic throughout his mind and soul.

But, on this occasion, he was a simple helper, and so he was eventually able to brush his more extreme emotions away.

The clever Miss Bentham had organised for half of her English class to visit one infants' school and the other half to visit a different one with another teacher. Harry went with Grace's half class along with Miss Bentham and a couple of helping mums. As usual the infants' teacher was a woman, so Harry was the only male adult. It was a little awkward to begin with, both for him and for the children who were not used to seeing a man in their classroom. He was assigned to 'look after' Grace and the group of infants to whom she was reading.

The infants sat in a neat circle around Grace's feet. They craned their necks round to look up at Harry with curiosity to begin with, but as soon as Grace began they fixed their attention firmly on her.

'Hello everyone. My name is Grace,' she told them with a big, glowing smile. 'I am going to read you a story called "Monica, the Little Lost Girl".'

Harry was not sure whether it was the confident way in which Grace could handle social introductions or the sincerity in her voice and smile, but she 'had them', had them right there in her hand. It was quite remarkable. And the story captivated them too. Of course, it did: Grace told it simply and honestly. She had no problems in pitching the story at their level; she seemed completely at one with the six- and seven-year-olds.

The story related the skirmishes and woes, and finally the joys, of a little girl who kept getting lost: lost at the shops; lost on the beach; lost in a new school; and lost all over the place. Of course, it appeared honest. It was! Harry had no doubt that Grace had been truly lost herself in all those places. She was telling it as it was, and the children loved it: loved to feel the fear of being lost, but within the security of their own classroom; loved to hear how the little girl was told off; loved the happy ending; loved the sincerity in Grace's reading; and loved the way she read with them rather than down to them, read as if they were equals.

The children clapped spontaneously when she had finished. Everyone else in the room looked round. Grace beamed benignly. There was applause at the end of most stories through the session after that, but more of the polite type, not quite like the spontaneity that had greeted Grace's efforts.

The readers were happy as they travelled back to their own school, pleased that they had done well. Some of them looked at Grace with just a bit of wonder.

Harry waited outside her classroom in the secondary school until the bell rang and Grace came out. He was slightly wary of bumping into the head teacher, but the man did not appear.

'You were great!' he let her know when she appeared. 'And I liked Monica a lot … better than Sascha!'

'Was I? Do you?'

'Yes, I do. Yes, you were. When we get you home, I'll wait and tell your mother how good you were … if you'd like that.'

Then, as he ushered her along the corridor, there was a polite call from behind.

'Oh, Mr Harry!' Miss Bentham came gambolling down the corridor to meet them.

'I just wanted to thank you for all your help. It was really good that you were with us.' She hesitated and wiped a stray strand of hair from her forehead. Although pulled back quite severely, Harry could see that her hair was luxuriantly dark, but with an undertone of red that brought life to the curls that were straining to escape. Her face had pinkened too, and to his surprise it seemed to be more in embarrassment than exertion. He worked hard to keep his eyes averted from the steady rise and fall of her bosom.

'I didn't do anything … really. Not like Grace … she was great wasn't she?'

'Yes, she was,' agreed Miss Bentham brushing her hand lightly and easily across the top of Grace's head in what Harry thought was a lovely gesture.

'It was a pleasure,' he told Miss Bentham.

'Yes, thank you. I hope we'll see you again.'

'Oh, yes. That would be … nice,' he managed to mumble as Grace and he made their way out of the school.

'Fuck it!' he thought to himself. 'Why do I always have to say 'nice'?'

MAY

'Oh, look!' cried Grace, 'the sun's come out!' It had for the first time in a week.

'You do not notice things until they stop!' Harry thought to himself. Now the sunshine appeared to be even more precious as it spread itself across the beach where they were walking, illuminating the wet sand and the water with sparkling jewels of light.

Despite the inclement nature of the previous weeks, the increased hours of daylight had allowed Harry to take Grace out in the evenings more regularly, rather than chase illusive progress with schoolwork within the confines of the house. On some very wet days they still worked half-heartedly with books and paper, which tended to drift into storytelling, but whenever the weather was not too wet they set off on a walk somewhere.

And, as on this day, the beach was their usual destination. It was easy to get to, most often empty of other people, save the obligatory, odd fisherman, and it had a great sense of openness and freedom. He felt the light breeze on his face and listened to the silence beyond the rhythmic fall of the waves and the ever-present calling of the birds. It seemed to Harry that it set them free.

'Smell that breeze, Grace!'

Grace and Harry always enjoyed walking the newly wet strand that was left as the tide went out. They made a special point of watching the many birds that made their life's existence along this thin margin. Out to sea black-headed gulls dominated, but right along the water's edge was a variety of little waders. Harry tried to remember the ones Moses had told him: orange beaked oystercatchers; speckled dunlin and sanderling; sandpipers, terns and ringed plovers. They loved to see the birds scurrying along the wet, mirroring sand, little legs flickering and double-imaged in the light of their own reflections. Harry thought that his and Grace's inner spirits flittered among them as if they were there to share the seabirds' world for those moments.

Those times on the beach were like a shared secret between them and always they would return to Bede House flushed with happiness and satisfaction. Being with Grace gave Harry purpose as well as company. It chased away the lurking monsters of dejection and hopelessness that had roamed so often around his inner thoughts. He had come to believe that the anger was to do with the mess he had made of his life. At least that was how he had begun to come to terms with having such anger. It made him feel better to have a reason, even if it was not the correct one. He was still very inept at looking inside at his own feelings.

The regular sessions with Grace provided a framework of purpose around which he could begin to build a pattern for his days. Life had grown increasingly more bearable and, like a reprieved man, he had ceased to dread the advent of each new day.

On a few occasions over the past weeks he had even set off in his own time to sketch and paint in the open. His subject was most often the view from cliff tops across the beach and sea. The resulting pictures were invariably disappointing, however. He wanted desperately to be able to capture that special combined sense of freedom and tranquillity that he had found together with Grace there, but he could never quite get it. He thought that perhaps the lack of specific detail had robbed him of focus. It was illusive to him. The components that made up the coastal scene were so simple and constant, just sea, strand and sky, but there was an openness and an atmosphere that he just could not manage to put down onto the canvas. He decided that his failure was what made the difference between him and the really good painters.

One day he was watching Grace poking around with a short stick that he had just picked up for her. She was using it to turn over pebbles and shells, her face wrapped in intense purpose and concentration as she whispered quietly to herself, or maybe to Sascha, about what she was doing. He realised that he would need to include her in his compositions if he was to have any chance of capturing that special atmosphere.

'What are you doing?' he asked her.

'I'm looking at the pictures on the stones,' she told him. 'There are all sorts of pictures on them when they are still shiny.'

Grace's interjection had planted a seed in Harry's mind.

'Next time we come down to the beach I'll bring my big rucksack and we can take a few stones home with us,' he told her.

The delectable sunshine that Grace and he had enjoyed on the beach that day proved to be something of a rarity as showers and sometimes more persistent rainfall doggedly pursued the passage of days through the middle of the month. A day came, however, when Harry decided that they could wait no longer to collect those large stones for painting.

Despite the greyness of the sky, the morning lay surprisingly tranquil before them. They kept close to the sea's edge and away from the sodden clay cliffs that appeared particularly dark and foreboding. Wandering northwards from the town's edge they searched indolently for the perfect stones: 'large as a good-sized Easter egg and smooth all over' was what Harry told Grace they were looking for. These particular stones appeared to be surprisingly rare, however, and they had trekked for quite a while before they came across an area containing just what he was looking for.

Finally, Harry was satisfied with four large, pebbly stones that he dropped into his old, blue rucksack along with some smaller pebbles chosen by Grace. He felt them rumble together in his rucksack as he gained his feet, though any discomfort from their weight was totally forgotten as he turned to see in great shock that the tide had crept silently but swiftly in to lap against the very shingle upon which they were standing. He could scarcely believe that the sea had advanced so far up the beach, and scarcely believe that he had been so stupid in not taking care to notice. His chest and throat seemed to freeze for an instant, but he forced himself to think more calmly.

'Right, Grace, we're going to pretend that we are in a race. Let's see how quickly we can get up the beach. You know … where the yacht club gulley is!'

The margin between land and sea was barely a pavement's width, but it was only around three hundred metres to reach the track that led up to the clifftop. Harry's optimism made him believe that they could make the distance comfortably, even though, as if on cue, the wind had risen to blow hard against them. It was not a great distance, but just the like heavy-legged running of his worst nightmares, the soft shingle pulled hard at every stride, and their progress towards the gulley was much slower than he had imagined.

There was still a full hundred metres between them and their destination by the time the water actually reached Harry's feet. It scared him. He veered in towards the black mud that had been tumbling down the cliff face all week, but, straightway, realised the error as Grace began to slip and slide in its cloying grasp.

It was all Harry could do to keep her upright and moving. He felt the stones in his rucksack lurching from side to side and thought about dropping them, bag and all, except that he was too frightened to let go of Grace's arm.

He really did begin to fear for their lives.

'A quick breather!' he shouted at Grace, who looked tearful and clung to his arm desperately. They were forced to wait for each wave to ebb before they could make a little more progress along the beach, which had become no longer a beach, but more of a frantic frothing of salt water right up against the crumbling cliffs.

The waves seemed to grow ever deeper and the wind ever stronger. There was no time left for hesitation. With one final, monumental effort, Harry picked Grace completely up in his arms and ran staggering and lurching to reach the slightly raised section of beach that marked the beginnings of the glorious track that climbed up from beach to the clifftops.

On reaching relative safety, Harry fell face down against the gravelly track, grateful beyond his former imaginings to be on dry land. He began to retch as the effects of his extreme effort took hold, but, even then, he struggled to control it in fear of frightening Grace any further. For some moments Harry just lay there. Despite the relief, he had no wish to face the moment.

He became conscious of a patting on his head. It was Grace, of course. He twisted round towards her, expecting to be confronted by tears and hysteria. Yes, her face was marked by tears, but she appeared calm.

'Grace. I'm so sorry!'

'You did your best,' was all she had to offer, and Harry was pleased to accept.

They got to their feet as it began to rain again and moved off along the bridleway towards Bede House.

Maude was at the door to open it before they had chance to ring the bell.

'We're very wet,' Grace chimed. And, before Harry could even begin to reel out one of the excuses that he had been rehearsing in his mind on the wet, cold walk back, the old woman had whisked Grace away up the stairs to look after her delicate, young charge.

Harry was left at the front door. He felt dismissed: completely dismissed. He pulled the door shut, turned around, re-adjusted the heavy rucksack and headed back to the cottage. He felt, however, quite happy to have been so dismissed. It could all have been so much worse.

*

A few days later Harry set to work on the first stone. Despite appearing smooth to the eye, he soon found that the actual surface of the rock was rough and grainy, so that it was difficult to move pencil or paintbrush across it with confidence. The stone itself, however, held such quality in its shape, and such texture and colour, that he was inspired to try to complement it rather than to enforce his own designs upon it. To a large extent the qualities of the rock dictated the form of the images that he managed to create upon its surface and, although he had started with some initial concept, he soon found that the lines and forms of the design seemed to emerge almost of their own accord. He was shocked to find that, by the time he had completed the work, it was well into the small hours. Harry went to bed feeling tired, but unusually satisfied.

In the morning he set himself the task of covering the previous evening's paint with a coating of transparent lacquer. Then later that morning, as he lifted the finished, dried stone for inspection, the design before his eyes quite enthralled him. To his own mind it was far, far better than anything he had imagined it would be. His abstractions of sea and sky were held within Grace's hands to create a vivid contrast between bright sunshine and a gathering storm: a patterned sequence of raindrops, clouds, sunbeams, waves and birds had been inscribed within the shapes of her hands to an effect far better than he had conceived in his own mind. And, to his pleasant surprise, amazement even, enveloped around the curves and contours of the humble rock there was a sense of space and light: a sense of space and light that he had been hitherto unable to capture on canvas.

Harry sat and stared at his surprise accomplishment for some minutes simply enjoying the pleasure of having created something so pleasing. He knew full well that it was completely self-indulgent, but he did not care. He had been thinking of giving the stone to Grace, but for reasons unknown he decided to keep it for some day in the future when … But he was unable to complete the thought.

*

Despite the regularity of the rain, he had still spent a lot of time working with Moses. They had established a regular routine of working for three mornings a week in the gardens of what they called Moses' 'friends': an army, it seemed to Harry, of old people who no longer had the strength to keep up with their gardens, but who were reluctant to lose them. Many of the 'friends' gave presents or donations to Moses, but he never did their tasks with any form of reward in mind; he just did it out of friendship. There was always a lot to do in the garden during May and the extra rain that spring had resulted in a veritable explosion of greenery. There was too much work to do to allow soft rain to deter them.

Moses drove from place to place in his old box of a Volvo estate. Harry could drive but had not got round to thinking about a car of his own. Most of the jobs were within or very close to the town, but there were occasions when they would travel further, even out to the Wolds. The roads were always empty out there and Harry loved the same sense of space and freedom he found there as much as he did when on the wide beaches of the coast. The empty green heart of the East Riding was, Harry thought, a special secret of its own.

He had soon determined that he would take Grace to some of the places there later in the summer: perhaps she could ride a bicycle or maybe he would be able to persuade Moses to drive them out there. He knew she would like the spaces and he was keen for her to see the lambs before they had grown out of their cute innocence. Unfortunately, with the persistence of grey skies, it looked as if the cute, woolly lambs would reach relative maturity before the weather improved.

Harry looked out of the window. They had driven well into the Wolds on this occasion to visit an ailing, old man who Moses simply called Bob. Moses and Bob had, it became clear from the banter in the car during their journey, been close associates in their younger days.

'Don't think we've been quite this far before,' Harry commented to Moses as they headed north-westwards along a quiet lane out of Driffield.

'Well, it don't seem far nowadays wi' cars an' all,' he replied nonchalantly, 'but back while we was young, it felt a pretty mile to cycle way out 'ere. We was best mates at school, but then 'is father got management of a farm ... this 'ere farm we's visitin' ... an' that was us split up fo' the rest of our lives. 'Cept, o' course, fo' the few days in me life when I had enough energy to pedal mes'en over ... an' that weren't often, I can tell thee. You young 'uns seem to tek travel fo' granted wi' all the cars an' planes an' things, but back then we never went far. 'Cept fo' the war o' course. I went a long way then ... but I wished I hadn't!'

Harry left Moses to reminisce and let his own mind wander across the long, smooth lines of the hills around them. It appeared to be a land empty of people: an uninterrupted blanket of rolling greenery; green and green and green as far as the eye could see; a little sombre, even melancholic in its present state of wetness, but very beautiful in its own way.

"Ere we are now. It's just up 'ere.'

From a distance, as they approached, the farm looked neat and attractive: the old stone house stood out against the backdrop of white apple and pear blossom on the trees in the gardens surrounding it. Close up to the property, however, the ever eager fingers of neglect and disrepair were clearly evident.

'He don't do much farmin' nowadays,' Moses interjected as if reading Harry's thoughts.

'Seems like a stroke took away 'is short-term memory. 'Is daughter visits 'im just about every day ... it was 'er what got in touch about 'is garden. Perhaps she'll visit while we're 'ere ... She's a grand lass ... I wish I 'ad someone like that to look after me in me old age.'

'You're not allowed an old age, Moses ... too much work to do. That's what you tell me!'

Bob soon answered their knock on the door. He stared at

Moses for a few seconds before he greeted him warmly. At first his incapacity was indiscernible. He joked and chatted easily, and he and Moses even reminisced about incidents from their boyhood past.

'Remember when old "Split-pea" chased us round the churchyard?' Bob had asked Moses out of the blue.'

But as their time with him progressed, Old Bob's lack of short-term memory grew more and more obvious.

'Fancy a cup o' tea?' he asked Harry for about the sixth time in as many minutes.

'No. Thanks. I'll just finish this edge.'

'Yes, you're makin' a right good job o' that. Would you like a cup o' tea?'

'No thank you, Bob. You just asked me that!'

'Did I? Silly old bugger!' He smiled at his own self-deprecation and averted his eyes to look wistfully across the empty hills: a few petals of white blossom had lodged themselves into his thinning hair to add pathos to his appearance. After a few seconds he turned back to his kitchen door.

'I'll just go and put the kettle on, then.'

They spent several hours there in Old Bob's garden before more rain drove them inside for, finally, a cup of tea before they departed. As they were drinking their tea, and completely out of the blue, Bob fetched a photograph from the drawer of the kitchen's large wooden dresser.

'Look at that,' he demanded with a smile as he placed it in front of Harry.

It was a picture of a little girl squinting into the sunshine. The photograph was clearly very old and the image was rather indistinct. Harry looked up at Bob waiting for him to elaborate on the purpose of this interlude, but he was simply staring back at him. Moses interrupted to fill the void.

'That's your Emily,' he reminded Bob, 'When she were a little girl.'

'Yes,' continued Bob as if his mind had just slipped back into gear, 'She were on a day trip from Hull where she lived while she were a lass. They was at the Tatton Sykes memorial an' she 'ad 'er picture taken. Funny thing was, she were just a couple o' miles from the place where she would live fo' the rest of 'er life!'

'That's right,' added Moses, who obviously knew the story well. 'Years later you met at Driffield market, fell in love and got married: didn't yer, Bob?'

'We did.'

'An' you brought 'er back 'ere to live on this farm.'

'I did.'

'She were a lovely woman. You did well to marry 'er, Bob. 'Ere, put this back in the drawer along with all your other memories.'

Moses stood, and to Harry's surprise, put out his arms to embrace Bob in a big hug. The two men held each other for some moments as if holding on desperately to their memories of younger days. At first it seemed out of keeping with the Moses Harry knew, and, he guessed, was not exactly common amongst tough, old Yorkshiremen. But then the sincere tenderness of the two old friends made it seem like just the right thing to do.

'Cheerio then, pal. 'Appen we'll see thee in a couple o' weeks,' said Moses. 'You be alright?'

'Me? Yeah I'll be fine. Our Janet will be round soon. She looks after me all right … she makes a good cup o' tea.'

'She does. You're a lucky man.'

As they drove off, Harry could see in the wing mirror that Bob had remained at the gate until they had disappeared around the bend and out of sight.

'That's a bit of a relief,' he commented to Moses as the old man accelerated along the road. 'If he asked about a cup of tea once, he must have asked me a hundred times!'

'Well, perhaps 'e did, lad. But there aren't any point getting aggravated. He don't mean to repeat himself ... He just don't know 'e's already asked,' Moses replied.

Harry felt mean for not having been more accommodating.

'Why, ol' Bob, 'e were a right un' in 'is day. Wit as sharp as a wet whip.'

'Yeah, I'm sorry I wasn't more ...'

'You don't need to worry, lad ... All you sees is a fadin', old man, but when I looks at 'im I sees all the things 'e's been over the years ... 'e could make me 'elpless wi' laughing. An' brave! Brave? ... 'E once giv' big Larry 'Enson such a thump to save me 'e did, an' it were my fault an' all ... 'E were a lad alright!'

To Harry's surprise Moses decelerated and pulled off the road. He got out, and stood against the dry-stone wall that marked the edge of the fields. A faraway look appeared upon his countenance, but when Harry approached he stretched out to point across the landscape.

'Look yonder, jus' past the end o' that line o' beech trees. Look, you can see the top o' the spire on Tatton's Memorial.'

'Who was Tatton Sykes?'

'Oh, I dunno' ... some rich landowner I imagine who wanted to 'ave 'imself remembered ... an' look there, lad ... see them birds there?'

'Yeah, plovers aren't they?' Harry added, trying to impress Moses with his ornithological knowledge.

'Tha's right. They are plovers … or pewits or lapwings. We used to call 'em tewits or tuets while I were a lad. Back then the sky used to be full o' them … an' when they wheeled in the sunlight it were like the sky wus a mirror shatterin' into pieces … there were so many flapping wings.'

And, indeed, as Harry looked, a flickering shaft of sunshine, escaping between the threatening clouds, fell upon the birds' wings in spectacular shards of brightness to verify his point.

'Sometimes nostalgia wraps 'er arms around me 'eart so strong, it's enough to burst it. It scares me that them times 'ave gone fo'ever … but nothin' stays the same: not Bob, nor Tatton bloomin' Sykes … not even the birds … nothin' stays the same.'

They stood there for a while, looking across the fields and back to where Bob's place lay. For an instant the sun fell with brilliant luminosity upon the fresh, green leaves of the beech trees, but even then there was still a sadness, it seemed, across the whole scene.

Back in the car Harry was cajoling Moses into telling more tales of his adolescent escapades with Bob.

'And what about Split-pea?' he asked him.

'Split-pea?' Moses answered through chortled gulps of laughter. ''E were a funny ol' bloke 'e were … One day we pinched a couple o' carrots from outside 'is shop. Thought we was clever an' out o' sight we did. But ol' Split-pea saw us … nothin' got past 'im. 'E were out that shop like lightnin'. Didn't think the ol' bugger could still move that fast! 'E chased us up t' road an' straight after us into the churchyard … the ol' vicar came out as I remember an' shouted somethin', but we never stopped, none on us. Me an' Bob was too intent on savin' us skins, an ol' Split-pea was intent on getting' 'is carrots back. Mean ol' bugger he were! Tha's 'ow got 'is name, Split-pea! When 'e weighed out vegetables on 'is ol' scales an' it were 'alf a ounce out … rather than gi' you an extra pea pod or carrot, or whatever it were … 'e'd cut one in 'alf. Split a pea pod 'e would out o' meanness. Tha's why people called 'im Split-pea! Yeah, ol' Split-pea, mean as witch's curse, but we took many a pea pod off 'im, me an' Bob … I could tell thee!'

And Moses dissolved into laughter again.

It seemed strange splashing along through the wet lanes in a torrent of laughter, but it was infectious, and Harry was soon laughing as much at Moses as he was about his past escapades with Bob.

Moses had been left a tray of fresh eggs by Bob's daughter as a thank you. He invited Harry round to his kitchen for one of his 'special' omelettes.

After whipping up the egg whites and then mixing in the yolks, Moses fried the omelettes with generous measures of fried vegetable and cheese.

'Ooh, great!' Harry told him. 'I love Spanish omelette.'

'Don't know about Spanish,' he conceded, '… my Rose used to cook 'em like that, an' to my knowledge she never went to Spain. Anyway, it were good o' Janet to leave us a present like that. She's very thoughtful. It must be a real blessin' for Bob to 'ave a lovely daughter like that.'

'You would have made a good father,' Harry told Moses. 'How come you never had children?'

'I did,' he said flatly.

Harry did not know why he had assumed that the old man had always been alone.

'I 'ad two children, but … I lost 'em …'

'What do you mean "lost them"?' Harry asked open mouthed.

'We had a daughter … our Elizabeth. She were just like her

mother, kind and gentle, and lovely. But she died, she did ...'

He turned away again to stare out through the window into an unfocussed distance.

'Only fourteen she were. Little angel 'ad a 'ole in heart. Wouldn't be no problem these days probably. But then they couldn't do nothin' to save 'er. None of us could ... Just watched her fade away. My Rose were never the same after that. An' when our Alec went off, then my Rose ... she sort of gave up on life. Seemed like she'd totally lost 'er purpose for livin'. She died a year later. They said she 'ad 'eart trouble too. Well I 'spose she did ... only it were a broken heart ... nothin' medical. Then we lost our Alec too.'

Harry waited for the old man to continue, but nothing was immediately forthcoming. He had never spoken so personally to Harry before and he looked drained by it.

'I'm sorry, Moses,' Harry told him.

'Well, you don't need to be sorry,' he sighed. 'It were my fault anyway.'

'What do you mean, 'your fault'?'

Harry spoke to his back since Moses had turned once more to resume his contemplation of the distance. It seemed that he had some difficulty with this conversation. But then he spoke again.

'Our Alec, that's our lad ...e had this woman ... She were older than 'im. She had 'er own children too ... not that I minded that ... only she never loved 'im. I could see it plain as plain; she just saw 'im as a way out. I could see it, but 'e couldn't 'o course. I ... I wouldn't 'ave 'er in the house. So 'e left. Never put foot in the house again, either of 'em. Sent a card to 'is mother. Said they'd emigrated to Australia. I haven't never seen 'im since. 'An that were thirty year ago.'

'Bloody hell, Moses! Thirty years ago? And don't you mind?'

'Oh yeah, I mind all right. But I can't undo it can I? I know I should never 'ave interfered. Should o' just let 'im get on an' mek 'is own mistakes. But I never realised that then. Now it's too late.'

'Why don't you write to him or something?' Harry asked naïvely.

'Don't know where 'e is!'

'Well, doesn't he write or anything?' Harry persisted.

'They wrote Christmas cards for a few years. To 'is mother o' course. 'E never knew she were dead, see. Then, some years after that ... a postcard ... just from him ... said 'e was fine, but only 'is name on it. Picture 'o Perth on the front, but only 'is name on the back. I still got it, upstairs. But that was many years ago.'

Then he just stood there looking vulnerable. Harry supposed he could have put his arm around the old man's broad shoulders, but he thought that might have been too intrusive for him. Or, perhaps, it was just too much for Harry. Harry just stood there and shared his silence. It seemed that neither of them knew how to conclude the moment.

'Sorry,' Harry told him again. 'I never knew you had all those things inside you.'

'We all got things we keep inside! My Rose used to say that everyone 'ad a 'ole boxful o' secrets inside 'em, so it's no surprise you got a few ... Come on, lad, you can 'elp me carry these pots out.'

Harry walked home in the rain feeling disconsolate. He continued to ruminate on the way he made so many false assumptions about other people and still got upset when others could not see the heartache inside of himself.

*

Time passed, then, after days and days of wet weather, Harry was woken for a change, by the brightness of early morning sunlight. For a while he just lay there listening, not realising he was listening, until he heard the milkman pass. Unusually, around the Holderness there were still deliveries of milk to people's doorsteps. It reminded Harry of being in his childhood bed, waiting for the Great Western hooter to tell him that it was time to get up for school. In those days the whole of Swindon had moved to the sounds of the Great Western Railway Works. Half of the men in the town worked there then; his father included. That was until it all closed down and his father was made redundant. It broke him, Harry could still remember: broke the family too. It did, or he did. His father was never the same after that.

Harry took a cup of tea out into the garden, where he sat watching the newly arrived swallows and martins flit industriously across the sky before and behind the softly waving branches of the big ash tree. The ash branches seemed to have been the last of all the trees to burst into life, but, finally, even they had been replenished with a full coat of green as tiny leaves and keys had unfurled on the tip of each and every twig.

For a while Harry could imagine that the morning was just for him. The air was still full of birdsong, which, paradoxically, made the whole scene appear even quieter and more peaceful. For the first time in a long while Harry felt pleased to be himself and pleased to be living.

The good feeling carried Harry through the morning as he set up his easel and painted vigorously to express the vitality of the season on canvas. The result of his labours was not a masterpiece by any means; it was just a view of the garden and the sky beyond the ash tree, but there was life to it and Harry determined to send it off to Howard to let him see the improvement in his painting as well as his whole being.

Harry's efforts had left him feeling really hungry and he was amazed to learn from the radio as he ate that it was already late into the afternoon. It was, in fact, time to get prepared for his session with Grace.

He stood for some moments after his arrival outside the door of Bede House in confusion. No one had answered his ringing of the bell or banging of the ornate Victorian knocker. The house appeared to be empty. Then he remembered that Mrs Hall had said something about going away at Whitsun. Had they reached the last week of May already? The days of the past weeks had passed so quickly, and he had no idea at all of what date it had reached. He resolved to check with Moses, though Harry suspected that his real motive for going around to the old man's place had been to seek company, since he had found it a disappointment and anticlimax to find himself not seeing Grace.

Predictably, Moses was working in his garden. 'Just the man,' he told Harry as he appeared around the end of his garage. 'I were needin' someone to 'old t'other end o' this ladder.'

'Oh, what you up to now?' Harry asked in mock nonchalance to disguise his pleasure at being needed.

'I were just lookin' to pinch out the young leaves on ends o' them quince branches.' And he looked upwards along the length of the twisted tree that had been trained across the brickwork of the old outhouse at the furthest end of his garden.

'Oh, it's a quince tree is it? Looks healthy enough to me,' Harry told him.

Harry had not really noticed the tree before, but indeed, it did look well with its pale pink blossom and its dark oval leaves.

'Might look reet to thee,' said Moses with exaggerated Yorkshire accent. 'But such things of beauty need proper tendin'. Me father planted this tree when I were nought but a lad. 'E said 'e'd brung it back all the way from Mesopotamia, where 'e'd been fightin' fo' the British Army in the Great War. Me mother, then my Rose after 'er, used to make jams an' jellies out o' the fruit. I don't make no jam meself, like. But I like to look after the tree. Seems like I'm preservin' a bit her,' he sighed. 'Lettin' all them young twigs run riot would tek too much strength out o' the old tree. So that's what I'm adoin'.'

It pleased Harry to help him for a couple of hours.

'You workin' with Grace tomorrow?' Moses asked as Harry was leaving.

'No. She's gone away with her mother for a couple of days. It's Whitsun.'

Moses suddenly brightened: 'Well get yoursen round 'ere again day after tomorrow, lad. I'll tek yu' for a little treat!'

Bank holiday Monday: a car boot sale. It would not have been Harry's choice of destinations or activities, but he had to admit that there was certainly vitality and colour to the throng of people and the tables of wares that they gathered around. From a distance the trestles and tables had an attraction and allure, though up close most of the items appeared pretty ropey to him.

'Never know, lad. One man's junk is another man's treasure!' intoned Moses.

'Yes,' Harry thought to himself, 'I'm sure there are bargains and treasure amongst all that tat, but I'm not sure I can be bothered to ...'

And then he saw it.

There was no good reason why he came to be standing in front of that stall and its particular pile of junk, but the second he saw it there beside all the other tat, Harry knew that it was perfect. Strange, he had not been looking for it. He had not been looking for anything. But instantly he knew he had to buy it.

The colour, a sort of pale mauve, put him off just a little, but that was almost an irrelevance. He knew inside that it would be perfect for him and Grace.

'Oh, yes. Yes! Yes! Yes!' he announced into the morning air.

'By 'eck, he's alive!' observed Moses drolly. 'Thought you didn't want anything! Thought the last thing in the world you wanted to do was visit a pathetic car boot sale. Thought wild 'orses wouldn't make you tek other people's old crap 'ome, let alone pay money fo' it!'

'Yeah, OK I was wrong … again … but look at it … what a beauty!'

'Well, what we lookin' at?'

Instead of replying Harry walked over to the tandem that was propped against a table piled high with garden implements.

'How much d'you want for this?' he asked the bored-looking bloke standing behind the pile.

'Sixty.'

'Sixty quid for that ol' thing?!' exclaimed Moses. 'I'll gi' yee ten for it.'

'Sixty.'

'Yee could get a moped for that!' said Moses getting into his stride. 'What? 'As it got silver wheels or summat?'

'Fifty.'

'Fifty? This is East Yorkshire, lad, not East Sussex!' Moses chided.

'Fifty will be fine,' Harry said to kill the discussion.

And before Moses could protest any further he fished the notes out of his wallet and held them out to the man, whose eyes showed interest for the first time. No doubt, Moses would chunter on about his ineptitude at haggling, but Harry was interested only in wheeling the tandem off and away from the maelstrom of the car boot sale.

'Drop in for a cup o' tea on your way back,' he called to Moses over his shoulder. 'You can show me your bargains.'

Harry's comment would have been 'one up' for him over Moses if it had not been for him having to wheel the tandem round to Moses' place that afternoon so that the old man could help him with the more difficult aspects of getting the tandem back into shape.

Moses seemed, however, to beam inwardly at Harry having need of his expert advice. Of course, there was not any real rivalry between them: the balance of craft, knowledge and expertise was too heavily skewed in the old man's favour for that to be the case. And, typically, Moses worked every bit as hard as his younger apprentice to get the work completed.

Not only was every component of the vehicle checked, cleaned, oiled and fixed perfectly into place, but Moses came up with a pot of navy blue enamel paint that they used on the rougher areas of paintwork to complement the existing pale mauve of the framework. At the end of their labours the vehicle did not look exactly new, but it did, to their eyes at least, look good.

'Nice!' Harry said to the old man with a challenging wink.

'Nay, lad,' Moses lingered over his expression before announcing with unexpected gusto, 'Splendid … reet splendid!'

'Yeah,' Harry agreed with him, 'reet splendid!'

*

Moses had been happy to work at fixing the tandem, but he was obstinately steadfast in his refusal the next day to accompany Harry on its maiden journey around the streets.

'I will not, lad,' he told Harry. 'The streets'll still be full 'o Wessies eatin' ice creams and struttin' round like they owns the place!'

Moses had a thing about the people who drove over from the West Riding to spend some time next to the Yorkshire coastline. 'Wessies' he called them.

'You can't tell me they're any different to people round here.'

''Appen I can, lad ... You ever bin to the west o' Yorkshire?' he asked.

'Well, I did go to a wedding in Huddersfield once.'

'Reet, lad, then you should 'ave noticed ... them 'ills round there ... they're like bunched knuckles ... all 'ard an' knotted. While over these east lands ... the 'ills are smooth and rounded like ... the limbs o' children.'

Moses looked at Harry as if he had made his point, but Harry refused to acknowledge it. Moses grimaced. 'Diff'rent 'ills ... diff'rent people! Stands to reason!'

'You do talk some rubbish, Moses. Fellow brothers and sisters from "God's own county", and you're too condescending to share a drop of sunshine with them!'

'Say what you like, lad ... I aren't going on it ... an' that's that! If you want to parade your arse about on your new flyin 'machine, you'd best do it on yer own. Now get on wi' thee!'

Whitsun week, along with the other bank holidays, was one of the few times when the little town got really busy, so perhaps

Harry had not chosen the best day for a test ride. But he was anxious to try out the tandem. Within the first half mile between Moses' house and the promenade, he came close to a serious altercation with one of the many caravans on the road but escaped without damage. He had to admit to himself that it did feel strange with half an empty tandem behind: not just the weight of the extra frame, but the very idea of riding it alone without a second person. Other people must have thought the same since a number of catcalls followed him down the roads: 'Oi mate, you've lost yer missus!'; 'Don't look now, but yer engine's buggered off!' were typical.

They made Harry smile and feel that he was sharing part of their holiday cheeriness. He decided to indulge in more holiday spirit by stopping along the front for an ice cream. There was more banter from the crowds as he stood beside the tandem licking great mouthfuls of soft ice cream.

'Any chance of a ride?' asked one particularly pleasant voice.

'Oh … hello … I wasn't expecting to see you here!' he answered.

It had taken him by surprise to be accosted by such an attractive woman who he soon recognised as Miss Bentham, although she did look different. Her hair was loose around her shoulders. It billowed around in the breeze, allowing the sun to highlight its redness.

She must have been reading his thoughts.

'Ha … you're as bad as the kids … expect teachers to fade away at the end of the school day … just like vampires!'

'Do you live here then?' he asked, trying to recover.

'Not here, but not far away … just down the road in Beverley. I must admit I don't usually come here on non-school days, but my brother's staying with me for the week. Thought we'd have a day by the sea. He's trying to teach me to drive … poor beggar!

He says you can't tell teachers anything … 'spect he's right … I'm not a very good pupil.'

She stood there smiling while Harry just gaped. She had said more to him in one minute than anyone, apart from Moses and Grace, had said in the past month. He must have looked shocked and stupid, but Miss Bentham did not seem at all put off.

'Well … what are the chances then?' She smiled at him.

'Chances?'

'Yeah! What chance of having a ride on this thing? I've never been on a tandem.'

'No … nor me,' he told her somewhat bashfully. 'I mean … it's my first time too.'

'Well, let me on then. It must be easier with two … that's what it's for isn't it? A bicycle made for two?'

And without further enquiry or encouragement she swung her leg over the bar to straddle the front section of the bike. She was wearing shorts and Harry could not help himself from noticing that her legs looked in pretty good shape, much better than he would have guessed from her previous appearances in school-teaching attire. In fact, her shapely, strong thighs fairly mesmerised him for a few moments as she stood there with the bar between her legs. He sincerely hoped that she was not able to read all his thoughts, though the look on her smiling face suggested to him that she probably could.

'You'll be better off on the back,' he told her.

The rear half of the tandem was constructed without a bar, in the orthodox manner for females.

'OK,' she said over his shoulder as she remounted. 'You'll have to tell me where we're going.'

'I don't know. Where are we going?'

'Anywhere!' she answered breezily. 'What about your garden? Grace tells me you've got a really beautiful garden.'

'Yes. Well … OK … It's not that beautiful, actually …' Harry began before his brain managed to tell his mouth to stop making himself sound like such a boring, old fart. 'Yeah, right. Let's go … ready?'

They made a disjointed start: scooting, missing the pedals, and generally mis-coordinating their efforts, but within a few seconds they were up and pedalling well together. The first bend almost brought disaster as they struggled to balance and ended up oversteering before finally making their way around it, but then they managed quite well. And all the way their progress was marked by Miss Bentham's shouting, shrieking and generous laughter.

'Oh, call me Molly!' she had demanded when he brought out tea to her on the garden bench.

She continued to talk enthusiastically as they drank, which pleased Harry and allowed him to relax in a more passive role. It was difficult for him to believe that she was the same woman he had met so unfortunately in the headteacher's office those weeks back. She almost burst with appreciation when he brought out the scones he had made the day previously: they had been made for Grace though he wantonly ignored that.

'Oh, you're so clever,' she told him. 'Me? Can't cook … can hardly do anything that's practical … books, books, books! That's all I'm any good for! You should hear my brother moaning about my driving … Ben! … Bugger!' she suddenly remembered. 'He'll be wondering where I am!'

They decided against relaunching the tandem, but Molly was happy for him to walk back with her to the seafront. She located her brother who was still sitting with his back against the timbers of the groins that struggled to hold the beach in place. Harry declined to join them.

'Well, come and see me in Beverley,' she told him. 'I'll show you my garden. It's not very big ... it's not very good either ... I don't think you'll like it much ... but do come and see me.'

'Yes. OK. I'll come over next week.'

'No. I'll be at school next week. Come tomorrow! Ben's going home in the morning. You could come for lunch ... Could you? Will you?'

It felt wonderful to be invited so enthusiastically. Warmth spread through him. 'Yeah ... sure ... great! I'll come tomorrow.'

'Where do you live?' he called after her as she descended the steps down to the beach.

'Monks Lane,' she smiled back. 'It's opposite St. Mary's ... number five ... you won't forget?'

'No. I won't forget,' he said to himself with a rare smile as she was skipping between people on the beach on the way back to her brother. Harry watched her go. She waved briefly, but then turned to gesticulate and talk animatedly to the young man still slouched against the timbers.

Harry made his way back to the cottage, still shaking his head in disbelief at the whirlwind that had suddenly blown across his day.

The next day arrived for Harry full of expectation. He took his bicycle, rather than the tandem, and cycled into Beverley. The town appeared as a bit of a sprawl to him as he approached from the coast, but then, as he cycled into its old centre, he found it quite beautiful and full of charm. Moses had warned him to look for the tower of Saint Mary's Church rather than the huge magnificence of Beverley Minster itself, and Harry found it easily.

Harry had to admit that the façade of the church was mightily impressive in itself and could easily realise how people might have confused it with something grander. Despite the church's glory Harry's eye was drawn to an art shop across the road where he looked into the window to marvel at the exquisite technique evident in the watercolours displayed there. He read that they had been painted by a local, but clearly professional, artist and their quality made Harry feel desperately inadequate about his own painting abilities. Eventually he allowed his gaze to be drawn away from the painting display to concentrate on finding Molly's address.

Monks' Lane was, indeed, directly over the road from the church. Number Five was one of a small block of three-storey town houses, somewhat nondescript, but enjoying a particularly pleasant setting amongst the old buildings of the narrow lane. The sound of her front doorbell brought a flurry of footsteps down the stairs and into the entrance hall.

'Oh, you're here!' she welcomed him. 'I wasn't sure that you'd come.'

It was an odd welcome, but she expressed her pleasure in seeing him by placing a kiss on his cheek as she pulled him into the house. Then she stood back hesitantly as if the kiss had been a step too far.

"Course I came,' Harry assured her, not wishing to lose the momentum of the unexpected kiss.

'I'm so pleased you've come, but I've got a little bit of a problem,' she told him.

'See … I was a bit muddled and … I'd booked a driving lesson. It's in about twenty minutes … I'm sorry.'

'Don't worry. I can walk round the town or something.'

'You see … I hoped you'd come, but I wasn't sure … and then

I remembered that I'd booked up … and today is the only chance this week … and it's in about ten minutes … and … and … I'm really sorry!'

Sometimes she talked like a machine gun.

'Look, stop worrying. I'll be fine,' Harry smiled, simply pleased that it was her and not him who had messed things up.

'I'll have a walk around. Is there somewhere I can put my bike?'

'You didn't come over on the tandem!'

'No, just on my bike, but I can't leave it out in the road.'

'No … yeah … I mean no problem. I'll open the garage. But look, if you've just cycled over, I can't push you out into the street again,' she worried.

'I'll be fine.'

'Why don't you come with me? I don't want you to go … just when you've got here. Come with me.'

'What? On your driving lesson? I can't do that.'

'Yes, of course you can. I want you to … I mean I'd really like you to,' she implored him. 'I'm sure the instructor won't mind. Say you'll come.'

As it happened the instructor did mind. 'It's not authorised. He's not insured,' he whined.

Molly got into the seat next to the instructor. As she spoke to him she placed her hand on his thigh, unusually close to his sensitive regions. 'Look, I'm sure it will be OK,' she informed him looking into his eyes and squeezing his leg. A look of sheer panic passed over his face.

'You see, my client from the previous lesson is already in the back,' he stammered.

'Well, there you are then,' Molly told him with sickening sweetness and with a firmer squeeze of his thigh even closer to his wedding tackle. The instructor had become helpless and his protestations ceased.

So Harry found himself not only in the back of the instructor's car, but also sharing the rear seat with a surprisingly old woman in a surprisingly bright tracksuit.

'This is a nice crowd isn't it?' the old woman observed to him pleasantly. 'Are you next?'

'No ... I'm with her.' Harry told the old woman in fluorescent pink. Molly smiled back over her shoulder at his comment.

'Let's just keep our minds on the driving shall we?' piped the instructor.

Molly started off reasonably well and Harry began to relax a little. The instructor was less relaxed. 'Check mirror ... watch the approaching traffic,' he whined, more nervously than routinely.

They had moved into a one-way system around the centre. There were tempting glimpses of the old market place between buildings and Harry thought it would be useful to see something of the town. Moses had frequently spoken of it.

'Thought it was about time I learnt ...' chimed the old woman. ' ... now he's gone! I need to get some independence ... need to get on with my life.'

She presented herself as a cheery soul, in contrast to the instructor who appeared to be getting increasingly agitated, even though, to Harry's mind, Molly was driving quite confidently and well.

'He's gone. He?' Harry asked the old woman gently.

'My husband! He's gone! Thirty-six years together ... then he's gone .... no warning ... no nothing!'

'Oh, I am sorry.'

'Don't be sorry, Dearie ... we all got to go sometime ... you never know when you'll be ...'

The sentence was left incomplete as they both jerked to the sound of Molly's scream.

'Oh God … I hit it!' she shrieked.

'What? What was it?'

'A pigeon … a poor, little pigeon! Look I can see it in the mirror … it's still flapping!'

Harry turned to look through the back window. Sure enough there was a pigeon in the road, flapping one wing, but otherwise not moving.

'Change down … check mirror … observe the traffic island ahead,' piped the instructor.

'I'll go back round,' said Molly, almost tearfully. 'How do I get back round?'

'We're not scheduled to go back round …' the instructor began.

His attitude made Harry instantly angry. He leaned forwards between the seats to grab his shoulder. 'Never mind your bloody schedule! Just direct the lady back to where she wants to be!' he bawled at the instructor.

There were a few seconds of silence in the car. The poor man appeared to shrink even smaller, but he did then direct Molly around the town centre and back towards the spot where she had first struck the unfortunate bird.

As they approached the bird came into view, still flapping in the same place.

'What shall I do? What shall I do?' Molly worried in some state of anxiety.

'Well, Dearie … I think you'd better put it out of its misery,' suggested the old woman.

'What? Run it over?'

'It's the best way. You don't want it to suffer. My husband got run over … he died straight away. They said he didn't suffer at all.'

But by the time she had related her sad tale the moment had been lost. Molly had swerved around the bird and was again approaching the traffic roundabout.

'Reduce speed … change down … check mirrors,' intoned the instructor, sneaking furtive glances in Harry's direction in case he should revert to more angry behaviour. Then, for a third time, the poor instructor directed Molly in a circuit around the town as the old lady persuaded her that running over the stricken bird was the kindest thing to do. By the time they had approached the bird again Molly had succumbed to the old woman's persuading and steeled herself to do the awful deed. She gave a little, inward scream as the wheel bumped over an obstruction. The instructor gave a louder scream.

'Open your eyes, Ms. Bentham … open your eyes!'

'Did I kill it?' she asked quietly as Harry looked back through the rear window. The bird was still flapping.

'Sorry. I think you missed it.'

'But there was a bump … I felt it bump!'

'I think you swerved across the cat's-eye in the middle of the road,' he told her.

'We'll have to go round again, Dearie.'

'I can't go round again!' lamented Molly.

But they did: silently. Even the instructor was passive with anxiety until they reached the dreaded spot.

'You have to keep your eyes open, Ms Bentham!'

'It's all right for you …. you don't have to …' They stopped with a sudden jerk.

'Ooh look, Dearie! … It's on the path!'

They all looked to see the pigeon walking about on the pavement, seemingly recovered from its trials.

'Good job you missed it after all, Dearie!'

After the pigeon ordeal the instructor swapped places with Molly and drove them all back to Monks Lane. The return trip was silent. Harry followed Molly into the house to watch her make tea. He observed her movement around the kitchen and again had to wonder why he had not noticed the extent of her attractiveness on previous occasions. She bent to place a sky-blue mug full of hot tea on the table between them. She did not seem aware of Harry's surreptitious watching or the heightening of his senses as he watched.

'I suppose you have to see the funny side of it,' he joshed with her despite the silence that had grown between them.

'Oh yes. I can see that now,' she acknowledged. 'Though it was awful for me at the time. I can't imagine how I let that old woman persuade me to try and kill a poor, defenceless pigeon … I don't really like pigeons that much … but it's a living thing isn't it? I wouldn't want to kill anything … I know she had positive motives … she's probably a very good person …

And that poor instructor, I thought he was going to die of fright. You really did scare him you know!'

'Him?' Harry could not believe that she was siding with that whining mouse.

'I was just trying to look after you!' The terrible combination of increased testosterone and self-dislike raised his anger immediately and by the end of the sentence he was shouting. He had managed to keep his ugly, pointing finger under control, but the words had crashed out like violent intruders.

Molly did not overtly react. She just looked at him.

Harry desperately wanted her to step around the table, to hold him in her arms and tell him that everything was alright. Of course, she did not. How could she? She hardly knew him. Harry did not know how to remove himself from the scene. They just stood there silently as the shadows of heavy clouds outside the window continued to move silently across the polished beechwood tabletop.

Molly broke the silence with words that penetrated right into Harry's heart.

'You were angry the first time I saw you ... then when you came to the primary school with Grace I saw such a kind side to you ... I thought to myself that there must be a kind and gentle person inside of you ... now ... why are you so angry?' she concluded.

'I don't know,' Harry whispered.

He left straightway and headed for the coast, but, before he had even reached halfway home it had begun to rain. Everything: the sky; his mood; the landscape; had turned to grey. The blinding red of his anger had dulled to the violets and indigos of self-loathing within his mind, but even those were submerged into the grey emptiness before he reached the cottage. For some obscure reason Harry pictured the sky-blue mug and wondered if it was still standing there on the polished beechwood table full of cold tea or whether its owner had emptied, washed, dried and put it away from sight. He suspected the latter.

JUNE

June, of course, heralded the approach of the summer solstice. The sun dawned, as ever each morning, across a land almost devoid of people, and all those early hours of its precious light were lost to the vast majority, who slept through to breakfast time.

It rose, on this first day of the month, in a clear sky above an unwatched sea before racing in to spread its light, unwitnessed, across the Holderness: in across the empty beaches and the vacant spaces of the promenade; down upon the quiet houses and gardens; over the fields and hedgerows, the silent dikes and ditches, and the waters of the Hull; and on and on to illuminate the lovingly-masoned towers of Beverley Minster, whose regular chimes fell upon the unhearing and sleep-filled ears of most inhabitants.

Harry was up and about by six. The human day had hardly begun and, had his mood been better, he might have been able to savour the quiet of a still largely sleeping town. The favour of such early access to the day was, however, lost upon his troubled demeanour, and he could manage little more than to stumble, tea in hand, in a short circuit around the garden before returning to sit on the bench.

He sat there for some time, brooding. On the roller coaster of his emotional being, his spirits had gradually climbed over the previous couple of months, but now, since the disastrous outburst in Molly's kitchen, they had plunged dramatically downwards again.

Later he forced himself to cook boiled eggs for breakfast in an attempt to cheer himself up, but he still felt unable to paint or consider anything else constructive. He simply returned to his seat in the garden. Things may have continued to spiral downwards had it not been for a little 'hello' that hailed him some time later from the other side of the fence. It was Grace, accompanied by Maude. He remembered somehow that it was Saturday: and surmised, accurately as it turned out, that something must have cropped up for Mrs Hall.

To his surprise, he did not get annoyed. In fact, he was slightly shocked at how pleased he felt to see them and relishing the thought of company.

'It's OK,' he told Maude later, 'I'll keep Grace with me for the day. I'll bring her home in time for her tea.' He imagined that was what had been intended. In tease, he even invited Maude in for a cup of tea. Naturally she did not speak, though he was able to tell from her expression that she declined the invitation. As a parting shot, moreover, Maude indicated with her eyes that Grace was carrying something in her hand: a bunch of wrapped flowers.

'Oh, a present for me!' he exclaimed taking them into his own hands. And then he felt a little guilty that he had treated Maude so badly. 'I'll go and put these into water straight away and then I'll make some tea,' he called out to Maude feebly as she walked away.

Grace watched Harry studiously as he unwrapped the 'present', which was a bunch of tulip buds. Harry put them into his only vase, which was rather too large for the thin bud-tipped stems and they fell a little forlornly against the glass edges.

'They'll soon perk up,' he told Grace.

She smiled and then she did have a cup of his tea, also some toast dripping in butter and honey. He told her that the local honey would do her good and protect her from hay fever. She smiled at him indulgently as she ate the toast, though she did leave some of her crusts.

'Eat your crusts!' Harry chided her gently. 'You'll get straight hair and curly teeth.'

'You mean the other way round.'

'Not if you don't eat your crusts!'

'I was saving them for the birds,' she let him know.

So, they crushed them up and put them onto the bird table in Harry's garden. Then they sat and watched quietly until some birds did arrive at the little wooden platform. There was soon a whole collection of what ornithologists would have called 'little brown jobbies': sparrows, chaffinches, greenfinches, and a single robin.

Harry could not quite fathom out why or how Grace's simple chatter and company managed to make him feel more comfortable with life and himself. Somehow she encouraged a gentler, saner and happier mood from within his troubled being.

'I like the birds,' she told him. 'Would they come to my garden if I had a table like yours?'

'I dare say they would … you can help me make one if you like!'

He was soon smiling to see her beam so widely.

'We'll go round to Moses and pinch some of his wood.'

Straightway, and strangely, her face lost its glow.

'I didn't really mean that we'll steal it!' he reassured her, though her face retained its troubled countenance. By the time they had walked round to Moses' place Harry was almost dragging her along.

'Come on, Grace … Moses will be really pleased to see you.'

And, of course, he was.

'So, this is the lovely Grace,' he charmed, holding out his hand to greet her.

Harry had forgotten that they had not met face-to-face before. Grace hid behind him. She would have nothing to do with Moses and remained there stubbornly despite Harry's coaxing. He felt embarrassed for himself and for Moses, who attempted to resolve the situation by removing himself to make cups of tea.

'Come on,' Harry cajoled her again. 'Moses is my good friend. I'd like you to be friendly to him at least.'

'Is that his staff?' she asked tremulously looking in the direction of Moses' stick that was leant against the wall. 'I don't like serpents!'

'What do you mean, you don't like serpents?'

Then realisation dawned upon him.

'He's not going to turn it into a serpent! He's not the *real* Moses!'

'Well, he looks like him!'

Moses reappeared, unaware, through his kitchen door with a tin of biscuits. The sun lit up his face and gleamed down upon the silver curls of his hair and beard. Harry had to admit to himself that Moses certainly was reminiscent of the benign, anglicised old men he had looked at with wonder in the picture bibles of his childhood, though the thought of Moses' elevation to biblical status did send him into convulsions of laughter.

'What?' Moses asked, staring helplessly.

When Harry had recovered enough to be able to speak and explain, the three of them shared the joke. Grace smiled a little, but continued to regard Moses with some scepticism, while he displayed utmost gentleness towards her.

'Have you told lass 'bout the surprise yet?' he asked.

'No, not yet. Today's for making bird tables. What is today, anyway?'

'It's Saturday.'

'We'll save the launching 'til Monday.'

By the end of the afternoon a handsome bird table stood ready for Harry to carry around to Bede House. And, by that time, Grace had just about come to accept and trust Moses. He had completed most of the work while Grace and Harry had looked on enthusiastically, and additionally he kept them entertained throughout that time with an endless supply of fascinating details about the birds Grace was likely to see on her very own bird table.

'Will I see robins?' she had asked him in earnest. 'They're my favourite.'

'I'm sure you will, princess. Those robins like to visit bird tables. Those robins are the bravest of little birds. Do you know, sometimes when I'm digging a little robin I know will 'op up right onto the top prong of my old diggin' fork?'

Grace pursed her lips with wonder as Moses went on. 'Do you know, those robins will defend their territory against any other birds what comes into it?'

'What's territory?'

'Territory is the area what the robin makes for his own. An' 'e don't let anyone else in. 'Ceptin' 'is own hen an' chicks, of course. An' if any other bird comes in 'e'll fight 'em. Even other robins.'

Grace smiled at the thought of such bravery.

'Sometimes those robins will fight to the death!' Grace's smile had fallen at that, but Moses was sensitive enough to notice and the rest of his asides were kept very cheerful.

'Thank you, Mr Moses,' Grace chimed as they departed, and Harry could tell by the look on Moses' face that he took it as ample reward for his afternoon's labours.

Back in the garden at Bede House Harry worked hard to set up the bird table for Grace. She clapped her hands in delight when it had been properly positioned and set in its place upon a spot where a small block of paving stones had been laid.

'Just below the garden's smile,' she had told him, though Harry had not understood her comment.

They were still gazing at their achievement when Mrs Hall appeared at the rear entrance of the house and descended the steps to join them on the lawn. As usual, whenever Harry saw her, she was dressed for work in an elegant suit: although the dull, grey pinstripe did little to enhance her pale colouring, the balance of the equation was rescued by the broach on her lapel, which was inset with three small stones the colour of her own eyes.

'Well,' she exclaimed. 'You have been busy. Where did this splendid bird table come from?'

Grace told her in a rush of excited detail.

'I must thank you, Mr Harry … and your friend Moses,' she began. 'I had to go into York this morning … to work.' Harry thought she was going to explain, but she did not. 'Of course, I'll be happy to make some recompense for all your trouble,' she offered.

'Mrs Hall, it was no trouble at all … it made the day for Moses and me to have Grace there,' Harry replied with sincerity, but with the sort of formality that he usually reserved for bank managers. 'I do not require payment. And I'll be around to work with Grace as usual on Monday.'

And with a smile to Grace he started to leave. Just in time he remembered to add, 'Oh, by the way … if it's alright with you … I was thinking of taking Grace out into the countryside … on a bicycle …'

'On a bicycle? I'm not sure that Grace is able to ride … 'er, can you ride, Grace?' Grace looked blankly at her. 'I'm not sure that she's ever been on a bicycle …'

'What? Never been on a bike? What sort of ...' And he just managed to choke down the anger that had begun to rise in himself. 'Well, in fact, it's not a bicycle ... it's a tandem.'

'A tandem? Oh! I'm really not sure. You would have to be ever so careful with ...'

'Of course ...' Anger was building again. Harry spread out his fingers and then brought them together, as in prayer, and blew his exasperated breath into them with as much control as he could manage. 'Mrs Hall ... of course I will be careful ... as careful as I would be if she was my own daughter.' More controlled breathing on Harry's part, more effort to be reasonable and amenable. 'I just think she needs to get out of this little town sometimes ...' he was adding.

'Grace needs to ... or is it you that ...?' Mrs Hall left the thought unsaid, though it did strike Harry, not for the first time, that often other people, especially women, seemed to know what was inside his thoughts more than he did.

But, before he could brood on this any further, Mrs Hall had looked across to Grace's bewildered face to take a change of heart.

'Yes, Mr Harry ... I think it would be wonderful if you were to take Grace around the countryside on a tandem,' she said. Then she smiled a wide, genuine smile that Harry had not seen before and which lit up her pale face with warmth and unexpected beauty.

'OK,' he managed to stammer and then he left before anything changed. On his way around the side of the house he could hear the two of them laughing together in the garden.

On Monday, after school, Harry collected Grace from Bede House and took her on the short walk to the recreation ground. She was, of course, full of questions and Harry hoped that his refusal to disclose their destination and intent did not build up too much intrigue. Moses was there to meet them with the tandem. Grace seemed pleased to meet him again.

'Hello, little princess.'

'Hello, Mr Moses.'

'Well,' Harry interjected. 'What do you think of it?'

Grace looked around. She looked at Harry, she looked at Moses and she looked at the sky. She smiled her big smile that meant she did not have a clue what Harry was talking about.

He picked up the tandem from where it leant against the pavilion wall.

'Look. This is a tandem!' he announced with just a little exasperation.

Moses raised his eyebrows at him in reproach, so Harry carried on a little more gently.

'This is a tandem for us. Me and Moses cleaned it up … and painted it … and got it ready for us … to go out on trips … to ride in the countryside.'

Grace continued to smile benignly. Harry continued to talk like a teacher who had bewildered and lost the class. He started again.

'You've seen people ride bikes, haven't you?' he asked.

Grace thought. 'Yes,' she conceded.

'Well, this is a bike for us … for both of us … to ride together out into the countryside … where we can see birds … and flowers … and all sorts of things! You'd like that wouldn't you?'

'Yes.'

At last they had joined together on the same thought line.

'Now then, have you ever been on a bicycle before?'

'I don't know. I don't think so,' she replied, smiling as widely as she could to hide the anxiety and uncertainty that lay beneath it.

They were on the outfield of a well-mown cricket pitch.

Harry thought the grass might save Grace from damage if they encountered the occasional mishap. Having already adjusted the saddle to its lowest position, Moses held the rear of the tandem so that Grace could mount.

Unfortunately, Grace did not have any idea about how to go about this. First she put her foot onto the mudguard and then between the spokes.

'Like this, princess,' Moses told her as he moved round to demonstrate. After a few more false starts Grace managed to put her foot onto the pedal and step up onto the saddle. Moses and Harry soon learned not to take anything for granted as within seconds she had lurched awkwardly to one side to dangle from the saddle by the crook of her left knee. Moses gently lifted her back up onto the saddle.

'Oh dear, Grace. It doesn't seem like you've got any sense of balance.'

'Haven't I?'

Moses was able to see the funny side of the situation and soon had Harry laughing as well. Grace joined in, but a little more hesitantly. And, thankfully, that laughter set the tone for the evening's trials and exertions. Any passers-by must have wondered at the 'crazy gang' that they comprised, but they persevered, and, with Moses' lead, laughed their way through the best part of two hours.

The greater wonder was that neither Grace nor Harry suffered any injury. She had no experience of such activity and showed no sign of having developed any sense of balance. It was just as well that the cricket pitch offered them such wide, open space as well as relatively soft landings.

The learning curve was steep for both of them. It took many

false starts, for instance, before they discovered the necessity of starting with the pedal raised on the same side of the tandem and each of them with their same-sided foot on it. Luckily, having Harry's greater weight at the front of the vehicle enabled him to exert some control over their direction.

That they finally managed to set off across the grass, however, with both of them seated and balanced, was a wonder comparable to the Wright Brothers' first flight in Kittiwake. Harry laughed out loud in the genuine joy of their forward momentum.

But that was just a start. It was harder going for his legs than Harry had imagined across the cricket outfield and he had to grip with every sinew as the grassed space before them diminished and he was forced to steer into their first corner. Harry had expected Grace to lean with him into the curve of their turn, but she remained bolt upright, causing the tandem to slew from side to side as Harry fought gravity in the fear of cut knees and a telling off from Mrs Hall. Due more to luck than judgement, they survived.

'I think that'll do for today,' Harry told her, between heaving gulps of air as they dismounted from that final manoeuvre. 'We'll have another try tomorrow.'

Harry was left to push the tandem as Moses walked hand in hand with Grace across the velvety, green sward. They walked the short distance to Bede House. Moses and Harry watched Grace down the path, waved as she turned into the door that had been opened by Maude, and then the two friends strolled off down Scarborough Road.

'You fancy a pint tonight then?' Harry asked Moses as they drew level with the cottage.

'Already booked, lad ... Monday! ... Dominoes night! Ye're welcome to come along and watch'

'No ... thanks, but no ... I'll give that one a miss tonight. See you tomorrow then?'

Despite having such an enjoyable day, Harry felt lonely as he stepped into the cottage. There was, however, an unexpected welcome for him on the windowsill of the kitchen's side window. The tulip buds had burst out into an explosion of deep magenta that seemed to fill not only the vase, but the whole window with vibrant splendour. He determined to paint them the very next day.

*

The weather stayed fair and warm and the swallows and martins flew higher and higher into the clear skies as the week progressed. Harry looked forward to the evenings of cycle practice with Grace and Moses. Though the days still passed slowly, the balance of his emotions had undoubtedly improved as well. He was able, for example, to find energy for painting. After relative success with a quick water colour sketch of the vase of tulips, he had even managed to get out with paints and easel on a couple of occasions, lugging them along the path to the loneliest corner of the lake's edge where he had little chance of being pestered by passers-by looking over his shoulder. It seemed that everyone expected him to be a completely expert artist and often they expressed outright disappointment at his less than expert efforts. Naturally, he did not like being watched.

One of the paintings worked quite well: a study of the town from the far side of the lake that just managed to capture a hint of the tranquillity. That evening he gave it to Moses, who, to his further disappointment, was quite critical.

'You've missed out lots of 'ouses!'

But, Harry could soon tell that, underneath the gruff exterior, the old man was rather pleased. But, 'It looks like the sort o' place where everyone lives 'appily ever after,' Moses mused. 'Pity they don't! Still, I'll 'ang it on t' wall, lad.'

By the end of the week, Grace and Harry were able to ride around the perimeter of the recreation ground without too much fear of falling off.

'We'll have to venture on to the roads next week,' he told her.

'What's a "venture"? Is it like an adventure?'

'Yes, I'm sure it will be an adventure,' Harry said with just a hint of worry.

'But will I be captured and ransomed? Will there be a castle?'

'No! Not that sort of adventure … well, maybe a castle … but just sort of quiet … little adventures.'

'You 'ope!' Moses had chipped in.

'But, if they are little adventures, will we still live happily ever after?' Grace pursued in such a way that Harry could not tell whether it was naïvety or subtle facetiousness.

Moses and Harry exchanged glances.

Harry's visions of gliding around the countryside of East Yorkshire on a tandem were to prove more difficult to achieve than he had initially imagined. Their maiden cycle along the lanes was short: cut short by a snapped chain that left Harry pedalling in 'fresh air' for a half second before the lack of resistance caused his foot to slip from the pedal that then scraped itself along his shin, taking a layer of skin with it.

'Fuck!' said Harry, 'the bloody chain's broke!'

'Ooh,' said Grace, 'you shouldn't say bloody!'

'You weren't meant to hear … all that!'

He began to get a little angry. Thankfully, Grace took no notice of his sulky misdemeanour.

'Look at all the flowers,' she told him with wonder and without warning.

Harry was surprised that she could be so observant, although when he did stop to look, the burst of colour across the fields was really striking. The previously plain green cloth of the land a few weeks previous had been painted, seemingly overnight, with patterns of, not exclusively, but largely, gold and white.

They left the tandem against a gate that they opened into a roadside field and Grace held his hand as they waded knee-deep into luxuriant growth. So deep was Grace's enjoyment and so startlingly beautiful the flowers that all Harry's anger disappeared. He sighed deeply at himself for being so myopic and stupid. Grace wandered round happily and soon decided that she would pick some flowers for Moses.

'OK, just one of each,' Harry told her with mixed feelings about taking wildflowers. 'We shouldn't take too many.'

'I'm sure the field won't miss a few,' she told him with what seemed like overwhelming sensibility.

So he sat down in the field while Grace danced all around him in pursuit of different flowers, picking in adherence to Harry's request for just one of each variety. Harry laid back in relaxation to allow his stare to drift up into the endless firmament beyond the swaying fronds of grass. In a while he focussed on a giant flock of small birds wheeling, randomly it seemed, above him in an ever-changing cloud of black confetti against the pure, cobalt blue backdrop of the sky: a murmuration he learned later. He thought to tell Grace so that she could enjoy the spectacle but decided that she probably had more than enough to occupy her mind and kept it to himself like a secret.

In some ways it was lucky that they had broken down so soon on their excursion since the walk back to Bede House was not too long. Harry sat upon the step outside while Maude fussed around Grace inside. Eventually Grace stood before him in the striking array of pink tones that Maude had dressed her in for the rest of the day, but also with a substantial bunch of wild flowers, and they were ready to go. They must have looked an odd couple walking back to Moses' place: Grace clean, tidy and beaming at her wild flowers; Harry with oily hands after his attempts to fix the tandem.

Moses exclaimed pleasure at seeing them both. This pleasure reached overflowing proportions when Grace presented him with her bouquet. She took a stem of buttercups from the bunch and held them under Moses' chin.

'To see if you like butter,' she told him.

'I certainly do, princess. Can you see a glow?'

Grace nodded.

'Now when I were a lad, me grandfather would rub them buttercups on the cows udders … to make the milk whiter 'e used to say!' They both smiled at the shared knowledge. 'And them daisies … them ox-eyes … me granny used to rub them on me chest when I had a bad cold.'

'Did they make you better?'

'Don't know … can't remember … I only 'member she used to do it.' Moses went on to name all the flowers, 'Saxifrage, cranesbill, clover, campion … and tom thumb … I knows 'em all. Even my old teacher used to be impressed. We used to pick them with me gran'mother … me and our Daniel … an' our ol' granny, … she 'ad a use for 'em all,' he informed Grace, before adding confidentially to Harry from behind his hand, 'Me grandfather used to say that she was a witch!'

'Was she?' asked Grace, all ears and eyes as wide as saucers.

'Oh, I don't know,' laughed Moses. ''Appen she were!

One day me ol' granny 'ad a pot full o' bright red poppies an' me grandfather says to 'er "What you adoin' wi'—"'

'No! Stop!' Grace interrupted. 'I don't want to talk about poppies!'

The two men looked at each other open mouthed at this strange interjection before Harry recovered his composure. 'Come on, Grace. Let's get you home before Moses fills your head completely with stories.'

'But I like stories. I just don't like …' But the thought remained unsaid.

Moses had helped Harry to fit a new link into the chain the next day, so that the day after he was ready to venture out with Grace again.

'Since you like castles, we could ride up to Seawick. There's the site of an old castle up there according to my map,' he told a beaming Grace as they sallied forth into the countryside on a warm and quite sultry Monday evening.

*

They travelled along the quietest of lanes through farmland pregnant with sap and greenery. The wide verges they found along the lanes were edged with the frothy white lace of the tall cow parsley that grew in every place that had not been carefully cultivated. The sun broke through at irregular intervals to light up these lacy edges and when it did so the heat rose up sharply from the road surface so that the sweat ran into Harry's eyes. But Harry knew it was worth all the effort as Grace hummed along tunelessly behind him and the smell of summer greenery filled not only his olfactory but all of his senses.

Although he could glimpse Grace's feet moving round on the pedals, she did not appear to be making too great an impact on their forward motion: not that Harry minded – he needed the exercise and was grateful to move along the lanes without incident or mishap. He was further grateful to meet only one vehicle on the roads until they reached the main road at Seawick, and that was a mobile library van moving slowly between the villages.

The castle site turned out to be something of a disappointment. There was a small mound that had once been the motte and some depressions across the fields where some other forms of fortification would have stood, but nothing to give Grace a more vivid impression of the castle that had stood on the place centuries before.

'Not much to see is there?' she commented. 'Perhaps we should have an ice cream!'

It was a good idea, so they left the tandem where it was and walked into the village. Harry did not think that they were ready for cycling on busy roads yet.

Sure enough they found a village stores and were soon enjoying cool refreshment. The sun had withdrawn behind thick, billowing clouds, but it was still warm and humid. A little worryingly, before they had finished the ice cream, there was a distant rumbling of thunder from the direction of the Wolds, where a tinge of yellow had stained the underbelly of the clouds.

'Mmm ... long way away,' Harry mused.

'What is a long way away?'

'Home,' he lied to her. 'Come on, gal ... we'd better get back to that pedalling machine.'

'Do I have to pedal all the way back as well?' she asked.

'That's a bit rich,' he thought to himself, since he had not noticed her pedalling too hard on the way there.

'We'll be back in no time,' he assured her.

But they were not. The incoming storm was preceded by a strong wind that pushed into their faces and dragged at Harry's legs so much that they hardly seemed to be moving forwards at all. There had been more dull rumblings of thunder, which he was pleased Grace had not appeared to have noticed, but then came a more distinct flash. Harry counted the seconds until the sound of thunder arrived: twelve seconds: less than two and a half miles away. Harry's calculations were barely completed before there was a second, almost blinding, flash. It came with a crashing bellow of sound that made Grace jump in her saddle so violently that Harry thought they would tumble.

'I don't like it!' she choked as he brought the tandem to a stop.

'It's only a bit of thunder,' Harry tried to joke. 'Nothing to worry about. Come on, let's get pedalling!'

'But I don't like it!'

He could tell that she was on the brink of tearfulness, so he stopped and turned round to face her.

'Look, I know you don't like it, but I'm here and I'll look after you … I won't let it hurt you. Do you understand that?'

Harry knew the words were empty promises, but he said them anyway. What else could he do? There was no point continuing to stand there in the openness.

Grace nodded. She blinked back the tears and squeezed her lips together in braveness. Harry had simply smiled too, but a deep feeling of pride had rushed up inside of him.

They resumed their struggle into the wind. Harry was hoping against hope that the storm would somehow pass them by, but that proved to be too much to hope for and soon drops of rain began to splatter against them: huge drops of rain that left tracer marks across their clothes the size of pennies, giant drops of rain that quickly drenched them in water. Being so wet and with lightning all around them, Harry did begin to worry.

By the time they had reached the small village midway between Seawick and home, the rain was falling so heavily that it was difficult to see further than the next bend in the road. Luckily, there was an old, traditional telephone box in the village into which Harry was able to squeeze the two of them for temporary shelter. They huddled there while the torrential rain beat its frenzied percussion upon the telephone box roof, dripping their wetness on to the floor and staring out into the world through a distorting wall of water that ran opaquely down the sides of their shelter. He could just make out the mobile library parked along the verge and an old woman staggering down from its entrance step with a bundle of books under her arm. Harry began with a thought, but, before he could crystallise it into action, both van and woman had departed.

When Harry glanced down into Grace's face he was shocked to see how cold she looked. She did not speak, but simply stared at him. He imagined she was wondering how someone she trusted could lead her into such an awful experience. There then followed another, sudden flash of blue-white light and another resounding crash that trembled the air all around them. It felt as if the sky had ripped.

'Just wait there, Grace. I'll find us somewhere warmer.'

With that Harry dashed out headlong into the deluge and ran up the nearest pathway to knock urgently on an unknown front door. There was the sound of barking, which eventually became more distant, as if the animal was being shut away somewhere.

Then, after what seemed to be a very long time the door opened slightly and a voice enquired as to what he wanted.

'Actually I was after a bit of shelter. My young companion's got really wet, and she's really cold, and I don't think she's very well really!'

'Oh really?'

The door opened a little more and an old woman's face looked at him as if in recognition.

'Yeah, really.'

'Well, don't stand there like some mooncalf … fetch her in!'

Harry quickly did so and within a short time they were sat in a warm cottage room with a cup of hot tea in their hands. The old woman had quite tenderly wrapped a blanket around Grace.

'What's a dolt like you doing taking a young maid out in that torrent?' she asked.

'Well, we were on a bike ride you see an—'

'Oh, a bike ride was it? You don't seem to have much luck with bike rides do you? … The last time I saw you, lad, you were laid out half dead next to your bike!'

Then Harry remembered the old woman out by the ruined nunnery a few months back.

'Oh, it's you … No, I don't do I?'

'Any road, never mind that. I don't think this little lass should be out cycling again today.'

'No. I think you're right. She is a bit delicate … she's a … she's a little bit … sort of special … I mean she's not quite like …'

Harry was getting nowhere quickly, but the old woman rescued the situation.

'Of course she's special! Any road, I can tell she's a bit delicate … I might be old … but I'm not stupid.'

Harry could tell that she was not.

'Perhaps you'd better telephone someone to come and fetch the lass in a car. I don't drive myself anymore.'

So Harry used her phone to call up Moses. The old woman must have overheard Harry speaking, since he could soon hear her in the background.

'Oh, Moses is it? That wouldn't be Moses Farrow would it?'

He was soon struggling to maintain two conversations at once: one with her about Moses and how he knew him, and the other with Moses who was asking for directions. Harry asked the woman for the name of her house.

'Just tell him it's Eadie Springthorpe's house ... he'll remember!'

Harry passed on the information to Moses, who replied emphatically down the telephone that he did, indeed, know the house. Harry held the telephone expectantly to his ear, but, other than that, Moses said nothing and the line went dead. Harry thought that surely the old man was not upset about being asked to fetch them.

'What did he have to say?' the hostess enquired once he had put down the telephone.

'Nothing much,' Harry answered truthfully.

The old woman looked disappointed.

'Anyway, thank you for your help, Mrs Springthorpe.'

'Oh, I'm not Springthorpe any longer,' she said with an enigmatic smile as she went out to the kitchen to make more tea.

It was not too long before they heard Moses' big, old Volvo pull up outside. The horn sounded once, then a few times more urgently. Harry started towards the door, but the old woman waved him back down into his seat.

'No, no! Let 'im come to the door,' she insisted.

It took a while longer, but then a firm knocking sounded from the door. Again Harry started towards it, but again the woman waved him back.

'Let me answer my own front door.' And she opened it to the rain and Moses.

'Well, well, Moses! Come in won't you?'

Harry could hear him prevaricating outside the door.

'Nonsense!' they heard her say, and then the very little woman pulled the very large old man into the room.

'Thanks for coming, Moses,' Harry told him.

Moses barely flicked his eyes towards Grace and Harry before returning his stare to the old woman. He stood there nervously thumbing his wet hat and staring at her. She returned his stare steadily as the glimmer of a smile danced around the corners of her mouth. Clearly, this elfin creature had some special power to disable and humble the hulking, normally confident man before her.

'Now then, Moses, not seen you in a long while,' she smiled into his downcast face.

It took a few seconds for him to find his voice.

'No. Not in a long time,' he replied finally.

Then he broke away from the grasp of their visual engagement, turned, picked up Grace, and carried her out to the car. Harry was left to stare in his place.

'Well, thank you again, Mrs Springthorpe … I mean, Mrs …'

He left the sentence for her to finish, but she simply smiled back in return to leave him answerless. Though there was a smile on her lips, Harry was unable to tell what lay behind her eyes.

He followed Moses and Grace out to the car and they were soon driving through the now faltering rain without speaking. The set look on Moses' face and the rigidity of his shoulders warned Harry from questioning him further at that time. It was only five minutes until they had stopped outside of Bede House. Harry helped Grace from the car.

'Are you OK?' he asked her.

'Yes,' she replied with one of her brave smiles.

'There was a storm,' he told Maude, who had opened the door to them.

The old woman's mute reproach was about to ignite Harry's temper, but Grace interrupted with a torrent of excited words.

'We were in the thunder ... we went in a phone box ... we went into a lady's house ... she had a dog ... she gave me a blanket ... we had a venture!' she told Maude, who said nothing, but took the blanket from Grace and proffered it to Harry.

'I'll get back to Moses then.'

But when Harry had turned from the closed the door and walked back to the gate, he discovered that Moses and his car had already departed.

Though great mountains of turbulent cloud still chased across the sky, the rain had stopped, and it was the clinging wetness of Harry's clothes that chilled him as he walked in some state of bewilderment back to the cottage. The building's familiarity welcomed him more than a little, though the tulips in the window had faded to the last remains of their short life: they lolled across the expanse of the vase like drunken old men unable to stand, let alone retain any semblance of their former glory. They epitomised, it seemed to Harry, the decline of fortune that had befallen the evening's expedition. He picked up the vase in a decisive gesture and deposited the wilted flowers in the compost heap, but then he had to return to collect the handful of dried petals that had fallen to the windowsill. As he scooped them up he noticed that pollen from the dropped stamens had scarred the white paintwork with deep orange stains.

He decided to light the stove and the routine of its lighting helped to restore some balance to his disturbed state of mind. He drank hot tea and stared out into the garden at the remains of the evening. It was unfortunate that Harry's mood was so black that it stopped him from venturing into the garden: the sky had cleared, the air had calmed to a mere whisper and a lone blackbird sang a melancholic but melodic chorus from the top of the ash tree to celebrate the passing of the storm.

Though Harry remained untouched by the beauty outside his own back door, he was, thankfully, determined not to let his spirits drop too much and by just doing so had cheered him a little.

Still, he wondered about Moses. Sometimes you think you know someone, he thought to himself, and then another time you think you don't know them at all. He thought about Marianne, and wondered if he had ever really known her. He thought about the sensual Miss Bentham and regretted that he had never got to know her at all. And he wondered about Grace: he just wondered about her.

Harry woke the next morning to remember that the tandem was still leant against the wall beside the telephone box: leastways he hoped it was still there. After breakfast he took up the old woman's blanket from the back of his chair and set out to walk the lanes to the village where he and Grace had taken shelter. He felt good walking through the countryside: there had been so much gardening work, what with all Moses' friends, and then the cycling on top, that he felt fitter than he had for as long as he could remember. He smiled broadly.

The countryside looked no less than radiant: the previous day's rain had washed everything so clean that the vegetation shone.

Harry was surprised to note that the wheat and barley growing beside him was now waist high. The fields bent and rippled as the light wind ran across them, sending shimmering waves of silver across their pale green sea. As a casual passer-by, to Harry the fields appeared to be immaculately managed: everything looked so well ordered and correct so that the consequent air of wellbeing filled his senses to make him feel just as harmonious and content.

So taken was he with the freshness, the fragrance and beauty of the surroundings that the village seemed to come upon him before he had any chance to realise it. And, thankfully, there was the tandem where he had left it.

The old woman received the blanket and his thanks with hardly a response. He tried to engage her in conversation about Moses and how they knew each other, but she was reluctant to share any secrets with him. 'Perhaps it was a mistake,' was all she would say.

She closed the door and Harry turned away, but as he was mounting the tandem a neighbour walked to his gate pushing an empty wheelbarrow.

'I were wondering who'd left a tandem parked there,' he told Harry cheerily.

'Yeah, we got a bit of a drenching.'

'Course you did, lad … you can't dodge raindrops that big.'

Harry wondered if they were all smart arses round these parts, but he decided upon generosity in his approach to the stranger.

'Would have been worse if your next-door neighbour hadn't taken us in. It's nice to know there's still kindness and generosity around.'

'Aye, lad. You were lucky to pick on old Mrs Farrow's door … she is a kindly ol' soul. There's many round 'ere wouldn't 'ave opened their doors for you. I should know. I'm one on 'em!' And he turned away before Harry could thank him suitably for his sarcasm.

But then it struck Harry what the neighbour had called the old woman, and he cycled off from the scene in something of a daze.

It did not take him long to reach the cottage, but on being there he was soon restless. The intrigue of Moses and the old woman and the nature of their meeting was worrying him. After a short while he was soon on his way round to Moses' house. Moses was not at home, however. Harry checked the garden and the sheds and the greenhouse, but it was all still and empty. There was no great mystery to Moses not being at home, though Harry did begin to wonder whether or not the old man was avoiding him.

Moses did appear the next morning, however. He simply wandered into the garden while Harry was hoeing out the weeds between the rows of newly emerged potatoes that Moses had helped him plant some weeks earlier.

'Them taters looks like they're comin' on fine, though you'll need to ridge 'em up a bit. An' I'd put some soapy water on them broad beans too … it'll discourage them blackflies.'

'Yeah, I think it's great growing your own food,' Harry replied honestly and nonchalantly. 'Sit yourself down on the bench and I'll make us a cuppa'.'

And with uncharacteristic meekness, Moses did just that.

'Now then, Moses, what's this about some fine woman living up the road with the same name as you? You're a dark horse and no mistake.' Harry told him with a laugh.

'Well, she is a fine woman … but it aren't nothing to laugh about.'

'Come on, Moses, I'm not laughing at you. You should know me better than that by now.'

Harry could tell that Moses needed to talk, but, as usual, he was finding it difficult. Even for a man who was slow to share his secrets, Moses seemed particularly agitated by this situation.

'I'm your friend … I like to know things about you,' Harry encouraged.

'What if the things are bad?'

'Then, so what? Bloody hell, there's plenty of bad things that I've done!'

'Yeah, 'magine so!' Moses mused, staring into somewhere beyond the focus of his eyes. The old man sat for a few moments just staring, as if he was picturing and composing his memories.

'Go on then, Moses … what about her? What's the mystery about this other Mrs Farrow? What's the story? '

'It's no mystery … I loved her … isn't that always the story?'

'You loved her? I thought you loved your Rose!'

'I did love Rose,' Moses replied calmly. 'But she were later … she came into my life later: an' I'm blessed that she did. But … before that … I loved Eadie!'

'Right … how come … did you marry this Eadie as well then?'

Moses took Harry's question with outward composure, though his eyes appeared troubled as he continued to stare into the unfocussed distance.

'Eadie were two years older than meself,' he began. 'She were the prettiest girl we ever did see. We all dreamed of 'er … me an' all the other lads in the school. An' she set 'er eyes on just one … that were my brother, Daniel. I remember watching them together, and, though I loved me brother, I couldn't help wishing it were me that were 'oldin' her 'and an' not him. I used to curse him in me mind for bein' older and damn him for being so lucky. But, o' course I were wrong … an' in the end, he never had the chance to love 'er properly anyway! They got married in a rush at the start of the war before we went away ... me an' our Daniel ... but 'e never come back ... only me what had cursed 'im for his good luck!'

A glint of light lit up the moisture in his eyes.

'Then, in those years while I came back 'ome from the war meself ... I started to go round to 'er ' ouse ... that ' ouse that you was sat in yesterday. At first it were just to say sorry about our Daniel dying an' all ... I were sorry for 'er and guilty for me ... But then it were just 'cos I wanted to see 'er. And soon I knew I was in love with 'er ... and ... I think ... she with me!' Moses stuttered through his unplanned explanation.

'So how come you didn't live happily ever after, then?' Harry pursued.

'Well, we wanted to, but it weren't possible. Turned out that it were against the law to marry your sister-in-law or your brother-in-law ... so we couldn't ... and it sort of broke our 'earts. And one day she told me not to come back to the 'ouse ... And I never did ... leastways, not while yesterday!'

'But that's crazy! It was against the law to marry her!? It's not as if you were related by blood.'

'Yeah, I think they've changed the law since then to reflect some sanity. But that's how it were then, an' that's how it stayed for us ... Some years later me an' Rose found each other ... and I were blessed for that ... funny how life works out.'

They sat quietly to finish their tea. Harry could not help but reflect that he had gotten by with Moses' support ever since he had arrived on the old man's doorstep, and in all that time he had been preoccupied with his own problems. Moses' life looked so calm and orderly on the surface that Harry had imagined that it had always been that way. Life is like that, he thought to himself, when people have problems: everyone else's lives appear as if they do not have a care in the world, but it never is that way.

'Not been much of a friend, have I?' Harry offered at length.

'Reckon you'll do, lad.'

And in that moment Harry felt quite complete.

*

By the end of the week the weather had improved to its summer best again. After school on the Friday, Harry took Grace out on the tandem. He retraced their way along the lanes to Skipsea once more but passed the castle site and the village and pedalled out further to where the road runs along the cliff tops above the beach.

There the constant battle against erosion was particularly evident. Parts of fields, caravan sites, paths and buildings were falling into the sea just as they had done throughout the year every year as the relentless tides ate their way steadily inland. At several points bits of old road ended abruptly to leave great hunks of tarmac suspended a hundred feet or so in the air, before that final trickle of water came to take away another slither of mud, to allow the whole lot to slide and crash down into the sea.

All along the Holderness man has made attempts to hang on to the land. But against the indomitable power of the sea, the remains of man's pathetic efforts to hang on to the land serve only to litter the cliffs and beaches with ugly debris. The muddy, debris-strewn cliffs are not objects of beauty, though, once the sea has completed its cleansing job, the beaches below them certainly are.

So, with little delay, they climbed down the set of steps that had been newly installed on the fresh cliff edge for that summer, and were soon walking on a wide beach beside the sea. Even on such a clement evening they virtually had the beach to themselves. The water was a long way out leaving a wide expanse of untrodden, unspoilt sand upon which they wrote a pattern of easy footsteps.

It felt to Harry as though the whole strand was theirs alone to enjoy. They revelled in the deliciously fresh air and the delight of late, golden sunshine. Harry wondered at how precious these long evenings of English summer were. They stared at the sea and the sky and laughed at their good fortune to be alone in such congenial rapture. A small, pale blue butterfly had found its way mistakenly out from the fields above to flitter across their path beside the sea and they watched its erratic progress.

'It's so beautiful!' exclaimed Grace.

'Yeah. What's it doing down here on the beach? It must have been blown over the cliffs by the breeze.'

'Didn't it want to come down on the beach like us?' she enquired with innocence.

'Well, I don't image butterflies actually think it through like people. They just sort of get blown along by the wind and don't have much control over where they're going,' Harry tried to explain. 'Not like people.'

'Do we have control over where we're going, Harry?'

'Good point, princess!' he had to concede. 'Now, remember what it looks like and we can look it up when we get home,' Harry cajoled to change a subject that appeared to be slipping from his control.

With time on his hands back at Bede House, Harry looked through Grace's books to see if there was anything that might identify their butterfly, but without success.

'Mummy has some nature books in her office,' Grace informed him.

Harry did feel like an intruder, but when Grace led him upstairs to the room in the tower he followed with unrestrainable curiosity. It was a very attractive room with its octagonal shape and immaculately neat shelves of books. There was a solid wooden desk placed to look out of the window and along the lines of the avenue, and upon it a very modern-looking computer and telephone.

Harry did not wish to overstay his intrusion, so he briskly found an appropriate tome of encyclopaedic information and was soon able to identify their lepidopteral visitor as a 'chalk-hill blue'. He was ready to retreat from the room straight away until his eye was caught by the door. It was a very substantial structure made of solid wood like oak or some such timber. Besides that, there were no fewer than four large bolts with which to secure the door once it was closed. It seemed to him to be completely incongruous within a domestic building such as Bede House and he wondered about its significance. He was not keen, however, to discuss his intrusion into her study with Mrs Hall so the issue remained unraised.

Since that day a few weeks before, when Moses had opened up his inner secrets to him, Harry felt some compulsion within himself to declare to Moses some of his own hidden skeletons. It made Harry nervous to think of exposing his most shameful experiences to someone whose friendship he valued and who was bound to think less of him for it. But within the intimacy of shared labours he managed to find enough courage to make a beginning. He began by questioning Moses about Eadie in her big, lonely house up the road.

'How d'you know she's lonely?' Moses challenged.

'Make's sense. She wouldn't have made you go round that day

if she hadn't wanted to see you. Surely she means something to you?'

'She did once, but that were then an' now's now! 'Appen I only got room in me 'eart for one woman, an' the way things worked out that's got to be my Rose. I can't change that.'

Moses bent into his work emphatically as if to let Harry know that the issue was no longer up for debate, but, having come this far, Harry wanted the conversation to develop further.

'Yeah, it is strange how life works out,' he began. 'Sometimes things happen when you're least expecting them. And almost, like ... beyond your control ... leastways, that's how it seemed to me ... The thing that broke Marianne and me ... well what happened ... what I did ... it just happened.'

Moses looked up from his labours to stare, but Harry could not read his eyes. He did not know whether Moses was still lost in his own reveries of Eadie Springthorpe, whether he was affronted by Harry's own interjection, or whether the old man was simply inviting him to continue. Harry took a deep breath and ploughed on.

'Of course, I never meant for it to happen ... it just did. A woman I worked with ... I had known her for years, but never thought of her in that way ... you know, sexually. End of term ball, for the students. I only danced with her out of sort of politeness ... well, not politeness ... that sounds wrong ... just to join in with the spirit, to make the students think we were joining in ... I can't even blame drink: I hadn't had a drop ... it was just that we danced and she felt beautiful, and somehow I knew she ... well ... well, knew she wanted me. And that sort of "lit my touch paper". This sort of excitement spread through my body, then it was as if I wasn't in control. I can imagine that sounds corny, but that's how it was … as if my loins had taken over from my brain. We made sure we left last and then we did it … there, on some gym mats behind the stage curtains … no finesse, no love even …' Harry continued more to himself than his confidant. 'It was just base lust! I remember looking into her eyes … Vicky … she was … I mean she is … a nice woman. But we looked at each other, lying there, and we didn't know what to say, or what to do. It was like eating the forbidden fruit – the very second we had done it, we knew it was wrong. But, by then it was too late.'

Harry stopped at last, as if exhausted by the effort of relating the shameful incident. Moses remained quiet for a moment before speaking to him gently: he had been listening carefully after all.

'And was that the end of it?'

'The end of it? No that was just the bloody beginning! … I mean, not with Vicky, neither of us ever wanted it to go on. No, I mean it was the start of all the trouble. When we left that night … when we got to the cars … I had given her a kiss: not with any passion or anything; just to say, sort of, sorry … but someone had seen us. The next day at school, it was the last day of term … I had told some students to stop messing about. They'd had some mistletoe … I told them to put it away, when one of them pipes up "You could use it on Miss Gayle, sir!" Then I knew … it wasn't much … but it was out … and nothing was ever the same again!'

Moses remained quiet. Harry closed his eyes and sighed deeply: he felt exhausted, but better for having finally told someone, though also a little frustrated that Moses had made no judgement.

'You don't seem shocked or surprised,' Harry told him.

'The only thing that surprises me is that you think I might be shocked,' Moses replied with surprising compassion. 'We all got secrets an' shame inside us, but it aren't something to be too 'shamed about … We're only men … just weak men.'

Harry supposed there was not a lot he could say to follow that, but, although somewhat relieved of his own burden, he was reluctant to leave the mystery of Eadie Springthorpe suspended in the air.

'You going to see Eadie again then?'

'No, no, lad. I reckon not. That was then and I were in love with 'er. But not now. I got me memories of my Rose … an' that's enough for me.'

'Yeah, know what you mean.'

'No. No you don't, lad … You're still young, an' seems that you never exactly had the wonder of an 'appy marriage, did you? No, lad, you still got that to find … I can see you got capacity to love in you, an' you need to find someone to share it with,' he told Harry.

'Oh, capacity to love is it?' Harry laughed back at him.

'You mark my words, lad. You'll find someone … you see.'

When Moses had gone Harry sat and wondered about his time with Marianne. For sure, he knew that his memories of their life together would not be enough to give him any real satisfaction. Looking back a little bit more coolly and dispassionately than previously, he realised that most of their years together had been a long way short of great. In fact, a lot of the time it had not been good at all.

The pace of their break-up, however, was something that still shocked him. He could picture so vividly, the two of them stood together in their bedroom in those first early hours of the new millennium, just eighteen or so months before; yes, they had been drinking, but he knew they were so happy right then. And he remembered thinking how lucky he felt right then to be spending his life with this wonderful woman. But then just a few months later it had taken only days for them to fall completely apart.

He reflected that, though they had now been separated for more than a year, he still could not step back from the painful longing and look at things completely rationally. Some people, he knew, could do that, step back and look at themselves objectively, but not him. He had always got his nose pushed up hard against the window glass of raw emotion: never fully in control, and slave to his baser feelings. He wished he was more the man he wanted to be, but that had always been the case for him.

Eadie Springthorpe, or Farrow as she had become, sat quite still in her favourite place in the garden; an old lean-to bench knocked together from rough planks of elm wood. She remembered that the wood was elm; she remembered her father telling her, she had been just a girl then, that the elm would weather well and last a long time. It had. Certainly, it had already outlasted her father and still looked as sturdy as ever. Though the edges of the timber were rough and hard, it was a place of comfortable memories and she sat there often.

Eadie still missed her father, who had managed, besides a busy life as supervisor of an abattoir, to bring up herself and her sister, Cecilia, from quite a young age when their mother had died from scarlet fever. She wondered now, though she never thought of it as anything other than normal when she had been a girl, at the complexities and wonders of life whereby a man who killed so regularly in his work could be as sensitive and gentle as a father.

After the sad events of her early adulthood when she had lost both her young husband and then practically his loving brother, it had been nothing less than relief to become responsible for looking after her father and his house. It had sheltered her from life outside and at that time she had needed just that.

Against the odds of frailty from her own brush with scarlet fever and the blatant discrimination of the times, her sister, Cecilia, had studied hard through scholarships and university to become a solicitor. Eadie had taken great pride in her sister's achievement and substituted it for her own lack of intellectual or social fulfilment. It seemed, though, that the sisters shared susceptibility to ill luck in love and partnerships, since her sister's only romantic attachment was reserved for a senior partner whose professions of love and promises to leave his wife never materialised. By mid-life, physical frailty had condemned her sister to early retirement, spinsterhood, shortness of breath and reliance upon a wheelchair. When their father died, Eadie had slipped easily into the position of carer for her sister. Conversely, in many ways it had been the happiest time of her life: they enjoyed each other's company; were comfortably off; and they were free to pursue their mutual interests in life, which revolved largely around the church and their love of books. They were well-respected and well-liked women who lived a full life within the confines of their own small circles.

Their happiness and contentment together had been cut short, however. The indiscriminate, deadly kiss of breast cancer had superseded Cecilia's existing frailties to end her life even more prematurely. Eadie had never managed to come to terms with the unfairness of her sister's cancer and the painful distress of her dying set Eadie at odds with the beliefs that had held her so firmly until then. She could no longer believe in a kind and loving God. In fact, she could no longer conceive that there was a God at all. Though such a void existed in her beliefs, there was still room in her life for her need to do good things for other people. She ploughed her energy and need into supporting those who continued to fight the illness that had taken her sister and became an ardent fund-raiser for all the campaigns against cancer.

Eadie picked up the embroidered fabric bag that lay beside her. It contained all her various coloured threads that she now regularly used to occupy her time with cross-stitch or embroidery. In fact, they had virtually all belonged to her sister, who had been such an enthusiast for all things fabric and who had taught all she knew about it to Eadie during her bed and wheelchair-bound years. And truth be told, it was really in fond deference to her sister's passion that Eadie actually used the needles at all.

So, Eadie sat on the old elm bench, threaded her needles, and considered her existence. She considered it to be, in so many senses, unfulfilled. When she had heard that cyclist man mention the name of

Moses it had instantly stirred up in her a maelstrom of indeterminate, yet painful feelings. For the briefest of moments she had entertained a tumult of hope and excitement. Then the firmness of his rejection had left her prostrate and empty. It had taken her days to recover. In those days her hurt had transformed into first guilt at her own selfish actions and then into anger. She had been so angry that he had rejected so blatantly the attachment that had existed between them.

The past few weeks had allowed the anger and confusion to moderate into a sense of realism and acceptance: indeed, she remembered that it had been her and not him who had ended their affinity all those years back. For a little while she had resigned herself again to her quiet and increasingly lonely life, but now she felt moved to challenge all that again. What was she doing? Just waiting to die?

Something was telling her to take responsibility for herself for once. For so much of her life she had been content to allow opportunity to pass her by, but now she looked upon the situation with renewed determination. What did it matter if she made a fool of herself? What had she to lose?

JULY

As the school holidays approached and the beautiful summer weather continued, Harry began to feel happier than he had for a long time. He was encouraged to believe that the corner had been turned towards better times. He should have been wary, however, of anticipating so much emotional progress. And once again it was a bird that signalled the peril of relying upon such optimism. Perhaps birds were fated to be Harry's own, personal harbingers of misfortune.

Just after breakfast there had been a gentle knock on the living room window, so he went across from the kitchen to see who had tapped, expecting Moses, of course. There was no one to be seen. But then Harry could see that a bird had flown into the glass pane. It lay on the path outside. An exploded tuft of small feathers was left drifting in the air. One had caught on a thread of spider's web, where it trembled gently between beads of dew.

On closer inspection Harry could see that the stricken bird was a hen thrush. It was still, but not yet dead. The silky feathers of its breast and underbelly were shaking with each panting breath and its eyes began to flicker with panic. Seconds later it attempted to move. Its struggle to gain an upright position seemed futile, since the left leg was not functioning properly and its neck looked to be at a wrong angle. It lay still again and the eyes seemed to lose life. Another of the downy feathers had drifted down to rest upon the bird's beak, giving it a slightly ridiculous appearance. Harry sighed at the little tragedy. Perhaps the incident of the stricken pigeon in Beverley had made him more sympathetic.

But, suddenly and without warning, the bird hopped to its feet, where, for a full minute, it just stood, stock still. Harry wondered whether to help it. He was content, he thought, for the natural cruelties of nature to take place; at least, as long as he did not see them. But he was anxious to protect this particular bird from all the predators that prowled the garden. The kettle started to scream, however, and reluctantly he returned to the kitchen, where, through the window, he could see next door's big black tomcat stalking past the bole of the ash tree, nonchalant and sure. Harry was pleased that the ruthless, old tom had missed the golden opportunity at the side of the cottage, so far at least.

Harry returned to the living room just in time to see the thrush fly off: low at first across the grass, but then climbing to reach the branches of a hazel tree opposite, and finally away over the gardens to continue its tenuous existence. All that remained to mark the incident was a single, creamy blob of thrush shit.

Harry wondered what would be left to mark his own passing.

Later that day, when Grace had returned from school, Harry took her round to see Moses in his garden. Harry had spent the afternoon helping him to plant a whole box of young cabbages, cauliflowers and broccoli plants: what Moses called 'his brassicas', and which he swore gave him strong blood. The new, weak plants had needed plenty of water in the hot weather, but Moses was confident of rain later in the day. It had been hot work beneath the sun and they had finished, for Moses, quite early.

'Bring the lass round later,' he had told Harry. 'I'll make some elderflower squash.'

'Do you mean elderflower presse?'

'No I don't, cleverclogs … I mean squash … That's what my Rose called it when she made it, an' that's what I'm acallin' it too!'

Grace later wrinkled her nose at the squash, but carried on drinking and smiling bravely. The touch of fresh ginger was clearly a little strong for her keen, young taste buds, though perfect for Harry's own.

'You don't 'ave to drink it, lass ... I'll feed it to the cat.' Moses always said that when anything was left over, even though he did not have a cat.

The mention of cats reminded Harry to relate the morning's incident concerning the stunned thrush, which he did. He thought to tell them about the pigeon in Beverley as well, but Moses had already begun to gently tease Grace about the dilemmas of nature and Harry thought that two bird tragedies in one go would be too much for her.

Moses had gone on to explain to Grace about how cats would prey on birds and all sorts of small animals. She was incredulous at first that a cat could eat anything as innocent as a bird.

'Aye, lass, them cats will eat anythin' little: mice, shrews. I've even seen 'em drag back rabbits,' he pressed a little too relentlessly. It surprised Harry that even for a grown man there was something attractive to Moses about Grace's innocence and vulnerability, and it had enticed him to go too far.

'Well, not a full grown 'un, but a bunny!'

Grace winced at the thought and Harry changed the subject quickly. Moses and he continued to share conversation, though Grace remained a little quiet after the bunny episode. As they sat there, in the now slightly tarnished idyll of Moses' well-kept garden, the evening turned humid and cloudy as the land threw up its heat into the sky with turbulent abandon. When Moses mentioned that it looked like 'one o' them summer thunderstorms brewin'', Grace was instantly ready to return home.

When Harry dropped Grace off at her house, there was a letter there for him to collect. He slipped it inside his jacket and returned to read it in the quiet of his own kitchen. Once there, however, like the room, Harry felt rather empty, so he went to bed early. Being mid-summer, he was still well within the hours of daylight, but he felt tired with the day and wanted sleep to leave it behind. In fact, the evening had turned quite dark beneath a billowing stack of dark storm clouds so that he did not even bother to close the curtains.

It was not long before the gloomy bedroom was lit up in the silver-blue neon of sudden lightning. As its accompanying thunder rolled slowly over the town and out to the sea, he thought about Grace's sad end to the day and wondered who would be there to comfort her, Maude or her mother.

Soon rain was falling in torrents. It is one of nature's miracles that the individual droplets fall so softly, but together the multitude is able to create such a crescendo of sound that the house was soon enveloped by a blanket of deep, growling noise. Harry himself began to marvel at the power of nature, but before long sleep had dragged its own deep blanket across his mind.

Not unexpectedly, the following morning was grey. The garden lay wet and still from overnight rain. Harry felt as dark as the skies. He had thought the east of England would be drier, but this was proving to be a particularly wet summer. In the mirror his face was scrunched up in sour contempt, his first cup of tea stood cold and untouched, and he stared sullenly out into the garden, lost in his own dark thoughts: dark thoughts that had been further induced by the contents of the letter he had picked up from Bede House the previous evening, but had only just thought to read.

Mrs Hall's note had asked if Harry would attend Grace's end of year 'parents' evening' later that week. The request had instantly annoyed him and, by the time he had sat down to face breakfast, this annoyance had grown into an anger of irrationally large dimensions. If anyone had happened to call in upon him then, no doubt, his anger would have burst out in sullen fury. But, of course, there had been no callers, allowing all that vile passion to sink deeper and deeper into his head. So there he sat in such heavy and thunderous countenance, staring out into the wetness.

Ultimately, Harry snatched up a coat and stomped out into the street. Without conscious thought his indignant footsteps took him along wet roads, along the puddled bridle path, and out towards the sea, where his petulant escape was soon confronted by a sudden drop over muddy, rain soaked cliffs. The sea should have been in tumultuous rage like his own, but it was not. Despite the previous night's storm, the air was by now still and the sea spread towards him in silver flatness from a murky, indistinct horizon. It left him feeling indecisive.

The reasons for his rage began to filter through his confused and troubled mind. There was an intangible anger within him towards Grace's mother, maybe towards all mothers; there was anxiety over having to face Molly, Miss Bentham, after their last, disastrous meeting; there was Marianne, there was always Marianne; and, not least, there were raw, aching thoughts of term endings and Harry's distressing departure from teaching altogether.

The night's disturbing dreams began to re-materialise. As always for Harry over recent months there had been that haunting dream of classes out of control. And not just dreams: real memories as well of those harrowing months before the end.

When rumours of his affairs with Miss Gayle had begun to circulate and spiral, there had commenced an unstoppable whirlpool of decline. Even good kids, good classes, had been unable to resist the opportunity to challenge and rebel. It has always been like that in teaching: children have an incredible ability to detect any form of weakness no matter how indefinable, and, once detected, an irrepressible compulsion to drive home their advantage to the point of destruction. That is what had happened to Harry. He could so easily recall those sickening moments when both he, and the classes before him, had realised the chink in his confidence and control: a chink that had quickly crumbled into an unbridgeable chasm. And so it was that, from being a good teacher, he was suddenly struggling with all forms of control, self-respect or ability to continue. And that was when, more even than from his estrangement from Marianne, that Harry's whole being had fallen into that dark, dark cell of over self-critical, self-imposed depression.

If he had imagined the post driving lesson affair in Beverley to be a downward plunge on the emotional rollercoaster, Harry now knew that it was inconsequential compared to the way he felt at this moment. It was as if all those memories of classroom chaos had been buried by denial, buried until this current crisis of self-examination had returned them to his conscious awareness.

As he stood on the cliff top, all the confidence and contentment of the past month fell away, just like the boulder clay at his feet which was breaking away from the cliff edges. Tears began to course down Harry's face just like the streams from the sodden fields. Perhaps he would have crumbled completely if not for the arrival of Moses, who, for some reason inexplicable to him, cared about his welfare, and who for some other inexplicable reason just happened to stroll along the same path right then. Harry saw him through the mist of his troubles, stood there resting his weight comfortably against that old, forked stick of his.

'What are you doing here?' Harry stammered.

'Oh, some little bird said they'd seen you walking down this way. An', 'aving nothing better to do I thought I'd be keepin' you company.' That was all.

Harry allowed Moses to put a fatherly hand against his shoulder and to push him in the direction of his own back parlour, where they were soon sat behind mugs of warm tea.

'Na' then, lad ... you don't want to go fallin' out with the world. What's troublin' thee?'

But Harry could not face going into all those thoughts that had been filtering through his mind: the pain was too raw. Then for some obscure reason a memory from childhood came into Harry's mind and he told the gentle, old man that instead.

'When I was a kid ... I don't know, maybe nine or ten years old ... I went out walking with me dad. We went up on the Downs by Swindon. Me dad lived in a village on the Downs when he was a boy and before he came in to work in the railways. He used to take me up there sometimes. Anyway, this day we were up on the high hills walking and there were rabbits: perhaps there were lots of them, I don't remember. But he stops me, quietly, and he points out a rabbit, right there in front of us. It was sat in a little clump of thistles or something. And it was petrified ... I mean really petrified, like stone. It was sat there looking at us, staring and not moving a muscle ... apparently rabbits do that. And me dad whispers for me to take his stick and to walk round in a circle to get behind the rabbit. And I did ... walked round so that I was stood right there behind it ... with the stick raised above my head, ready to bring that it crashing down on the rabbit's head. And I stood there ... but I couldn't do it. And then at some point the rabbit finally bolted off. Then me dad came up and smacked me round the back of my head. "You're bloody soft, our David ... just like a big girl," he said.'

Then Harry stopped talking. His eyes had filled up with tears again and he could not speak any more. Thankfully, Moses did not comment. He just sat there, they both did, until Harry felt more in control.

'I don't know why I told you that little secret,' he said to Moses at last.

'Don't worry, lad. We all got stories like that inside us. Dads can be strange animals. I know mine was!'

Moses' words were unexpected and just a little baffling. Harry drank the tea, which by now had become quite cold. Suddenly, from walking on the Downs he was, in his mind's eye, stood atop a high cliff, and was uncertain what to think. Despite a feeling of tiredness, Harry knew it was important to do something, anything, constructive.

'Got any jobs that need doing?'

'Always got plenty of jobs, lad. Them gardens don't wait for no one.'

They were soon lifting up bulbs from the wet earth, daffodils, hyacinths and tulips that had already flowered. Then they laid them out to dry in Moses' big greenhouse so that later they could be stored ready for replanting later in the year. It was unexciting, maybe even tedious, work, but it helped Harry to get his mind back onto a steadier track.

Back home, after lunch, Harry fell asleep in his kitchen. He awoke with aches in both his mind and body. Thankfully, the imminence of his session with Grace forced him up from his chair and out into the remains of the day.

Despite the bouts of patchy rain that still fell randomly from a covering of grey sky, and wrapped in waterproofs, Grace and Harry made their way to the sea. The tide had brought the water in right up to the sea wall, making it a less attractive scene in every way, but there was still enjoyment to be found, dancing out of the waves on the margins of beach and even sitting out the worst showers in the shabby shelters along the promenade. Grace liked to sit there and play games with their dreams. Besides, Harry thought back to the afternoon when they had been caught on the beach by the tide and had decided that the promenade would be a lot safer.

'What will I be when I am a lady? Will I be happy? Where will I live?'

It amused Harry to tease her imagination, though there was sadness in knowing that adult life was likely to be more trying, even nefarious, for one as delicate as her. Perhaps he should have been preparing her for a crueller and less forgiving world, rather than feeding her dreams with hope and romance, but, sat together in the cosiness of the shelter and their imaginations, it seemed right to make her happy and unafraid of what might lie ahead. It made Harry happy too. Their dreams and stories were like waterproofs against the showers of uncertainty that threatened the future.

On returning home at the end of their walk, Harry felt far calmer and more cheerful than he would have imagined possible at the start of the day. There was even a rose-coloured tint to the evening sky promising more stable weather for the day ahead.

'Perfect for rides out into the countryside,' he thought to himself.

By the time Harry arrived at Bede House the next day, Grace had already changed out of her school uniform and into what had become her cycling gear: mid-length trousers, blouse and cardigan, plus a very sensible sun hat with a tie under the chin to stop it flying off; all in varying shades of pink. She looked as healthy as Harry had ever seen her, with the blush of the last few days' sun spread across her freckle speckled cheeks and forehead.

'You must have read my mind!'

'Did I?' she asked with a coy twist of her head.

Soon they were pedalling along the quiet lane past Eadie's house. Grace asked if they would be stopping there.

'Not this evening,' Harry called back over his shoulder. 'Not unless the heavens open again.'

But, there appeared to be no danger of that. The sky was clear blue save for a faint spread of cirrus that floated like gossamer way up high.

'Look at those beautiful mares' tails.'

There were no real hills in the area, though there were bumps and lumps in the thick layer of glacial moraine that comprises the Holderness. As the odd couple on the tandem enjoyed the ease of free-wheeling down one of the longer slopes, with the sun on their backs and their lungs and souls filled with the sumptuous summer air from all around them, Harry thought that it was about as perfect as he ever imagined it could have been.

Then, without warning, a big, black Land Rover, or whatever it was, swept by them with such noise and speed that they came right off the road and into the thick vegetation of the verge.

'Fucking idiot!' Harry cursed from where they lay amongst the long grass and the cow parsley. He was ready to leap up from his prone position to launch into a full rant, but, luckily, his concern for Grace stopped him. His fears were soon allayed as she turned round to him and smiled.

'You shouldn't say idiot!'

It was soon evident that no damage had been done and they resumed on their way.

About half a mile further on, however, they spotted the offending vehicle parked on the driveway of a large house set back from the road. A man was closing the five-bar gate that led into the driveway.

'Private: Keep out' it read on the expensive-looking sign on the top rung of the gate.

'You just about forced us off the road!' Harry shouted out to the man without too much venom.

'If you're not stable you shouldn't be on the road,' the driver retorted without even turning around.

'He's not very nice is he?' called Grace loud enough for the man to hear. 'Good job there's a gate to keep him in.'

'Yes, you're right … let's not bother.'

If asked, Harry would have sworn that he had not mean to do it, but, as they pushed off again on the tandem, he broke wind rather loudly. Harry could actually sense the man behind the gate stiffen, although the man was determined not to give the perpetrator of the fart the satisfaction of making him turn round.

'Pardon me!' Harry offered.

Grace started to giggle straight away and was soon laughing loudly and openly. Her laughter set Harry off as well, so much so that they soon lost control of the tandem and found themselves floundering in the long grass of the verge again.

Grace sat up in shock at falling off, but soon realised that she was OK.

'Oh, pardon me!' she mimicked and soon she was rolling about again in more uncontrolled laughter. They both lay back in the luxuriant vegetation and laughed up into the warm evening air, right up to the mares' tails. Just for good measure Grace stood up and blew raspberries at the house into which the pompous driver had disappeared.

'You're not very nice!' she mimicked at herself, then collapsed into laughter again under the weight of her own wit. 'We'll tell Mummy about the laughing ...' she concluded some minutes later, as she sobered into some form of seriousness, 'but not about the trumping.'

Then they cycled home without further incident.

*

Harry and Grace made regular incursions into the warm, verdant summer countryside along the little network of roads that lay just inland from the coast. They both became fitter and far steadier on the tandem. As they cycled along Harry would pass on all of his limited knowledge of the natural beauty around them. He did not know if Grace took any notice: she was usually quite quiet while they were actually cycling. She did join in the conversations, however, when Harry managed to spot any animals, domestic or wild. And she was still fascinated by the future and the wistful possibilities of reincarnation.

'Perhaps I'll be a baby horse,' she had pondered after they had passed a mare and her foal up to their fetlocks in a sea of kingcups and ox-eyed daisies.

'Yes ... that would be nice, though you might get fed up with being in the same field.'

'Mmmm ... maybe not then!'

Another time when they had seen a fox dart across the road,

'Perhaps I'll be a fox … I'd be quick and clever!'
    'Yes … though foxes do kill things!'
    'Not a fox then!'
And another time … 'I could be a bunny!'
    'Yes, nice: as long as the fox doesn't get you.'
    'Isn't anything safe?'

*

Harry had not seen Mrs Hall for a few days, so he was more than a little surprised that she came to see him in his own cottage garden one warm evening rather than wait for him to come to Bede House to meet on her home territory. It had started as something of an awkward meeting.

They sat at opposite ends of the bench, avoiding direct, face-to-face confrontation. Mostly Harry tried to stare fixedly across the lawn and away from her, though, unusually, she was dressed quite colourfully in a suit of blue that drew his eyes back towards her in surreptitious but irresistible glances. The subtlety of the blue unsettled him: it was poignantly familiar in some way, though he just could not place what it was that reminded him of the exact shade.

Harry had just finished cutting the lawn when she had arrived and the perspiration from working made him feel distinctly unclean next to her cool presence. Her smell was both fragrant and familiar, but he could not remember exactly what it was: his mother would have told him clearly that it was the essence of lilies of the valley, since it was a scent that she very much favoured herself, but for Harry it just confounded him. He sincerely hoped that the strong smell of severed grass around them would mask the strong odour of his own perspiration and prevent any comparison between them.

They sat there for a while in the stillness of the garden. A bird was singing in the ash tree. It was a blackbird or a song thrush: Harry was too distracted by female presence to recall exactly which it was.

Mrs Hall drew back her shoulders to begin her explanation of wanting Harry to attend Grace's parental consultations evening. Later he considered whether it had been a feeling of hygienic inferiority, fatigue from anger, frustration at not remembering that memory of blue, or some other subliminal reason that enabled him to listen passively to her petitions, but he had managed to do so.

She set out her request in such cogent and logical progression that Harry felt like a privileged business client listening to an unmissable opportunity. She began with apologies for her written request, then entreaties on how valuable his time was with Grace, and, finally, reasons why he could understand the school's comments better than her. None of it brooked any particular favour with Harry, but then, without any influence from him, she faltered and changed her tack completely.

'Mr Harry ... I know this is all a bit unreasonable ... I know you must think I'm a bad mother ... but I'm not, really. I love Grace, dearly ... but ... I have to admit it ... I just cannot face that school at the moment. It's just ... I ... they ... would not be able to understand why she needs to attend that school ... and I just don't feel able ...'

There was genuine anguish on her face as Harry turned to meet her plea. She looked lost and vulnerable, and in that vulnerability, quite beautiful. Harry wanted to express his concerns: that she was not going to be there as the parent; that he was anxious himself over facing Miss Bentham again; that he felt vulnerable and inadequate himself. But, in that instant, and in the face of such delicate candour, he suddenly wanted to protect this vulnerable woman before him, and his resistance caved in.

'OK, I'll go.'

Mrs Hall appeared incapable of expressing her appreciation or, indeed, anything else. She simply sat there for a few moments and stared into Harry's face. 'I just don't know how to ...'

'You don't need to,' he told her. 'There are lots of things that I couldn't explain to you. But I know that being with Grace has been ... how shall I say ... good for me, since I met her. And, if I can help by attending those school consultations, then I will.'

'You're a kind man, Mr Harry. I can see that.' And she smiled.

After she had gone Harry allowed the compliment to turn slowly through his mind a few times, just to enjoy it. Small things like that meant a lot sometimes, and at that particular moment his fragile persona needed all the support it could get. Well, that is how it felt to him then, though perhaps it had just been masculine weakness in the presence of an attractive woman. He thought about it as he lay in bed waiting for sleep to take over.

The next week Harry was there at the school awaiting his appointment at the parental consultations. Even if he had been placed there with his eyes closed, he would have known that he was in a school. It was nothing auditory, since the pupils were not there. Perhaps it was the unique smell, or maybe it was just feeling, but even without pupils around it was unmistakeably familiar. Paradoxically, on this occasion it felt unfamiliar too. Harry was used to sitting behind the desk, not in front.

Harry had time, sitting in the waiting area, to think back to all the sessions he had attended over the years. He had always got nervous. He had always harboured anxiety that something would go wrong and that there might be difficult parents, but, invariably, the evenings had passed pleasantly and well. He surmised that there should not have been too much surprise in that, since usually it was only the parents expecting good news who bothered to attend.

On this evening he was not sure what to expect to hear about Grace, but, nevertheless, he was intent on being pleasant to Molly, who was Grace's form tutor and the only appointment on his schedule. She was seated behind her nameplate in a soft dress of what Harry guessed was fine silk: tiny cream polka dots on a dark blue background; elegant but understated. She might have looked a little colourless had it not been for the vague hints of red in her hair. And as she looked up at him over the top of half-moon reading glasses, her large, dark irises looked quite beautiful against the startlingly clear whiteness of her eyes. Harry looked closely in an attempt to determine whether they widened to see him or not, but in the poor lighting of the school hall he struggled to detect any expression at all. She held the silence as he sat down and waited for him to fall falteringly into it.

'My eyes were always tired and bloodshot by this time of the term ...' Harry announced, not knowing where the statement had come from.

'What?'

'Sorry!' he stammered realising how ridiculous his comment must have appeared. 'When you looked up just then,' he forced himself to continue in a saner manner, 'your eyes just looked so clear and ... and ... nice ...'

Harry thought she must have been braced for something more confrontational or aggressive, but his eccentric compliment seemed to take her off-guard and her set expression softened just a little.

'I'll try to be clear about Grace's progress,' she began, reverting back to serious teacher mode and looking intently at some notes before her. 'To be frank, Mr Harry, I don't think she has made too much progress at all this year ...'

'Not made progress! You must be joking! What about her storytelling in the primary school? That was brilliant for her ... just getting through the year in a big school like this is an achievement for her!'

It was all coming out in a bit of a rant. Miss Bentham's wide eyes widened even further. Harry stopped to take breath before continuing in a gentler manner.

'She's a delicate and vulnerable child ... she's different and special. I know she's not very intelligent in the normal sort of way, but she's a sensitive person. And ... she is a person! She feels all the frustration and pain just like we all do ... she is a real person! She deserves the same chances as anyone else!'

Although he had spoken quietly, his thoughts came out with a passion that took them both by surprise. He had not rehearsed his thoughts or feelings, but now he had stated them, he was ready to defend them against any challenge or censure.

For a moment Harry thought she was ready to blast back at him and he tensed himself for the combat, but then, without warning, her face broke into a wide, generous smile.

'Yes, of course she is ... well I guess we'll just have to try a bit harder to accommodate her, won't we? Though, and perhaps I shouldn't say this, there might be a better choice for Grace ... There are some great courses, for example, at the agricultural college. You should visit it with Grace ... would you like me to arrange something?'

'You mean you don't think Grace is fit for proper schooling?'

'No, I don't mean that at all … Look, I think some of the courses there could be just right for Grace … You leave it to me and I'll arrange for you both to visit. How about that? … And if you don't like it, then I'll talk to the head … and persuade him that we should do something a little more appropriate for Grace here.'

And she smiled again, but conspiratorially now. Harry smiled too; relieved that it would be some other unfortunate man at the receiving end of her feminine wiles this time.

'Thanks, Molly … I mean Ms Bentham … I think, perhaps … I owe you a favour.'

'Yes, Mr Harry, I rather think you do.'

They faced each other in silent appraisal before she awarded him a third unexpected smile. 'How about you buying me a drink after this?'

'Yeah, course!' he returned, thinking it might be ungrateful to shirk his share of feminine wiles after all.

Harry felt strange going back to the cottage and then out again to meet Molly at the pub, but as he did so there was a whirl of excitement in his guts that had not been there for a long while. A bit later, as he stood at the near-empty bar, he began to get a little nervous about what to say to Molly when she arrived. He was wondering whether or not he should apologise for his anger the last time they had been together or rather to just let it just pass like water under a bridge.

Molly did not arrive until nearly ten o'clock so he had plenty of time to consider his quandary, though Harry need not have bothered.

'Half a pint o' shandy, a nice smile … and none of that angry stuff!' Molly announced as she pushed up against him at the bar.

'Yeah … look … I'm really sorry about that,' Harry stated lamely. Molly must have recognised his anguish.

'Don't be daft! I'm only joshing you! I always do that when I'm nervous,' she smiled meekly before continuing. 'It's all an act you know! All this brash banter … I don't go meeting fellas in pubs every day of the week!'

'Don't you …' Harry was about to make another self-effacing remark when, thankfully, he realised how dull he must have been acting. He decided that reciprocal smiling on his part would probably advance his cause far more effectively than talking too much. When he asked himself why it was that he wanted to advance his cause anyway, a little bit of honesty allowed him to realise that it was simply a treat to sit there in the company of such an attractive woman. And Molly certainly fitted that description once she had removed her rather ordinary woollen coat to reveal the silk dress again. It was simply cut, but stylish enough to accentuate the well-shaped curves of the body beneath it. In terms of modern acceptability, Molly was probably two or three kilos the wrong side of perfect, but to Harry she looked even more attractive for it.

Despite her confession of shyness, and in between gulps of shandy, Molly talked almost garrulously. Harry had always felt more comfortable in the company of women who took the lead in conversation and he enjoyed being her attentive audience. Mostly he enjoyed the delicious normality of sitting there with her in the pub. It made him realise how abnormal his life had been for the past year. More than that, his own beer consumption had lifted his usual cloak of gloom and inhibition to the extent that his senses were beginning to respond to her attractiveness. Fortunately, there was not time for him to fall into the trap of reckless advances before she concluded the reunion.

'Thanks for the drink … It was good to see you again. But …' she said through a yawn that made her eyes water, 'got to get up early. Some of us have to work in the morning!'

'How are you getting home then?' he asked her.

She held up a set of keys and jangled them impishly. 'Oh, ye of little confidence! Passed me test first time! … Pigeons of Yorkshire, look out … here I come!'

And with that she slid out from behind the table and slipped on her woollen coat. 'Bye, then!'

Harry groped around inside his slightly befuddled brain to find some witty or even charming throwaway lines with which to engage her for just a little longer, but the reserve was empty. So, he merely nodded, smiled back and watched her walk away. Though he felt relieved that she had managed to overlook the disastrous ending to their previous encounter and had bothered to meet him at all, Harry was acutely disappointed that this meeting had ended so soon.

His eyes were still fixed sorrowfully on the door through which she had just exited, when, to his surprise, it opened, and her face popped back into view again.

'Don't suppose you fancy helping me with a little bit of gardening Saturday morning!'

'Yeah! Yeah, I'd love to!' Harry replied quickly once he had snatched his breath back.

'Right, Saturday morning then. Ten? Eleven?'

'Yeah, great! Ten.'

Harry walked home through the still balmy evening, cheerfully whistling and looking forward to draining tea from the sky-blue mug on the polished table again.

*

The next day was Friday. Harry met Grace after school and they walked by the sea. It was still hot, as it had been through the day, and they strolled very slowly, enjoying the warm touch of the sun upon their skin. Grace looked as healthy as Harry had ever noticed before. There were even freckles on her pale arms and face.

'Every time you kiss your boyfriend you get an extra freckle on your nose!' he told her stupidly. 'Let me count your freckles. If you've got an extra one next time I see you, then I'll know!'

'Don't be silly, Harry,' she retorted rather solemnly. 'Mummy says I mustn't let boys kiss me or take advantage of me or anything like that.'

'No, of course not,' he reassured her hastily, realising that it really had been a mistake for him to say that and remembering how very vulnerable she must be.

'No, it was a very silly thing for me to say. I'm sorry. Shall we just forget I said it at all?'

'Said what?'

'You know, what I said about fre— You know, Grace, you're a bit clever sometimes!'

'Ha … I am sometimes, Harry,' she laughed, looking wonderfully happy and pleased with herself.

'Come on, I'll buy you an ice cream.'

And they were still in high spirits as they returned to Bede House. So too, it seemed, was Mrs Hall, who met them at the side gate.

'What are you two laughing about?' she asked rhetorically. 'You both look a little hot. There's some cold lemon if you'd like it.'

'Yes please, Mummy,' Grace cried in her usual polite way. 'Harry and I are really thirsty, aren't we, Harry?'

'Well, I ...'

'Yes, come on, Mr Harry ... we'd love you to join us.'

There were garden chairs and a table beneath a large sunshade at the back of the house. It all looked new and rather expensive too, even Grace approached it hesitantly. Mrs Hall must have read Harry's mind.

'Thought I'd splash out. No point having a secluded garden if one never sits out in it!'

Harry smiled in agreement, though he was surprised at her choice of adjective to describe the garden. 'Still, better than "nice"!' he thought to himself.

'Please sit down, Mr Harry,' said Mrs Hall.

There were three chairs and Harry wondered for a moment if she had put one out just for him. 'I'll fetch another one if Maude wants to join us,' she continued, clearing that doubt. 'Though I don't expect she will join us if you're here ... no offence, of course, Mr Harry. She's just not that ... comfortable ... with visitors.'

'You can say that again!' Harry thought to himself, raising his eyebrows metaphorically if not physically.

The lemon drink was refreshing and, to Harry, it felt really good just to be relaxing there in the sunshine. Grace, in particular, seemed very content and was absorbed in watching a large bumblebee so heavily laden with nectar that it appeared almost drunk. Regardless of its heavy burden, it continued to make its cumbersome journey in and out of each flower on a tall, though rather ungainly, single hollyhock that stood alone in what might formerly have been an herbaceous border.

Despite his affectionate feelings towards Grace, Harry had to admit to himself that she too was a rather ungainly flower. All of which clashed quite dramatically with the appearance of her mother, who appeared relaxed also, but stylish to the point of chic without effort, in her casual clothes of linen shirt and long Bermudas. She sported not just a wide-brimmed straw hat, but sunglasses as well. And all that pale simplicity was set off so perfectly against a silken tie of such exquisite pale blue and golden swirls in her equally pale hair.

For a change Mrs Hall was happy to exchange small talk and pleasantries.

'I suppose the garden deserves rather better treatment … not very exciting is it?' She said nonchalantly. 'I never get round to gardens much whenever we move.'

'Do you move a lot then?'

'Well, not … we've had to move a few times.'

She stopped rather abruptly as if on the defensive and the conversation lulled somewhat. In fact, it stopped altogether until Harry attempted to rectify the situation by returning to the subject of the garden.

'You have a nice, big patio,' he surmised. 'You could easily fill up a few pots with flowers or shrubs. And you can see that there used to be some flower beds … you could fill one of those in the garden. Might put a smile on its face!'

'Put a smile on its face?' Grace interjected. 'The garden already has a smile!'

Harry had almost forgotten that she was there. They both smiled at her, but passed over her remark.

'Mr Harry means that it would cheer up the appearance of the garden, Darling,' explained her mother before turning her head in Harry's direction.

She kept her head low and her eyes hidden behind the combined defences of her glasses and the brim's shadow. Harry regretted not being able to discern her fuller expression. He imagined that he was being admonished for his unsolicited advice, but, so it turned out after a brief pause, this was not the case.

'And, do you know? That is a splendid suggestion, Mr Harry. Some flowers would make a real difference! Wouldn't it, poppet?' she added to Grace.

'Yes, flowers!' exclaimed Grace leaping to her feet and clapping. 'Let's have flowers!

'But, it's July already,' stalled Mrs Hall. 'We're not too late for flower planting are we, Mr Harry?'

'No, of course not … not yet … I mean, I'm not really an expert … I could ask Moses. I'm sure he'll know what's good for planting now.'

'Oh, super. I'm free tomorrow. We could get planting straight away. You'd like that wouldn't you, poppet?' Grace beamed at this and the whole idea.

'Yes,' she shouted delightedly. 'Harry will help us, won't you, Harry?'

Harry was uncertain and shot a look across to judge the expression on her mother's face. Unfortunately, the shadow of hat and glasses precluded any signs from there.

'Yes … I'd love to help, but …' he began before hesitating again.

'Oh, but what?' intoned Grace.

'Well, not a "but" really … it's just that I've already arranged to help someone else on Saturday, and …'

Harry was desperately keen not to disappoint her, and something was telling him not to miss the opportunity of spending some of the weekend with them.

'Look, I'll go and see Moses this evening … and then I'll let you know … and then you could buy things tomorrow and … I could help you … on Sunday!'

'Yes, that would be ... perfect,' said Mrs Hall's voice, though Harry could not tell from her face if she really meant it.

'Oh, why can't you help us tomorrow, Harry?' Grace asked quite dejectedly.

'Grace! You mustn't be rude!' her mother admonished immediately. 'Mr Harry is busy. We can't take up his whole weekend.'

'No! Look! I'd love to spend Sunday with you.' It came out a little too strongly. 'I mean, I love gardening and I'd be pleased if you would let me help you on Sunday ... and ... besides ... I need to talk to you about Grace's schooling for next year.'

The warm air seemed to quiver in anticipation. Harry stood to break the spell. 'I'll get off and see Moses right away. Then I'll let you know ...'

'What ... what about your lemonade?'

'That's OK. I'll finish it another time.'

In his flight from the garden Harry realised that it had been a foolish thing to say, but for some nebulous reason he had felt claustrophobic in their garden and had just wanted to get away.

But he did not go to see Moses immediately. First he went home to the cottage. The evening felt too warm and the coming weekend too pressing. Parts of his brain were whirling too quickly so that he felt unbalanced and out of control. Harry went upstairs to stand under the shower. He loved that shower; its jets poured down so powerfully that they almost hurt. He found its harsh flow to be therapeutic even on normal days, and at this time it felt like a downright life saver. The steady rhythm of the water onto his cranium gradually helped his pulse to slow and his equilibrium to return. It worried him to be a grown man thrown into panic through a few simple requests for his time: and by things that he really wanted to do. It was worse for Harry in that he had been, in former times, a person well in control of situations.

Harry tried to explain all about his stupid dilemmas when he eventually got to Moses. To begin with Harry had been unable to find Moses in his house. Instantly Harry had thought that his friend would be at the pub and the thought of going there in his own fragile state of mind had appeared too daunting. Not long afterwards, though, Harry had spotted the old man hovering in a sheltered corner of his garden. Moses seemed to be simply wandering round to stand in front of each plant growing there so that he could stare into its foliage. Intermittently he would reach out to touch a leaf or blossom with his fingertips. At some points Moses even seemed to be talking to them.

'You talking to the flowers, Moses?' Harry asked softly.

'Oh, it's you,' he observed dryly after starting just a little. 'Nay, lad, I aren't talkin' to 'em … jus' noticing 'em … See, lad, you can go round every day an' not even notice the things that's right there in front o' your nose … well, yer eyes. An' sometimes I likes to 'ave a real good notice of 'em. Else what's the point o' growin' 'em?'

Harry had to smile at his logic.

'Well, Moses, besides a cup of tea, I could do with a little bit of your best advice,' Harry told him in as matter-of-fact tone as he could manage.

'Oh, aye … you coming to me for advice! Not sure I knows nothin' worth knowin'!'

'Not sure you know *anything* worth knowing,' Harry arrogantly corrected him. Moses paused.

'Well, if you're so clever, how come you're askin' me?'

'Yes. I'm sorry. Can we start again?'

'Course we can, lad … Sit yer sen down. I'm sorry too … look, just wait two ticks an' I'll fetch us a drink. I got plenty o' that elderflower *presse* left.'

It really did seem like the perfect drink for a summer's evening. While they drank Harry asked his old friend about a list of plants for the Halls' patio.

'List? Yer don't need no list! Jus' tell 'em to get down Bev'ley market an' whatever they's got on the stall then that'll be fine … jus' tell 'em to pick out whatever they fancies.'

Harry nodded at his logic again, though he was a little disappointed not be the source of that advice.

'Still, tell yer what,' added Moses with relish, 'I got some things what'll get 'em started!' He led Harry over to one of his many herbaceous boarders. 'See these wallflowers … well, I got to thin 'em out any road, so there's plenty o' them for your little lass an' 'er mother,' Moses began.

After collecting those Harry followed Moses into the greenhouse.

'I got plenty of extras. Grows 'em case anyone needs a few more.' And Moses had soon amassed a fruit boxful of little pots containing plants ready for potting: fuchsias, peonies and pansies.

'That's great, Moses,' Harry told him, 'They'll just love them.'

'Course they will. Everyone deserves some little treats now an' then,' the old man declared with a satisfied smile. 'Talkin' o' treats … I got jus' the thing fo' you an' me!'

Moses returned a minute later with an old whiskey bottle.

'Don' worry, it aren't whiskey! Nothin' as strong as that. Just a little drop o' medicinal mead,' he told Harry, holding up the bottle so that the low sunlight could illuminate the treacle-coloured liquid inside.

'Medicinal?' Harry laughed. 'And what is mead anyway?'

'Mead? You dunno' what mead is? Mead's what we makes in the country, lad. It's made with 'oney: 'oney to soothe the soul! That's what this is ... an' this 'ere bottle's ... crab-apple mead. I saw this tree full o' crab apples while last year, up Honeysuckle Lane. Loaded it were ... an' them crab apples ripe as autumn itself ... an' I can't bear to see the bounty of the countryside go to waste. So, I picked 'em! Got an 'ole sack full. An' I looked in me books ... an' there was a recipe fo' crab-apple mead. So, I made it ... an' 'ere it is!'

Moses poured them half a tumbler each and sat down on the bench next to Harry. The bottle must have been stored somewhere cool, since the glass and the liquor itself was cool to Harry's lips: cool to the touch, but warm to the palette. The warmth and tasty smoothness of the mead surprised him very pleasantly.

There they sat in the warm embrace of the balmy evening, calmly downing the golden mead. As soon as their tumblers had emptied, Moses had poured some more of his magical nectar. Harry protested, but only as a token of politeness, of which Moses took no notice, of course.

'Relax, lad: it's Friday ... I got no crib tonight, an' we can just enjoy this beautiful, still evenin'.'

It was beautiful, the ambience enriched, no doubt, by the congenial impact of the mead. They sat and watched the last rays of sunlight pass slowly across the upper boughs of the quince tree and by the time darkness had fallen they had imbibed enough alcohol to allow their conversation to flow in whichever way their subconscious demands dictated.

It did not take too long before they were talking of women. Surprisingly, it was Moses who began this line of conversation by announcing that he had decided to visit Eadie.

"Appen she'd appreciate a 'and with her garden,' he considered.

"Appen she would,' Harry confirmed to him, intrigued, but not wishing to pursue the reasons for the change of mind at this delicate stage. Or, perhaps it was just preoccupation with his own concerns that held Harry back. He became introverted into silence for a moment.

'An she's 'ad a little setback just now ... since 'er poor ol' dog 'as gone an' died on 'er ... poor ol' gal ... I expect she'll be appreciatin' a little bit o' company and 'elp right now.'

Harry remained quiet, as if in thought.

'An' what about the women in your life?' Moses enquired of him.

Once Harry had begun to tell Moses of his arrangements to meet both Molly and Mrs Hall over the weekend, all sorts of thoughts and ideas seemed to fall from his mouth without any control, as if someone else was using Harry's voice and, indeed, his brain as well.

'You see, Molly,' Harry heard his voice telling the old man, 'she's a very attractive woman!' Harry stopped, waiting for the inner voice to inform them both further, but nothing came.

'An',' pursued Moses, growing a little impatient at Harry's temporary reticence, 'you think this Molly might be the one fo' you?'

'No,' Harry told Moses with an emphasis that made him sit up and listen to his own thoughts. 'No, I don't think she's the right one for me. But she is a very attractive woman, and ...'

'An' 'appen you feel a bit guilty wantin' to sleep with her when you don't love 'er?' Moses interjected again in an attempt to read Harry's mind for him.

Harry thought about this premise for a while. The inner voice was not allowing him to reach any conclusion on that score. He stared into the sky, which had by now filled with stars. 'Do you know?' he informed Moses absently and in a complete change of direction, 'There are more stars in the universe than there are grains of sand in the world.'

'Oh really..? An' what about this Mrs Hall woman?' pursued Moses ignoring Harry's distractional tactics. "Appen you want to sleep with her too? Attractive woman is she?'

'She is a beautiful woman,' Harry considered wistfully, 'but, no. I've never thought about sleeping with her as it happens. You know, I don't think she even likes me … And, I'm not sure she likes men very much at all.'

'Any road,' Moses concluded, 'you'd better get off wi' them plants while you can still walk straight, else you're gonna please 'er an' little Grace even less.'

'Tha's a good idea,' Harry told him and straightway picked up the fruit box and set off towards Scarborough Road.

A little while later, Harry stood with some uncertainty on the path leading to the front door of Bede House and he looked up at the lighted window of the tower room. For a moment he began to wonder at what might be behind the lighted curtains. But then his eyes were drawn up to the myriads of stars that seemed to whirl around ever so slightly in the endless darkness above the building's tower.

'Do you know, there are more stars in heaven than there are grains of sand on earth?' he said in a voice that could only have been audible to himself.

Later Harry would remember putting the box of plants on the step, and he would remember searching for some scrap of paper upon which to write. But that would be all he would remember about the end of that particular day.

Molly returned home from school, made herself a cup of coffee and sat down at the table to stare out of the window. The wisps of steam from her sky-blue mug drifted into her face without being noticed as she gazed vacantly into a clear sky of slightly paler hue and, without conscious thought, she picked out a chocolate truffle from the opened box on the table there. She could have easily spent the next hour consuming these chocolate globules of guilty passion, but then, in an instant, she stiffened into a far more resolved attitude, pushed the confectionery away and stood up. Downing the hot coffee quite quickly, she moved across to the stairs, where her telephone resided. Then, settling herself onto the lowest step, she moved her pressing fingers rapidly over the buttons to tap out a familiar number.

'Hello ... yeah, it's me ... ...

Yeah ... yeah, I'm fine, what about you? ... good, good ...

No, not yet: next week. In fact, just four days to go, well, three and a half really, then that nice long holiday stretching out. ... Yeah, I know ...

No, no problems at school, school's fine ... Yeah ...

No, no problems at all ... What? ... Well, there is one thing ... What? Yeah, it is a man, but ... What do you mean, "It's always a man"? Dad, that's mean!

No ... I'm not at all "worried about men" all the time! ... Yes, I know you are, but sometimes you still treat me like ...

No, I know you didn't ... No, it's alright, I know you didn't ... Yeah, I know it was always Mum's dearest wish, bless her ...

No, he's not ... I don't know ... I sort of liked him, and he seems real nice, but he gets sort of angry sometimes ...

No, not like that Michael did! No, he's not really violent ...

I know ... but I just felt sort of sorry for him ... ... Yeah, sorry for him ... that is allowed!

... Dad! ... Yeah, I know she used to say that about you, course I remember ...

Well, I asked him round tomorrow and ... and ... now I've sort of changed my mind!

Do you think so? Oh, thanks, Dad ... No, I just can't get myself bothered with someone who gets angry, that's all. You know, it's the end of term and I just feel exhausted. But ...

No, I can't. He's not on the phone: least, I don't think so. I don't know his number if he is ...

So, I was wondering if I could come over for the weekend ...

Oh, thanks, Dad ...

Yeah, I know it would, but I just haven't got the energy. You know, end of term and things ... yeah ... oh, thanks, Dad ... you sure it's not incon ...

Oh, great ...

No, tonight! That's if it's ... Oh, good ...

No, I'm going to get on the train ... Would you? Oh, that would be great ... I'll ring you when I get close ... Yeah! "It's me! I'm on the train!" ... yeah ...

Yeah, course we can go down the Fox ... Yeah, I know they are ...

Yes, of course, I can say something other than "yeah"!

What? Yeah, I know you do ... Yeah; I love you too ... ... yeah ... yeah!'

*

Harry awoke quite late to find that the Saturday weather was disappointingly dull: everything outside the window appeared hazy and grey. He had planned to cook himself eggs for breakfast, just to start the day off right, but in the event he felt a little sick in his stomach and settled for just toast. It was not until he began to eat that Harry remembered the mead from the night before. He sat restlessly in his chair until it was almost half-past eight and time to leave for Beverley. He thought it would take about an hour to get there, but he gave himself a good ninety minutes to be on the safe side. Despite the greyness of the morning he had decided to brave the elements in shorts and he felt a slight chill as he took the bicycle out of the shed and set off into the mist on it heading for Beverley.

Just a few miles away from the coastal strip, however, the misty greyness had completely evaporated to reveal a cloudless sky into which the sun had climbed to pour down its light and heat. And by the time Harry had climbed the very slight slope that rises to the centre of Beverley, he was wet with perspiration. So, rather than go straight to Molly's, he steered into the area of the market.

Right on the edge of the market was a stall selling plants and garden equipment, where he bought a plant to present to Molly. It was not quite 'a' plant: in fact, it was a collection of small white lilies that he imagined would look attractive in some corner of her garden. For some reason the lilies had beckoned to him though he could not find the connection in his mind as to why, but leaving the marketplace Harry felt rather pleased with himself to have thought to buy her a gift.

Harry rang Molly's bell at least four times and his mood changed quickly from happy expectation to frustration and concern. He waited as long as his patience would allow before ringing it once more. Then he noticed an envelope stuck behind the little knocker in the centre of the door. It took a little time for him to realise that the envelope might be for him. The note inside was brief, just a simple sentence to tell him that Molly was sorry, but that 'something' had cropped up.

The brevity of the note stunned him. He could not work out why had she changed her mind. He looked around to see if anyone else was there to witness the humiliation that filled his insides, but there was no one around. With clenched teeth, Harry dumped the lilies on the step and turned the bicycle around for the return journey. The last time he had cycled home from Molly's house his mood had also been red with rage and he was angry enough this time, though his mind was also clouded with purple shades of doubt and confusion.

Harry retuned to the cottage hot and hurting from both physical and mental labours. At first he just sat in his garden and stared angrily into the space before him. It was, no doubt, the soothing effect of the garden's greenery that helped to neutralise the flashing reds within his brain so that, after a while, he was able to recognise his own company as probably the worst thing for him at that moment. He did the sensible thing and walked round to Moses' place again, where, not unusually, there was a little game of hide and seek before he finally found his old friend.

Moses was in the old barn-like outhouse at the end of his garden, bent over a flickering flame. Harry scraped his feet on the doorstep to avoid startling the old man and then went in to intrude upon his studied exertions. Harry could see that Moses was holding a little, flat tin of dark liquid over the top of a candle flame. The usual mustiness of the air inside the old cobble walls was shot with the redolence of a far more pungent nature.

'What sort of wicked brew are you concocting now?' Harry ventured to ask.

''Ello, lad. It aren't no brew, it's just an old tin o' Cherry Blossom what'd gone 'ard.'

'Cherry blossom?'

'Yeah, Cherry Blossom … polish, lad! You know, Cherry Blossom polish that you puts on yer boots … leastways, I do. It 'ad gone all crumbly like, so I were just melting it and letting it settle down into somethin' smooth again. An' that's not all,' Moses continued. 'While I'm 'ere rummaging … I got summat in 'ere somewhere to show thee, lad … but let's 'ave a cup o' tea first while you can tell me what's eating you up. I'll make the tea … an' while I'm at it you can water me pots an' borders. It's a bit early in the day, but I might be busy later an' not 'ave time.'

Moses always watered his garden from a whole series of butts, which collected rainwater from all the roofs of the house and its many outbuildings. He insisted that everything be done through his big, old galvanised watering can so that each plant received a gentle sprinkling from its wide rose rather than a sudden dousing: 'jus' like raindrops' Moses would tell Harry. It was a simple job, absorbing in its own way, and therefore soothing upon Harry's troubled mind, which was, of course, exactly what Moses would have intended.

Over tea Moses listened to Harry's complaints: the wasted journey to Beverley, the insensitivity of Molly's brief note, and the way that he seemed to be forever damned in his contact with women.

'No one ever said it was easy,' the old man sighed.

'Ever said what was never easy?'

'Anythin' worth 'avin', lad!'

They drained their cups and sat for a while in secluded thought. When it seemed that Harry had come to the end of any useful purpose to his contemplations he reminded Moses that he had promised to show him something. Moses led the way back into the outhouse and across to a workbench below an arched and heavily cobwebbed window. There were shelves all around it filled with cans, bits of wood, boxes, ancient machinery, tools and all sorts of bric-a-brac.

'You ought to sort this lot out, Moses, and take what's worth having up to that car boot sale. There's probably some valuable things in amongst that lot,' Harry told him.

'You aren't wrong, lad. There are some valuable things ... they're valuable to me! I like to 'ave these old things around me. They're part o' me life, an' part o' other people's lives too. Like what I'm about to show thee!'

Moses picked up an old, but simply framed picture from the bench.

'I were wanting to put that painting o' yours up, an' I were thinkin' o' usin' this old frame what 'ad another picture already in it. It were one o' me father's old prints o' flowers. It were a bit washed out an' I never did like it too well ... any road, when I takes out the old print, what do I find at the back of it than this old photo what were used fo' backin' the print?'

Moses handed Harry the photograph. It was a wedding group of around a dozen people stood in a row either side of the young bride and groom. They were stood in a summer garden in front of an old house with a windmill behind. It must have been a working plate for the photographer for round the edges were little, neat notes about the colours that he would need for tinting the otherwise colourless print. 'Hazel eyes' it noted for many of the subjects: 'manganese blue!' it stated for the eyes of the bride and the shorter woman beside her.

Harry studied it for a few minutes before the evidence fell into place like jigsaw pieces from the scraps of information he had picked up from Moses. Two of the young men looked quite alike in face, stature and expression.

'So that must be your brother's wedding,' Harry told the old man gently.

Moses nodded then gathered himself to point out his brother, Daniel, his father and mother, Eadie's father, her sister, and a few aunts and uncles.

'Bloody 'ell!' Harry told him, indicating to the auburn haired and blue-eyed bride beside his brother. 'She was a really beautiful girl … no wonder you both fell for her! But where is it? Where was it taken? It looks a bit like here,' Harry concluded.

'It is 'ere, barmpot. Course, most o' the windmill's gone now; jus' part o' the tower left. You can see it if you go round the back o' Mill Cottage. I were thinkin' o' takin' the photo round Eadie's when I goes to sort out 'er garden. What d' you think?"

'Dunno. Depends what you think you want to happen, like, with you and Eadie … What do you want to happen?'

'Dunno, lad … me brain tells me jus' to leave things lyin', but there's another part o' me longs to … well, make contact with 'er again.' Moses shook his big, snowy head. "Ere I am, almost in me eighties … an' still can't think straight about women … I'd like to tell yer it gets easier an' more straightforward, but I dunno. Don't know what I do know sometimes.'

That made Harry smile, which pleasantly surprised him at the end of a woebegone day.

Harry did not know why, but he felt nervous about his visit to Bede House the next morning to help them with their gardening. They had not mentioned a time and he decided to arrive at ten so as not to disturb them at breakfast or anything like that. To his surprise, when Maude had opened the front door and led him around the house to the garden, Harry could see that they had already started. In fact, they were just tidying up the last couple of plant pots.

'You started early.' Sometimes, he thought, he could be really imaginative with his small talk.

'Come and look, Harry ... come and look!' cried Grace excitedly, having rushed up to pull at his arm as soon as she heard him arrive.

Harry happily allowed her to drag him around to inspect each and every pot, plus a crescent of reclaimed border that they had planted with Moses' red and orange wallflowers.

'Look, we planted them in the garden's smile,' Grace cried out excitedly.

When Harry looked he could see, indeed, that the crescent shaped border was like a large smile in the middle of the lawn.

'Yes, you're right, Grace! And, I can't believe you've done so much already,' he managed to stammer in nervousness.

'Yes, one of us was up rather early this morning,' smiled Mrs Hall.

'Well, they do need a lot of watering,' Harry offered in an attempt to be of some help. 'I could help you do that.'

And he did, with Grace helping closely at every step: so closely that before they had finished she was quite wet with water from the can. Her mother sent her off with Maude to put on some dry clothes. Harry stood on the patio rather helplessly once she had departed.

'Come and sit down, Mr Harry,' Mrs Hall invited and he took one of the new garden chairs. 'I'd like to thank you.'

'I don't need thanking ... I've only watered a few plants'

'No, I don't mean for today, although we are grateful for the plants you brought on Friday evening … along with the cryptic message!'

'Cryptic message? Me?'

'Yes … there was a little note we found with the plants on the doorstep. "Go to Beverley" it said,' she teased him with a laugh, 'nothing more!'

'Was that all I wrote? You must think I'm stupid.'

'No, we don't think you're stupid, Mr Harry. No, what I wanted to thank you for … was all that you have done for Grace. She really hasn't been so happy for a long time.'

Harry was embarrassed and lost for words. It was as if all the social skills he had ever developed over his fifty odd years of living had suddenly disappeared and he was starting again, like a teenager. Thankfully, he remembered about the possibility of Grace attending the agricultural college and told her mother about that. Mrs Hall wasn't sure, but said she was happy for Harry to investigate. She corrected herself: she would be grateful if he would investigate with Grace.

Grace came running back into the garden to join them, but with the gardening completed Harry felt at a bit of a loss to be sat there with Grace and her mother.

'Why don't we go for a walk?' chimed Grace.

Neither Mrs Hall nor Harry could think immediately of a good excuse not to, so they both sort of nodded and smiled and agreed.

'Where shall we go?' demanded Grace quite urgently as if wishing to confirm the arrangement before her mother or Harry could change their minds. 'Let's go to the sea!' she decided before they could offer any ideas.

'Yes, alright, darling,' Mrs Hall affirmed to placate Grace. 'Where would you like to go, Mr Harry?'

Harry dithered: Mrs Hall continued. 'Perhaps somewhere new? We could go in the car. You must have been to every beach near here. What about somewhere a bit further?'

More dithering from Harry.

'You've been to Bridlington haven't you? Where's past there?'

'Past there … Filey, I think,' said the ditherer at last. 'I've never been to Filey.'

'Right, Filey it is then,' Mrs Hall announced in an authoritative, almost triumphant, tone.

Within ten minutes all the necessary 'bits' had been gathered up and put into the boot of the car, and they were on their way to Filey. Harry sat in the front to navigate from the pristine road atlas, though finding the way through Bridlington took quite a while and by the time they had reached the approaches to Filey an hour had already passed, which was a long time considering that conversation between them in the car was rather formal and a little stilted.

At first the little town appeared uninspiring, but when they eventually found their way to the seafront the resort revealed itself to be a real gem. They parked in a road of white-façaded Victorian hotels that clung to the cliff sides, then made their way downwards through manicured gardens to the promenade that gave access to a beautiful, sandy beach which curved away southwards for miles. As they began to make their way along towards the cobbled slipway to the beach at the northern end of the promenade, Harry's senses were caught by the savoury aroma of seafood and fish and chips from the kiosks clustered there, so he suggested he should treat them to lunch. He was trying hard to be relaxed around Mrs Hall and he sensed that she was trying hard too, but there was still an air of tension around them.

Grace was desperately keen to get to the sands, so she and her mother wandered down past the landed fishing boats to the beach, while Harry queued for their lunch. He later followed down the slipway laden like a circus juggler with a balanced collection of food packages between his hands. Unfortunately, his concentration on the packages enabled him to unceremoniously trip over the last stone block of the slipway and to propel himself uncontrollably forward. At first a frantic dance of eccentric steps allowed him to maintain an upright posture, but then he caught his foot in a sandy pothole and plunged ungracefully downward, face-first into the sand.

All the pent-up tension of the previous two hours gushed up into Harry's head in an angry surge of blood and embarrassment. He felt ready to explode, but with clenched eyes and equally clenched teeth managed not to. He just lay there, face down in the sand wishing that he could have been a long way away from this scene of ridiculousness.

Then he heard them laughing. At first it was just sniffles and snorts as they tried desperately not to laugh, but then it grew and grew until they were both convulsed in uncontrolled, unabashed hilarity. And, by the time Harry dared to lift his eyes from the sand, mother and daughter were laid back helplessly as each one's shrieks encouraged the other to further and deeper mirth. And, amazingly, their laughter finally found its way into Harry's own miserable countenance and he began to laugh too. Then, strangely, laughing at himself enabled him to reassume his dignity, which allowed them to stop laughing too. They all stopped laughing, but the tension that had dogged their excursion thus far was miraculously dispelled into the fresh, seaside air.

They chatted idly through lunch before setting off to walk

along a rocky promontory that they heard called 'The Brigg'. A steady stream of people was making its way to and fro between the beach and the furthest limits of the promontory. The path was slippery in places, but manageable. And there were all sorts of wonders along the way: crabs and fish in crystal clear tidal pools; limpets and mussels; bits of driftwood; even a perfect starfish that Harry held up for them all to inspect.

Harry had to call to Grace in order to gain her attention to look at the starfish as she seemed lost in a dream world. He watched her carefully. She was engrossed: not with the sea breaking against the wet rocks; not with the marine treasures of the rocks and pools; not with the stunning scenery along this spectacular stretch of coast: none of these. She was unashamedly staring at, and studying, the other children, and there were quite a few, who were there with their parents. All through the afternoon she appeared lost in the fascination of watching other children, especially, Harry thought, those who were there with their fathers.

It did not take any form of genius to guess at why she found them so fascinating and Harry's emotions were in considerable turmoil when at one point she walked between her mother and him and reached out to take both their hands. Harry felt a surge of warmth towards Grace at the thought of what she might have been feeling but wanted at the same time to recoil from the possibility of arriving at any associations with her motives. Harry's insides burned with embarrassment, though Mrs Hall showed no signs of such embarrassment or that her thoughts had moved along the same lines as his own.

When they had returned to Bede House at the end of their sun-filled and, for Harry, idyllic day, Mrs Hall's farewell to Harry was light and completely nonchalant.

'Look,' he offered to Mrs Hall, 'I'm happy to take Grace out in the day … you know, while the school holidays are on … I mean, if you're happy with that!'

'Yes, I'm sure she would derive great benefit from spending the day walking or playing … no … I didn't mean "playing"! No, I'm sure she learns a great deal from her tutor time with you.'

'Well, no … I don't mean tutoring exactly … just walks and trips out now and then when I'm not busy with Moses,' Harry clarified.

'Yes, thank you, Mr Harry. She loves her trips out with you. And thank you for today: perhaps I could join you again sometime … when it would be convenient … when I'm not working, of course … if it fitted in.'

'Yes, that would be fine,' Harry assured her. 'I'll look forward to it.'

Then he turned for home before the conversation became any more involved.

*

During the next week Harry found a note sitting outside his back door. It was from Molly saying that she had arranged an appointment for Grace and him to meet the admissions tutor at the agricultural college later that week. It felt like a punch in the stomach for Harry to see her name and remember the way she had just given up on him. He felt like throwing the note into a bin but decided for Grace's sake that they should carry out the visit.

As always, Moses was pleased to help and drove Grace and Harry out into the countryside just beyond Beverley. On arrival Harry was shocked by the scale of the college and the excellent facilities it had to offer. Grace too warmed to the place. She loved seeing all the animals, though in truth, they frightened her a little and they soon settled on a horticultural course for her in the coming September. She was able to charm their host at the college with her accounts of planting out her mother's garden. There had been a slight impasse when the admissions tutor discovered that Harry was not Grace's father, or even her guardian, but he was left assured that Mrs Hall would very soon be in contact with them to sign all the papers.

They all returned in Moses' car in high spirits.

"Ere we are, back over the river an' into the 'olderness!' Moses called out with pride as they drove over the river bridge at Tickton.

It prompted Harry to explain to Moses about the gnawing sense of frustration that had been building within him. He explained that, apart from this main road to Beverley, which would have been too dangerous for Grace, there appeared to be no road bridges across the River Hull until much further north by Driffield and, that, although their stamina and the length of their cycling ventures had grown, they were restricted by the river to just the coastal strip of the Holderness. And, pleasant as their journeys to the coast were, Harry had a real yearning to break beyond the Hull and westwards to the open hills of the Wolds.

'You barmpot!' Moses accosted him with affection, 'why didn't you tell me afore? I knows a bridge, an' just right for cycles it is too!'

A few minutes later Moses swung off the road home and ventured northwards along the country lanes to a small settlement called Hempleholme, where, just as he had said, there was a narrow bridge over the river.

Harry got out of the car in a trance of wonder. Across the bridge a couple of gated lanes led to farms beyond. Indeed, as they stood there, a Land Rover with a horse box passed gingerly over the bridge and made its way to one of the farms.

'Can you get through there?' Harry asked a fisherman sat beside the bridge.

'It aren't open to cars, like, jus' fo' the farm traffic,' the fisherman told Harry, 'but you'd be alright walkin'.' Harry's eyes widened.

'And where does it go to?' he pursued.

'It goes through to Hutton an' Cranswick,' the fisherman informed him.

'You sure?'

'I ought to be ... tha's where I lives!' the amused man replied.

*

The very next day Harry had Grace back there on the tandem. They made their way awkwardly over the bridge, through the gate and then on past the farmhouse where, thankfully, no one bothered to challenge their passage. Within twenty minutes they had reached the village green of Cranswick, where they sat to lick ice-lollies bought from the post office. It was a most pleasant setting, but what really made Harry smile was the gentle rise of the hills beyond.

'What are you smiling about?' asked Grace from cherubic, lolly-reddened lips.

'Oh, just ventures.'

She smiled as if that had been the answer she had been expecting.

One morning, a few days later, they made their way back over the bridge at Hempleholme and down to the gated lane.

'Through the magic gate!' Harry chimed to Grace.

'Is it magic?'

'It might be.'

They were soon in Cranswick, where they stopped once more to buy drinks and flapjack at the post office beside the green. Then, after refreshment and just a few minutes later, they turned off the main road and climbed up, out of the village, to reach the brow of a hill. Harry stopped in awe. There before them, stretching out into the distance, lay the Wolds, empty and inviting like a secret park.

The couple cycled off towards the blue horizon and spent a whole hour on quiet tracks and lanes before they saw a single vehicle. It was all simply gorgeous. Harry's legs felt strong and the miles just slipped past. So eager had he been to taste the openness of these empty hills, that he had not noticed the passage of time. Grace needed to remind him that they should stop for lunch.

They sat on a grass verge beside a field of ripened barley to eat their sandwiches. It appeared that the harvesting of this field was overdue: the sun-baked stalks and whiskery heads of the barley scratched dryly against each other as a light breeze played across the wide expanse of standing corn. Tall poppies grew in speckles amongst the barley to give a contrast of vivid red against the pale, sun-bleached crop of cereal. After what had been said in Moses' lounge, Harry kept his thoughts about the wild blooms to himself, and so was rather shocked when it was Grace herself who brought them unexpectedly into their conversation.

'Maude says that poppies are the blood of young soldiers who died in the wars,' Grace solemnly announced out of nowhere.

Harry mused on this romantic, but morbid notion. It began to explain some of Grace's reaction previously, but he felt unsure about how to handle the issue, so he let it pass without comment.

Once stopped, he had felt twinges of tiredness in his legs and realised that he should not press Grace too far physically, even though she had so far not complained.

After devouring his sandwiches, Harry lay back on the grass and closed his eyes. It was so pleasant lying there in the warm, fresh air with only the sounds of the crackling cereal, trilling larks and the occasional humming of hymn tunes by Grace. There was a sense of calm within Harry that had been absent for a very long time.

Perhaps he had fallen asleep or perhaps he had just been in thoughtful contemplation before Harry was brought to his senses by a persistent irritation on his nose. He sat up to rub it vigorously before taking in the notes of the hilarious laughter behind him. Of course, it was Grace who had been tickling his nose with a long stem of grass. She thought it was the funniest trick in the world. Harry jumped up with a pantomime roar and began to chase her across the grass. Grace ran, shrieking in delighted fear. Sadly, Harry had forgotten her physical frailties and in no distance at all she had tripped and fallen.

By the time he had reached her she had regained her feet. She was ready to laugh and run again, but Harry put up his hand to caution against it. Tiny specks of blood had appeared upon her knee and soon there was a little trickle of blood. Thankfully, the wound was small and inconsequential, though Harry praised Grace's bravery as she sat there holding a tissue against her knee to stop the bleeding.

'You're just like one of those soldiers that Maude talks about,' he told her.

'I won't die will I?'

'No, of course you won't,' Harry laughed. 'Least, not today anyway!'

'But I will die one day, won't I, Harry?' she questioned him with such deep seriousness in her eyes.

'Yes, of course ... we all die someday. But it's not something to worry about.'

The little accident persuaded Harry that they should return home. Along the way Grace's knee stiffened up and he told her to just freewheel for the rest of the journey. It made the cycling a bit more difficult for him, but the return journey was predominantly downhill or flat so that it was not a great concern. Besides, Harry figured that their longer-than-usual journey had been taken to satisfy his own indulgence, so it was only poetic justice that he should labour somewhat on the way back.

When they reached Bede House, Harry handed Grace over to Maude's care. She gave him a somewhat reproachful look when he explained about Grace's accidental trip, but, of course, said nothing.

'Harry said I was brave like the soldiers,' Grace chirped in, which again brought a strangely sad look to Maude's eyes. Harry began to beat his retreat through the front door.

What Grace had said during the day did not strike home to Harry until later in the evening. He challenged her about it when he next saw her. They were in one of their favourite positions lounging against the promenade rails as they gazed down at the holidaymakers on the beach below them.

'You know what you said about the poppies?' Harry began, 'About Maude saying they were the blood of soldiers ... well ... did she actually say it to you? I mean ... did she speak it to you?'

'Course she did, silly.'

'But that means that she spoke to you. I mean ... does she really speak to you?'

'Of course, she does, silly Harry.'

'But I thought she didn't speak … I mean, she does speak then?'

'She speaks to me. She speaks to Mummy. She doesn't speak to Granddad though,' Grace concluded.

'Mmm … interesting.'

'Is it?'

Maude returned to the house after taking Grace to school. It took her no more than an hour to complete all the household chores: none of them in the house made much mess, not even Grace who had by now been well trained to keep her own room tidy.

She made tea with leaves: Darjeeling, as always. She felt comfortable with routine. The most recent move of house had upset her again. She felt aggrieved that they had to move so often, but she accepted the necessity.

The tea was black. She drank it while it was still hot and felt the warmth spread across her chest. One might have expected the old woman to relax into the drink's soothing effect, but no. She was up out of her chair as soon as she had finished the tea, moving to the bookcase where her hand moved slowly and affectionately across the worn spines of neatly placed books.

Probably, she could have named each volume with eyes closed, but she enjoyed the familiar flow of titles and authors as her look ran across them. She had read them all many times. No modern authors could match her favourites.

This time she chose Austen, like her she felt, a woman living on the edges of society: and her very favourite, Sense and Sensibility. As the pages parted her eyes took up the text without hesitation and within seconds her mind had gathered in the context completely, so well did she know the prose. She allowed herself to fall into the heart and soul of Marianne longing for her Willoughby, though she knew that in reality she had been far more of an Elinor.

If only she had had the strength and honesty of the novel's Marianne, then perhaps she would not have allowed herself to become such a victim of a man's cruelty. The prose became a dream, which itself became a recollection of a time passed, a time she visited so often in her mind. The only time that really meant anything to her.

In a while the book slipped from her hold. She sat up abruptly. She *would not allow herself to fall into laziness. But she had to allow for the gathering of wetness in the margins of her eyes. It blurred her vision just a little as she stared out across the furrowed lawn and wondered at the vagaries of living which had brought her to this moment where living did not seem to be so very important.*

In order to stimulate her consciousness, Maude reached across to the small wooden box beside the lamp on the room's desk. The beechwood box had been quite crudely made but had been polished so regularly that the wood almost glowed. She took out the single sheet of paper within and read it once more. Her pulse quickened as usual, but it was only a short while before her mind began to drift again. Sometimes the past seemed as real as the present.

She read the old letter and there she was in her mind's eye as a young woman. It was the most exciting day of her life. She was in London, not for the first time, but for the first time without close family members to chaperone her every movement.

It had been a surprise when her brother had allowed her to join the party of women volunteers who had travelled up to London from their quiet villages by the Suffolk coast to lend their hand tending to those many, many casualties who had returned from the terrible beaches at Dunkirk to overcrowd the hospitals in the south of England.

Ever since their parents had died, her brother, Winston, had taken such a strict sense of responsibility for her welfare as if wishing to make up for his lack of experience with an overbearing adherence to moral surveillance. He had arranged for Maude to stay with their widowed aunt, who was a nursing officer with the Queen Alexandra Imperial Military Nursing Service.

Being in her aunt's care was almost as stifling as that of her brother's, but she enjoyed the work that her aunt had arranged for her at Paddington General. She had been sent to co-ordinate the care of men returned from

Dunkirk. She had worked tirelessly to ensure that these men had as much comfort as could be arranged and, indeed, she had created effective channels whereby some of them could return home to be tended by their own loved ones.

She had also spent long hours listening to and comforting the sick and wounded. Many of them made light of their experiences and draped their misfortune in jokes and boyish bravado. Some of them looked lovingly into the pale blue eyes of her handsome face, but none of them took advantage of her youth or innocence. There was something about her sincerity that forbade them to do so.

Despite her aunt's strict regime, despite the ominous threat of an impending German bombing onslaught, and despite the weariness she felt from long hours at the hospital, Maude enjoyed her summer there: the summer of 1940. She enjoyed the camaraderie she had found with the other women working around her. But all through that summer she had been secretly searching for her Arthur, the Arthur who had seemed to have been there for her every day of her life until the call-up of 1939 had snatched him away to army training and then out to the fields of France.

It had been such a wrench when Arthur had left. Although he belonged to the ranks of those serving their house and, even though he was a year older than her, Maude had always played with him and his sisters. She was able to talk to him like no one else. By the age of sixteen she knew that he was the man to whom she would give her heart. If only life should be so simple. First, she had stood up against her brother, Winston, when he was unjustly berating Arthur for the mistreatment of a horse to cover up his own ineptitude, and then she had allowed him to discover one of her unfinished letters to Arthur during his training period. On reading her impassioned words to the young soldier, Winston had been enraged. No sister of his would be allowed to disgrace the family through such an intimate relationship with the lower classes, he had stated with ferocity.

And from that time she received no direct communication with Arthur, though, before she had moved up to London, she had been able to surreptitiously glean from his sisters that he had returned injured from Dunkirk's beaches where, she had since learned, so many had been maimed. She had since visited so many of London's rest centres in church halls, schools and other redundant buildings that she had lost count, but without finding him.

In the end it had been Arthur who had managed to trace her through his sisters and who, out of the blue, had arranged for her to meet him. She had burst into tears for the first time since leaving home when she read the brief letter, and had then poured out her tender feelings uncontrollably. Eve, her messenger, had listened carefully and sympathetically, but with growing indignation. 'If you don't mind me saying so, Mam, your brother sounds like a complete bastard!' The unexpected expletive had shocked but amused her and they had laughed together through her tears. Eve had warned that her clothes were not quite appropriate for the occasion, making her look 'too much the lady' and Eve had insisted that she borrow her own WVS uniform.

The change of clothes had excited her. She felt like some kind of agent and pulled her dark beret low over her eyes. Crossing over the Lambeth Bridge to the southern side of the Thames felt to her almost like crossing into a foreign country, though she walked with pride: pride in the borrowed uniform that she wore; pride in herself as a resolute woman serving others and her country; and pride in her mission to see the love of her young life, no matter what her brother thought.

Despite her pride and determination, she approached their meeting place with some trepidation, uncertain of the territory into which she was moving.

It had been easy for her to pick out Arthur in the little park behind St Thomas' Hospital, even though he was facing away. There he was at the base of a strong cable that floated up into the ether, where it tethered a billowing barrage balloon. And the sky was so blue! Her heart leapt to see him and she knew it would always do so whenever she pictured the scene.

Their union was necessarily formal amongst the many pedestrians out to enjoy the weekend and the unexpectedly fine September weather, but it was achingly joyous. She had not realised how lonely she had been for the past year until she saw him again.

'Hello, Maude,' was all Arthur was able to manage.

'Hello, Arthur,' she replied, before taking his uniformed arm and allowing herself to be walked back over the river again.

They stopped on Westminster Bridge to gaze into the dark waters and then her pent-up words burst out in a shower of unrelated thoughts.

'Isn't the price of food shocking?' 'Do you know the sea froze over on my birthday?' 'Eve says the Germans won't attack until springtime.'

'I really missed you, Arthur.'

At the last statement, Arthur, who had remained silent through the outpouring, spoke at last.

'I missed you too … Did it really freeze?'

'What? The sea? Yes it did, and on my birthday too!'

'The twentieth of January.'

'Yes … you remembered.'

'Yes … of course I did!' then his eyes had filled with tears so that he had been forced to turn away.

She smiled and held his arm even tighter as they traversed the bridge and turned eastwards along the Embankment. Maude remained bright and cheerful though she found it difficult to extract much in return from Arthur.

'There's Tower Bridge!' she exclaimed. 'I've never seen it before. Have you?'

'No.'

'Are you alright, Arthur? You're not unhappy with me are you?'

'No, Maude. I am not unhappy with you at all.' And he smiled into her questioning face. It hurt him that he was not making her laugh and smile too, and he tried harder.

'I couldn't be more happy than to be with you. You are so beautiful, so wonderful. Just like I always remembered you!'

'And you are the most wonderful and brave soldier!' she beamed.

'Am I?'

Maude could not help but notice that though he smiled and tried to look happy, there was something brittle about his smile, and, indeed, about the whole of his appearance and demeanour.

'Oh, Arthur! How selfish I am,' she burst out. 'I haven't even asked you about your injuries. What happened to you? Tell me about Dunkirk.'

'Don't let's worry about that on such a beautiful day ... I'm fine now. "Fully recovered" the doctors say ... I'm back to the unit in a few days' time.'

His fragile smile widened across his face, but there was no disguising the watery gleam that flawed the brightness of his eyes once again.

For a moment Maude was able to do nothing more than stare into his sad eyes. She was unable to guess at what lay behind them, though she wondered deeply.

'No. Let's not waste a sunny day,' she exclaimed brightly. 'Look, there's the Tower.'

'I could take you for lunch,' said Arthur, but Maude told him she felt too excited to eat. 'Well, what about a drink then?'

Maude felt just a little disappointed. All she wanted to do was to hold on to Arthur and walk through the sunshine, but she did not want to decline all of Arthur's invitations so she acquiesced with half a smile.

They walked past the Tower then into the streets of small houses near the docks at Wapping. There Arthur guided Maude into a public house.

She felt a tingle of emotions both good and bad, since she had never been into a pub before. The room appeared dark and a little scruffy, but there was loud and cheerful chatter. She was pleased to hide behind the anonymity of the plain green WVS uniform she had borrowed. Arthur bought two glasses of beer and ushered her to a table in the shadowed recesses of the room. Maude tried to be brave and drink the dark beer, but it was too bitter for her to taste without pursing her face into creases of aversion. Arthur laughed, the first time she had heard him do so for so long and the sound took her back to their childhood play in the garden.

'I'm sorry I'm so silly,' she told him.

'No. It's me that's silly: silly to bring you here,' he told her tenderly. 'I just wanted to be able to talk to you ... like we did before ... I want to tell you everything, but I can't seem to tell you anything.'

Maude felt tearful. She had not expected all this, but at least she could tell that her 'old', dear Arthur had returned to her. Her stupid, romantic mind had led her to picture some blissful scene of idyllic splendour.

'But this is wartime London,' she told herself inwardly. 'You are a grown woman with responsibilities ... act like it.'

And it was with this resolve that she unexpectedly agreed to Arthur's ultimate request that they should book into a little hotel.

'Look, one of the lads said we should do it,' he told her as the disinterested proprietor had closed the door of the shabby, little room where they found themselves moments later.

'I don't mean no disrespect, Maude ... I just wanted to be with you ... I got to go back to the bloody war on Tuesday.' His eyes filled with tears.

'No ... I know you didn't mean any disrespect,' she told him.

And then she pulled him onto the bed to hold him while he wept into the comfort of her body. At last he allowed his emotional anxiety to escape in shuddering sobs.

'It was terrible ...' he confided at last. 'They flew right down on us

with their guns! We couldn't do nothing, just crouch there and pray that the next bullet didn't get us … we couldn't do nothing … where was our boys … where was the RAF? Them Messerschmitts just flew in and shot us to bits!'

Maude did not know how to reply. She felt helpless and yet wonderful to be there to hold her Arthur. She held him until his sobbing stopped and then she could feel him sleeping peacefully against her. She felt the warmth of his steady breathing against the soft skin of her throat before raising her head to kiss his hair.

She realised that she had never kissed him before and smiled to herself. She felt so good and so secure there holding him. She felt that nothing on earth could hurt them as long as they held each other so closely.

But she was mistaken.

Without warning a huge explosion shook the room: the windows; the walls; the bed they lay upon; and even the very air they gasped at in shock.

That first explosion was followed by another, and then more, whole volleys: volley after volley. It felt as if the whole world was going up around them. Maude's fingers dug into Arthur's back as she clung to him for safety. Her eyes were wide and her mind dumbfounded: nothing in all her life's experience could allow her to make sense of the sudden mayhem.

Arthur's scarred mind, however, was able to take it in all too readily. The terror of his time on Dunkirk's bloody beaches had never left his mind. Ever present below the fragile film of control he had managed to maintain through his convalescence, that terror now burst out into reality with such terrible effect that he lay beside her in total grip of raw fear. Hands over his ears, eyes shut tight and mouth pulled back in a silent scream, he curled up into a foetal ball. Though Maude shook and shouted he was unable to make a response.

Maude felt too saddened to panic. What had started as the most exciting and wonderful day of her young life had instantly disintegrated into the very worst.

She had held and caressed her beloved Arthur, only to have everything snatched away. Her life was to be forever wrapped in the cold grasp of tragedy.

Even though his body lay beside her, she knew that her young, brave Arthur had been taken away and that nothing would ever replace the dream that she had longed to share with him.

So deep was her sadness that the potential agonies of shame and embarrassment at what followed barely touched her. Cruel coincidence had brought them together at the very time and place of the Germans' first bombing attack on London: the very first day of what became known as 'the Blitz'.

Outside their shabby room half of the docklands were ablaze. In the chaos of the aftermath they had been taken in by the police and then the military. There was a fuss: Maude's details did not fit in with the uniform she was wearing; her aunt had to be called to verify her claims. And as Maude was questioned and identified, she had barely noticed Arthur's dispatch to his barracks; something that was to haunt her mind guiltily in the painful months that followed.

Back at her aunt's house, Maude stayed within the confines of her room, barely eating and barely noticing the stern conversations taking place outside of it. Within a few days, she could not be sure of exactly how many, her brother, Winston, had arrived.

He had burst into her room consumed with anger and righteous indignation that she had so blatantly despoiled the family's honour. Her aunt and whomever it had been beside her stood passively, almost approvingly, as Winston had ripped into her with his own volleys of detonating questions. She knew that she could never explain sufficiently to satiate his overwhelming desire to extract blame and retribution, so she said nothing.

Then, in frustration, Winston had slapped across her face so powerfully that Maude had staggered, despite her resolve to stand impassively against him. In a strange and perverse way the slap had strengthened her. She had stood erectly, stared through flaming eyes, and said nothing. She said nothing at all. And, strangely, she felt powerful in her silence. There was nothing he could do to violate her silent dignity: nothing at all.

Maude continued to say nothing throughout the journey back home to Suffolk and through the days that followed. She held her silence through the weeks and months and even through the years that followed. On the day that Winston informed her of Arthur's death in Northern Africa she had gasped, but still said nothing.

The family and its household grew accustomed to her mute existence and Maude felt no great desire to speak to them. She took in the events and passages of life in the family house where she spent all her time, but responded only in actions, never words. Occasionally she had been moved by the emotions of life there, but mostly she kept her emotions locked into her private thoughts and memories, rarely displaying them to others.

She had silently sympathised with the frightened and submissive wife that Winston had brought into the house, but had left her empathy unspoken. She had been pleased to help her sister-in-law with preparations for her first children: twins.

And, when the unfortunate young mother had died in childbirth with her stillborn second, Maude had felt great sadness for her and for the baby girl who had become motherless. Winston had named the surviving child Elizabeth after his own mother, though it had soon become clear that he had little stomach for further paternal duties, and it was soon established that Maude would become responsible for the girl's upbringing.

At first many in the family had been concerned that the child's welfare and development should be left to a loving but mute aunt, and many had recommended the hiring of a professional nanny, but Winston the father had been adamant that there should be no further help from outside the family.

As the toddler girl grew into a child and then a young woman, all were obliged to agree that she had been nurtured well into a thoroughly worthy and fine young person: more lively and open, and, almost certainly, happier than her sturdy, but remote father.

There had been speculation at how successfully Maude had been able to perform her role as surrogate parent so successfully when the task was hampered by her muteness. Winston said nothing to dispel the suspicion, though there had been many occasions when he had heard audible communication between the two.

'There, there, my Elizabeth,' he often heard through the door.

AUGUST

Having been a teacher able to enjoy long summer holidays, August had always been Harry's favourite month. Although he did not know it at the time, one day Harry would be able to look back on this particular August and say that it was possibly the very best time of his whole life. As summer spread its warmth and sunshine across the land, Grace and he made frequent forays across the bridge at Hempleholme and out into the wide, open spaces of the Wolds.

It might have appeared a little strange to the occasional walkers and farmers they passed to see a middle-aged man enjoying such contentment in the company of his childlike companion, but for Harry the relationship was just perfect. He knew that Grace enjoyed being there with him even if cycling was not necessarily her activity of choice, and the only responsibility he had in the whole world was to keep her safe and happy.

Drifting along those quiet lanes between fields of gently waving wheat and barley allowed them a seclusion and serenity of their very own. Harry never minded the pedalling and the perspiration. For him it felt like sailing across a green-gold ocean, and he would always remember it as a halcyon time in his life.

As a mark of his exhilaration Harry would sing out loud whenever they reached a downhill incline that allowed him to stop pedalling and to take a little more notice of the wonder all around. For reasons unknown to himself he usually launched into the chorus of Jeff Beck's 'Hi Ho, Silver Lining', which he could vaguely remember singing as a drunken student in the union bar.

He was hopeful that Grace would join in with him some time, though she never did until he asked her to sing one day. She thought carefully before quietly singing the first few lines of 'Onward Christian Soldiers', after which Harry declined to invite her again.

One fine day they found themselves having stopped to rest at the head of a path that was the opening to what a passer-by told Harry was called Pasture Dale. The green, grassy path wound its way along the floor of the dale, zigzagging between the interlocking spurs of the encompassing hills. It was such an inviting prospect that they left the tandem beside the metalled road and walked lazily down it into the dale, the roundness of each spur hiding from view whatever might be around the next bend.

In fact, there was not anything spectacular around any of the bends, but it was just beautiful in its simplicity, and it was so peaceful. The rich greenness of the path contrasted against the pale sides of the steep dale, where the russet grasses had been bleached almost colourless by the accumulated sunshine. They followed the path into the dale and stopped for a while beneath the branches of a single ash that grew in the very heart of the seclusion.

They had chosen a great day for their jaunt: the sky was strewn with giant, billowing cumulus, but there appeared to be no threat of rain. Harry allowed his eyes to ramble lazily across the hills and the sky.

'You like watching clouds don't you, Harry?'

'Yes, I do.'

'What are they?'

'What, clouds? They're just big, vacuous ... well ... clouds are made up of tiny droplets of water: millions and billions of little molecules too small to be seen, but together ...'

'Well, if they are too small to be seen, how do you know they're there?'

'How do I know? Oh, I don't know ... I just do 'cos I'm clever!' he joked.

Grace knew he was joking, but she was ready to compete.

'Well, if you're clever ... tell me where they go.'

'Where do what go?'

'Clouds! Sometimes they're there ... and sometimes they're gone! Where do they go?'

Harry had to admit to himself that he was not that clever.

The ash tree and its welcome shade had enticed them to stay for longer than Harry had planned, so in a while they made their way back to the tandem. They had been out from home for quite a few hours so Harry was determined that they should make some haste in returning. They headed due south looking for a way homeward, but by the time they had reached the second village he realised that they had become very tired and that they had drifted too far west. He sat them down to rest at the edge of the little village they had just reached, again seeking the shade of trees.

Across the rough pasture was a stream and cottages beyond. And as they sat resting they were quickly engrossed by the activity before them. A girl was walking up from the stream towards the nearest cottage, and behind her was a line of ducklings.

'Ooh, look!' cooed Grace. It was a rare and heart-warming sight.

'Is she their mother?'

'I don't think ... I really don't know. Sometimes ducklings do learn to follow people and ...'

But, before Harry could finish, Grace was up and had crossed the bridge just downstream to arrive outside the gate of the garden into which the young girl had disappeared. Harry rushed over to join her before she could become a nuisance to the people inside the house or garden.

A man appeared at the gate.

'We were just watching your daughter and the ducklings,' Harry began.

'Is she their mummy?'

'Why don't you come in?' asked the man kindly.

'Well, it's a bit late and ...'

'Oh, yes please!' squealed Grace and she was straightway into the garden before Harry could utter another word.

Harry was welcomed to a seat beside the shrubbery and the fishpond from where he could watch the girl show Grace how she fed the ducklings. The girl must have been younger than Grace, maybe not quite a teenager yet, but Harry could see that, as she explained to Grace about the ducklings following her, she had already assessed Grace's needs and vulnerability. She spoke to Grace like an adult, but with gentleness and with an engaging smile across her warm, open face.

There were two brothers in the garden as well: an older one who was absorbed throughout with cleaning and repairing his bicycle, and a younger, quiet boy with beautiful doe eyes, who seemed content just to observe.

And Grace? It was as clear as the day was bright that Grace had completely and instantly fallen for the beautiful mother of ducklings. She watched the girl with wonder in her face. Harry could tell what she was thinking.

'I'd like to be that girl with ducklings and brothers and a mummy and a daddy!' was what she was thinking in that inimitable way of hers.

Harry even thought to himself that he would quite like to be the man with his lovely family. It seemed, there and then, that the man's life must be so simple and happy. But, of course, what did Harry know about the man's or anybody else's life?

The mother of the house broke into Harry's thoughts with 'Would you like a cup of tea?' And almost before he could nod assent there were cups of tea and a plateful of homemade cakes.

'You're lucky,' quipped the man, 'Jan's just baked these!'

'Ooh, you are a fibber, Andy!' she admonished with a peal of giggles. Then to Harry over her shoulder, 'I've just got back from the fete in Pock' … they were selling these off cheap!'

No matter: they spent an idyllic half an hour in their country garden sipping hot tea and devouring the cakes, while the mother regaled Harry with tales of her schooldays picnics in Pasture Dale.

The garden they sat in, in fact the whole village, nestled in a valley between two lines of hills. To the east, the direction in which Harry and Grace needed to travel homewards, was the unbroken escarpment that marked the beginning of the Wolds. And beyond the beck and the meadow where they had first sat to rest, a narrow road climbed steeply to the top of the escarpment. It looked like a daunting ascent.

It was time for the visitors to depart. There was a moment for Grace to marvel once more as the girl led the ducklings back to their brookside home, then, similarly, the family followed them, one by one, out to the tandem. The man of the house had brought out an expensive-looking camera, which he appeared to be using with expert nonchalance. The two cyclists were made to stand together by the tandem for a photograph. Grace smiled her best smile. Harry tried, though his mind was clearly distracted by their imminent climb out of the valley. The man seemed to read Harry's mind.

'I wouldn't fancy riding up there on a tandem,' he declared mildly.

'Hmm ... no ... I ...' was about as much as Harry could offer in return.

'How far 'ave you got to go?'

'We've got to get back to the coast,' Harry told the father dumbly.

'What! You won't get there 'til dark! ... Why, I haven't been to the coast since last summer ... come on ... I'll give you a lift. Come on Beckie, do you fancy a ride to the seaside?'

His daughter quickly jumped up ready for the trip.

'Are you sure?' Harry intoned meekly, hoping that the man would not change his mind.'

'Course I'm sure! Got room for another one! Anybody else comin'?

Mind, I haven't got room for the tandem ...'

'Oh, that's OK. My friend will give me a lift over tomorrow to collect it ... if you don't mind us leaving it here!'

The man did not mind and soon everyone was strapped into the car; the man and Harry in the front; and Grace, the girl and her quiet brother in the back.

Throughout the journey Harry was worried about Grace being able to say goodbye to the friend of her dreams, but, in the event, that situation did not occur. As Harry looked back over his shoulder to tell Grace that she was home, he could see that she was fast asleep. So deeply was she asleep that nothing he did could wake her: not calling, nor prodding, nor anything else he could think of to do.

Luckily, the other occupants of the car thought that it was really funny. Harry's poor back did not share their humour as he eventually heaved Grace out of the car and he summoned up just enough energy to get her up the pathway to her front door and to ring the bell. Mrs Hall came to the door and, with Maude's help, they carried her to one of the leather settees. When Harry finally remembered the people in the car it was too late and they had gone. Harry leaned against the doorjamb and began to straighten his back.

'I'm really sorry, Mr Harry,' Mrs Hall began to tell him through her laughter, 'when Grace falls asleep ... she stays asleep! ... But where's the tandem? Is everything alright?'

'Yes. Everything is fine.'

'Except for my back!' he thought to himself. 'We had a really nice day.'

'Would you like to come in for a drink? Or something?'

'No. Thank you. I'll just get off home.' Harry was thinking about the warm shower, though later he mused on an opportunity lost.'

Moses told Harry with a sardonic grin the next morning that there was nothing he would like better than a drive across the Wolds to pick up the tandem. He said that it must have been whole years since he had travelled all the way across the hills and that he would show Harry some of his favourite spots along the way. He was, however, busy that day so the trip had to wait until the day after.

They did not take Grace because they needed to fold down the back seats of the old Volvo to be able to accommodate the tandem and, besides, Harry thought it would be a bit much of an imposition on the good folks' hospitality to take her back to the duckling girl again: maybe, one day.

Harry thought ruefully about Molly as they passed by Beverley, but did not mention it to Moses. Then they were out into the country lanes. Soon, and without warning, Moses brought the car to a stop beside the road they had just turned into and motioned Harry to join him. With one hand on his charge's shoulder the old man pointed towards the furthest end of the lane.

'Look at that, lad … If that aren't the loveliest spire in the land then I'd be pleased to see what is.'

It certainly was a beautiful vision looking along the straight road to where a needle-like spire graced the horizon. They soon passed by the church, but Moses did not want to stop and look inside. Harry would have enjoyed exploring both the inside and outside of the church, but Moses was content to let it simply stand as part of the landscape.

'I always feels like I'm intruding where I didn't ought to be when I goes in churches,' Moses explained without expansion and Harry did not press him.

But, when they did next stop later atop a hill that allowed them a wonderful panoramic view northwards across the Wolds, the old man was pleased to talk more expansively.

'See down there,' he confided while Harry gazed across the open downlands. 'That's where they 'olds the Kipling Cotes Derby.'

'It's so peaceful up here,' Harry told him, taking in as much as he could of the gently rolling patchwork of fields and hedges.

'They been 'olding an 'orse-race 'ere for five 'undred years. It's the oldest 'orse-race in England,' Moses continued.

'I love it … It's so peaceful.'

'Course, there's no grandstand or fancy finishing straight: just hard riding cross the fields and tracks.'

'It seems like just last week it was so green, but now it's every shade of brown and yellow … and …'

'You aren't listenin' to a word I says are you?' complained Moses.

'Of course, I am, Moses! I love the history of it all. I've even been reading up about your friend, Mr Sykes, and what he did to change the landscape. But, I'm just trying to take it all in. It's so beautiful ... it's like the loveliest picture that was ever painted ... or never painted ...'

And perhaps Moses was taken in by it as well. The pastiche before them was magnificent: umbers and ochres; hints of white and gold where the sun lit up the scene; and in the further distance, blues and greys and silvers that merged into the horizon.

'And the order of cultivation ...' Harry went on like he was some sort of poet. 'It's so calming.'

'You wouldn't find it so calming if you was to be driving the tractor or the 'arvester! Cultivation looks all very well from a distance, but up close it's just 'ard wo'k,' Moses retorted.

'Yes! But all that wheat and barley ... it's so ... fecund.'

'Oh, fecundity now is it? Come on, lad; let's get in the car before we both trip over some o' them big words. Those tea party friends of yours will be thinkin' 'bout selling that ol' tandem soon.'

Sadly, when they reached the cottage beside the beck, there was no-one at home. Harry was disappointed: Moses had introduced him to so many nice people and Harry had been looking forward to doing the same. After taking off the front wheel, Moses managed to squash the tandem into the rear of the car, Harry scribble a note of thanks on the back of an old envelope to leave on the front door of the cottage beside the beck, and they departed.

'Never mind, lad. Let's drop in on ol' Bob,' suggested Moses.

So, they did.

There was time for another week of tandem excursions in the

last week of August; or perhaps they should have called them 'incursions' as they invariably crossed the bridge at Hempleholme to explore new parts of the Wolds. Moses had promised 'fine skies fo' the back 'alf of August'. 'It's what the Wolds farmers relies upon. You won't catch much rain in East Yorkshire while August comes to an end.'

Indeed, wherever the two on a tandem went that week the fields were full of harvesting activity. Those fields left waiting to be cut were still waist high with corn bleached almost colourless by the sun. The dried-up leaves and stalks in them whispered drily in the hushed heat while the bursting ears of cereal impatiently crackled with ripeness as Harry and Grace cycled by. The sun was so warming that it made the shirts on the cyclists' backs smell like they had just been ironed. Grace often appeared to find it hard going on the sunniest days, but the heat bothered Harry hardly at all since he was relishing the freedom of the physical challenge.

That last week of the month and what Harry thought was the last full week of the school holidays should have been the best of all, but, somehow the atmosphere and the excitement had dissipated. Grace was wilting a little. She seemed somewhat reluctant on some days and, in fact, there was a general malaise about her.

The two of them were bustling along on the Friday of that last week when a little voice from behind piped, 'Harry, I'm tired.'

They stopped. Harry went for encouragement.

'Look at all the flowers, Grace!'

It was true, although the fields seemed to have dried up, the verges were still full of flowers. 'Let's count them ... there must be more than twenty different ones!'

'Mmmm,' she offered with a complete absence of enthusiasm.

'Are you a bit fed up with cycling, Grace?'

'No,' with even less conviction.

'Would you rather do something else?'

'No.'

'Is anything bothering you?'

'No.' But, there was just enough hesitation in her reply for Harry to be able to discern that something was bothering her.

'Are you worried about school … I mean college?'

'No … well … a little bit.'

'Are you worried about boys like Baz?'

'No.'

'Are you worried about doing the work?'

'No.'

'Well, what are you worried about then?'

'I don't know … Things won't be the same will they?'

Their conversation continued in tortured questions until Harry was able to illicit that Grace was worried that the closeness that had grown between them through their regular cycling excursions would not continue.

'Don't you worry about that!' he reassured her. 'We shall still have lots of ventures.'

'Will we, Harry?'

'Course we shall … let's have one tomorrow. Where shall we go?'

'To see the ducks!' she replied without hesitation.

'Oh, you mean the girl with the little ducklings? OK. But it is a long way to go. Perhaps Moses will come and fetch us. Shall we go round and ask him? I'm sure he would say yes to a pretty face!'

'Would he? … Is that me, Harry?'

'What, the pretty face? Yes, of course, that's you. Come on, let's go.'

Moses was in his garden, though by the time they had got

there the sky was darkening with the accumulation of heavy, restless clouds that were gathering threateningly above. The air had similarly become heavy and clinging as the humidity built. Slowly moving along the lines of vegetables in his orderly garden, Moses had at first appeared calm and untouched by the humidity, but as he rose to gruffly greet them Harry could see that his skin was likewise lacquered with perspiration and there was an almost pained look in his eyes. Moses noticeably perked up, however, as he noticed that Grace was there as well.

"Ello, princess,' the old man managed. 'Like to 'elp me pick some veg, would you?'

Harry watched as Moses fetched Grace a light basket. Even from a distance, the tenderness in his movements was palpable as he led her gently through the garden. Grace had a cough that intermittently burst quite harshly into the peacefulness of the garden, but Moses simply waited patiently for it to subside before continuing. Harry could not hear them, but could tell from her face that she listened raptly to everything that Moses told her. No doubt it was a mixture of wise knowledge and silly anecdotes that Moses seemed to adopt especially for her. It was clear that they had become good friends.

Despite the oppressive humidity it was relaxing and warming to watch their sedate progress around the garden. But then the peaceful reverie was broken by a hesitant 'hello' from around the side of Moses' cottage. They all looked around and stared. Grace was first to react, though she too was extremely surprised.

'Mummy!'

'I hope you don't mind me coming into your garden,' said Mrs Hall. 'I was knocking on the door, but nobody seemed to hear. I hope you don't mind.'

'Mind? No, course I don't mind. I suppose you're ...'

'Yes. Sorry!' their visitor offered towards Moses. 'I should have ... yes ... I'm Mrs Hall ... I mean Elizabeth ... I'm Grace's mother.'

'Yes, of course you are.'

There was a silence and a slight stand-off. Again, despite the humidity and the colourful abundance of Moses' garden, Mrs Hall, Elizabeth, looked crisp and elegant in her charcoal, pinstriped suit and high-collared pale pink blouse. Harry got up from his garden seat to rescue her from the impasse should she need it or not.

'Fancy seeing you here!' he cried, feeling dismally that his wit and sense of occasion were as lacking as ever.

'Well, I finished work early. And I thought I my find you here ... I mean, I thought I might be able to find Grace here.'

Despite Harry's efforts to ease the situation, he had managed to heighten rather than dissipate the awkwardness of the unarranged meeting. But then Moses intervened with surprising grace and sensitivity to dispel any growing tension.

'Now then, we're so pleased that you have found us. David here will fetch us some nice cool elderberry squash ... or presse even ... while you can 'elp me an' Grace collect some nice vegetables.'

'Yes, Mummy!' Grace cut in with great enthusiasm and excitement.

Harry had almost forgotten that she was there.

When he returned with squash and glasses on a somewhat old and battered tray, the three of them were still gathering from the garden.

'What are those?' asked Grace. 'They don't look very nice.'

'Them's broad beans. They might not look pretty on the outside, but jus' you look in 'ere while I breaks open the pod.'

Moses broke open the pod to reveal the cool, pale beans inside their perfectly protective pod.

'See ... them's so tender you can eat 'em without even cookin'. You jus' try one o' them, princess. An' you jus' feel that,' he cajoled Elizabeth, proffering to her the tender, velvety insides of the pod. ''Ave you ever felt anythin' as soft as that?'

All three of them appeared pleased with their various discoveries and Moses led them back to the garden seats and table.

'I mus' find you a bag to take them 'ome,' he told them.

'That's too kind!'

'No ... I alwus grows more than I needs. You cook 'em up for this little princess ... She could do wi' a little more colour in 'er cheeks.' If Elizabeth felt slighted by the comment she managed not to show it. 'You could do a plate for young David 'ere as well. 'E seems to be wiltin'. Or perhaps it's the damage of 'is own cookin'.'

Harry was pleased in a way that Moses had also included him in his disparaging remarks. Elizabeth appeared quite happy to take up the challenge.

'I don't do a lot of cooking, but I enjoy it when I have the time ... I'd be pleased to cook for the two of you if you could make lunch tomorrow ... I'll try to do justice to these beautiful vegetables.'

Harry was both pleased and surprised to receive the invitation, though when he looked across at Grace he could tell that she was remembering their plan to visit the girl and her ducklings. It was a dilemma, but one that Harry was saved from having to resolve by Moses' interjection.

'Sorry, my dear, but I've already got an invitation an' arrangements for tomorrow. But I'm sure the rest of you will 'ave a lovely meal together.'

Harry regarded Moses closely in expectation of elucidation,

but none was forthcoming. In fact, the old fellow made a point of not meeting Harry's eyes, which was unlike him, as he departed to fetch a bag.

'Any road, you tek this bag o' veg fo' Grace an' 'er mother,' Moses said on his return and by way of ushering them all from the garden.

The three of them stood outside Moses' house on the pavement. Not unusually, Harry dithered, but Grace took each of them by the hand and they walked back to Bede House. 'See you tomorrow then.'

Harry was relieved the next morning to wake once more to blue skies. Following a long bash in the shower and a particularly careful shave, he stood in the bedroom to peruse his wardrobe. It was uninspiring and he regretted for once having neglected his sartorial duties so completely. Finally, he managed to find a pair of trousers that were not jeans and a short-sleeved shirt. They would have to do. None of his jackets or coats came close to fitting the bill, so he left any further protection to chance: it had not rained for a while and he decided that he would probably be alright.

It was relief for Harry to find that Grace and her mother had not dressed too formally, though both looked a lot more stylish than him in their matching, tailored culottes. Grace took Harry straight into the dining room to show him the table that she had set herself. A discreet vase of flowers crowned the centre of the table and Harry regretted not having brought flowers or any other gift himself. Harry's eyes were drawn to the flowers. In amongst the pale-yellow roses and the germini were freesias whose fragrant aroma instantly bought an image of Marianne to Harry's mind: they were always her favourites. He realised that whole days had passed without him having thought of her and, suddenly, he felt unaccountably guilty for being there enjoying himself in the company of other women.

Maude joined them and they all enjoyed a pleasant meal. Conversation did not flow particularly easily until Harry and Mrs Hall had both drunk a glass of wine. Harry ate everything on his plate except for his portion of cabbage, which, he was forced to admit, remained from childhood as something of an anathema to him. He was able, however, to honestly compliment Elizabeth on the way she had cooked Moses' vegetables and, indeed, on the whole meal. Elizabeth went so far as to explain that she had learned to steam the vegetables, which helped to retain their full flavour, but that Moses' vegetables were so fresh that flavour was virtually assured anyway.

Grace took delight in letting Harry know that she had helped with the rhubarb crumble. Harry's exaggerated gasps of enjoyment at eating it were silenced by Grace's admonishment not to be so silly, but then she laughed and any lingering tension that might have been there, or might have perhaps been there only in Harry's imagination, completely disappeared. He was, in fact, willing himself to enjoy the sense of being part of a family occasion, though it did not come easily to him as he had few memories of family situations beyond times spent with Marianne's family, who had, in truth, never appeared as being close. Harry particularly remembered difficult times with Marianne's sister, who had always appeared antagonistic towards him.

Nevertheless, Harry was determined to make the most of this afternoon and was really pleased that both mother and daughter responded positively to his suggestion of going for a walk. He had suggested a saunter along the sea front, but Mrs Hall had countered that she would prefer somewhere less crowded. Harry had never found the sea front to be crowded, but readily acquiesced when Grace surprised them all with the idea of visiting the lighthouse at Flamborough: 'the light we can see on the horizon' as she put it.

The car journey took longer than expected since they had again become ensnarled with traffic through Bridlington, but the open spaces of Flamborough Head soon proved to be adequate reward. Harry had always loved the wide openness of the chalk downs.

They walked a while before sitting down together on the inviting grass. Harry could not contain himself from launching forth with his love of this geology and topography.

'I love these Downs. I grew up on them! … You know, there's a whole wave of them … They start on the coast at Dorset and travel all the way up through Wiltshire and then on into the Chilterns … and don't forget Kent and the cliffs at Dover … and right up through the Wolds in Lincolnshire … and then on across the Humber … and right up to the sea here at Flamborough!'

Grace and her mother looked at Harry in mild amazement: not at his disclosure of the vastness of the English chalk lands, but at the fact that Harry could sustain such enthusiasm about it. But Harry was not finished and ploughed on to express his own further amazement.

'And do you know what absolutely astonishes me? … What astonishes me is that every piece of chalk is made up of tiny microorganisms – tiny, little animals that lived in the sea millions and millions of years ago. And when all these tiny creatures died, there were so many that all their little micro skeletons made a thick white layer at the bottom of the sea. And it was these millions and billions of skeletons that were crushed together to make chalk. Just think of it!'

Almost like synchronised dancers, mother and daughter

simultaneously moved their heads in gentle motion to assert they were, indeed, thinking about it.

'Every single fistful of chalk is made up of millions of little micro skeletons! And look how many fistfuls there are in these cliffs ... there would be millions of fistfuls in any part of them. And all this chalk just goes on ... all the way across those hills we can see ... and on ... past Beverley and across the Humber ... and look how thick it is ... how many billions and millions of tonnes is that? How many fistfuls ...' Harry stopped rather abruptly: finally realising how long he had been ranting on about micro-skeletons.

He looked at the two blank faces opposite. 'I went on a bit, didn't I?'

Mother and daughter looked back at Harry, not daring to look at each other, maintaining a fixed, passive smile towards their lecturer. But then their composure broke. Grace began it with just the merest of sniggers, which provoked her mother into a whole snort, after which neither could stop themselves from rolling around upon the grass in uncontrollable laughter. For just a moment Harry was inclined towards offence, but the sound of their laughter was so delicious that it warmed even his insides too.

Despite the strong breezes the air was quite warm and they strolled happily together in the sunshine. Grace enjoyed the spectacle of the lighthouse, though she was completely disinclined to go inside and even more determined not to go too near to the massive drop at the cliff's edges.

'I'm glad she doesn't like the cliffs,' Harry confided to Mrs Hall as Grace stooped to inspect flowers hidden from the breeze in the grass. 'I always get this funny feeling inside when I'm by cliffs ... like I sort of want to ... throw myself off!'

'Oh, don't do that, Harry!' Grace cried jumping back up from the flowers in concern.

'No! No, I don't really intend to jump off … I just … sometimes … get this strange feeling that I might …' Harry stopped. He felt suddenly embarrassed by his unusual confession, though both females were sensitive enough not to burst out laughing again.

'No, don't leave us yet, Harry!' began Mrs Hall in kind support. 'We're just getting used to …'

Then she too lost momentum in her thoughts and stopped in mid-sentence. They all stopped. The breeze also had seemed to stop. Harry had a strange feeling that time itself had stopped. Perhaps the idea of them all being there so intimately together was too precious. Harry could not work it out in his mind. But then Grace was laughing again and chasing a pair of butterflies that came flickering like dancing pieces of sky through the air between them. Without warning, however, Grace became caught up in a fit of raw coughing and the spell was broken.

'They're corkill blues!' she whispered hoarsely to her mother.

'Chalk-hill blues!' Harry corrected, though Mrs Hall still regarded them with amazement.

'I should have brought a jumper or a jacket after all,' Harry was forced to admit quite soon afterwards, which made them all begin to notice the exposure, and they returned to the car.

The journey home was quiet apart from Grace's coughing. In the silences they all had time to appreciate those moment of intimacy back on the breezy cliff tops, but they were, as yet, unwilling to confront or share their feelings about it. On departing at Bede House, Harry had been keen to salvage something from the encounter.

'I was wondering if I might take Grace out on the tandem

tomorrow. I know it's Sunday ... but we might not get too many more chances. I was thinking ... I was thinking that perhaps you could come too!' Suddenly he felt as if he was standing too close to a cliff's edge and he stopped.

'Well, I don't have a bicycle ...' He sensed that Mrs Hall was trying to let him down lightly. 'But ... in any case, we are going to Suffolk for a couple of days ...' Mrs Hall, in turn, sensed Harry disappointment and feeling of being left out of their fledgling relationship. 'Look ... there's another whole week before Grace begins at the college ... so you might have lots more cycling ... perhaps, even ...' But, before she had committed herself, Harry jumped back into the conversation.

'I thought the schools went back next week!'

'Yes, I'm sure you are right, but ... Grace is a grown-up girl now, aren't you, poppet? She's going to college now ... and college doesn't start until the following week!'

Harry was silenced by his own inadequacy once more. He agreed that there would be plenty of opportunity during the next week and made his farewell.

And as he turned back into the tree-lined Scarborough Avenue, he noticed that the sky had darkened a little. Harry should have felt happy at having completed a proper social engagement so enjoyably, but, for reasons he could not clearly discern for himself, he felt rather vacant and indolent. So, on return to the cottage, he did what he usually did on such occasions and made himself a cup of tea.

Despite the gathering gloom he took the tea outside to sit in the garden. He could have drifted into selfish melancholy if it had not been for that single blackbird, which sang once more in such melodic grandeur from the top of the ash tree in challenge to the sombre sky, that he could not fail to take note of its poignant beauty. So he simply sat and allowed the blackbird's soulful anthem to sink into and take over his senses. It was a good decision. By the time the benevolent bird finally retired, Harry realised that, though his tea was cold and still untouched and that it was really quite dark, his mind, and, yes, even his soul, was a little lighter.

SEPTEMBER

As it turned out, opportunities for Harry to cycle with Grace during the next week did not materialise: Grace was away with her mother in Suffolk on the bank holiday Monday; it poured with rain throughout the Tuesday and Wednesday; Thursday was taken up by an induction morning at the agricultural college; and Mrs Hall had also reserved a special day off work on Friday to choose a whole new wardrobe for her daughter to wear at college. Harry had been pleased to be included for the induction day trip. He had even borrowed a tie from Moses to wear for the occasion and he took it as a compliment when Mrs Hall took the opportunity to adjust it for him as they began their morning's visit.

It was clear from the beginning that Grace was in a group of special young people who needed a lot of support with their learning. This seemed to please Grace and, indeed, the whole group of ten of them all appeared quite comfortable and secure within their shared vulnerability. Of course, it was difficult for Harry to discern just how comfortable Grace felt as she simply smiled benignly at everything put before her throughout the day. She did show particular pleasure at handling a selection of gardening tools that the group were able to try out in one of the horticultural areas, and related enthusiastically to everyone her experiences at planting out all the plants in her garden a few weeks previously and how she liked to help Harry in his garden.

At the end of their morning the tutor thanked Mrs Hall and Harry for attending. 'I am sure your ...` he had begun, but had then hesitated without knowing how to categorise the relationship between the three of them.

'Daughter,' stated Mrs Hall proudly.

'Special girl,' quipped Harry back to the tutor, 'my special girl!'

Grace beamed with delight at being 'a special girl', even though Harry knew that what she would really have loved would have been to be there as 'an ordinary girl, but with a daddy'.

Nevertheless, spirits were high and as they approached Beverley on their return Harry directed Mrs Hall to turn left and northwards rather than straight on through the town.

'Are we going on a venture?' asked Grace.

'Thought I would treat you two lovely ladies to lunch!'

The road northwards narrowed and emptied as they travelled out onto the Wolds and Harry soon asked the driver to stop at an empty layby. He assembled the two females on the broad roadside verge and directed their attention out across the soft, rolling hills.

'That's where we cycle,' said Harry proudly. And they stood for a while longer. As the spell of the scenery faded Harry realised that Grace had ensconced herself between them to hold each adult tightly by the hand. Both adults smiled contentedly at her, then contentedly to each other.

Thankfully, later they were blessed with pleasant sunshine as they sat outside a pretty inn to each their lunch. Harry made a plea to Mrs Hall for a chance to take Grace out for just one more cycling excursion before her term began. They agreed between themselves that Harry should take Grace out quite early on the Sunday so that she could be back in time to spend the afternoon with her mother, who needed to complete what she termed as 'final arrangements'.

Harry arrived at the agreed time on the Sunday, but Mrs Hall met him at the door with a glum face. 'I'm afraid she feels too poorly for cycling today. But come up and see her. I'm sure she would love to see you.'

'But, what's wrong with her?'

'Oh, nothing too serious. Just female problems … you know. But it seems to have taken her really hard.'

'But … Grace …'

'Yes, Grace!' Mrs Hall chided gently, almost amused. 'She is a young woman after all.'

'Yes, but I just … Yes, yes … of course, she is.'

Harry bounded up the stairs ready to overpower Grace's reluctance with his own enthusiasm, but as Grace lifted her head up from the pillow to attempt a smile, he could see that she really did not look at all well, so that his enthusiasm soon melted in sympathy for her.

'Never mind, special girl,' he told her. 'We'll go out next Sunday!'

Grace managed a nod before relapsing back onto the pillow. She seemed too poorly even for Harry to stand around and chat. He went out through the front door feeling, and obviously looking, really dejected.

'I even made us a picnic,' he muttered.

'Look. Why don't I come with you?' Elizabeth suddenly volunteered to shock Harry into a nervous stationary state on the steps.

'But you haven't got a bike.'

'Yes, but it's a tandem isn't it? Or if you would rather …'

'No, no … I mean yes … yes, please do come … Do you …'

'Look, it's fine! I can ride a bike you know … and Maude is more than capable of looking after Grace!'

'Well, if you don't have more pressing things to do,' Harry replied in a stumbling effort to take advantage of her unexpected offer.

'Well, I might have more pressing things, but on this occasion,' she challenged with emphasis bordering on sarcasm, 'the crunching of boring numbers can just take second place for a change ... and we can be back in time for me to sort out Grace later.'

'Yes then,' Harry managed, realising that he was in danger of losing an opportunity to spend time with Elizabeth. 'Yes ... that would be great.'

She smiled.

'Do you have anything to wear?' Immediately he regretted such inanity and held up his hands as if in surrender. 'Look you get ready and I'll just go and check on the bike.' And he fled from the steps before making any more blunders.

They headed north through the country lanes to Rudstone. Harry had told Moses of his plan to have a final run out with Grace and the experienced local man had suggested a route that included Rudstone and a foray into one of the more northerly section of the Wolds, places that Moses had cycled himself when he had been just a lad.

'There's this huge stone in the churchyard at Rudstone: a monolith,' Moses had recalled. 'When I were a lad we used to 'ide 'alfpennies in the little 'oles an' pockmarks in that great stone ... high up like so no-one would find 'em ... an' mek a wish. Ol' Bobby used to say that in the dead o' night, ol' Split-pea used to get up there wi' a ladder an' steal all the coins, but I think 'e were jus' mekkin' it up!'

What Moses had not told Harry was that there were some sizeable hills to climb to get there. It was a cloudy day, but dry and warm enough for cycling. Now and again the sun had broken through to send patches of golden light racing along the hillsides. With the first tinge of gold on the leaves, the little patches of brightness seemed to emphasise the beauty of the countryside even more. And when they cycled in the sun it made them really quite hot. Elizabeth had discarded her windcheater and occasional glances allowed Harry to appreciate that she looked really quite trim in her pale khaki shirt and culottes.

By the time they had reached the churchyard at Rudstone they were ready for a rest. It had been quiet between them for the first part of their ride. Being so close together on the tandem created an intimacy with which they were not completely comfortable. Harry felt excited to be engaged in activity so close to Elizabeth, but incapacitated by not being able to see her beyond the occasional glance. Engaging in conversation in such circumstance had not been easy, so he had mostly kept his thoughts to himself. Elizabeth had been similarly quiet, perhaps for the same reasons.

They slumped down side by side with their backs against the rough stones of the churchyard wall. Although it was a Sunday, the church appeared to be completely unpopulated at that time. Harry could still feel the awkwardness of silence as they sat there together, but he also felt simply fortunate to be sat there with her at all. Despite her pale complexion, Elizabeth's skin, he could see as he stole surreptitious glimpses of her well-shaped legs, was smooth and, to his mind, very seductive. He had to bring his thoughts back from his imaginings to think about something to say. The monolith was right there before them, a great slab of stone more than five metres high, shaped, Harry thought, like some huge, mythical Norse shield. He kept his thoughts of mythical Vikings to himself, but related Moses' little story about the coins and the wishes to Mrs Hall.

'I even brought a couple of old sixpences with me for Grace to put into the holes,' he told her.

'Oh, that's so thoughtful of you, Harry … I mean David … I'm sorry, I always think of you as Harry! Do you mind?'

'Call me what you like. No … I mean, Harry's fine. I like Harry.'

'Yes, and please call me Elizabeth. Anyway, Harry. Let's put the sixpences up into the holes for Grace. She will just love it when I tell her.'

Harry supposed that it was down to his ineptitude in analysing his own feelings that made him clumsy in the nuances of relationships. And, of course, it is always easier looking back with hindsight, but he did curse himself later for not taking better advantage of the sudden, accidental entanglement that occurred between them in the churchyard.

They had begun with such innocent intent. Harry was careful not to embarrass Elizabeth as he roughly hoisted her up the face of the old monolith with small coins in each hand, and they were both laughing energetically at the ungainly spectacle that they must have presented to the silent cherubs and other assorted stone edifices that were all around to witness their efforts. It was not even a surprise when, without warning, they collapsed together into a giggling heap at the foot of the monolith.

What did surprise both of them was the opportune kiss that Harry pressed against Elizabeth's lips as they lay there with their faces barely inches apart. Harry later reflected that it must have been thinking of her legs and skin that had brought out the more base desires in him. For one glorious moment Harry had imagined that Elizabeth was eager to respond, but then in something of a panic, she broke away.

'It is Sunday … and we are in a graveyard!' she panted.

'Yes, I know it's Sunday! But people still ...' But, Harry did not finish his sentence for which he then felt relieved.

For a few more moments they just lay there in tangled surprise. Neither of them knew how to move on it seemed. Then, unexpectedly, a large cock pheasant dropped down into the graveyard from over the wall. It began a halting, haphazard strut across the paths and graves for no apparent purpose, halting and cocking its eye in all directions, showing off its beautifully luxuriant plumage and also its nervous eye. At least its erratic movement had managed to hold their attention. Then, just as suddenly as it had appeared, the pheasant was gone and their embarrassing moment with it. Harry considered that, one day, someone would find those old sixpences lying there and wonder how someone could have been so careless to lose them so.

Back on the tandem their progress through the countryside was even quieter than before the stop at Rudstone. After several silent miles and, in an effort to break the despondency between them, Harry brought the tandem and the pair of them to a stop beside a huge entanglement of heavily laden blackberry briers.

'Just one frost and they'll all be gone,' he told Elizabeth, indicating the berries, but without being able to resist the opportunity of thinking more metaphorically to himself. Elizabeth prised a plastic container from inside her backpack, and they soon began to fill it with dark, juicy fruit. It proved to be surprisingly therapeutic to concentrate upon just fruit gathering, and the mood between them lightened. As they were about to step back from the briars it was clear that Elizabeth had, however, become ensnared by their barbs. Helping her to become untangled was an obvious chance for Harry to appear chivalrous and kind, so he leapt to assist her, hoping that his efforts would not appear too blatant. He scratched the back of one hand quite badly in doing so.

'Look …' he began in an attempt to excuse what he had done in the graveyard.

Elizabeth held up both hands to stop him, but, when freed, she did a surprising thing. Placing both sets of her juice-stained fingers around Harry's own raised hand, she kissed him lightly on his knuckles close to the jagged scratch that had begun to ooze bright globules of blood. She held the hand tenderly, and then looked intently into his eyes to tell him, 'I'm sorry, Harry. I can tell that you are a good man, but you have no idea what damaged fruit I am!'

It was amazing to Harry that someone so practised in keeping her distance could speak so candidly and move him so easily. Given the slightest opportunity he would have melted into her pale eyes, but no sooner than spoken she had moved away. It had been a tender gesture, but too profound for him to do other than ponder it in silence, even though the surge of electricity that has shot through his whole body at the instant of the stolen kiss remained etched upon his mind and senses.

As they cycled back there was an unmistakeable sound of distant gunfire. Harry thought about the pheasant in the graveyard and how, ironically, it had been quite safe there. 'We all need safe ground now and then,' he thought to himself.

'Could I come in and see if Grace is OK?' Harry asked timorously on their return to Bede House.

'I'm sure she will be fine. Just give her a day,' returned Elizabeth and she disappeared into the house to complete the 'final preparations'.

The parting had left Harry with a profound sense of emptiness way beyond the vacant saddle behind him. He cycled round to

Moses' place, but the old man was not at home, so Harry returned to his own cottage. It was not particularly cool, but Harry decided on lighting a fire. He threw an armful of logs down to the floor beside the range.

Suddenly, without warning, the old anger, which had been dormant for all those beautiful weeks of summer, forced itself up into Harry's throat so violently that he kicked out viciously at some of the logs around his feet. They flew in all directions across the kitchen. One of them even flew high enough to smash his single vase on the windowsill. He had no great sentimental attachment to the vase, but slowly picking up the smashed pieces of ceramic did help him to the point where he was able to calm down. He had been devoid of such anger throughout the past summer of idyllic adventuring across the empty countryside of the Wolds, which had encouraged him to believe that his ugly anger might have gone, but now its reality was there to confront him quite brutally.

*

Grace began her course at the agricultural college and it seemed to go well for her. The bus that brought her back from the college each day dropped her off quite close to Harry's cottage and she developed a routine of stopping to have a drink and a chat with him before returning home each weekday. There was still plenty of work for Harry to complete with Moses each day, but he made sure that he was always home in time to meet Grace at the end of the afternoon. He always looked forward to seeing her.

Both of them, it became clear, enjoyed the security of being able to say whatever they felt like without fear of contradiction or condemnation from the other. Sometimes Harry surprised himself by relating, to his young companion, quite detailed accounts of events that had occurred previously in his adult life. Grace, on her side, liked to tell Harry about her time at the agricultural college, which she was enjoying. But, of course, it was never a clear, cogent account of the course or her days: just little snippets and cameos of whatever flittered across her mind, and often from a dimension unique to her own way of thinking.

'Why do all the cows stare at me at the same time?' or 'Who decides what colour the flowers will be?'

She did remember some things clearly, she often made really wise observations, and she was capable of occasional brilliance in her creativity, but, it seemed to Harry, that there was no conventional organisation to all her thinking and remembering. It seemed to him that most people assimilate new learning into a framework of what they already know, whereas with Grace everything seemed to float around in an almost random manner and without connection. Harry loved her for it, but it did make him fear for her ability to survive in any way independently.

One afternoon, as they were sat looking out onto the garden, a pair of magpies flew down from the ash tree to spread their brilliant chiaroscuro across the pale green of the lawn.

'One for sorrow, two for joy!' Harry intoned.

'What is?'

'That's just what people say about magpies.'

'Why do they say that, Harry?'

'It's just a little rhyme about magpies, those black and white birds there. One for sorrow, two for joy, three for a girl, four for a boy, five for silver, six for gold, seven for a secret never to be told.'

'I've got a secret,' she smiled at him.

'Have you? What is it?' Harry asked.

'Mummy says I mustn't tell,' she added without breaking her smile, though Harry could tell that she meant it.

'Well, in that case, you had better keep it to yourself!'

Grace liked to help in the garden as well and she was developing a real liking for plants: plants and cows were the things that she spoke about most to Harry. On a previous day she had been quite distressed about her day at the college and it transpired that, because of foot-and-mouth, several of their cows had been taken away from their herd and had been destroyed: it became clear that Grace did not learn of this directly, but she had been very upset at not seeing them again. Harry took her to the end of his garden to see the cattle there, but he was unsure of how to help her further.

He was, however, able to help her with plants. Moses had already set them on to planting sweet pea seeds ready for the next spring: he liked to call Grace his 'sweet pea'; and he had promised to supply them with crocus bulbs as well, but Harry had forgotten to bring them back to his own place. So Harry had sat them down to look at catalogues of plants for the new year. Grace relished the opportunity to sit beside Harry with the catalogues.

'I love your garden, Harry,' she told him, which was pleasing even though he knew there was nothing special about his garden: not like Moses'. He thought that, perhaps, it was more that she just enjoyed being with someone who enjoyed her company.

An idea came to him.

'I know, I'll paint you a picture of the garden, shall I?'

'Yes! Yes! With us in it!'

So, during the next week, he did paint that picture. He painted it from a bird's eye view looking down cheerfully on the field in the foreground, then centrally to the garden and the cottage, and then behind that to the town and then right out to the coast, with the sea beyond. He painted it in the vivid acrylic colours of a sunny September teatime. The ash tree was a giant sail of pre-autumnal glory around which the two of them ran as if in chase across the lawn. He painted in the black and white cows that grazed in the field at the end of the garden and, as a link to the black and white of the cows and to the mock Tudor facades of the houses in Scarborough Avenue, he painted the black and white plumage of seven magpies in the foliage of the tree and the hedgerows.

'Why are there seven?' Grace had asked when he showed her the completed painting.

'It's a secret!' Harry had replied.

Grace, of course, fully understood his little joke.

She and Harry had sat for some while to discuss the picture and as a consequence they had arrived at Bede House later than usual. Harry did not go into the house, but, as he was about to leave, Elizabeth stepped out of her car to stand before him. They faced each other like shy teenagers at a dance. Harry had not seen her for weeks: in fact, not since their tandem ride together, but the awkwardness of the kiss in the churchyard still hung between them.

'You must stay for a cup of tea ...' Elizabeth managed at last to wrench out from her anguished insides.

'Um ... yes ... OK ... thank you.'

Grace disappeared upstairs with Maude and Harry was left to wander around the garden until Elizabeth returned with a tray holding two cups of tea.

'You still have some flowers out,' he observed with as casual a voice as he could manage.

'Yes ... they're lovely ... I would like to have done so much more ... but I have been so busy. Look, Harry ... I've not been avoiding you ... it's just ...'

'You've been busy!'

'Yes!' They both managed a small smile. 'Grace loves coming to your garden ...'

'Perhaps you're free this weekend ...'

'No ... I'm not ... perhaps next weekend ... Yes, I'll cook you lunch ... how about that?'

'Yes ... Yes, that would be really ... nice,' dropped out from his mouth before he could regret his overuse of the mild superlative. 'And ... I could take Grace out this Saturday perhaps!'

They agreed to each other's suggestion and smiled again, but the awkwardness between them had not completely evaporated and the two shy teenagers had soon returned to the dance floor. Harry made a fairly quick departure from their pas de deux leaving Elizabeth to take away the undrunk tea. As he made his way down Scarborough Avenue, he failed to notice the worried expression on the face of the young girl who watched from the window, which was a pity since she would have been relieved to know that he did so with at least the start of a genuine smile on his face.

With the hint of a spring in his step, Harry made his way round to Moses' house rather than going straight back to his own cottage. The old man came to the door trying, with some frustration, to settle a newly knotted tie into his collar. It was unusual for Harry to see him so flustered.

'Got a date then, Moses?'

'Happen I 'ave, lad ... if you must know, I'm tekkin' Eadie to a choral recital ... she ... er ... likes that sort of thing!'

'Very ... nice! Your dominoes mates will be really impressed!' Harry could not resist from teasing until the stare that blazed from beneath Moses' furrowed brows encouraged him to quickly hold up his hands in contrition.

'No, seriously, Moses … I think it's great that you are seeing Eadie a bit more … regularly.'

And so Harry was soon on his way back to his own cottage after all. It came as something of a surprise to himself that he was able to detect just a tiny shard of jealousy dropping into his gut. He paused to imagine whether Elizabeth might feel the same about his relationship with Grace, though he reflected gratefully that the mother always seemed so content for him to be close to his young charge. Despite past months of torturing himself over Marianne, he realised that he was really not too good at self-analysis and he quickly decided that he would be better off going to bed early to seek the sanctuary of sleep.

On the Friday, when Grace dropped in after college, Harry surprised himself again on noticing how quickly she was able to lift his mood. She was just a little at odds with herself, however, when Harry asked her what she would like to do on the Saturday. Without her having to explain it out loud, Harry could guess at her dilemma: she would, without hesitation, have chosen to have visited the duckling girl again if it had not been for the task of having to cycle all that way across the hills to get there; and Grace had lost her energy in general, and her enthusiasm for the tandem in particular, over the past few weeks. Harry came to her rescue by suggesting another trip on the bus to Bridlington, which instantly appealed to Grace, who waved happily to Harry from her gate when he left her to return home.

Although the journey was, unsurprisingly, not quite as exciting as it had been for her first ever bus journey, from the moment the old double-decker appeared, Grace was as bright and breezy as her old self and as the sunny morning that greeted them on the Saturday.

They alighted from the bus a few stops before the centre so that they could wander in the sunshine down the long, open promenade. Of course, it took far longer than Harry had bargained for as Grace flitted like a butterfly around all the brightly coloured buckets and spades, sun hats and other assorted seaside paraphernalia that were still being displayed, somewhat forlornly Harry thought, outside every other corner shop and kiosk. Eventually, he was able to shake off his prejudices long enough to buy her a bright, multi-coloured 'windmill on a stick', which Grace held proudly before her on their walk towards the centre. Harry was not troubled by the childish innocence of her behaviour and appearance.

Before they had reached their destination, however, the brightness of the morning had deteriorated into greyness and then drizzle. Harry was pleased to note that Maude had taken the trouble to ensure that Grace had been particularly well dressed to insulate her from the unpredictability of east coast weather, and he wondered what it was that enabled women to think so much more soundly about those sorts of practicalities.

So, Harry had soon ensconced Grace on a bench within the security of a promenade shelter, while he dashed off to buy portions of hot chips. He had promised to return within a couple of minutes, but it had inevitably taken longer. He returned to find Grace in tears.

'A man came in!' she explained.

'Are you OK?' he asked in alarm, and when she had nodded he dashed back outside the shelter again, shocked, guilty about his own lack of care, and ready to accost anyone who might have committed the offence. There was no-one in sight.

'What did he do?' he asked her with forced calm above the obvious panic inside.

'Nothing ...' Grace conceded with fresh tears at having caused Harry such anxiety. 'But ... but he was ... looking at me ...!'

'But ... he didn't do anything?' Harry pursued as relief coursed through his senses.

Grace shook her head. 'I'm sorry, Harry ... I was frightened.'

'That's OK, princess ... don't worry ... it was my fault ... I shouldn't have left you.' Harry realised, with surprise that he had even forgotten, just how vulnerable Grace could be in such situations, and he was genuinely upset with himself.

But, the day needed to be rescued and he was soon chiding Grace to eat up her chips. They did both eat their chips, but silently in deep, unspoken thought. The only sounds came from the wind around the shelter, from occasional turns of the plastic windmill sails, and from the constant beat of the waves upon the strand, until Grace dropped a quiet question into their shared silence.

'Did you ever get frightened when you were a boy, Harry?'

Strangely, the innocent question set up all kinds of worries inside Harry's mind. Even though he was sat there safely with Grace on a seat within their private shelter, he felt a real surge of panic flash through his senses. Suddenly he was plunged back into his days of childhood. Harry's childhood days had not been a happy time: the latter part of his boyhood, in particular, had not been the joyous time that it deserves to be for young people. He had, indeed, very often been frightened: his memory was, in fact, instantly filled with a catalogue of frightening times from his childhood. He had hitherto kept them carefully stored away and he felt very reluctant to delve into that particular box of secrets.

Grace, however, was insistent, 'Tell me about when you were frightened, Harry! Tell me about when you were a boy ... please, Harry ... please!'

Harry groped around inside the melee of frightening memories that had been stirred up inside and settled for what he thought, at that time, might be a manageable dose of difficult memories for them both.

'Well, I remember when my mum and dad died.' Harry could not quite work out why that was important to tell her, but it was a starting point, and he had never been allowed to talk about it at the time, or, in truth, had never talked fully to anyone about it in his whole life.

'Do you … did they, Harry? What happened? Did it frighten you?'

'Yes it did … they died in a car crash …' Harry hesitated as the memory and its pain came flooding back into his mind.

'I came home from school one day … and our house was full of strange people … I mean people I didn't know … and a lady sat next to me on our settee and told me.'

'Did she frighten you, Harry?'

'No. She didn't frighten me … she was nice … I remember she smelt like one of those boxes of soapy things that you give to your mum for Christmas … no, she didn't frighten me.'

'What was it then that did frighten you, Harry?'

Harry was still reluctant, but then something urged him on to reveal what else had happened on that day and just what it was that had truly frightened him.

'Let me think … I was eleven I think … yes, I was eleven. It was when I had just started grammar school. And I remember feeling frightened because I thought I would always be on my own when I came home from school … left alone for all the rest of my life.'

'Yes. That would be frightening … were you left on your own, Harry?'

'No. I wasn't left on my own. I went to live with my aunt … my Aunt Thea,' he told her, almost choking on the name.

And right then Harry knew that there was to be no turning back from the full exposure. The story of that part of his life had been waiting to get out for a long time and there could be no turning back.

'My Aunt Thea didn't have any children … and she lived on her own on a farm. I thought it would be nice, but it wasn't.'

'Did she frighten you, Harry?'

Grace's question took Harry straight back to those days on the farm with amazing clarity: not just visual recollections, but everything: sounds, smells, and feelings, even inner ones – especially inner ones. And in those few minutes of beginning to remember it all over again, a cloak of cold, dark fear had wrapped itself around his insides: there was a fistful of spiteful hurt thrusting and twisting itself into his gut.

During all those years with Marianne, Harry had never talked about living with Aunt Thea. He supposed that Marianne had known about it but had not wanted to stir up all his memories of those unhappy years. And he supposed that he had gladly shoved them all back into the furthest recesses of his memory instead of talking about them. All those years they had been stored carefully away inside, and, uncannily, it was not until this moment in the promenade shelter that he felt able to talk about them. He did think about the paradox of revealing his own dark memories to a vulnerable girl who was being trusted into his care, but he felt safe with her and he felt that the trust between them demanded that he should tell her: somehow, it just felt right to tell her the whole truth as he remembered it.

'My Aunt Thea? Yes, I was only eleven, and she wasn't much bigger than me … but she could scare the living daylights out of me.'

Grace moved closer to him as if to add comfort.

'She kept dogs, big dogs, and somehow she made them sort of hostile to me … she used to shout at me in front of them … perhaps that's how she did it … Five horrible years I lived in that house … that horrible farmhouse! She didn't want me to love me … she just wanted someone to work for her! We used to get up really early … we had to feed her cows … she never trusted me with the milking machine, but I had to help her with the feeding. I had to cut the cabbages for the cows!'

'Did the cows frighten you, Harry?' Grace cut in, attempting to share some of his anguish.

'No,' he told her gently. 'I loved the cows … but I hated those cabbages!'

For a few minutes Harry retreated into himself. He could remember those cabbages so well: one cabbage for each and every cow each and every day. And there were about twelve of them most of the time. They were in a big field: the cabbages that is, not the cows. It was always cold, he could recall, in that field. He had to cut the cabbages off their stems with a really sharp, old knife and load them onto his aunt's trailer. And since he had been relatively small, it had been really hard to lift them up. He had been forced to roll them up onto his chest and push them on the trailer. And, he remembered with such vivid pain, in the mornings the big cabbages had always been so wet inside, so that when he lifted them up, all that trapped water would roll out of their big leaves straight onto his shirt. With every single cabbage he would get a shock of freezing water straight down onto his shirt or jumper, and onto his own skin and bone!

Harry remembered always seeming to have a cold in the winters then. But it didn't make any difference to her: even if he stayed off school, he would still have to get out there on the cabbage field and get wet all over again every day.

It came back to Harry just how much he hated that cabbage field, and just how much he hated that woman. She had stolen all the fun from his childhood: well, that part of it anyway.

'Is that what frightened you, Harry?' Grace chirped up to remind him that she was still there.

Harry had to think for a moment: search back in the recesses.

'No, Grace. That's not what really frightened me!' He felt even more unsure about telling her the rest, but he pressed on anyway.

'One day I came home from school … it was just before sitting my O levels. And she wasn't there. Eventually I went looking for her … and in the end I found her. She was just lying on the ground … lying on the ground with her dogs round her. They wouldn't let me near: though, probably, I didn't really want to go near … I could tell … she was dead! The police came … and an ambulance. They took her away.'

'Is that what frightened you, Harry?'

'No, Grace.' And Harry had to swallow hard before he told her.

'When the policeman was there, he looked at me and he said, "Did you have anything to do with this, young man?" And I hadn't! I found out later that she had something called an embolism: a heart attack. But, when he looked at me … I thought he could see right into my mind … and I almost said "Yes. It was me!" … because I thought about all those times in the cabbage field when I had thought about sticking that sharp, old cabbage knife in her! And I wished I had! That's what really frightened me!'

And Harry just sat there, still full of all those bad memories. He began to fear that it had all been too sordid and alarming for Grace's young mind, but after a while she simply smiled at him.

'No wonder you don't like cabbage, Harry!'

Harry laughed and laughed: anyone passing would have wondered at him roaring out like a madman. But he did not care about anyone passing by. He just felt free. He felt free and exorcised!

*

During the week that followed Harry found that he needed to quite frequently stop himself from asking Grace about her mother: he was thinking about Elizabeth increasingly often. By the time the next Saturday had arrived he had grown quite nervous, nervous he supposed about the possibility of not making the most of his opportunity to become closer to her. Standing outside the door of Bede House, he had been in a state of considerable anxiety, but once welcomed inside and into the kitchen he was able to relax into the security of a warm reception from both mother and daughter.

Grace was enthralled by the opportunity to help her mother in the kitchen and beckoned Harry over to watch. She was standing on a patch of floor covered in newspaper and was making quite a mess with her hands immersed in a large, brightly coloured bowl of thick dough, which she was attempting to kneed further.

'We're making hoppers, Harry!' she cried out excitedly to him.

The air in the kitchen hung heavy with the smell of spices, though Harry was very inexperienced with such ingredients.

'Hoppers? What's that then? … Frogs' legs!' Harry ventured before instantly regretting his attempt at humour.

Elizabeth simply raised her eyebrows at him and placed a newly poured glass of wine in his hand as she passed by. Harry watched in fascination as she scooped up the dough into a large pot-like vessel onto which she attached a top with a wide handle. It soon became apparent that the contraption was a press of some kind and the dough began to appear from it in long strings.

'Spaghetti!' Harry guessed, soon regretting a lack of reserve as well as wit.

'Not far off!' Elizabeth told him kindly, 'it is like spaghetti, but not quite so smooth. They're going to be string hoppers. You find them quite often in the sub-continent.'

'You must have been there on holiday,' deduced Harry indicating in gesture towards the shirt of elephants printed in batik that Elizabeth was wearing.

'That's from the elephant orphanage!' Grace cut in to join a conversation that her mother quickly brought to a conclusion.

'Go on, Grace. Run up and tell Maude that we shall be serving in ten minutes. I'll just put these in the steamer and then Harry can help me take everything through to the dining room.'

Harry was pleased to help and soon they were all sat down together to a meal that was some kind of chicken curry: Harry knew that much at least. Despite that much prior knowledge, however, Harry could not stop himself from coughing out most of his first mouthful in surprise. He was relieved that it caused amusement for the three women rather than offence.

'You'll have to get used to your curries hot if you are going to eat here regularly!' he was cheerfully informed, which served, in fact, to make Harry feel warmer inside than the curry.

Harry was beginning to learn that his little faux pas had the effect of allowing the women before him to relax rather than to become annoyed, as he might have done; and that, though it often fell upon stony ground, his attempt at humour was something they seemed to like in him. Thereafter, through the evening, he was able to regain his composure and they sat for a long time simply enjoying each other's company and talking idly about nothing in particular. Probably, Harry thought later, he had gone on too much about the tandem trips that Grace and he had shared over the previous month. When he had looked up at one point he saw that Grace had fallen asleep with her head on her arms at the table.

'I'm obviously more boring than I thought,' he joked.

'That girl. She could fall asleep anywhere. And you know what she's like once she's asleep.'

Harry did remember the previous occasion and felt for the small of his back where he had ached after lifting Grace from the back of the kind man's Volvo. But there was no resisting his inflated ego and, somehow, they managed to get Grace up and over his shoulder so that he could carry her into the hall like a fireman. He even climbed up the stairs with her before stumbling on the last step and sprawling across the landing floor. Because he had been concentrating on keeping Grace from harm he managed to slide across the carpet on his chin, taking off a slice of skin from it.

Elizabeth almost collapsed once more with laughing as she looked down upon him lying there. 'Seems to be your favourite position!'

Then Maude appeared and the two women took Grace into her bedroom.

'Yes ... falling flat on my face comes easy to me!' he mused to himself as he wandered downstairs. But sitting alone in the dining room made him feel restless, so he wandered further out into the garden.

It was not too cold outside, but after a little while he thought to go inside to fetch the duffle coat that he had carried with him to the house. To his surprise, Elizabeth appeared through the door before him, wearing her own coat and carrying his. But, as soon as she went to put the coat around Harry's shoulders, it was her turn to shrink back in surprise. But then she rushed up to dab at Harry's face with her handkerchief.

'There's blood all over your shirt!'

He allowed her to dab at his chin. Her face was close to his and he enjoyed breathing in her scent and the smell of her hair. It seemed so long since he had done that with anyone. When she lifted her eyes they were just a touch away from his. They held each other's gaze for a mere moment, unwilling, it seemed to Harry, to pull away, but too nervous to make a more positive move in any way.

When Elizabeth finally straightened and moved slightly away, Harry cursed himself inside for such ineptitude.

'I'd better be going.'

'No,' she said calmly and to his great surprise. 'Stay and share some more wine with me.'

Elizabeth returned from the house again with a bottle of wine. It had grown dark quite quickly. After so many summer weeks it seems like the long sunlit evenings have become routine, but as September arrives the shortening of such crepuscular luxury seems to suddenly accelerate. Darkness fell while they were drinking the last of the wine, then Elizabeth fetched coffee and by the time they had finished that, the transition to night time had been completed.

'Look at the stars,' Harry said in an effort to stay even longer into the slightly chilled evening. 'Look!' he exclaimed again in his slight tipsiness and in his enthusiasm to engage Elizabeth.

He soon began talking as if he was an astronomical expert, which was something he would later regret. 'There's the Plough

... It's amazing that ... though all the stars move constantly, or at least appear to move, the Plough always points at the North Star ... which doesn't move at all. And look, there's the Milky Way ... have you ever looked at it through a pair of binoculars? It's amazing!'

'Yes. Yes I have actually!' Elizabeth replied with what Harry thought was just a hint of irritation.

'When I was in Kandy ... we looked at them quite regularly.'

'What do you mean "in candy"?'

'In Kandy ... Kandy the city ... in Sri Lanka.'

'Wow, Sri Lanka!' he repeated in genuine awe. 'I'd love to go somewhere like that. When were you there?'

For some reason Elizabeth had gathered herself up, as if she had said too much, as if she had become suddenly very chilled by the air.

'It was a while ago. Before Grace was born,' she told Harry with what struck him as unnecessary austerity.

And Harry knew, right then, that their pleasant evening was over. The warmth and intimacy that he had felt from her earlier had rapidly dissolved. Whatever windows might have been open earlier were now closed tightly.

He could not think that he had said anything offensive in any way, but whatever had been there between them was gone.

'Thank you for such a pleasant evening,' he stumbled, but she was barely able to acknowledge him as he left.

Elizabeth could still recall with clarity the shock that had been her introduction to Colombo in Sri Lanka. It was not the clash of culture – she had expected that from her reading and research – but she had been simply affronted by the unpleasantness of the experience.

To her, the city appeared so loud, dirty and vulgar, and virtually devoid of any architectural merit. It was just a great urban sprawl, thrown up without any apparent planning or attempt to create something at all beautiful. To begin with she had found respite in the Viharamahadevi Park just across the road from her workplace at the British Consulate, or sometimes after a walk to the Galle Face Green, but there were just so few green spaces in the city. The chaos, the ubiquitous squalor and frenetic pace of the place had knocked her senses so far sideways that she had struggled to recover. She felt constantly guilty for it, but that was the way she felt.

There was shock too in finding herself so free and far away from home. At school and at Cambridge she had worked feverishly hard at her studies, unconsciously attempting to impress her unresponsive and unappreciative father. She had found limited time for socialising or for the incessant philandering that apparently obsessed so many of her associates. She was, fairly she thought, considered to be a cold fish, and it was something she recognised and accepted.

After initial training with the Foreign Office she had jumped at the chance to work in an 'exotic location', despite the known political tensions in Sri Lanka. But, besides the disappointment of not liking Colombo, she had found it difficult to create meaningful friendships or an enjoyable existence outside of work. On occasion she had travelled alone or with others to resorts further down the western coast, but had not felt really comfortable there.

Then one weekend she had accompanied a female colleague on a short excursion to first the renowned 'elephant orphanage' and then on to *the old capital of Kandy. The drive to Kandy from Colombo had been horrendous with such unruly and undisciplined driving by all concerned. The road was packed with traffic in both directions: it appeared to her like two wild and turbulent streams flowing in opposite directions within the same course.*

Elizabeth and her companion had enjoyed their short stop at the centre for destitute and abandoned elephants before being plunged once again into the turbulence of the thoroughfare. But, once in Kandy, the whole atmosphere was relaxed. And, the city, she thought, was beautiful.

There were busy spots and bustling markets within Kandy, but the city was centred upon its lake with gardens and promenades around, not to mention the spectacular shrines and temples. Elizabeth sensed a feeling of beauty and space, which she had found so sadly lacking in Colombo, while the surrounding hills and forest-clad mountains brought a serenity of their own to the scene.

Perhaps it had been the calmness of her guesthouse too that had allowed her to enjoy such inner tranquillity while staying there. The Donald Guesthouse stood amongst many others on a hill just above the lake with uninterrupted views down across the lake, the Temple of the Tooth and the centre of the city. Sitting upon its veranda for that first evening after all those frustrating weeks in Colombo she felt complete in her contentment.

It was not surprising that, despite the rigours of the calamitous road between the two cities, Elizabeth's visits to Kandy and to her favourite guesthouse became a regular feature. She had even worked extra shifts to enable her to fit in more visits.

Mr Da Silva, or Jay as she came to know him, was the proprietor of the guesthouse. One might have correctly guessed that the calm and well-ordered atmosphere of the guesthouse was a close reflection of his own temperament and demeanour. Though gentle and modest, he had both charm and the ability to make guests feel completely secure. Straightway, Elizabeth felt more at ease with this slightly older man than she had ever done before in male company.

For his own part, Mr Da Silva made a point of discretely, but regularly, intercepting his most beautiful guest whenever she made the short journey from her room to the dining room or veranda. Although it would not have been obvious to the casual observer, he had become completely entranced by Elizabeth's startlingly fair complexion and understated beauty. He struggled perpetually to disguise the degree of his attraction to her: partly due to his modest, unassuming nature, and partly because he could tell that any blunt and obvious approach towards her would not have been well received.

Over months the two of them gradually became closer. It was clear to both that they had a natural affinity, which they were happy to nourish. Jay became her regular guide around the city and on visits to the many outstanding natural and cultural attractions in the area. It became an accepted expectation that they would meet for evening meals during her visits to the guesthouse; she was even welcomed into the kitchen on quieter occasions, before sharing long hours together on the guesthouse's cool veranda.

As it does in tropical regions, the darkness of night came swiftly and early. It was natural that they should discuss the clear, starry skies beneath which their feelings for each other grew. Jay had a considerable knowledge of the stars and planets, which he had purposely supplemented with extra reading for Elizabeth's benefit. They had, indeed, looked with binoculars into the mesmerising depths of the Milky Way and wondered at the beauty and purpose of the whole universe. Perhaps it had been in response to this vastness and the feeling of being so insignificantly small that they had grown closer to each other. On many occasions there had been power blackouts across the city and, without the ambient light, the celestial bodies had shone even more brightly to awe the couple with their romantic essence. On one such occasion Jay had kissed her fully on the lips with unreserved passion. Elizabeth had felt her whole being leap towards him in response, though dark fears of the unknown had made her pull away before anything further developed.

For Jay the sense of falling in love with his most regular and welcome visitor had come quickly and easily, but for Elizabeth the gradual realisation had arrived with a plethora of conflicting emotions. Although restrictive in many ways, the formality of her upbringing and all its attendant expectations had brought a stability to her life that disappeared when facing the boundless array of possibilities in a life with Jay. She was shocked and excited, happy and scared all at the same time. For the first time in her life she regretted not having the comfort of a close female friend with whom to share her whirling thoughts and expectations. Despite her concerns they made love beneath the stars.

During the early English summer of that year Elizabeth had returned to Suffolk to visit her father, or, rather more pertinently, her surrogate mother, Maude. She had argued bitterly with her father during the stay, even though she had kept her affinity with Jay safely guarded from him. He had argued that the growing unrest between Tamils and Sinhalese had made it an unsuitable place for a young woman to live and work. Elizabeth knew quite clearly that her father's protestations were more to do with his own feelings of inadequacy and his need to assert authority over his daughter than they were of concern for her. She resolved that on her return she would explicitly express her love to Jay and let their relationship follow its path to whatever lay ahead.

Colombo still affronted her sensibilities on returning, but it was now clearly the key to her future happiness. Straightway from the airport and on to the consulate, however, there was a palpable atmosphere of danger due to the escalation of the ethnic tensions that had been growing

*before her departure. Within days of her return the consulate staff were
warned to be on constant alert and confined to their quarters. She was
so frustrated. Her telephone calls to Jay were a bittersweet combination
of joy and disappointment: it was torture for her to have to wait while
having made such firm convictions in her mind to reveal all of her
longings to him.*

*Before long the tensions of ethnic contempt broke across the country
in a storm of looting and vicious murder. In reprise to a Tamil ambush
and killing, mobs of Sinhalese vigilantes raged across the breadth of the
island in an orgy of concerted slaughter. Whole Tamil communities were
wiped out in the waves of atrocity that became known as the 'Black July'
of 1983.*

*It would have been bad enough just to have been in the country at
such a monstrous time, but the repercussions of such cataclysm proved to
be even more personally devastating for Elizabeth. She learned in terrible
simplicity from the tearful cook of the guesthouse, who had travelled out
of loyalty to personally inform her, that her beloved Jay had been brutally
murdered beside the once peaceful lakeside in Kandy. The dreadful irony
of his killing had been that he was Sinhalese himself, but had stood before
a crowd of them in vehement protest against their fury and bloodlust to
the point where they had turned upon him and slain him there in the
shadow of their own most holy temple.*

*Even now, after all those years, Elizabeth's inner feelings lurched and
ached at the memory of her loss. She often thought of Jay and could not
spare herself from recalling that moment of such devastating news. She had,
however, taught herself never to think further about the abhorrent personal
events that followed so quickly and so malevolently in its wake: that was
something she attempted to hide forever within her darkest recesses.*

*And, in her attempts to do just that, she learned that it was work,
feverishly dedicated and hard work, that afforded her a screen and refuge*

from wider consideration of her life's events both past and present. She did realise the limiting social repercussions of her stance, but she felt that it was the only way for her to survive.

Of course, through those terrible years that followed, she had learned to cope with the aching attachment and sentiments of motherhood. She recognised clearly that she could never attain to the orthodox images of that station: she had experienced neither the role models nor the emotional stability to do so. She was, nevertheless, committed to Grace's future happiness.

OCTOBER

Not yet fully dressed, Harry had been staring from the bedroom window for some time. He was thinking of how his mother used to sing as she completed her daily round of housework. 'The leaves of brown came tumbling down,' she used to warble, 'remember, that September in the rain.' Now climate change meant that the leaves did not start to fall until well into October.

Harry contemplated the view behind his cottage and recognise that it was, at last, succumbing to autumn. The first frosty night of the season had crept over the big ash tree so that now its leaves had paled to shades of yellow and ochre and its keys to dark sienna.

Just like the passing of weeks and days, Harry could sometimes stare and have no idea of how many minutes or hours have passed. Probably he would have stayed there a lot longer had it not been for the sound of something being thrust through the letter flap of his front door. It gave him little cause for curiosity since most his mail had so far invariably turned out to be offers of loans, credit cards and other inconsequential rubbish. On this occasion, however, there was something about the sharp outline of white, rectangular paper lying on the mat that caught his attention.

Bending down to pick it up, he was considerably surprised to read his own name typed on the exterior. For a second or two he enjoyed the tingle of expectation, but then his emotions changed as the ragged edges of the torn envelope were pulled back to reveal the neat black edging of the card inside.

John Earnest Bevan, beloved husband of Irene and father of Marianne, Evelyn and Roger, departed this world on Friday, 14th. October 2001. The burial service will be held in the Chapel of Kingsdown Crematorium at 13.00 on Friday 21st October.

That was all there was. Harry read the message twice, looked inside the envelope twice and stood there holding his chin for several minutes. 'Who had sent it? Marianne! Would she be there? Would she want him there?' flashed through his mind. And then 'Blimey, that's tomorrow!' he gasped out loud.

A whole catalogue of thoughts went racing through his mind. He managed to make himself a cup of tea, but got no further than that for a while. Images of Marianne bounced round his brain like demented pinballs, making him feel first excited and then guilty, so he tried to focus on her father, Mr Bevan, Jack they all called him. They were not exactly intimate, though Harry quite liked her father as a man who had always shown respect to him, even when his daughter and Harry had separated. He recalled it was unlike her mother, who had displayed an exaggerated indifference to Harry both before and after the event. He found it difficult to feel too sorry for that woman.

But there was no way for Harry to keep images of Marianne from whirling chaotically round in his thinking: what she might be wearing; what she might say; what she might do. He wondered what she might think of him being there and he began to torture himself with conjecture. As a result, he stumbled out in search of his trusty, old friend.

There was no reply to Harry's knock on the door so he made his way round to the greenhouse where the old man was planting daffodil and crocus bulbs into pots. The sweet smell of fresh compost hung in the air. It seemed like no time at all since Harry had been helping him lift those bulbs out of the soil. Moses soon roped Harry in to help and the steady rhythm of the work enabled them to talk through what was on Harry's mind. To a casual observer Moses' greenhouse might have appeared somewhat cluttered with plants, packets, boxes, pots and tools all competing for space on crowded shelves and the floor, but working with the old man revealed method and order. In much the same way, his patient listening, accepting his occasional caustic remark, allowed Harry to come to terms with his current situation and to begin to plan rationally for attending the funeral. This did not mean that Harry had overcome all self- doubt.

'What if I can't face all those people?'

'Now then, young David,' Moses told him. 'You've come a long way since the start of the year. Don't go getting too excited an' fallin' out wi' yourself. Stay wise ... an' calm too.'

'Yeah, you're right. I know you are ... seems like you always are,' Harry sighed with more sincerity.

Later in the day, Grace came knocking upon Harry's door. It did not take her long to realise that he was not his usual self. Taking the grown man under her adolescent wing, she walked him back to Bede House where Maude provided him with tea. They sat at the desk overlooking the garden, though all the flowers had disappeared from the beds so that even the garden's smile was absent.

'You look sad, Harry,' she said with her innocent bluntness. 'What's the matter?'

'Someone I know has died,' he told her.

'Oh, Harry. That is sad. Did you love them?'

'Them? Him? It's a man. No, I did not love him. But he is ... he was ... the father of someone I did love,' he told her in faltering sentences as he thought it through to himself.

'Did love, or still love?' he mused inwardly.

'Well, don't be too sad, Harry. If he was a good man then he will go to heaven.' Then, 'Do you think I'll go to heaven, Harry?'

'Yes. Of course you will. But that's a long …'

'And will you be there too?' she asked him quickly: rather too quickly.

'If I manage to be good,' Harry told her.

She looked at him with a crooked eye.

'Will I be clever when I get there?'

'Yes … yes you will. And yes, I will be there too.'

It was not what Harry believed, but it was what he thought she needed, what she deserved, to hear.

'Where will you both be?'

They both jumped, having not suspected that anyone was there to eavesdrop on their conversation.

'Oh, Elizabeth! What are you doing here?'

'I do live here you know!' Mrs Hall said with a forced smile.

'Yes. Of course, I know … But you're not usually here now!'

'Well, just for a change, I didn't have too much work on, and I thought I might just come home early. I didn't know that I would be interrupting anything … If I'm not welcome …' she intoned.

'No … Yes! Of course you're welcome!' Harry said quickly, and perhaps a little too emphatically. There was a slight pause that was in danger of becoming a long one.

'Yes. Of course you're welcome!' echoed Grace getting up to put her arms around her mother and relieving the tension that was in Harry's mind at least. Her mother smiled.

'Well. Where was it you were both going to be? Was it somewhere I might come too?'

Grace and Harry looked at each other. 'Actually, it was heaven!'

'Oh, heaven?' said Mrs Hall pulling a quizzical but smiling face. Grace laughed delightedly. For a brief moment Harry glimpsed a feeling of warmth between the three of them. But then he had to break it so resoundingly.

'You see,' he began to explain, 'I'm going to a funeral tomorrow. We were talking about it … and Grace was talking about heaven.'

'Oh. A funeral? I'm sorry … I hope it is not someone very close.'

'No, not too close … It's my wife's father.'

The words landed between them like breaking plates. Elizabeth, Mrs Hall, looked at Harry as if she had been struck.

'I didn't know you had a wife,' she said flatly.

'Well, I have got a wife … sort of. But we're not together any more … I haven't seen her for a long time.' The words still fell like delicate china … crashing and smashing onto the space between them.

'But, you didn't say!' retorted Mrs Hall.

Harry looked at her helplessly. It was not as if he had tried to deceive her. It was not as if he was trying to cheat on anyone: he would never do that again. Then he started to feel angry as the frustration of his relationship with Elizabeth surfaced. It was not as if she had made any sort of commitment. He had been patient. He had not tried to conceal anything, Harry reasoned to himself. It was just complicated.

'I'm sorry!' it came out as a shout. 'It's not bloody easy!'

'Mr Harry … You're shouting,' Mrs Hall said as calmly as she could, but using her daughter as an excuse for her own ire. 'You're shouting in front of Grace!'

Harry looked into Grace's pale face. Shame spread through him in a flush of red. He put his fingers up to his temples and tried to breathe deeply, but the shame and the anger would not let him. Harry's brain would not work clearly enough for him to begin to explain, so he took the only course of action left open to him and fled the scene.

Before Harry knew it he was outside on the pathway looking back at the house. It all looked so normal on the outside, but he knew that the mess he had left behind would be difficult to retrieve.

*

York Station was busy and, as ever, Harry was nervous about travel arrangements, even though Moses had driven him there in plenty of time. It had been dark when they had left, and Harry had helped Moses to scrape the frost from the car's windows. Harry looked around at the other travellers. No one seemed to notice him at all.

He gazed up at the great iron girders that supported the arched roof. They seemed like giant ribs holding giant lungs. It was cold. The great, grey lungs seemed to be holding in the frigid air and Harry was glad that the train soon arrived to exhale him out into the light and warmth of day.

Harry had enjoyed train journeys in the past, but at those times he had usually been travelling to somewhere that he wanted to be. Sure, he wanted to see Marianne again, but there was too much uncertainty to this journey. The call of Swindon was distinctly unalluring. So much had changed since the last time he had been home. 'Home'? The word struck him with both sadness and anxiety. The place he had left a year or so earlier did not feel like home anymore. And he certainly did not expect to be welcomed like some prodigal son returning.

The journey passed uneventfully. In other parts of the carriage people were talking enthusiastically to others they had never seen before or were likely to see again, but Harry's distracted and detached expression must have been enough to warn off any attempts at conversation and no-one had bothered to engage with him. He concentrated on looking out of the window, though he hardly saw the landscapes or townscapes that passed. They flickered by like a procession of frames in a film that was ever in the background, but rarely in his consciousness.

Just once, towards the end of the journey, somewhere between Reading and Didcot, the train stopped. By chance Harry was opposite a garden next to the line. A man and a woman were standing near the fence and, as the train halted, he happened to focus upon them, and they upon him. They held each other's stare. For some reason it was clear that the couple had been arguing. They looked shocked to be suddenly locked into this unwanted interchange: trains and passengers were meant to pass without noticing, not to intrude upon other's lives. A child moved in the woman's arms. It had remained unaware of the train or Harry and continued to move restlessly while everything else stood still. It broke the spell. The couple looked at the child, then at each other and finally back at Harry before turning away to walk back to their house, united it seemed against his intrusion, and their argument forgotten.

Harry watched them go and wondered whether a child shared with Marianne would have saved them from eventual separation. At first they had wanted children, a child. Then she had been pregnant but had lost the baby to a miscarriage. After that they never spoke of having children again. Harry had often thought of asking her about it all, but he had not been strong enough and the moment had never seemed quite right. They had never been great at sharing their thoughts or feelings about the things that mattered to them most.

The unscheduled stop had broken Harry's feeling of relative comfort, and his grip on calmness and reality felt less secure. It had also made him late, which was not altogether a bad thing since he had to rush and, therefore, had less time to think and grow more anxious.

Outside Swindon Station he bundled himself straight into the first taxi. The driver was full of inconsequential chat, which floated on a tinny stream of 'golden oldies' pouring out of a transistor on the seat beside him.

'Funny old day,' he told Harry. 'Had a bit of everything. Bit o' sun, bit o' wind, bit showery.' He trailed off as he edged the cab into the main road. 'Where is it, then, guv'nor?'

'Kingsdown Crematorium.'

'Oh, right,' said the driver, quietening in deference to his passenger's situation, and he concentrated on the traffic, though it took him a further minute to realise that 'Celebration Time' was probably not the most appropriate accompaniment for their journey and he turned his radio off.

'Sorry 'bout that mate!' he said, looking in his mirror for any signs of offence to his passenger. But Harry was already turning his attention to matters outside the window.

He had walked or cycled these streets many times in his childhood and youth. On this day they looked smaller, and a bit grubby. Without his noticing, the clear, blue day that he had left behind in Yorkshire had changed. There had been a shower recently, though the wetness had only served to dampen the scene rather than freshen it. The journey should not have taken long, but they were making slow progress out of the town centre through the lunchtime traffic.

"Bout time they sorted this out,' the driver interjected with a gesture at the road ahead.

'Right,' Harry replied in a way to let the driver know that he was not interested in conversing with him. In fact, Harry was beginning, for some unfathomable reason, to get angry with his driver. Harry's face was tight and ugly, and his fingers curled into tight fists. It took real restraint to stop himself from smacking the back of the driver's lank-haired head. Thankfully the hot reds inside Harry's brain cooled among the greys, sepias and paler reds of urban gloom before him outside, and soon they reached a short band of countryside, which hailed the entrance of the crematorium.

'Just stop here by the gates,' Harry told him.

''S all right, mate. I can take you right up to the ...'

'No! Stop here.' Harry pushed a note into the driver's hand, got out, and within seconds the taxi had turned in a tight circle and disappeared.

Standing alone at the gateway Harry breathed deeply. With face turned up, but eyes closed, he stretched and breathed deeply again so as to allow the bile to drain from him. He opened his eyes to watch clouds racing across the sky in the spaces between the bright autumnal foliage of the trees arching over the driveway. The trees did look wonderful he had to concede to himself. A whole variety had been planted at the crematorium over the years to constitute a veritable arboretum. These trees along the driveway formed a kaleidoscope of umbers, ochres, reds, golds and pale greens as he walked along beneath them.

Harry felt somewhat unreal. Even though he had changed trains in London, the journey seemed to have passed without him knowing: flickered past as frames on a film. Now, strangely, it was as if he was on the film, standing outside himself looking in at the figure standing in this pool of iridescent light, waiting for the next scene to commence.

Harry looked at his watch to confirm that he was late. The autumnal trees were beautiful. It was almost a beautiful place. Almost, but not quite: the two tall, aluminium chimneys that stretched up above the highest leaves could never allow for that.

People were standing in the space at the back of the packed chapel, so that few noticed his late arrival. Everyone was standing for the singing of 'The Lord's My Shepherd'. Harry was just able to make out the people in the front row: Mrs Bevan was supported on one side by her son and on the other by her daughter, Evelyn, who was Marianne's younger sister.

He could not help it even in such reverent circumstances, but his whole body gave a little jump when he glimpsed Marianne, who stood next to them, but a little apart. Her black coat hung elegantly from square shoulders, though he could not see her legs. Curls of red hair had escaped from beneath the fringe of her black hat. 'She always looked so lovely in a hat,' he was thinking to himself and he sighed deeply as the hymn ended and the congregation sat down. There was more music and singing: bittersweet singing. There was talking as well, but in tones sanctimonious and flatulent so that he took little notice. Then it was over, and the congregation began to troop out into the crematorium gardens outside.

It was clear and bright as they all emerged, though, clearly, another shower of heavy rain had just passed: the culprit clouds were still scudding low across the sky towards the Downs. Water droplets clung to the wreaths and other flowers that were displayed on the walkway and on the handwritten cards the ink had blotched and run. Harry studied the messages and the bouquets carefully; not looking for meaning, but too ill at ease to meet the eyes of others.

He looked up, finally, from the flowers to see that two sleek, black limousines were already leaving, one of them carrying away his beloved Marianne. He put his hand up as if to shout out after them, but the cry was stifled within a throat that seemed to have closed. His hand dropped to cover his face as both spirit and body sagged.

'Now, then, David, lad ... you'll be coming back to the house for a drink. Jack would've liked that!'

Marianne's Uncle Frank had his big, strong hands clamped around Harry's shoulders and the detached Harry allowed himself to be steered over to the car park and into Frank's car. Harry was struck mute with confusion and remained so until he reached the Bevans' house, though he was able to manage a nod when he was instructed to. 'Follow me, lad ... I'll make sure you have a glass in your hand.'

Harry did follow and soon he was propped against a door holding a tumbler half-full of sherry. He would not normally have drunk sherry, but he had to admit that when he took a couple of large gulps its warmth spread through him so that he felt instantly happier and more relaxed.

'Our Jack always kept a good sherry in the house,' Uncle Frank commented, replenishing the glass up to the halfway mark again once he had waited for Harry to down the bulk of his glassful. 'He was always good like that.'

For a while Harry was happy to stay lost in alcohol and the blanket of sound that had grown as the room had filled with people until, suddenly and without warning, this comfort blanket was torn savagely apart.

'You've got a bloody nerve ... coming here!'

The cold challenge had been thrown at him by Marianne's sister,

Evelyn, from across the other side of the hallway where she stood with spitefulness and venom written all over her face. She had always been aggressive towards Harry, though he had never known the reasons why. Harry had pushed her into the further recesses of his mind and had not predicted that she would be the one to challenge his attendance at the family gathering. And challenge him she did: standing there in resplendent provocation, unflinching from the attention of all the people crammed into the family home.

For a few seconds Harry was too numbed to do anything, not even breathe. His insides had petrified. Everything recoiled into a void of inertia, leaving him unable to move or speak. Then it erupted. Erupted like magma bursting though ice. His reply came in a roaring flow of bursting anger. The words spat out like spurts of machine gun fire.

'I've got a nerve? I've got a nerve! ... You've got a bloody nerve! Hardly set foot in the house for five years ... Too busy toasting your fat arse in the Costa del bloody Crime!'

Evelyn recoiled.

If it had gone quiet before, then the silence that followed Harry's outburst was positively crushing. The two of them stood there like prize-fighters surrounded by the crowd, only silent and still: a film frame frozen. For a second time that day Harry seemed to be outside himself, staring down on the ugliness of his angry pose and the spectacle of their malevolent squabble that now lay unwanted and grotesque before a houseful of respectful mourners. He had wanted it to stay frozen that way so that he could have crept away unnoticed and untouched, but a quiet sound was forcing itself into the desperate silence, a sound too dismal and distressing to be anything other than real. Sobbing was escaping in small breathes from the diminutive, black form of Mrs Bevan.

All eyes turned to her stricken, crestfallen form.

The scene was too harrowing to bear.

Then movement: Evelyn rushing tearfully up the stairs; people began to murmur; Harry's own mind returned to painful consciousness. He had no idea what he could do to rectify the vile scene before him. Then, once more, he was being led away out of the house and across to a car.

'Get in!' but this time it was not big Uncle Frank's voice commanding. It was unmistakeably Marianne's.

Arriving at the cremation had felt surreal, but that was nothing compared to Harry being driven to his ex-home by his ex-wife in the car that he had bought for her fortieth birthday. The most astonishing thing to Harry was that she showed no signs of being angry, let alone being ready to explode at him for his terrible outburst.

Marianne drove in silence and Harry was too numbed to speak either. They stopped outside the house they had shared for almost all of their married lives. Sat inside the car, Harry regarded the house with a fair degree of sadness and regret. He even felt shock at realising that what had been so familiar to him had now become so alien. His mood might have become seriously melancholic had it not been for the fickle October sun that, thankfully, chose that moment to break through the clouds and spread its radiance across the house and garden. So brightly did it pour down upon the filigree of yellowed leaves still clinging to the birch tree there that they were lit up like an arrangement of most wonderful, golden jewels. The surrealism was complete.

Harry watched as Marianne went to the boot of the car, then back to scan the seats.

'Shit!' she said: it was rare for her to use expletives and Harry prepared himself for the expected onslaught.

'Shit!' she repeated. 'We can't go back for it now!'

'What?' he managed. It came out in a pathetic whisper.

'Go back for your bag … your case … whatever it is you have. We can't go back now they'll be …'

'I haven't got one.' Harry interrupted.

'What? Nothing? What were you intending? What were you thinking?'

'Nothing … I dunno!' He had assumed the role of a helpless child.

'And I was told that you were getting better.'

'I'll never get better from losing you,' he told her quietly.

He looked into her eyes with concealed expression and she looked straight back at him in equally disguised passivity. Moments passed. It seemed like Harry's world was revolving slowly around in the patchy sky behind her head.

'I was thinking we'd just have a cup of tea,' she said at last, flatly and unexpectedly.

Harry just sat there, looking into her wide, green eyes. They still looked so beautiful to him. Then her image grew blurred as tears started to course their way down his face. He managed not to sob, but the water continued to run from his eyes.

'Come on,' she said. 'Let's go and have that cup of tea.'

The house felt the same, yet different. He suppose the only big change was that he no longer belonged to it. Marianne brought the tea in and they sat there sipping it quietly. They were both, it seemed, reluctant to start the conversation. Harry guessed that he was waiting for her to set the mood since he still assumed so deeply the role of culprit. He remained completely surprised that she did not appear angry with him.

As ever in their games of silence, it was Harry who broke first.

'I'm sorry for making such a scene,' he said at last. 'She just made me so angry ... I don't suppose she deserved all that.'

'What? Our Evelyn?' Marianne smiled. 'You certainly gave it to her! I don't know what hurt her the most ... insinuating that her Jeff is an ex criminal ... or inferring that she has a fat arse! I expect you're right on both counts!'

'But, your poor mum. And you too ... with your Dad just dying,' Harry continued to apologise. 'You must be so upset to lose him.'

Then she really jolted him.

'Sorry? No I am not!' she said in quiet but cold tones as she got up to look out through the living room window. 'I'm glad the old bastard's dead!'

'How can you say that?' Harry was unable to believe that his Marianne would ever speak in such a way.

'I can say it because it's true. He is a bastard! ... And they know it ... our Evelyn and our mother ... they know it! They know it's true ... and they know what he did to me!'

'What do you mean ... "What he did to you?" ... what did he do to you?'

Marianne held Harry's stare. She breathed deeply as if to compose herself.

'Abused me!' she managed to say at length. 'Abused me for years! I was only seven, or eight, or something when he started ... but that didn't stop him ... He did it! The bastard!'

Harry was unable to find any words with which to reply. He was stunned. All those years and he had never known. She had never even suggested. He felt unable to move again. He could barely believe what had happened in the day so far, and now this revelation. All he could do was to sit there open mouthed and watch her. She remained in the window, motionless. Well, for a while she appeared motionless, but then he could see that her shoulders were shaking ever so slightly. There was no sound or movement from her, but she was trembling like a leaf on the birch tree outside.

Harry got up and moved towards her. He put his hands on her trembling shoulders, just lightly.

'I'm so sorry, Marianne ... I never knew ... I'm so sorry ... you poor thing.'

His sympathy seemed to open the gates, and as he spoke, the trembling in her shoulders grew, gathering momentum like an avalanche down a slope. It grew until she was openly sobbing and shaking. Harry simply held her in his arms: so quickly the comforted becoming the comforter. But her need was greater even than his, so he braced himself and simply held her.

He was not sure how long it was, but he held her until the shaking and the crying stopped. He held her until she was still and silent. It felt wonderful to hold her. A sexual surge rose up in Harry, but he ignored it as best he could. This was for her, not for him.

'I'm OK now,' she said some time later, gently pushing herself away. Harry wanted to protest, but let her go.

'I'll get us a proper drink,' she called back over her shoulder.

She returned with two glasses in one hand and a large bottle of golden looking liquid in the other. She held it up to him. 'Gran Liqueur' was written on the side.

'Brought this back from the Costa del Crime on me last visit!' She winked. 'Been saving it for a rainy day. Think it's just about fucking "poured" today! Don't you?'

She did not make many jokes so Harry smiled and nodded.

They drank and talked into the evening. At some points, early on, Harry had tried to talk about 'us', but each time Marianne told him that 'that sort of thing' could 'wait until the morning'.

So, not wanting to spoil the pleasantness between them, he just followed her down winding lanes of nostalgia and dreaming until they were both too inebriated to care or properly understand.

Looking back, there was no doubt in Harry's mind that it would have been the best way for the day to end. But, parts of his brain and body were screaming out to be with the woman he still loved.

It all happened so disastrously.

He might just have managed to contain himself had she had not kissed him. It had been just a light kiss on the cheek, a light, friendly kiss to thank him for being so understanding. But the drunken Harry saw it as a sign to put his arms around her and pull her closely into himself.

'I still love you,' he told her. 'I still love you, Marianne!'

For a short while she allowed him to hold her close. And it felt sublime to him to be holding her again. But, the base desires within him took no time at all to take hold, and within seconds he was trying to kiss and touch her.

If the drink had allowed, Harry might have stood outside himself for the third time that day, to recognise the error of his untimely lust. Not that he should have blamed the alcohol, he thought later. It was just him. And, he thought, just the way men are. Sometimes sex just takes over male minds, and their bodies.

He struggled to hold her, but then a cry broke from so deep inside Marianne that her body shook again. She pushed him violently away.

'No, Davey! That's not what I want!'

That should have been sign enough, but he was too full of drink, dull thinking and blind arousal. The sudden anger that had seeped into his persona earlier that day and in the weeks previous erupted again.

'You don't want! You don't want! Well, it's what I fucking want!'

And he stood there like some finger-pointing monster. Stood there until the look of fear and revulsion across Marianne's face shocked him into some kind of sensibility. Then, the surging flow of emotions that had once more brought him to the brink of disaster died to nothing, and he dropped like a dead leaf onto the settee. Harry closed his eyes and let the blood thud in a thunderous pulse through his head. When it finally stopped he was alone.

Thankfully, drunkenness and sleep soon overcame him, so that at least he was spared temporarily the usual recriminations and self-loathing.

Naturally, Harry felt ill in the morning. As he stood at the bathroom sink, a reel of shocking scenes from the previous day and evening flashed through his consciousness in a flood of painful realisation. He wanted to be sick. He wanted to vomit up all the terrible things he had said and done so that they could run down the plughole. If only his life had been that simple. He was desperate to see Marianne, but dreaded it at the same time. He did not know how he could possibly apologise.

When he stumbled into the kitchen Marianne was already there.

'Look … I'm so sorry. I'm so sorry,' he began.

But she stopped him before he had hardly begun.

'It's OK. Really, Davey, it's OK!' she placed her hands on the outside of his arms and said it so emphatically that he knew she meant it.

In fact, Marianne seemed quite bright. She made Harry eat: grilled smoked salmon with brie cheese on top of toasted bagels, topped with a spoonful of cranberry jelly. She had learned to do that, Harry remembered clearly, on a holiday to see a friend in Canada. It had become his favourite breakfast, though he had not tasted it for a long time. And, it seemed to work: he felt slightly better after that.

'I need to talk to you. Properly!' he suddenly threw out at her.

There was a pause.

'Yeah. I know,' she said gently. 'But not here. We've had too many rows here.'

'I don't want to row!' he snapped angrily.

'No ... no, I know you don't. But let's go somewhere ... somewhere nice, eh?' she spoke soothingly and calmly.

Harry's anger subsided instantly. She seemed a different person to the woman he had lived with before and he was not sure how to handle her calmness. He struggled with himself for a moment.

'Yeah ... course,' he managed. 'Let's go somewhere nice!'

Soon they were out into the cold of morning. Remnants of frost hung like pearls to the tops of grass blades, though most of the birch's leaves had died overnight to lie in a fallen bouquet around its bole as a warning of winter soon to come.

It took twenty minutes to leave the ugly urban sprawl of Swindon behind them and 'somewhere nice' turned out, instinctively and without them saying, to be the Downs: another of Harry's favourites. They drove along the narrow road that threads its way through the line of villages that have stood along the spring line at the foot of the hills for century upon century, until, at last, they climbed up the steep escarpment to stop in the car park beneath Uffington Castle.

Then, leaving the car, they trudged up the steep incline of the ancient hill fort and along its rim to the mystical lines of the chalk white horse. The markings have lain there for eons, ever since the

Neolithic tribes made these chalklands the demographic centre of Britain. The ancient horse etching is beautiful, though standing directly upon the simplistic trench lines it is not possible to see or comprehend the whole image or picture. And, that is how it was between Harry and Marianne on that morning.

For a while they looked out over the patchwork of rural idyll that stretched away across the Thames Valley to a pale horizon. They had come to talk, but so far they had hardly exchanged a word. In some ways it was enough to be there together in the open countryside. The long, smooth lines of the pale chalk hills always seem to calm the eye and mind, but Harry already knew that they would not be enough.

Though it was a clear October morning, the wind there on the edge of the escarpment was chilling so they descended back down to the Ridgeway path. At this higher elevation, the hedgerows beside the Ridgeway were already almost bare of leaves though the prickly branches of blackthorn and hawthorn were still heavily laden with berries that spread blushes of soft purple and brighter carmine red along the avenue of the Ridgeway that they followed to Wayland's Smithy, the remains of a Neolithic long barrow.

It is a site of legends. The huge sarsen stones that comprise the ancient tomb have stood there for millennia. They have a way of putting the short span of people's lives into a better perspective. Perhaps it was that which enabled Harry to take in something of what Marianne had to tell him.

At first he had wanted to interject and protest, but gradually he coerced his restless insecurity into submission so that he was able to simply listen to her tale. She told it simply too.

Marianne had thought through her life carefully. She told him with tenderness how her father's abuse had left her loving men, loving him, but hating them, hating him, at the same time.

'But it was me that hurt you!' Harry had protested eventually.

'No ... not like that ... but, yes, you did hurt me! I felt devastated when I learned that you'd had sex with that pathetic woman ... though now I can see how much I had hurt you and damaged you too,' she told him with simplicity. 'I didn't mean to hurt you ... and you didn't complain ... you just let me do it.'

'But you didn't do anything wrong. It was me!' Harry protested.

'Poor Davey. You were never any good at recognising emotions were you? Not yours, not anyone else's. Always had someone to tell you how to feel. First your mother, then your cruel Aunt Thea ... and then me.'

'I know emotions! Course I know about emotions!'

'Yes. Perhaps you do. But you only see them on the surface. You don't know how people work underneath. You just try to please them,' she told him with pain in her green eyes, before adding, 'and I love that in you now.'

'But you don't love me!' he said quietly.

Marianne looked up into the soughing boughs of the tall beeches that surround the monument to search for the right words. The sun was still shining, and the withering leaves had changed, with deep browns clashing against flames of cadmium yellow.

'No ... I don't love you in the way you mean ... the way you want me to love you ... I just can't do that ... It's not your fault, and it's not mine either ... it's just the way I am ... the way that old bastard made me. I can see that now. And I'm sorry, Davey ... I really am sorry.'

There was a hurting inside Harry so violent that he did not know how to control it. He stood up with hands clenched into fists, but there was nothing for him to do with all that tension and energy except to kick out at the stones. 'Why do I always fuck things up?'

Marianne stood to put her arms around him. Her hold was gentle, but firm. Harry continued to struggle for a while, despite wanting her to hold him, but her embrace was calming.

'Look at me, Davey. It's not your fault! Please remember that! ... You had no chance. It's not your fault ... not even that sordid, little affair ... You were hurt. We were both hurt. We didn't mean to hurt each other ... It's just the way we were ... the way we are.'

Although Marianne's words had shocked Harry again and his insides were twisted in disappointment, there was a feeling that at least some of what she had said was true. He couldn't take it all in then, but he began to understand some of the truth of what their relationship had been. He let her hold him a while longer. It felt good despite all the pain. Harry still wanted to make love to her. He wanted her to love him too. And he wanted her to be the woman she had been before: at least, the woman he thought she had been before. But he knew that none of those things were possible. Still, it felt good and he let her hold him a little longer as the skeletons of dead beech leaves fell silently around them like tears.

Harry loved the autumn in a scared and fragile way: he found its colours to be so beautiful, but he knew it was just not going to last.

Sadly, large clumps of billowing cumulus had gathered to push their way across their sky just as misfortune had clouded their past. In the clouds' shadows the air grew colder and so the separated couple walked back together to the car. As Marianne settled behind the wheel Harry let his eyes take in a last, long look along the lines of the hills where they had walked as if their words would lie there on those gentle slopes. He realised that they had spoken more deeply in that brief time than he could ever remember, but he knew that there was far more that had been left unsaid.

They drove back to the house that had been their home, but where he now felt like a visitor. There was more tea to drink.

'I need to get to the station,' he told her.

'Can't you stop another day?' she asked.

'No. I've got to go. Got to see Grace.'

Marianne looked startled.

'Who's Grace? Got yourself a new girlfriend already!?'

'No. Grace is the little girl I teach … Well, she's not so little really. But she's the girl I teach.'

'That's nice,' said Marianne. 'But stop another day … It's only Saturday. You can tell me about Grace. And I can tell you about the other things I … I … need to tell you.'

Harry's mind reeled at the thought of what other 'things' Marianne might have to tell him, but there was a pressing need for him to leave. He did not feel able to face whatever else there was to tell. For some reason he just wanted to get back to the relative normality that he had begun to create in his new world back at the cottage.

'No … I'll go now,' he said with surprising calmness. 'You can write to me … I hardly ever get letters. You could send me one … I'd like that.'

'Yes. OK. I'll write to you.'

Harry sat passively on the train back to Yorkshire wondering why he was so keen to return. An old man approaching eighty and a delicate maid in her mid-teens waited for him there: not the most conventional combinations on which to base the bedrock of his life, but he knew inside that they managed somehow between them to give him comfort at least. And, yes, more than just comfort.

Sometimes he wondered what he was doing here on earth, as if he was just floating around on the surface. But he realised that it was connections with people, like with Moses and Grace, that held him down to reality. When he lost Marianne and retreated from life, there was no-one and nothing with whom or with which he connected, but now he had those two.

He looked around the railway carriage and again wondered why everyone else's lives looked so simple. Of course, we all know the answer to that – we only see the exteriors that people attempt to portray, and little sign of the turmoil beneath. Whatever, he was looking forward to seeing the old man and the maid.

'But what of Elizabeth?' he thought to himself. In the confusion of detaching himself from any chance of reconciliation with Marianne it was impossible for him to properly consider what might happen with Elizabeth or even what he hoped might happen. That she was a beautiful and virtuous woman was certain, but whether he could ever have been able to break down the barriers between himself and her was far from certain.

*

During his time away clear night-time skies had allowed more heavy frosts to spread their icy blankets across the fields and gardens of the Holderness. And, seemingly overnight, the trees and hedgerows had been robbed of their autumnal glory. It had become winter.

The clocks had just 'fallen back an hour' so that the evenings had lost their light and it was already dark by the time Harry reached Bede House to visit Grace. It had been the thought of seeing Grace again, and perhaps the outside chance of seeing her mother also, that had kept the winter cold from seeping too deeply into his spirits. Despite all that had passed between Marianne and himself, he had managed to remain positive about Grace if nothing else.

His ring on the doorbell had been answered by Maude, who straightway proffered an envelope into his hand and began to shut the door. In shock he pushed back against the door to question Maude.

'What's this? Is Grace OK?'

But Maude made no reply. She simply pushed against the door once more. Even as his anger rose Harry realised that he could not continue pushing the door against such an old woman, and he allowed it to slam shut in front of his face. Thankfully, there was no one to witness his dejection and humiliation, so, with lack of a reasonable alternative, he painfully turned himself around and walked home.

He did not know how long he sat in the dark of his kitchen before he could bring his thoughts back to the present, but he finally broke from his dejection to the consciousness of still holding an envelope. It was as much as he could do to open the envelope such was his dread of what the communication inside might contain. It was brief, which was a blessing since, despite staring at the words intently, it took some time for him to focus on what the words actually said. It read simply that Mrs Hall wanted to see him the next evening.

The hours of the next day passed slowly despite that he was helping Moses with his garden. They were spreading top dressing across his lawn. The light sand and soil was blown into their eyes and the crevices of their faces by the wind. Moses worked on with disregard to wind or cold. Though he paid little service to the delicacies of perfection in his garden, he did like to keep his lawn in first-class order.

'You going to play tennis on it next summer then?' Harry said, forcing himself to jest with the old man since he was keen not to disclose the depth of his upset about the note and the imminent meeting with Elizabeth just yet. Moses rested on the broom with which he was brushing the mix of sand and loam into the grass, his dusty face looking thoughtful.

'Always had a tidy lawn,' he commented at last, wiping his eyes with the back of his hand. 'My Rose always liked a tidy lawn … said it added a little civility to a working garden. She liked it like that. I've always kept it tidy … even after she died … Dunno, I 'spose I keep it tidy for her … 'case she might come back.'

He looked into a place beyond the focus of his vision. 'Funny. All these years, an' I still think she might come back.'

Then he did something almost unheard of for him and sat down on the bench before he had finished the job. It was Harry's turn to lean on his brush.

'Been thinking 'bout our lad, our Alec, lately … since we talked of it, like,' said Moses. 'Been wondering if he's alright,' he paused to gather his thoughts. 'Perhaps he were hurt when that floozie left 'im … been thinkin' that he should 'ave 'ad 'is mother there to look after him … I just been wondering.'

So, there was the explanation for Moses being unusually unaware of Harry's own internal turmoil.

'Yes, but that was a long time ago, wasn't it?' Harry offered.

'Oh aye, a long time ago. But those things still hurt, even after a long time … an' I just been wondering about him.'

A new facet of the old man's personality was revealed to Harry as Moses hesitantly spoke about his lost family. It felt strange for him to be listening to his more senior friend for a change, rather than the other way round. Selfishly, he was not sure that he wanted the balance and pattern of their relationship to change. Harry had grown comfortable with Moses as his support, and now he suspected that he should reciprocate. Moses continued.

'It's easy 'nough to look back and judge yo' own parents, but when you're doing it yours'en, then ... I don't know ... I never meant to be a poor father ... it was jus' 'ard. There's no-one to tell yer what's the right thing to do. 'E were such a loving boy while 'e were little ... then ... I 'spose everybody sees through their dad at some point ... jus' gotta 'ope that they learns to see through themselves as well. Course, lookin' back now, I can see I was wrong. What 'e needed were someone to guide 'im ... not challenge 'im an' turf 'im out like I did.'

'Well, perhaps you should do something about it,' Harry suggested rather vacuously.

Moses looked at him, and then simply raised his left eyebrow ever so slightly; sweat had turned the dust into tiny rivulets of mud in the wrinkles of his brow to heighten the dramatic impact of his gesture. Harry could not tell whether it was a signal of sadness, helplessness or even contempt. Harry considered that perhaps Marianne had been right: perhaps he was poor at discerning emotions other than those blatantly on the surface. Looking back, he knew that he would always regret the paucity of his understanding and support. Sadly, Harry allowed his own emotional priorities to overtake those of his dear, old friend and the moment passed unrequited. They resumed their brushing.

The meeting with Elizabeth, when it arrived, was brief and painful.

They sat opposite each other in their accustomed positions on the leather furniture like opposing chess players, except that they were both black in their attire. Harry regarded Elizabeth. There was not the slightest concession to wanting to appear attractive: no jewellery; no apparent trace of make-up; even her hair was pulled back into a tight, mean knot. Harry knew that he had seriously upset her before departing for the funeral and the anxiety he had been feeling about it deepened as he regarded her stiff expression.

Mrs Hall came bluntly to the point.

'You get so angry,' she told him. 'But it's not that. The thing is ... that I don't ... I no longer feel that I can fully trust you.'

The sentiment of her premise cut into him deeply, but what could he say? He could see clearly how it appeared to her that he had broken her trust. Harry tried to look into her eyes. They were averted and distant. He had not been expecting good news or pleasantries, but this and the feeling of desperate emptiness that filled his insides like iced water was more than he had bargained for.

'You know I would never do anything to hurt Grace, or you!'

'Mr Harry, I know how much Grace likes you. And I know you would not intentionally hurt her,' Mrs Hall continued in her deliberate and controlled manner. 'But we can't leave ourselves open ... we just cannot contemplate any vulnerability to ... men ... to people, who might let us down.'

Elizabeth could say no more.

Harry sat on the settee, crushed by the weight of his disappointment, unable to speak or move. He wanted to deny that he could ever make them feel vulnerable; wanted to explain that he was not that sort of person; wanted to appeal that he was too kind, too honest, too gentle. But then Harry had visions of the angry, ugly man that had surfaced too often over the past few months for him to be able to sustain such a defence. The stark realisation drained him of defiance or defence. He sat there like an empty shell. Not even the Persian rug could distract him from such disappointment and emptiness.

After some seconds Mrs Hall turned to look in his direction. For a moment there even seemed to be gentleness in her eyes before she instantly regained her tone of cool control.

'I'm sorry, Mr Harry, but I resolved a long time ago never to allow myself or Grace be in a position where we could be seriously let down by anyone ... not ever again.'

In retrospect Harry supposed that she had been bracing herself for one of those shameful outbursts that had regretfully punctuated the times when they had met in this room before. It struck him too that he should be so passive and quiet.

Well, whatever either of them had been expecting, it did not happen. Harry just sat there for some further seconds absent-mindedly rubbing his top lip between his index finger and thumb and sighing into his hand.

'I'm really sorry,' he said, perhaps more to himself than her.

Then he stood up to walk silently across the hall and out into the cold evening. He did not hear the door, but he knew that it was closing on more than he wanted to think about at that moment.

*

Less than a week later a further communication arrived to confront him and to compound his misery. It was from Marianne. It was brief and it cut brutally into his still raw sensitivities.

Dear David,
It was good to see you. This is not the letter that I promised to send you,

but things have happened quickly and I feel that there are lots of things that you need to know. And I need your help.

The house has been sold. One of my former colleagues had already shown interest and wants the sale to go ahead as quickly as possible. Please agree, David. You will see some forms for you to complete. You will get half of everything.

If you agree and the house is sold then a firm of house clearers will come in and sort it all out. There might be things you want to keep. I have given a key to Howard. Please talk to Howard. I have spoken to him and he will explain things. You will need to come and collect things soon. I am really sorry. In two days' time I am going to Canada: to live there. I care for you, but I have to go. Please help me. Please complete the forms.

Marianne.

The letter had been badly formed and badly written, which was not like Marianne, though it was her name clearly enough scrawled beneath the type. If Harry had not been hurting so badly inside himself, then he might have wondered at the state of poor Marianne's emotions, which had allowed her to write something so poorly composed. But he was not in a sufficiently composed state to be able to consider her feelings at all.

Harry sat there in a stupor trying to work out exactly how he felt. What was uppermost? Was it anger or disbelief or betrayal or simply the feeling of not being loved anymore by someone with whom he had shared part of his life?

After re-reading the letter several times it was the sense of betrayal that stuck in his gut most severely. She must have known all this when he had been with her in Swindon. He could not imagine that she could just sell the house like that in a moment. 'How can you just go off and live in bloody Canada in the next couple of days for God's sake!' he wondered out loud to himself. It was difficult for him to consider that if she cared for him then why didn't she tell him all this when they were there together, face-to-face. He thought about Elizabeth and her own feelings of being betrayed by him were more understandable.

Harry checked the date at the top of the letter again. It was three days previous: Marianne was not just going to Canada – 'She's bloody well gone!'

Harry did what was becoming natural for him and went round to see Moses, but, unfortunately, his comforter was not there. Back in the cottage again, he felt too down to put on the lights. It would have been easy to slip back into the dark cell of the year before, so Harry sought solace in sleep to stave this off. The temporary balm of sleep lasted until morning when he was able to get up and walk around to Moses.

'Where were you yesterday?' Harry asked him accusingly.

The old man simply looked at him from beneath vexed eyebrows until Harry was able to gather for himself that it was unreasonable to expect Moses to be there for him at all times.

'I'm sorry!' Harry managed. 'I'll go an' mek tea.'

After twenty minutes interrupted solely by the quiet slurps of tea, Moses raised his eyebrows again and Harry began on his account of the unfortunate communications that fallen upon him over the past days. Moses then listened patiently while Harry gave him his thoughts on the letter and Marianne's departure. They sat in silence for a while.

'Come on. You can help me with a little job ... then you can give our ol' pal Howard a ring.'

Just a couple of days later Harry was back in Swindon again, having previously spoken to Old Howard on Moses' phone. They had arranged to meet in the bar of the Great Western Hotel just across the road from the station entrance. Despite his old mentor and friend being the only person there, it had taken a double take for Harry to recognise him perched delicately on his barstool, since he looked so small and insignificant compared to the larger than life figure of Harry's recent past that he had been expecting. Naturally, Old Howard recognised the surprise in Harry's expression.

'Don't ask!' he warned before Harry had chance to speak. 'Here, take my keys. I've just had a wee dram ... so you can chauffer me round for the rest of the day.'

'Thanks for coming,' Harry told him as they sat in Howard's car.

'Don't mention it, dear boy. It's a real treat to see you again. Don't suppose you've brought me any paintings have you?'

'No. Sorry ... I haven't. But I do think of you when I am painting ... I'll bring you one for sure next time.'

'You had better make it soon,' Howard quipped. 'No! Pretend I didn't say that! Come on, just drive ... I take it you can still drive?'

In fact, Harry realised, he had not driven for more than a year, but it came to him fairly easily and twenty minutes later they were parked outside the house of his and Marianne's failed marriage. She had been gone for less than a week, but already the house looked forlorn and uncared for. Even the formerly golden birch tree outside the house now looked sad, lonely and skeletal.

'Come on,' said Howard. 'I'll let you in. Bring that box will you?'

Howard got out of the car with some difficulty and Harry followed slowly with a square cardboard box containing, he could see, milk and tea bags, a bottle of scotch, and a crisp, white paper bag.

'Let's have tea first, shall we?' Howard suggested, and Harry nodded his consent.

'I've brought you a treat!' he smiled, pulling apart the paper bag. 'Lardy cake!'

Lardy cake is something of a Wiltshire speciality: a heavy, doughy concoction laced with currants and rendered lard that is baked into a crisp, sticky, and caramelised block of cholesterol-laden bread or cake. It might sound terrible, but on a cold, somewhat dismal morning it was perfect for them.

'Do you remember those Friday lunchtimes?'

'Yeah, course ... Arkle's ale and lardy cake!'

'Proper fart recipe!' and they both laughed at the shared memories.

'Look,' said Howard as they shared their makeshift lunch, 'I've talked with Marianne ... It's not my business, but I know she's hurting as well! I'm sorry it has come to this ... You two were the next best thing to children for me and I hate to see what's happened ... I really am sorry!'

'You don't need to be sorry, Howard ... No, I'm OK ... Course I wish it had worked out different, but what's happened has happened. I just wish she'd told me ... about everything. Sometimes I get really angry, but other times I can see that she just needs to ... I don't know ... do her own thing!'

'Yes. Anyway,' Old Howard cut in, 'I put the heating on yesterday, but today the electric has to be turned off, so you had best make a start. I can make a list if you want ...'

'No need for that. I don't want the furniture or anything. You make yourself comfortable and leave me to have a look around.'

Harry felt distinctly uncomfortable looking around his old house. Although it had been his home as much as Marianne's, he still felt like an intruder.

Marianne had clearly taken very little. She had obviously wanted to make a fresh start and Harry supposed it would have been difficult to take too much all the way to Canada even if she had wished.

'Whereabouts has she gone in Canada?' Harry asked Howard as he rifled through all the drawers he could see downstairs.

'She's gone to stay with Lucy,' Howard replied quite cautiously. Lucy had been a colleague of theirs previously. She and Marianne had got on really well, and she and Harry had even visited Lucy there together some years back.

'What, British Columbia? Revelstoke still?'

'I believe so. You don't seem to have found much,' Howard added to change the subject.

'No, just these photo albums. I'm surprised Marianne didn't take them.'

Harry and Marianne had never been great ones for photographs, but he was surprised that she appeared not to have taken any of their photograph albums with her.

'I'll take these … I don't want anyone else looking through them.'

It was the same upstairs. There was nothing Harry really wanted.

Then, as Harry pulled back the sliding doors of their shared wardrobes there were dresses of hers left hanging there. He stopped and touched one of them: it had been a birthday present from him to her. The skin on his neck prickled and to his surprise his eyes filled with tears. He could still see her in this and other dresses. And more than that, he could remember, even feel, little cameos of time with her wearing those dresses. It felt too real. It was too sad to feel those lovely times shared with her. It hurt him so much that she had not wanted to take those dresses and those times with her. Harry's whole being lurched with the feeling of loss and for a moment he sat there on the carpet with his face in his hands.

Time had, however, created some distance between them and after a little while he was able to stand, go downstairs and begin to block those times from his mind.

'No,' he commented out loud to Howard, 'there's nothing here for me. I'll just take these photo albums ... Marianne said she had sorted out some house clearance people.'

Howard was still sitting where Harry had left him, though he had taken the scotch from the box and had already downed a good portion of its amber liquid.

'You still love her?' Howard asked, proffering the bottle to Harry.

'No,' Harry mused to himself, 'I don't think so any more ... not her ... just the dream! No thanks,' he said to the offer of whiskey, 'Too early for me. Bit early for you too isn't it?'

'Nothing's too early for me.'

The alcohol had clearly loosened Howard's resolve to keep his secret from Harry.

'What is it, Howard?'

'Cancer, dear boy ... bloody cancer!'

A brief resume from Howard revealed that he had shied away from all the signs until an inevitable visit to the doctor had led to a diagnosis of advanced cancer that had spread though his lymph glands to just about all parts of his body.

'They offered me chemo and radiation and all that, but I said no. I couldn't face all that ... I'm not brave enough ... I watched my mother go through all that and I know I'm not strong enough.

And, anyway ... I don't want to prolong the agony ... I don't want to live any longer than I have to ... like this! ... And this stuff,' he added referring to the scotch, 'this stuff makes it a bit more bearable.'

Harry was stunned even though it had already been obvious to him that his old friend was quite ill.

'How long?'

'What? How long left? Dunno! Weeks? Months? Dunno ... not long I don't think!'

'But it's ... it's not fair!'

'Fair, dear boy? Of course it's not fair ... life's not fair! Though I have to say, I've had a good enough life.'

He raised the scotch bottle to Harry in a silent toast.

'How about you, Davey? What about your life just now? Is that fair enough for you?'

Harry could not answer. Howard did not, however, wish to hold Harry's thoughts to ransom.

'Come on, lovely boy. Take me home. How's that? Fair enough?'

Harry bundled the photograph albums into the cardboard box and followed Howard out of the house for the last time.

NOVEMBER

Harry knew some people who could reel off whole reams of famous verse, but he had never had that ability or desire. There was one short burst that came to him and he always thought of it whenever he turned the calendar to find November staring back malevolently at him from the page:

'No warmth, no cheer, no healthful ease ... No ... vember!'

That is, at least, what his teacher, Mr Archer, had always snarled at them as they cowered in the front row of the primary class, and it was his old teacher's wicked enthusiasm rather than all else that made it stick in Harry's mind. So Harry had been quite disappointed, when he had looked it up later in life, to find that the only line of verse he had ever remembered from childhood was, in fact, a significant misquote. Mr Archer had obviously thought that his own abbreviated version held the essence of Hood's words if not its exactness. Whatever the quote, it certainly embodied Harry's own dim view of November. It always left him dispirited.

Moses had the ideal remedy for the malaise that hung over Harry in the week after his dismissal from Bede House and the horrible day in Swindon.

'Been feelin' me back these past few days,' Moses told him, 'an' all that digging to be done. Gotta get that earth turned over in time for them frosts to work into it an' break the soil up ... Mother Nature an' the weather can make it 'ard enough. Got to use 'em when we can, lad ... but it just needs you to get things moving.'

So Harry dug stoically. Then, after the digging, it was treating the wooden fences with protective paint, then building compost heaps, and relaying paths. Moses was never at a loss to keep him occupied through the days, but Harry did not want to miss any opportunity to repay the old man and he knew that the physical effort would ease his mental turmoil, so he leant himself to the task quite readily. And, of course, it worked to improve his spirits. Well, it worked through the day. The grey emptiness of evenings was a different proposition. That was the most difficult time for Harry, especially since, with the sun going down so early, the evenings were so long.

Sitting around on his own and doing next to nothing was bad for Harry, he knew, but he felt too miserable to get stuck into anything productive. Harry could never get himself to paint when he felt down, and he had also lost the will to read at length.

On a couple of occasions Moses had dragged Harry down to the pub with him, where Harry sat mutely watching him play cribbage with his friends. Harry found it difficult to talk to him there. There was little conversation between the group of them. They concentrated on their cards, and on cheating! They had a complex code of facial twitches and small hand movements that sent messages to their partner: each raised eyebrow; each scratch of an ear or cheek; every sniff; even a flared nostril; each was a covert sign to exchange information between partners. They all did it so carefully and surreptitiously, as if the other pair did not know exactly what they were doing, which of course they did!

'Why do you all do it?' Harry asked Moses once.

'Dunno what you're talking about,' Moses had replied. 'Anyway, it's all part of the fun.'

'Yeah, but that's stupid! It's not fair!'

'Don't take it so serious, lad. 'Sides they might tell each other what cards they want or got, but they're tellin' me an' my partner too! It don't do 'em any good ... 'Sides, I aren't bothered about who wins! It's jus' fun.'

On other evenings Harry simply sat and stared into the fire. Often he listened to the CDs he had borrowed from Molly. He felt guilty for playing what he should have returned to her, but the tragic lost loves of Joni Mitchell and Van Morrison that were captured in their melancholic words and music seemed to fit his own mood so completely.

Sometimes Harry even grew angry at his romantic misfortune. It seemed to him that he had this great capacity to love inside of him, but not the woman upon whom he could lavish all that feeling. He often thought to himself that it was just punishment for his misdeeds and weaknesses.

He said as much to Moses while they were sat in his greenhouse on a cold, wet day.

'Don't be so stupid!' Moses retorted: the depth of his annoyance quite shocking Harry. 'Don't think life is so fair or simple. Don't think there's no big plan or record sheet. We just do what we do an' get on with our lives ... that's all! An' that's what you need to do too!'

Then he had just stomped off into the rain and cold leaving Harry open mouthed and alone in the silence of the greenhouse.

For a while at home Harry felt angry, and then very sorry for himself at having to receive such an outburst from the person he depended upon so much. Thankfully and gradually, reason began to sink into his mind. It made him wake up and take stock of his pathetic state. He knew that he needed to do something, but he did not know exactly what.

Finally, Harry pulled the bicycle out of its shed and rode out into the remains of the day. The rain had dwindled to little more than dampness in the air, but it was cold. He pumped his legs as hard as he could and set his direction for the empty lanes. In films such wild activity always seemed so romantic as the hero or heroine disappeared into the glory of a perfect sunset and orchestral rapture. In Harry's own reality it just got colder and more painful as his muscles tired. Within half an hour the light was diminishing rapidly, and he began to feel more than a little stupid. It was reminiscent of a situation some months before when he had cycled out into the mists. The return journey took longer than his outward mad dash and it was dark by the time he returned to the cottage.

As Harry completed an arduous dismount from the bike, Moses stepped forward from the shadows of the garden.

'What's this, then? Tour de East bloody Riding?' he said as cheerfully as he could manage.

'Thought I'd just get out and ... sort of purge me se'n,' Harry offered in mock colloquialism and also with as much cheer as he had left.

'Reckon you'd be best purging yourse'n inside ... with a cup of 'ot tea.'

If Harry had felt better he would have smiled, though it did occur to him that this was Moses' way of saying sorry for his outburst earlier in the day. As it was Harry simply let himself be led into the cottage where Moses not only made tea, but also built up a raging blaze in the stove.

'You need to tek care o' yourself, lad,' he said, before adding, 'I got plenty more jobs left for you!'

Harry smiled and nodded.

'Seriously! You need to tek care o' yourself.' Moses repeated, and then surprised his younger charge by putting a fatherly arm around his shoulder. He had never been so demonstrative. It felt strange to Harry, though good and warming as well.

'Yeah, I know I do,' Harry told him honestly. 'But I don't really know how.'

'Well jus' gi' it a try ... an' tek' destiny into yer own 'ands, lad!'

Later in the evening the feeling of being held came back to Harry. Overall he felt more composed and generally better, though it made him realise how much he missed having a parent, or a wife, or someone of his own with whom to share his feelings. And now it was worse without his regular tutoring sessions with Grace. Harry wondered how she was feeling without them. It seemed such a waste in Harry's mind for both her and for himself. He decided to try something, anything rather than sit passively back and mope.

Showering, shaving and putting on a clean shirt made him feel more positive and he stepped out into the evening with the thinnest veneer of confidence.

There were lights on in some windows of Bede House including the window of the tower, but there was no response to Harry's ring at the door. He rang again, pressing his ear to the door so that he could hear it resounding inside the house. For a second time there was no response, and he stepped away from the door to look up into the windows where there was light but no sign of life. A moment later, however, as he was about to leave, there was movement from the curtain of the window above the door and then, after a few further seconds, the door opened.

Given the chance to guess, Harry would have expected it to be Grace who had sneaked down to the front door, but it was, in fact, Maude who had opened it to him. At first she was motionless, but then she pointed upwards above her head, leaving Harry to believe that Mrs Hall was in her special room in the tower. Maude motioned Harry to come in and close the front door before making her way slowly but steadily up the stairs. He heard her knock on the door and then the intermittent sound of Mrs Hall and herself talking together. For a while there was only the faint sound of footsteps and it seemed a long time to him before Mrs Hall descended into the hall to stand facing him.

She was wearing a plain black cardigan that would have surely drawn all the colour from her face had it not been for the warmth that radiated from the amber droplets of her earrings: amber droplets at the end of silver rods that fell gently beside her throat to emphasise its slender smoothness. Despite the effect of her simple jewellery, she looked tired and Harry thought to tell her so before dismissing the idea as far too personal and presumptuous in the given circumstances.

'Mr Harry,' she said stood with her hands clasped together like a reproving schoolmistress.

'Mrs Hall,' he reciprocated.

Then she waited for him to continue.

'Would you mind ... do you think we could sit down?' he asked.

She unclasped her hands to indicate the way through to the living room where they sat in their two usual places at either end of the Persian rug like opposing chess players again. He stared down at the rug to wonder why he had brought himself to this point. The colours and patterns were so fine, intricate and balanced that, as usual, it began to calm his mind.

'It's a very beautiful rug ... I've always thought so.'

'Mr Harry, surely you have not come here to discuss the rug. Perhaps you could get to the point.'

Harry nodded in agreement, though he still struggled to focus upon what he wanted, what he needed, to say. And now it seemed that even those stylised birds and animals from the rug were staring back defiantly.

'The point is … the point is … that I would like to apologise … and explain,' he sighed, placing his fingertips together and stroking his nose. The statement came as a surprise not just to her, but to Harry as well. He had not had the slightest idea that he was going to say it, but as soon as he had, he realised it was the truth and instantly he felt much better.

Harry breathed deeply waiting for Mrs Hall to encourage him, but she made no attempt to speak. She simply sat there and looked at him. It seemed hopeless, but finally he made the effort and began.

He started to speak, simply and without careful thought, just allowing words to tip loosely from his mouth. Strangely, they seemed to flow of their own accord, without, even, any reference to Harry's conscious thinking, and in bursts and rushes like a mountain stream between rocks, that grew and grew into a great torrent of words.

It was amazing, even to Harry, that so much had been locked inside him waiting to burst out. And it all came out in a great flood of swirling emotions: the loss of his parents and the agony of his time with Aunt Thea, even the cows and the cabbages; then his life with Marianne, the affair, and their break-up; then his depression, the funeral, and even the recent words between Marianne and himself. It all came out to lie exposed before them.

At first Harry had expected Mrs Hall to recoil from the ugly deluge that had poured from within him, but she had just sat there quietly without comment or condemnation. He thought it was this that allowed him to keep talking. Some of the things he said had surprised and even shocked: thoughts and ideas seemed to drop from his lips as revelations, not just to Elizabeth, but to Harry as well! It was strange how simply the act of talking allowed him to discover feelings that had lain so long beneath the surface of his own conscious thought.

'I don't think I liked my parents very much,' he eventually heard himself say to her. He realised straightaway, of course, that he had never, ever thought that to himself before, let alone said it! Yet as soon as he heard it he knew it to be true. And it was then that he made the great discovery.

'I don't think that they were ever very kind to me,' he heard himself tell Elizabeth. 'Then they left me! I know they didn't mean to die, but what about me? I had to live with my horrible auntie! That wasn't very nice for a little kid! I hated it ... I hated her ... it wasn't fair!'

Harry had for a while forgotten all that, forgotten the misery of feeling alone and unloved, forgotten all those tedious days sitting quiet and still like an unwanted ornament in his aunt's cold, miserable house, forgotten all that pain. It all came back to him, his cold childhood in that house of cold austerity, learning the litany of how grateful he should be to have a respectable roof over his head, repeating into insensitive, adult ears how much he loved his parents who were now passed away. Of course, as a child he knew he loved his parents; all children loved their parents, that's what children did. But now Harry knew that for him it had been a lie to those adults' own respectability, confusion and guilt.

'That's what I've been angry about!' he told Elizabeth, almost whispering. 'I was never really loved by my parents, and their death took away my chance of a proper childhood. It wasn't fair!

And when I lost Marianne that took away my chance of a happy adulthood too! That's what I've been angry about, and I never knew it! Well, not until now.'

Harry sank back into the settee, tired, shocked at his realisation, but, somehow, relaxed that such a huge emotional boulder had just been rolled from his shoulders. He wanted to close his eyes and drift away on a cloud of newfound peace. In fact, he wanted to sleep. But then he remembered where he was, remembered also that he had just revealed all this to a woman who had recently curtailed his services and who may not have appreciated such candid exposure. He looked blankly across at her, not knowing what to expect.

'Well, Mr Harry,' she said at last after realising that he had concluded his ramblings. 'Now you have told me!'

It seemed an over simple thing to say, though just what anyone is supposed to say after listening to someone unburden themselves so is difficult to guess at.

'I don't know how to reply.'

'There's no need to reply,' he told her. 'I'm just grateful that you let me tell you.'

'And why have you told all this to me?' she asked.

'Because I wanted to, I needed to … and it seemed right … and I want you to … to be able to trust me … with Grace … and with you too.'

Harry let his rationale hang there in the air between them, like some kind of plea. Mrs Hall did not respond and he allowed his gaze to drop once more back down to the Persian rug. They continued to sit, both of them, it seemed, preferring to lose themselves in the intricacies of the rug, which divided and connected them at the same time.

'It's got a mistake in it!' Harry blurted out suddenly.

'What?'

'The rug! That beautiful rug. It's got a mistake in it right there!'
She did not bother to look at the rug.

'Of course there is a mistake in it. Though it's not there by
mistake! The carpet-makers are Muslims. They would not dare to
attempt anything that was supposed to be perfect. That would be
an insult to Allah. So they always make their rugs with a deliberate
imperfection. I think it is a wise idea. Nothing is perfect: none of
us are anywhere near perfect ... so ... so, perhaps it was unfair for
me to expect you to be perfect, Harry!'

Slowly, Harry allowed his eyes to travel up again and across to
Mrs Hall. She looked, well, perplexed.

'I've upset you,' he concluded to her.

'No ... no, I'm not upset ... I think I might be ... shocked!'

'Oh, shocked. Shocked by all the things I've done wrong?
Shocked to learn that I'm such a bad man?!' he concluded further.

'No! No, I don't think you're a bad man. I'm not shocked by
what you've done ... I'm just shocked that ... that you told me.'

'I thought you wanted me to tell you!' Harry exclaimed.

'Well, perhaps I did. Yes, I'm sure I did. But no one ... well,
maybe once ... has ever spoken to me like that before,' she told
him quietly.

'Like what?'

'So personally ... so privately ... like you've let me into your
private feelings.' She lifted her eyes to look into his. 'Look, it's not
a bad thing! It's just that no-one has ever done it before.'

'What? No one? Not your parents?' Harry asked.

'No.'

'Not your close friends?'

'No.'

'Not Grace's father? Or your husband, or whoever?'

'No ... especially not him!' she let out bitterly.

'Oh, I see,' he told her. 'The first ... I'm the first! Well ... I'm sorry.'

'Don't be sorry,' she said, lightly touching his arm. 'I'm pleased you told me.'

They walked through the hall to the front door without talking further. Harry realised that he was still wearing his faded duffle coat.

'Well, do you think you might be able to trust me to work with Grace again?' he asked at last anxiously.

'Yes ... I think that would be fine,' she replied simply.

Harry sighed deeply with relief, and then managed to smile at her.

'Goodnight then,' he said.

'Goodnight, Harry' she replied. Then she kissed him lightly on the cheek.

So bemused was Harry by what had happened that when he returned to the cottage he went straight to his bed. He laid there staring at the ceiling until sleep fell over him like a heavy blanket, even though he had not undressed or drawn the covers over himself. The night passed for him undisturbed and, unusually, dreamless.

*

Harry awoke feeling reprieved and happy to have a place back in the cycle of life at Bede House. He was not exactly sure of his position with Elizabeth, but he was prepared to hold himself somewhat in reserve to allow her room to invite him into whatever relationship lay ahead rather than to force himself into a situation that was not yet clear. His position with Grace was, happily, much clearer. She came round to his cottage straightway after her first day back at college after half-term. Showing no inhibition, she wrapped her arms right around Harry to hold him in a warm hug. Though his natural instincts as a teacher would have warned him against such close physicality with a teenaged girl, he knew that there was nothing less than complete innocence on both sides. He allowed her to hug him like a daughter and wished that life could have been that simple.

It came as a pleasing surprise to be invited for lunch again on the coming Sunday.

Having travelled into Beverley with Moses on the Saturday morning on their way to collect a repaired hedge cutter, Harry had taken the old man's advice to buy some flowers.

'Perhaps a plant would be more appropriate,' Harry had thought to himself in his new mood of careful reserve.

'Oooh,' said Grace when she took the wrapped poinsettia from Harry at the door, 'thank you!'

'Actually, it's for ...' but Harry could already tell from the sparkle in her eyes that she was only playing with his nervousness.

'Mummy will love it!'

Elizabeth did, indeed, love the plant even though the gift made her blush deeply. Harry blushed also to see her so touched; he could not recall that she had done so on the previous occasion when he had brought flowers. Their discretion towards each other sat palpably within the silence. Fortunately, Grace allowed herself to use their pleasant impasse as an opportunity to assume the role of hostess, taking the adults to the table and organising them to help themselves to a creamy white soup served with crusty hunks of bread. The adults shared a smile to see her so happily engaged.

'This is delicious!' Harry enthused over the thick cabbage and potato broth. 'What's it called?'

Elizabeth said nothing, but turned her eyes to Maude, who had clearly been the cook. She, however, declined the invitation to speak, so it was Elizabeth who had to tell Harry that it had been, in fact, 'soup Normande'.

'And coq au vin!' Harry was pleased to be able to tell them over the main course, and, though his hosts showed their pleasure, he realised that his relief at recognising the dish had simply served to illustrate the limitations of his culinary experience.

'I'll have to cook something for you all,' he offered as cover, even though their quick acceptance made him feel distinctly vulnerable. Then he settled down to enjoy the rest of the meal and the accompanying red wine. He had heard of Chateau Neuf du Pape, but could not recall having actually drunk anything quite so smooth and satisfying before.

Perhaps under the influence of wine, Harry had been insistent upon taking advantage of the unusual warmth of the afternoon to take a walk down to the sea.

'It's a shame the weather is so gloomy,' Elizabeth had commented.

'We can't let a few clouds stop us!' Harry had countered gallantly, and Grace had immediately jumped up excitedly to support him.

'Please, Mummy!' she begged.

And so they set off into the remains of the afternoon.

It was an excursion soon cut short by an increase in both rain and wind that managed to quickly cool the geniality between them. Harry thought to use the opportunity to his advantage by gathering the two of them under the large umbrella that he had brought from the stand in the hall, but in the wind and rain it proved too ungainly, and he was to complete the swift return to

Bede House with just Grace under his wing. In fact, Harry felt such a sudden distance appear between himself and Elizabeth that made him, in sulky retaliation, decline an invitation to re-enter the house for tea as they stood at the front door. He felt quite hurt that her warmth towards him could have cooled so sharply. An excuse was made for needing to drop in on Moses and he left with barely another word to his hosts.

On the short walk home he decide against visiting Moses and instead spent the evening huddled beside the warmth of the stove. Unsurprisingly, he failed to pull himself out of moody contemplation of his plight and, cocooned within the dulling of wine to his senses and the pounding of rain upon the rooftiles, he fell once more upon his bed and into restless sleep.

As if by arrangement, Harry's walk round to Moses' place the next morning was cut short by the older man pulling into the kerb to meet him. 'Where are we going?' Harry had the temerity to ask as he bundled himself into the front seat of the old Volvo, but Moses was not able to bring himself to reply until they had reached the empty roads of the Wolds. And it was not until they reached the familiar road to Old Bob's place that Moses felt able to prepare Harry for their arrival with an account of Bob having been moved into a home for the elderly on the edge of Bridlington, where he had found it difficult to fit in at first, but where he now, apparently, felt quite safe and happy.

'I feel reet sorry for ol' Bob an' for 'is girl … she 'ates not bein' able to look after the ol' devil, but she got 'er own family, an' it were jus' too much … a 'ome was the only answer. Me an' Eadie went to visit the ol' lad. The place was all reet, though it were really sad to see ol' Bob there … 'e was always so full o' beans. Now it's like he's just a shell o' the real man. 'Ope I never gets like that.'

The terrible thought of such a fate awaiting either of them hung over Moses and Harry as they went for a desultory wander around Bob's house and its outhouses. It even smelt of decay. The buildings felt like shells too: they were still standing and intact, but without Bob's presence they were empty and for Moses, who had so many vivid associations, quite melancholic.

After Moses had completed his check of the property they left. As before, though, Moses stopped the car a distance down the road so that they could stand against the dry-stone wall and regard the farm from a distance. He said it was like looking back on their memories.

'I know 'e's not died yet … an' I aren't one fo' morbid talkin' … but it seems like 'e's already gone … poor ol' fella. An' … it makes you think about yourse'n … it do. We don't know 'ow long we got any of us … It's one o' the reasons I bin seeing more o' Eadie. Don't go raisin' yer eyebrows at me, David, lad … we're both round about on eighty, an' we both needs a bit o' companionship … an' that's all we needs! But it's like we both missed so much along the way … an' now there's no time left to fit it all in!'

'No time?!' retorted Harry. 'You're both as fit as fiddles! You've got time for lots of things … you've just got to want to do them enough!'

'Really? You might like to listen to your own advice sometime, lad! Though perhaps you're right … we just got to want to do them enough.'

Later in the day, Harry was really pleased to see Grace arrive at his cottage on her return from time at college. She was pleased to see him too, which made him feel really good. He had been intending that Grace would help him with some gardening jobs, but lately she seemed to be even more lacking in energy. After simply walking to the cottage from the bus stop she seemed quite out of breath. Harry sat her down in his big chair beside the kitchen window.

'Maude says I'm still a bit peaky,' she told him. 'What's peaky?'

'I think it just means that you are a little bit poorly. Come on I'll make you a nice cup of tea.'

'"Nice" tea, Harry? Maude says "cheery".'

'Yes, madame ... one "cheery" cup coming right up!' and Grace managed a small laugh, which, unfortunately, developed into coughing.

They drank the tea with little conversation and stared out into the garden. Most of the view was taken up by the silhouette of the ash tree against a pale grey sky. Its haphazard tangle of branches and twigs seemed to fill the window like a Pollock painting. The arrangement of branches and twigs denying pattern or reason, with boughs bending in all directions like arms with dislocated elbows.

'It's not the prettiest of trees,' Harry commented absent-mindedly to Grace.

'I think it is,' she contradicted. 'Its spaces are like magical windows.'

Harry regarded her with mild amazement.

'If you close your eyes you can see them,' Grace encouraged.

Harry knew what she meant and squinted through half-closed eyes to see. The lines around the spaces between the boughs and branches were, indeed, quite beautiful. He had never looked at trees in that way before, looking at the spaces rather than the tree itself, and, not for the first time, he wondered what it could possibly be like inside Grace's mind.

Before the sun set completely, he escorted Grace back to Bede House. He had hoped to see Elizabeth, but she was clearly not going to arrive at home imminently, so once more he set off for the comfort of Moses' parlour. But his old friend was not at home either. It was a dull evening. Later, however, as he pulled the curtains across his bedroom window, Harry could see a slim crescent of moon hanging in the sky westwards behind the ash tree. At that very moment it was framed perfectly by one of Grace's 'windows'. It was, indeed, beautiful and special.

*

It was not the coldness of the month that bothered Harry so much as the shortness of the days and the general lack of daytime hours and brightness. So his eye was particularly caught the next morning by a flicker of pale, but startlingly clear violet going past the kitchen window where he was sat inertly at the table before an array of, so far unused, paints and brushes. The pale violet turned out to be Eadie's shawl, casually appearing, though probably carefully draped around the top of her plain, grey coat. He was pleased to receive the distraction of a visitor. He was surprised to see that it was Eadie, though, in truth, any visitor other than the three people currently so central to his life would have been unexpected.

He welcomed her in and straightway made tea for the two of them.

'What a beautiful shawl!' he managed to say some time later as they sat beside the comforting warmth of the range. 'What lovely, deep colouring.'

'Thank you. It's a pashmina,' Eadie informed him. 'My sister brought it back from Kashmir for me ... She was always more adventurous than me ... She went there once to see where our grandparents had been missionaries.'

Harry told her light heartedly of his surprise that Yorkshire could be a hotbed for missionaries.

'I don't know that it is or ever was! My mother's parents were Welsh Presbyterians. My dad used to say that he rescued my mother from "death by chapel" when he brought her up here from Wales. He met her when he was working down there as a temporary slaughter man ... courted her for two weeks ... then the next year went down to marry and bring her back here ... Things happened quickly in those days.'

'And, did she like it here?'

'I don't know really. She died less than ten years after coming here. Sad I suppose, though I've never thought about her life really. It was just what happened ... and I accepted it then.'

They both sat silently for a few minutes in their own reveries. Harry felt pleased not to have pressed Eadie into an explanation of why she was visiting, since she came to it in her own time.

'I brought you a little present,' she told him bringing out a package from a small rucksack that had been hidden under the shawl.

There were three jars in a small wicker basket. Harry took them out carefully to examine the labels that had been so neatly written by hand upon them. There was a jar of tomato chutney, a jar of blackberry jelly, and a third jar labelled 'Chilli Jam'.

'Wow! They look nice!' he exclaimed, ever inventive with his choice of adjectives. 'You made them yourself?'

'Yes ... I like to use produce from the countryside ... "Nature's bounty" is what my sister always called it. That's one of her recipes ... the chilli jam.'

'Did she bring it back from one of her travels?'

'Yes ... from a delicatessen in York I think!' Eadie smiled.

Harry set them in a row on the table, beside the paint pots. It had been a really thoughtful gesture, though he wondered why Eadie had gone out of her way to reward him so well on that day.

'I've been thinking about a present for Moses ...' she told him. 'He's eighty next month ... and I wanted to talk to you about it.'

Of course, Harry knew that Moses was approaching eighty, but he had not really registered that the old man was quite so close to his birthday. Moses did not disclose that sort of thing to Harry. 'Or anyone!' Harry would have imagined.

Eadie went on to explain that she had discussed a birthday party with Moses. It came as no surprise to Harry to learn that the old man was not keen on the idea. But Moses had, Eadie continued, agreed to what he termed 'a birthday Sunday tea', since his birthday was, in fact, on a Sunday this time around.

'He said he didn't want any fuss, and just wanted a quiet "tea" with me and you. He said he didn't want any of his drinking pals there to make jokes about his age and to generally get silly ... and he wondered if you might like to bring Grace and her mother along.'

Harry told Eadie he thought that Grace and her mother would probably be delighted to attend, and he smiled inside at the thought of Moses scheming to arrange a situation for Eadie to meet Elizabeth at last.

'You'll enjoy meeting them,' he told her.

'Well, I've already met the young lass! Don't you remember? Drenched and cold in my living room! But I haven't met her mother yet.'

'Yes, of course. Now what do I need to do?'

'Well you can leave all the food and that side of it to me. You try and get your friends to attend and I'll sort out the rest. But, now ... I was wanting to talk to you about my present for Moses!'

They did just that.

Afterwards Harry sat down and thought intently: partly about the enormity of Eadie's present; and partly about what his own present could possibly be. Before the light had begun to fade he had decided upon a painting for Moses and exactly what it would be. The implications of Eadie's present for Moses left Harry, however, feeling decidedly uncertain.

DECEMBER

Harry awoke to the sound of a cow complaining loudly in the field behind his cottage. For just a moment he was transported back to the dingy attic room where he used to sleep at his Aunt Thea's house way back in his childhood, and for just a few seconds he imagined with horror that he was actually back there under those old, cold, grimy sheets. He felt sick to his stomach before he was able to return to the reality of his own comfortable room.

He went gingerly down to prepare his simple but satisfying breakfast of toasted wholemeal bread saturated with rich butter and honey followed, of course, by strong tea. And he ruminated all the while on the wonders of memory and the human brain.

Until he had spoken to Grace, and then her mother, about them, those horrible days of childhood had remained deeply hidden in the recesses, but now they had just reappeared so vividly. It amazed Harry that he could bring to mind every detail of days so long passed: the setting and the scenery; the weather and even the feel of the air; who had been there, what had been said, and even words left unsaid; the way he had felt, and the things he had thought. There were so many amazingly complete memories locked away in the brain, just waiting to be revealed by some trigger or other: a word or a question, a picture, even a line from a song.

And what amazed his vulnerable brain most this particular morning was the thought of all those memories, good or bad, that might remain hidden forever just for the lack of a chance incident to trigger them off. It was enough though, he was able to conclude by the end of his breakfast, to be able to decide which memories to share or keep locked away, without worrying about those which did not even come to mind.

His rare philosophising came back later in the day to haunt his mind as he sat waiting for Grace to arrive at the end of college, but she did not arrive.

After a while he went to Bede House to enquire about her and was not too surprised to learn that she had become too poorly to attend college. Maude was happy for him to visit her in her bedroom, but, by the time they reached her, she had already fallen asleep for the evening. He did think of waiting for Elizabeth, but thought she might be late herself, tired and more concerned about Grace than anything he might want to share, so he just took his leave with a rare smile to Maude.

'I'll come round tomorrow afternoon once I've finished with Moses,' he informed Maude who likewise rewarded him with a tight smile. He could tell that she was worried about her patient.

True to his word, Harry arrived the next day as soon as he could after finishing his morning session with Moses. Maude welcomed him in and straightway led him up to Grace's room. The first thing that Harry noticed was that the poinsettia had been placed on the bedside table in her room. The second thing was how pale she looked against its deep crimson redness. After an enthusiastic welcome from Grace, Harry persuaded her to lie down while he read to her. She chose Enid Blyton's *Shadow the Sheepdog* which was her favourite, even though he had read it to her more than once before. She snuggled contentedly into the blankets with a brave smile, but, less than twenty minutes later, when Harry looked down he could see that she had fallen asleep.

To Harry her innocent face looked even paler than it had before, perhaps too pale, and her breathing was quick and shallow. He went downstairs to find Maude in the kitchen and she followed him up to look at the sleeping girl. After feeling Grace's brow for temperature and then, quite expertly it appeared to Harry, checking her pulse, Maude's expression became anxious.

'She's very hot. I think we should summon a doctor,' she said simply in a soft whisper of a voice. It was the first time she had ever spoken to Harry, but he was careful to show no hint of surprise.

'Would you like me to call?' he asked and she nodded. Harry looked into her worried eyes and by chance in such stressed circumstances recognised the older woman's likeness to Elizabeth.

After securing the promise of a doctor's visit, Harry this time waited in the house until Elizabeth had returned home from work. It made him tingle inside to see her again, but she was preoccupied with Grace and the doctor arrived soon after. She did manage a nervous smile as Harry made a quiet departure since he was feeling just a little superfluous.

Not unusually, Harry returned to sit in the quiet of his kitchen with a troubled mind, though this time his thoughts were for someone else's problems rather than his own.

Moses had been anxious for Harry to miss working the next morning, knowing that he was concerned about Grace and also because the day had started with such a heavy frost, but Harry had insisted on helping since he knew it would keep his mind occupied. He did, however, skip lunch so as to arrive at Bede House quite early in the afternoon. Maude ushered him into the hall with a welcoming gesture, but a concerned expression. She stood close to Harry so that he could hear her quiet voice clearly. She informed him that Elizabeth had gone with Grace the previous evening to the hospital in Hull and had not yet returned. Maude looked tired and frightened herself, but nodded to Harry that she was alright when he had asked how she was.

For a few moments Harry stood outside Bede House in a daze of indecision. Of course, he then set off to find Moses, whom he imagined might give him a lift to the hospital, but, as had happened increasingly more often in recent weeks, Moses was not at home. Harry thought about buses, but then decided to cycle into the city. He knew there was a cycle track all the way there along the route of the old holiday railway line, so he decided to follow it.

In fact, the cycling track that had replaced the old iron and sleepers was in pretty good condition, perhaps helped by a morning frost that had persisted to keep the mud and puddles still frozen into ice. There was a steady northerly breeze behind him so he made good time in reaching the city.

Unfortunately, he had not thought to find out where the hospital was, but after asking a few passers-by he found it without too much bother. The next setback was a little more disconcerting though, as the main city hospital informed him after some time investigating that Grace was not there but at the Castle Hill Hospital some miles westward and out of town. The cycle to that further site finished steadily uphill and Harry was feeling quite tired by the time he had dumped his bike and stood outside the arrivals desk.

The woman on duty did concede to him that Grace had been admitted, but, after he had confessed to them that he was not 'family', he was informed that it was not possible for him to see her. After pleading and dramatically describing his efforts to get there, the kind woman at reception did agree to inform Mrs Hall that he was waiting in reception.

Sometime later Elizabeth appeared in the doorway from an adjacent corridor. She looked very tired and, herself, even paler than usual.

'You look tired!' dropped out of Harry's mouth with a stunning lack of sensibility, sensitivity or subtlety.

Elizabeth chose to ignore his comment then closed her eyes for a moment like one about to address a child. But then she looked down at Harry's mud-splattered legs and asked more perceptively.

'Did you come all the way on your bicycle?'

He told her that he had and her whole demeanour softened.

'Thank you for coming, Harry. I'm sure Grace would have loved to see you, but she is sleeping and she is not allowed too many visitors.' She went on to explain that Grace had acute pneumonia.

'I could tell she was under the weather, but I didn't imagine it was anything so serious ... How serious is it?'

Harry had begun pacing around in a somewhat demented fashion, but Elizabeth pulled him down into a chair next to her. She explained that Grace did have very acute pneumonia, but, so far, nothing more: the doctors were completely confident that with rest and modern antibiotics she would make a full recovery. There did not appear to be anything more to discuss so they sat in silence for a few minutes.

'I'd better get going then,' Harry finally told her.

Elizabeth regarded him quite blankly at first, but as he started to stand up she grasped onto his arm. And as Harry pulled her up to his own level, large tears curled into the corners of her eyes to fall in tiny rivulets down her pale cheeks. In such a state of vulnerability and dependence, she instantly appeared to Harry as the most beautiful woman he had ever known.

'Harry ... I feel frightened ...'

'Don't worry ... She'll get better ... I know she will!' he told her with a conviction in his voice that he did not feel.

In fact, what he was feeling most of all was the desire and

physical joy of holding this beautiful woman closely to himself. He was not so base, however, that he was not able to compose his thoughts and reject those baser feelings and unworthy thoughts for a more considered attitude towards a desperate mother and a sick child who meant so much to him.

'I'll call round to Bede House tomorrow, if that's all right.'

'Yes … of course it will be all right. Maude will … Oh my God! I haven't told Maude yet … I must let her know! I don't know when I will be home tomorrow. I expect I'll be visiting Grace. Perhaps I could call in … at your cottage.'

Harry told her that calling in on him would be fine. Then he retreated to the door and made his departure. He could feel Elizabeth's eyes upon his back as he walked away down the corridor and he turned to wave. Elizabeth was clearly distracted by thoughts of Maude as well as Grace, but moved her own hand just discernibly in return. It was a small response, but enough to lift Harry's spirits almost wildly.

And lifted spirits was exactly what he needed. It was beginning to get dark by the time he started to cycle and, as he turned northwards away from the city and onto the road to Beverley, rain carried by a stiff wind cut into his skin with icy effect. Pulling himself up the hills past the old windmill at Skidby encouraged the blood to flow through his system and that, plus the excitement he still felt from having held Elizabeth so intimately, helped him to feel warmer for a while.

The constant stream of heavy traffic along the main road, however, felt threatening and dangerous as impatient drivers in a rush to get home whisked by with just the narrowest of margins to spare. Though Harry knew it would increase the distance, he pulled off the main road at the earliest opportunity in order to approach Beverley by way of quieter country lanes. He had no knowledge of these lanes, but, by using the town lights and the now lit up outline of the magnificent Minster, he was able to keep some sense of direction and find his way to what he recognised as the approach to Beverley across its open common. Taking the quietest of road options, he arrived down narrow lanes and streets into the very centre of the town.

By this time the rain had turned to sleet. He felt soaked to the skin and so cold that there was little feeling in his arms or shoulders. Shops and cafes were still lit up warmly, but, with great regret, he realised that he had left for the hospital without sufficient thought and definitely without any money. In his own perverse way, Harry had so far been almost relishing the challenge of cycling miles into the wind and rain, heading for the ethereal outline of the Minster, but his spirits dropped considerably as he was forced to recognise that this sort of inept thinking was, sadly, so completely characteristic of him, and he had cause to curse himself once again.

Lost in such sad reverie, it took him some time to realise that the person who had just walked over the pedestrian crossing in the town centre before him was, in fact, waving and shouting at him from under her umbrella on the pavement. It took even longer for him to realise that the person was someone he recognised. It was Molly.

'Harry! What are you doing here? You must be mad! You must be frozen!'

Harry didn't know what to say, but even as he began to reply, he realised that he could barely move his lips, let alone make intelligible language.

Getting back to Molly's place and into a hot shower remained a bit of a blur to Harry, though he could clearly remember the base and disreputable thoughts of sex with Molly that he allowed to roll around in his imagination as his brain thawed in the stream of hot water in the shower. He felt shocked that the sudden urge for sex could take over rationality and control so suddenly and so completely. He would have liked to believe that his fantasies were no more than just fantasies, and that he would not have been tempted into anything unworthy of the trust that was just beginning to build between Elizabeth and himself. But, as it turned out, no such temptation was placed before him.

When he did emerge from the bathroom, in a pinker than was called for robe that Molly had placed there for him, she found his appearance in her old dressing gown to be far more comical than romantic. Any notions that Harry had entertained for having sex with Molly disappeared with her laughter and her own uncanny recognition of what she knew had crossed Harry's mind.

'What?!' he challenged back to her knowing look, but without being able to supress a blush of shame.

'You boys ... you're such martyrs to your instincts!' she threw back, though not without a forgiving smile that confused Harry's thoughts even further. Then she found some old clothes left behind by a former boyfriend that just about fitted the bill for Harry's frame.

Molly listened patiently and with genuine sympathy as Harry related the details of Grace's illness and of his journey so far. Of course, he thanked her for rescuing him from the cold and then for letting him use her phone to call Moses before the old friend could disappear to the pub to meet up with his cribbage mates.

"'S alright, Harry ... I think I owe you one for letting you down the last time ... You're not angry with me are you?'

Harry was able to laugh it off: a lot had happened since that day.

'No. Trying not to get angry anymore!'

'Well, let's drink to that … friends, eh?'

Moses was rather bemused, but at least a little amused as well, to find his wayward charge sipping a large glass of rose wine when he arrived at Molly's house. He was not able to stay long, however, due to the call of the evening's cribbage game.

'I'll bring the clothes back some time,' Harry threw over his shoulder as the two men moved out through the door.

'No … don't bother … I don't think he'll be coming back to claim them … but do call in on me some time, Harry … you can let me know how Grace is getting on!'

'How Grace is getting on?' Moses interjected with concern, since he had remained unaware of her illness. Later he took in carefully what Harry had to tell him about Grace, but on leaving he almost tripped over himself as they walked away down Monks' Lane for allowing his gaze to linger too long and too fully upon the allure of Molly.

'Well?' he enquired with a quizzical raising of his eyebrows that allowed Harry perfect understanding of his unasked question.

'No … No! Nothing like that! We're just friends.'

'Friends eh? Nice to know you got some friends then!'

'Yeah … real nice!' Harry told him in a way that not just continued their play on the word, but which Harry hoped would also allow Moses to realise how much he appreciated his old mentor's friendship as well.

'Right then, friend!' Moses retorted, 'just 'appens we're one short for cribbage this evenin' … You'll be able to stand in then!' and he smiled at Harry's show of exasperation.

'You only thinks you're tired!' the reliable old friend laughed as they set off through the Bar Gate and out of Beverley.

Actually, it transpired on the journey back to the coast that needing Harry to fill in at the cribbage table had all been no more than a joke on Moses' part. He dropped Harry off at the cottage with another warning that his young charge should look after himself more.

'You'd be best setting yourse'n a fire, lad,' was his departing shot.

Harry had managed to do just that and again, after a lazy day since Moses had been otherwise engaged, repeated the operation the following evening. He was pleased to have done so when Elizabeth arrived. He enjoyed being able to welcome her into a warm, fire lit room.

'I've just popped home to see Maude and to fetch some clothes for myself,' Elizabeth began, ensuring that Harry realised that she would not be stopping long.

'The doctors say that Grace is doing well, but she will have to stay in hospital for a while … maybe another week or so … until her fever is under control and until she has regained some strength. They say I can stay over there for another day or so at least … so I will.'

Elizabeth was keeping herself, Harry could tell, under tight control. She did, however, become tearful as she told him that Grace might need a minor operation on her lung if things didn't progress well. At that moment she allowed Harry to hold her by the shoulders to tell her again that everything would be alright. As she lifted her face he felt himself almost falling into those pale blue eyes gleaming as the firelight reflected in the tears. She held Harry's gaze and smiled, but then she was off like the woman on a mission that she was. The cottage became still and silent apart from the crackle of the fire, though inside Harry's mind uncertainty rumbled and crashed like a winter storm.

He should have had more faith and optimism. Two days later Elizabeth arrived to ask if he would like to accompany her to visit Grace in hospital. It was the start of them 'doing things together', and, thankfully, the start of Grace's slow recovery.

*

A new rhythm to the days developed for Harry over the next week: working with Moses in the mornings and accompanying Elizabeth to visit Grace at the hospital in the evenings. Gradually in the afternoons he managed to draw or even get some paint onto a surface or two. He knew that some practice was needed before he attempted his 'birthday present painting' for Moses.

On one of the more clement afternoons that week Harry pulled his bike out of the shed and set off for the Wolds with a large rucksack on his back. It took a couple of hours for him to reach Old Bob's farm since he had stopped en route in Driffield to fortify his art supplies with a good quality pad of watercolour paper, and also to buy a couple of Yorkshire delicacies: one of his favourite curd cakes; and a nice, big, treacly slice of parkin.

On arrival at the lane before Old Bob's place, it was all he could do to leave the cakes in the rucksack, but he was determined that they would remain in the sack as a promised treat until he had completed a half satisfactory drawing of the farm and its surroundings.

Pulling out his new pad and enjoying the velvet touch of its opulent surface, Harry managed a surprisingly accomplished sketch at his first attempt. As an amateur he was never confident of 'getting things right', particularly at first attempt, so he was really pleased with it. He knew also that he did not have the skills that some practised artists have of being able to paint in the field, especially in wintertime, so he made a really big effort to try and remember the scene in his mind, knowing that he would have to complete the work once he was back in the comfort of his own kitchen.

Despite having been really quite warm and rosy from the cycle ride, standing still to sketch had allowed his body to cool down rapidly. He ate his two cakes quickly and washed them down with hot, cinnamon-spiced 'apple tea' that Maude had prepared for him that morning: she often made it mid-mornings at Bede House and he had already grown partial to it. The hot drink warmed him up long enough to stand and gaze for another five minutes whilst he tried to metaphorically drink in the sights and sounds, even the smells all around. He hoped his memory would be working as fabulously as he had surmised earlier in the week. He stood in the lane to take in one more swallow. For just an instant Harry fancied that he could hear the calls of Bob and Moses in their youthful carousing through the fields and hedgerows, but, of course, it was just fancy.

On the afternoon of the next day Harry settled in his kitchen studio to attempt the completion of his picture for Moses. Looking back afterwards, Harry thought that it must have been chance above all else that had allowed him to finish with a painting that pleased, at least his own inadequate eye, so well.

Taking a lesson from the Persian rug, he had attempted to create harmony through using a simpler palette of only cadmium red and yellow, sepia brown, and a Prussian, rather than his usual cobalt, blue. His initial intent had been to paint simply a 'wet on wet' watercolour, but lack of technique had forced him to supplement this with further working, even though he knew the dangers of overworking a picture. First he used Indian ink to outline and bring out the contrast of the farmhouse's angular shapes against the gentle folds of the landscape, then to capture the wild disorder of the fruit tree branches, and also to draw in the merest impression of two human shapes within the composition. Secondly, he had needed to resort to gouache, which he applied to soften the fields and more distant hills into their paler winter hues. A second application of gouache lightened the cloud formation to suggest, he really hoped, a burst of sunlight breaking though upon the bucolic scene. It was the final balance of light and dark that appealed to Harry's own judgement most.

Though he knew that he had worked with intensity far beyond his usual efforts, he was still surprised to see that, by the time he had finished, darkness was already gathering outside. Harry put on the light so that he could inspect his finished work again and was surprised all over again: surprised that he had been able to create something that looked far better than he had imagined he could achieve. It was just as well that no-one else was around as he stood there for quite a while smiling at the painting and smugly congratulating himself, which was a perhaps deserved change from his usual more self-deprecating manner.

That evening at the hospital Harry informed Elizabeth and Grace of the forthcoming birthday party for Moses. They were both pleased at the prospect, particularly Grace. Her mother told her that she would need to get well soon.

'What must I do then?' Grace had asked in her customary simple, yet pragmatic manner, to which she was told to eat up all her vegetables and get to sleep early. They already knew that Grace had, surprisingly, slept well: more than one of the nurses had let them know how much they enjoyed her quiet, peaceful face when she slept.

During the visits Grace was keen for both of them to read the stories that she had written during her more comfortable moments. They were just like the ones Harry had witnessed from their visit to the primary school that time. He was pleased that Elizabeth did not question Grace about 'who Sascha was'. He told Grace with some sincerity, but also a little guilt in the back of his mind, that he would take the stories to show her old English teacher some time, which made Grace even more eager to write.

On leaving the hospital, Elizabeth mentioned that Maude was feeling unwell and likely to have gone to bed early. Harry knew that, back at Bede House, Maude liked to cook for them in the evenings. Her meals did tend, however, Harry had once agreed with Elizabeth after joining the two of them on a couple of occasions, to be a little plain. So, he seized upon the opportunity by suggesting that they should go to a restaurant. Elizabeth was unsure. As they approached Beverley in her car on the way home she conceded that she did not really feel like being out with other people. Harry was relieved that it was other people and not him that made her uneasy.

'Come back to the cottage then.'

'Have you got any food in?'

'Not specially … sausages?' he grimaced.

' … Yes … fine … I'm sure they'll be … lovely!'

Harry was not so sure that sausages would suit what he imagined might be the more refined tastes of Elizabeth, but he was pleased for her to come back to the cottage and to prolong his time alone with her. There was a bottle of wine waiting, which he had bought when out with Moses a few days previously in case he might have needed it as a present or something like that. He sat Elizabeth down beside the stove with a large glassful from it whilst he began cooking.

'Maude's not a great cook, but she does bake really excellent cakes,' Elizabeth informed him as he was preparing. 'I'm sure she would love to make one for Moses' birthday ... yes, I'll get her to make one. When is it exactly?'

'That'll be great!' Harry replied, feeling really happy that they were able to enjoy casual small talk. 'I think it is exactly on ... the Sunday ... the Sunday between Christmas and New Year.'

Then he turned his concentration back to his cooking. The sausages were from a local butcher, who was well recommended by Moses, so he knew they would be tasty, and he was confident about his bubble and squeak: there were not many things for which he could be grateful to his horrible Aunt Thea, but bubble and squeak was one of them. One of his frequent tasks during his time with her was to cook their simple evening meal. Harry had learned his cooking, quite fearfully most of the time, by trial and error, but had found that presenting her with something tasty was one of the few ways in which he could please her. Leftover potatoes and other vegetables, well-seasoned and mixed up with chopped onions before being fried on a high heat could, he had learnt, magically turn themselves into such a tasty treat. Thankfully, there was an abundance of vegetables left over and pressed upon him from a meal with Moses, which included sprouts and kale, both of whose slight bitterness would, Harry thought, be a perfect balance against the sweetness of the onions. Bubble and squeak with sausages: fit for a king, or queen. Then he hit upon a minor brainwave by placing two of Eadie's jars on the table with their labels away from Elizabeth.

'What are they?' she asked with a smile that had been induced, he hoped, not just from the wine, but also from the relaxed company.

'You'll have to guess!' Harry teased. 'Put them on your plate and try them.'

It had grown fairly late so they were both aching with hunger. Harry knew that, failing all else, their hunger would sustain their appetites. Being late was a good tactic with food he thought.

'It's delicious!' she informed him as they ate.

'What? The 'sauce'?'

'No, Silly! All of it!'

'Thank you. What do you think you are eating then?'

'Well, sausages, and bubble and squeak, of course! I might be from a ... sheltered ... background, but I know a good bubble and squeak when I taste it.'

'And what about the 'sauces'?' Harry was enjoying their little food quiz.

'Mmm ... well, that's a tomato chutney or pickle, or something ...'

And this ... it's nice ... adds a little ... piquancy ... mmm ... not sure. It's like jam with spices in it.'

'Very good, Madame. And which spices exactly?' he pursued in fun.

In fact, Elizabeth appeared to be very good at her spices.

'Well, there's chilli, that's for sure. And ... ginger, I think. And, of course, it's in a jam of some kind ... strawberry or raspberry. And, there's some lemon or lime in it ... am I right?'

Then Harry had to admit that he did not really know. He passed her the jar. 'It's called 'Chilli Jam' ... Eadie brought it round last week. I'm glad you like it.'

Later, Elizabeth found some sachets of drinking chocolate from within the depths of her bag and he mixed them with boiling milk. Sadly, from Harry's perspective, there were only hard backed chairs in the room, so it was difficult for him to sit with her rather than beside her. When he did move his chair right up next to hers, however, she appeared pleased rather than threatened or alarmed. Harry decided in his mind that it was time they became more intimate, although, probably unintentionally, her next words halted this plan.

'Thank you, Harry,' she began. 'Thank you for the meal, and thank you for being so … kind … and supportive … and … and … patient!'

He smiled into her pale, lovely face. Against the tumult of desire that was rising inside, he managed a calm exterior, which he realised was a dramatic contrast against the awful, uncontrolled, angry man he had presented to her on so many previous occasions.

'You're welcome.'

His reward was the laying of her hand upon his arm as they sat there in his quite bare kitchen. He hoped she had no idea of how much such a simple gesture on her part could sent such tremors of electricity through him, whilst he concentrated on simply enjoying the moment until she left.

He enjoyed it … patiently.

*

The next week Grace returned home. Harry was pleased to spend time with her each afternoon and to become altogether a more frequent visitor to Bede House. He helped Grace to sort out her stories and to put them together in a folder. She was very excited about the party for Moses and they had decided that her present to him would be a story written by her. It was about a kindly old man who travelled round the countryside with his dog and cat in a special car helping any lost or otherwise needy children. Harry was sure that Moses would love it.

The hours of daylight continued to diminish and the two of them, rather than sit beside their upstairs window, would more often work and talk and play around the large table in the kitchen. Quite often Maude, and occasionally Elizabeth, would be preparing or cooking food there, which always created an ambience of warmth and intimacy.

Despite the year not having yet reached the nadir of its 'shortest day', Harry's spirits had been lifted by the increased opportunity to spend time with Grace and her mother. He was beginning to think to himself that getting through this winter might not be so bad after all. Since becoming more attached to the everyday goings on at Bede House, he had begun to awaken to each day with a growing sense of contentment and purpose.

Harry had even risen one morning with a firm intent to sort out his cottage and the muddle of his belongings within it. His initial enthusiasm, however, had been brought to an abrupt halt as he came across the box of photograph albums that he had retrieved from his old house in Swindon. He hesitated over re-opening it, worried that it might contain images that could in some way threaten the wellbeing that he was beginning to enjoy. Life was getting better, but he was cognisant that his path through it was still quite fragile and uncertain. In the end, he decided to take it with him to Moses' place.

Moses was already busy when Harry arrived pruning back the branches of the quince tree.

'Yer needs to cut out the dead wood,' Moses admonished with

a mischievous grin. 'But I aren't goin' to get all metaphorical on yer, lad! Go an' put that kettle on the 'ob for me … an' you can mash us both a nice cup o' tea.'

Harry knew better than to do other than what Moses told him at that time of day.

'You know those old photos you showed me a while back?' Harry warned Moses as they sat down together. 'Well, how about looking through some of these?'

'What yer got there then?'

'Just photos. You know … family stuff.'

The album opened up with pictures from Harry and Marianne's wedding. The old man naturally commented on how young they looked and how pretty Marianne had been as a bride.

'Very nice!' he commented. 'Is there anythin' from your childhood?'

'No, nothing … just me and Marianne together.'

'An' you're showing them to me 'cos …?'

'Well … because I didn't want to look at them on my own really!'

They continued to look through the pages. Harry realised that nearly all of them were of Marianne and him together or with her family. A few of them were of the two of them with friends. It was as if each of them had been frightened to stand before the camera on their own. Harry pointed out the members of Marianne's family.

'That's her father,' he told Moses, ' … what do you think?'

'What? Of him? Tell the truth, he looks a bit shifty … like he don't want to be there!'

'That's right!' Harry agreed with Moses. Then he realised that he had wanted Moses to think that all along. 'That's right … he didn't want to be there … he didn't want his image to be there once he'd been discovered as the evil bastard he was!'

And then, of course, Harry told Moses all about the abuse that Marianne had suffered at her father's hands.

'I'm sorry, Moses … I guess I just needed to unburden myself.'

' It's no problem, lad … it's 'ard to imagine a man can abuse 'is own daughter like that.'

Moses then became very quiet and thoughtful.

'Though I reckon I abused our Alec!' he suddenly revealed in some distress.

'Course you didn't abuse him!' Harry countered.

'Well, course I didn't abuse him like that … but I knows now how I must 'ave 'urt him … I didn't mean to 'urt him, like … it were jus' me own ignorance and stupidity … but I did it all the same!'

An awkward silence fell across the garden for a few moments.

'Sorry, Moses … I didn't mean to stir all that up!'

'Course you never, lad … come on … I got some jobs to keep us occupied! You been paintin' lately? 'Cos I got a little paintin' job for yer … it's only monochrome mind!'

They went via the garage to pick up some rough brushes and a large tub of creosote before Moses led Harry down the side of his house to the high wooden fence that needed treating.

'Try yer skills on that, lad!'

Harry thought it was fair repayment for having Moses there for him to turn to, though the simplicity of the work left him with perhaps too much time and opportunity to think. He completed the task with mixed emotions and a slightly empty heart. The prospect of having Grace 'back into his life' was certainly good for Harry, but there was still a slight feeling of emptiness hanging over him. Perhaps he thought to himself it was just wintertime. He had never been a big fan of the wintertime. For him it has always been something of a penance to be endured between the more pleasant periods of the year. When he had been working at school there had always been Christmas to look forward to: not that Christmas had ever been an especially good time for Marianne and him he had pondered. He thought the absence of their own children had precluded that. But at least there had been the end of term and a holiday to look forward to. Now that he was on his own even the anticipation of Christmas was a little daunting.

Harry might have become really maudlin had there not been an arrangement in place to meet up with Grace and Elizabeth that afternoon. An appointment had been made for Grace to visit the college before the end of term, as she had missed so much time through illness. Elizabeth had, for a change, booked the day off from work to take her, but had, nevertheless, asked if Harry would go with them. He was pleased to do so.

Harry's in-built worry over being late meant that they were more than an hour early for their appointment at the college, which he then used to his advantage by suggesting 'a little drive over The Wolds'. The two females had looked at each other with a knowing grin, but had been pleased to acquiesce. Harry guided them towards a circular route up through Driffield and out across the emptiness of the area that he had grown to love, though he allowed Elizabeth to make her own way back through the network of quiet lanes that led them southwards and back towards the college.

At one point a dawdling tractor forced them to pull over into a track entrance beside the road, whereupon Harry suggested they should get out to stretch their legs for a short time. Their stroll brought them before a giant deciduous tree that dominated the quiet stand of trees behind it. For some reason, and despite the wintery bareness of the trees, the scene struck Harry as being particularly serene and beautiful. His companions stood patiently beside him as he gazed upon it for a while.

'I think I could spend the rest of my life looking at that view!' he told them with a sudden filling up of passion and emotion.

Elizabeth regarded him so intently that he was forced to look away. Then he felt Grace's small hand find its way into his own. She stood between them to hold both their hands.

'We could stay with you and be a family!' she announced to them with a sublime innocence that was difficult to face.

They stood, each in their own contemplation, before it was time to move on, though the memory of that place and thought would linger in Harry's mind for a very long time.

It had been a good idea to arrange this preview trip for Grace. She was pleased to be reacquainted with the place and took pleasure in pointing out things to the two adults, especially many of the animals that she remembered. They met with one of Grace's tutors for a brief interview during which Elizabeth explained that Grace would not be fit enough to start until the new term in January, but there appeared to be no insurmountable problems. The tutor thanked them for attending and said how good it had been to meet both parents together. Elizabeth and Harry simultaneously launched into an explanation of them not being married, but then the funny side of the situation and Grace's comment hit them and they all fell into laughter. Grace found it particularly amusing and even enjoyable, but there was no doubt in Harry's mind that being an ordinary girl with two parents was what she most wished for in life.

As they left, and once more to extend the bonhomie between them, Harry suggested lunch together in Beverley. They found a sunlit table in the courtyard room of the Beverley Arms and sat down together to decide upon 'sandwiches all round'.

'What's your favourite?' Harry asked Grace.

'I don't know ... what is my favourite, Mummy?'

'I'm not sure, darling ... you are a ninny sometimes!' her mother smiled.

'I know,' answered Grace with a laugh at herself. 'Maude calls me her mooncalf ... what would you call me, Harry?' She loved this game. Harry took his time to answer: partly to tease; and partly because he could not think of just the right word.

'I would call you ...' he stretched it out. 'I would call you ... the apple of my eye!' He could not bring to mind anything more apposite.

'I'm not an apple, Harry! Am I, Mummy?'

'Harry doesn't mean that you are a fruit, darling ... I think he means that ... that you are ... very special to him.'

'Do you, Harry? Am I special to you?' she asked with her inimitable innocence and candour.

'Yes ... you are very special to me.'

And just the simple act of saying it brought a tightness to Harry's throat and a watering to his eyes that he had to fight to control. It was just a tearful day for Harry. Grace smiled and Elizabeth rested her arm gently upon Harry's to show the sensitivity of her feelings towards him at that moment.

'Am I really, Harry?'

'Yes: of course you are!' he answered, though it came out as a whisper as the realisation filled him with an unwarranted sadness that he could not fathom.

Harry's comment and show of emotion brought another moment of silence, though there was no sense of unhappiness between them. It just seemed to add to their collection of important moments that day.

Elizabeth broke the silence.

'We were wondering … if you could come with us at Christmas.'

'With you at Christmas?' Harry struggled to take the invitation in.

'Yes! Yes, I would love to come with you at Christmas,' he assured them swiftly. 'But, where would we be going?'

'We go to Grandfather's … we always go to Grandfather's at Christmas,' Grace chipped in, though, strangely, without her usual enthusiasm.

'Yes then … I would love to come to your Grandfather's … Father's … for Christmas … it'll be great!'

'Well …' Elizabeth intervened to warn with words that she seemed struggling to find, ' … it might not be 'great'! You see, my father, Grace's grandfather, is not the … warmest of hosts. In honesty, it is usually a bit of a struggle to get through the few days. He is rather … well it would help me if you were there, Harry.'

It did not take too much of Harry's imagination to appreciate that their family relationships might not be so wonderful, but it certainly felt great for him to be wanted.

'Of course, I'll come with you. There is nowhere I would rather be!' Harry was able to tell them honestly.

As they left the last crumbs of their sandwiches and the hotel behind, Harry smiled to himself at the curious episode that had unravelled over their lunch, knowing that he had more to look forward to than he could have previously imagined.

Unwisely, Harry had allowed his expectations for Christmas to swell during the week running up to the event. He could not recall, ever before, wanting so earnestly to buy presents for people. He allowed his imagination to plunge ahead under full sail, forcing Moses to take him into Beverley not just once, but three times. And, had it not been for another unexpected communication arriving on his doorstep, then he would probably have ventured too closely if not completely over the edge in his imaginings. As it was, the large brown envelope that the postman handed to him outside the cottage's front door had the effect of not only taking the wind out of his sails, but also dangerously stirring the waters of his newly found contentment.

*

It was something of a surprise for Harry to encounter the postman at all, since he could not recall having ever seen him before. But the real shock was in the contents of the envelope, despite that he had examined the outer covering sufficiently to recognise the stamps as Canadian and therefore the package to be from Marianne.

Firstly, amongst the contents, Harry opened the small, enclosed envelope that he presumed correctly was a Christmas card. It expressed not exactly 'love' from Marianne, but her wish that he had a happy time over Christmas. He confirmed determinedly to himself that he would, indeed, have a very happy time and that perhaps he did not need her love any more anyway. Her phlegmatic greeting had disappointed, but not totally surprised Harry, but the other two contents did.

An even smaller envelope fluttered out from somewhere between the card and the substantial inner foolscap item. It was not even gummed down, but inside was a cheque for what appeared to Harry as a staggering amount of money, and it was made out in his name. He quickly ripped open the brown foolscap wrapping expecting to find a formal typed explanation, but there was only a sheet of numbers and an untidy, handwritten sheet inside.

Dear Davey,

Sorry I have not written earlier. You can't imagine how busy I have been.

Thank you for signing the papers. I am sure we will both be happier in the end.

Here is a cheque for your half of the house. It was in my name so I have sold it and paid off the mortgage and all the other fees. But I want you to have half. That's fair I think.

Do you remember how we struggled to find the money in the first place? It's hard to imagine that prices have risen so much. It's crazy.

I am well. I am living with Lucy at the moment. I have got a job. There is a shortage of nurses here.

Anyway I am happy.

You would not believe how deep the snow is here. It's as high as the top of our front door. But people are very friendly and I am happy.

Take care,

Marianne.

P.S. I will write again once I am settled.

As usual Harry turned to his gentle giant of a friend for reassurance even though he knew Moses already had plenty on his own mind. Harry showed Moses the letter and the cheque, which he read without comment. Then, for quite a while after Harry had seated himself beside Moses on an easy chair in his parlour, they just sat and thought without speaking.

'Life's alwus full o' surprises, Lad!' Moses said at last.

'Yeah … I don't even know what to do with it.'

'Well, that's simple enough. Jus' stick it in the bank until you're ready t' mek a decision.'

Harry left to make his way ponderously back to the cottage. He was in quite a quandary over whether to feel pleased or offended at receiving all that money. What certainly irked him was the careless manner in which Marianne had informed him. It was, he thought, as if she did not care. More confusion swirled around inside Harry's mind. He did not know whether he should still care so much about Marianne, though her feelings towards him still mattered so much.

It would certainly have been more than an understatement to say that Harry's life over the past couple of months had been something of a rollercoaster.

Marianne had sat for a long time that morning trying to contemplate and compose the letter that she needed to write. Despite the gravity of her task, it was still a wonder for her to be located in Revelstoke at all. Indeed, her mind was still tempted to stray toward the distraction of the sparkling waters of the Great Arrow Lake beside which she now resided, or past the forest fringe to distant peaks of towering mountains which dominated the skyline beyond. Even though the whole scene was now blanketed in snow, she knew that come June and July the slopes of those same mountains would be alive with 'painted fields' as hordes of wild mountain flowers burst out into spectacular bloom. The scenery of British Columbia had always been the ultimate dream for Marianne and now she was living that dream.

She allowed herself to rest back in her study chair to conjure images of idyllic days ahead, though, right now in the background, Lucy was making enough noise in the kitchen to make Marianne's delicate task too difficult.

With the briefest of explanations to Lucy, Marianne donned heavy winter over-clothes and snow boots to set off on the short walk to Front Street where she found a quiet corner in the warmth of her favourite coffeehouse. Even the largest of cream-topped hot chocolates had, however, failed to fortify her enough to keep her attention away from the spectacular sunlit scenery outside. She so badly wanted to do justice to her own and David's feelings in a letter that she knew would inevitably be inadequate.

In truth, even the most eloquent of speakers or most cogent of thinkers would have found the task overpowering. How could she explain to the man with whom she had shared her adolescence and twenty years of married life that she was now blissfully happy in her relationship with the woman who she had probably loved latently for most of that time? How could she express the relief she felt at being six thousand miles from the town and family home where she had suffered such scarring and marring abuse?

At the end of her hot chocolate, though cold it was by then, she had quickly and, yes she would have had to admit, quite carelessly scratched out the lines of the letter which she had hidden beside the Christmas card to David, who had formerly been her David. She knew that he deserved far better, but at the time she had been unable to give more: perhaps one day, but not then.

'What have you been doing today, Harry?' Grace asked him as he took a seat at the kitchen table.

'Oh, just talking to Moses,' he told her, not wishing to go into details about his exceptional postal surprise.

'What were you talking about?' she asked.

'Oh, you know what adults talk about … everything and nothing … What about you?'

With proper attention to appropriateness and detail, Grace told him all about the Christmas pudding mixture that she had been helping Maude to make ready for the visit to her grandfather.

'Of course, we haven't finished it yet. We are waiting for you and Mummy to give it a stir and to make a wish!'

Grace arranged the bowl and the spoon for Harry and watched intently as he stirred, screwing his face up to give added gravity to the wish he was about to make. He had to admit to himself that it was a pleasant and gratifying feeling to be included and to make a wish. 'That this sort of shared happiness might continue' was all he had wished for. Grace's smiling innocence and enthusiasm had brought him a sense of happiness previously absent to the day. It increased when Elizabeth arrived to join in with the mixing and wishing ceremony.

Despite the plainness of Maude's cooking the meal passed happily between them.

'It feels like it's nearly Christmas!' Elizabeth exclaimed. 'Let's light a fire!'

She allowed Harry to take the lead as if lighting a fire in the hearth was within the masculine domain and he was pleased to do so. Then, sure enough, the warmth and light of the fire, once it had gained momentum, brought a wonderful feeling of togetherness to the room.

'We should have a tree!' Grace proposed, and she was beside herself with pleasure and anticipation when it was agreed that Harry should go to purchase one as soon as he could organise it.

When Elizabeth and Maude took Grace to bed Harry sat on the settee feeling more 'whole' than he had for a very long time. He piled logs onto the fire so that it would last for a while until Elizabeth returned to the sitting room. As she did so Harry put out his arm beckoningly along the back of the settee so that she might sit closely next to him. Thankfully, she did just that and, eventually, even allowed herself to relax into him. Although touching against each other, they sat in stillness and silence.

'I'm sorry,' she said at length.

'Sorry? What are you sorry about?'

'You know. I'm sorry … I'm … the "Ice Queen"!'

'Look,' Harry told her as calmly as he could, and in contradiction to the rising excitement within him, 'I'm not the best at these things! We'll just have to work at it together.'

She smiled warmly at him, then tucked herself back in against him. Harry had been hoping for at least a kiss but reasoned that he was pleased enough just to be sitting close up to her there. Unfortunately, and with some rancour, since he seemed to have an undeniable ability to put his foot in it, he spoilt the moment of intimacy by bringing up the subject of Christmas at her father's house. Perhaps he should have realised from previous times that mention of her father would induce a sudden touch of frost into the atmosphere, but it had not come to mind.

Elizabeth sat up and began to explain that her relationship with her father was what she described as formal and strained. She did not say why.

'Well … don't go there for Christmas then!'

'I have to go there,' was all she would reveal.

'And Grace doesn't seem to want to go either!' he persisted.

'Yes, it is a bit of a trial for Grace,' she conceded. 'But ... we have to go!'

Silence for a while.

'Surely he's nice to Grace,' Harry put in a bit churlishly.

'No ... I wish I could say that he was ... but ...'

Harry could see that Elizabeth was struggling to maintain her composure and that he had, perhaps unfairly, pushed her to the point of being upset.

'OK,' he said in retraction and as reassuringly as he could manage. 'I'm sorry if I was unfair.'

'No ... You weren't unfair ... It's not your fault, Harry.'

'No, perhaps it isn't, but I want to help. I must be able to do something'

She closed her eyes: he imagined to fight back tears. Harry felt so tenderly towards her then that it took great restraint not to do something grandly demonstrative in order to show her how much he cared. Unfortunately, he was so emotionally inarticulate that he did nothing. He knew, anyway, that she would not have welcomed some great gesture from him at that stage, so he just sat beside her quietly.

Eventually she was able to turn to him and smile.

'There is one little thing,' she conceded. 'You could teach Grace her three times tables!'

'What!?'

'It's this stupid thing! Every year he asks Grace "What is three times three" or "What is three times four?" I don't know why he does it. She never knows the answer.'

They sat and gazed at each other in shared incredulity. It struck

Harry that her father had already been able to spoil things for them, and he had not even met him.

'Right ... three times table! We'll give it a go!'

*

Grace and Harry sat at the desk beside the window overlooking the garden, though at this time in December it was already dark. She was fidgeting restlessly, as if she had some premonition that they were about to be dealing with her anathema of numbers.

Harry pulled a handful of small pebbles from his pocket to spread them haphazardly across the desktop, which at least gained a little of her reluctant attention.

The pebbles were all similar in their size, shape and colouring: egg-shaped beads of blood-red quartz, each one no larger in circumference than the width of Harry's little finger nail: that was how he had always explained centimetres for the children at school – about the width of a little finger nail.

Freshly wet from the sea, the pebbles had shone with gleaming opalescence when he had carefully gathered them in. Now dry, they had lost that gleam, but there was still a warmth to their pinky-orange skins.

Harry laid the handful in a row of first ten, and then another five.

'How many are there?' he asked cheerfully.

Grace feigned complete disinterest, while Harry cajoled her into admitting that there were fifteen. He had to nudge her arm to persuade her into arranging them into five groups of three pebbles each.

'Look! That's five times three – fifteen!'

Grace's total concentration was focussed upon showing not a single glimmer of interest or recognition.

Harry then removed six of the pebbles to leave three groups of three, and then tried again.

'Look! Three lots of three. That's three times three equals nine!'

She remained stony-faced and forced her gaze into another corner of the room, as if to close down the shutters completely. Clearly, Harry's carefully thought out approach was not going to work. He did flirt with the idea of presenting the exercise as some form of challenge to beat her grandfather, but decided against that as well. Then he hit upon a different approach.

'If you were a girl with nine little ducklings, how would you sort them out into groups of three?'

Grace considered him gravely from beneath scowling eyebrows. Then she allowed just the tiniest twitch of a smile to escape into one corner of her mouth. She held the scowl for a few seconds longer before replying very primly.

'I would talk to them very nicely!'

Without too much engineering, however, Harry was able to move them on. Soon Grace was quite happily moving her little ducklings into various numerical arrangements. She spoke to the little pebbles as if they were not only ducklings but long-lost friends even, while Harry attempted to engage her in mathematical terms.

'Do you think I would be able to look after little ducks as well as the real girl?' she asked finally, after wrestling for some time with the concern.

'I'm sure that you and your friend across the hills there would make an excellent pair of duckling handlers,' Harry told her. And he could almost read her happy thoughts as they drifted away across the rolling Wolds to rest beside that cheerful stream.

By using the small stones as make-believe ducklings, Grace allowed Harry over the next couple of days to rehearse her through the machinations of the three times table to the point where she could go through the first five or six workings of the table with some certainty. Though, of course, she was far happier simply using them in her imagination as a family of ducklings, and often he would arrive to see them lined up on her bedroom windowsill in a line behind her favourite Russian doll.

*

The number of days before Christmas was diminishing quickly so, on the afternoon when Elizabeth was taking Grace for a hospital check-up, Harry sat down in the cottage to write his cards. He had bought a box of ten, which he knew would be more than enough. It did strike him as being quite sad that there were so few people in the world who meant enough to him to merit a card, or, as he more pertinently assumed, so few people in the world to whom he mattered at all. Apart from those within his immediate group living on the Holderness, Harry sent cards to just Howard in Swindon and to Marianne in British Columbia, though he knew hers would arrive late.

Eadie opened the door to Harry when he arrived later at Moses' house. Harry told her how pleased he was to see her even though his immediate internal reaction had been one of slight resentment. Moses was pleased to inform Harry that he knew the ideal pal to supply a Christmas tree, so after dropping Eadie at her own home, the two of them travelled on across the winter hills of the Wolds. Moses' old friend was pleased to supply them with mugs of hot tea and one of the well-shaped spruce trees that stood stacked in his yard.

During their journey home, the wonderful aroma from the boughs of their captured tree enticed Moses into a whole string of amusing tales about his Christmases as a boy, not least his annual fear at having to perform a song or poem for the rest of the family: strange that what had frightened him so much back then could make him roar with laughter now. Moses then insisted that they should return to his house before delivering the tree so that he could search out some old Christmas decorations from within the depths of one of his outhouses.

Back at Moses' place, Harry made more tea while Moses was rummaging about and they drank it while the old man sorted through two boxes full of salvaged decorations.

'Aah, look at these,' he sighed, opening up an old tobacco tin. 'Know what these might be?' he asked, proffering Harry a handful of dull crystals.

'Them's myrrh,' Moses informed Harry without waiting for a reply. 'Me father used to light them for us when we were kids. He said they used to light them when they wus in Mesopotamia.'

Moses liked to say the word 'Mesopotamia' as if it held some magical quality, which it probably did for him. Later, when the two had arrived at Bede House, Harry issued the word again with an equal amount of satisfaction. It did not take too much persuasion from Grace to entice Moses into a demonstration. Grace thought it was magical indeed that 'these stones from the Bible' could burn and give off such a fragrant smell. She said it was like being in the stable by the manger; her innocent sentiments reminding them all of just how 'magical' she, and probably all children, could be at Christmas.

Moses had enjoyed being at the centre of the activity of setting up the tree and its decorating as well as the magic of the myrrh crystals, though he declined an invitation to stay and eat. Strangely, for one who was so generous to others, he found it difficult to accept the same generosity towards himself.

Harry went round to Moses' house on the morning of Christmas Eve to wish him well for the season, though the old man accurately guessed that Harry's own need for reassurance lay beneath the excuse.

'Jus' be yourself,' he chided. 'That should be good enough fo' anyone.'

The approach to the Georgian building called Creake Hall was grand, though diminutive in comparison to the more celebrated mansions in that area of Suffolk. From the road a hundred yards of tree-lined driveway ran between lawned garden flanked beyond that with tidy fields of arable land. The front of the substantial house was stone clad and very attractive Harry thought.

'Wow!' he said, 'what a place!'

'Don't be too impressed,' warned Elizabeth. 'Initial appearances are not all they seem to be. This place has seen hard times for the past twenty years.'

Harry soon learned that all the land beyond the garden had been sold off to local farmers, that most of the lime trees in the avenue were stressed and in dire need of pollarding, and that behind the façade the fabric of the building was literally crumbling to dust. It was a similar picture inside the house, where beyond the entrance hall and main lounge, closer inspection revealed furnishing and decor well beyond its replacement date. Whatever had formed the basis of the family's previous good fortune; it had clearly faded and diminished over more recent years.

They were ushered into the house by an older woman who kept her eyes averted from direct contact and they awkwardly stood waiting in the hall.

'Major Duncan-Hall will be with you soon,' she murmured in retreat.

Harry, who had rolled his eyes at the announcing of the Major's double-barrelled surname, was mildly surprised that his female companions had simply stood and waited without daring to throw themselves into the arms of their previous home. But wait they did and soon a small, rather aged man entered the hallway. He had silver hair and a clipped moustache, and clearly resembled the subject of the portrait that hung on the wall of Bede House's hallway. He wore a suit of broadly pinstriped navy blue with wide legs and very square shoulders which appeared to be a size too large for his frame, and which made Harry smile to himself as he thought it would have been more fitting to have been worn by one of the Chicago gangsters he remembered from the days of black and white B films.

The major kissed both Elizabeth and Grace perfunctorily upon the cheek, though Maude had been careful to retreat into the recesses of the hallway and away from attention before he did so. Then he came across to Harry.

'You must be Mr Harry,' he said warmly, though there appeared to be little warmth in either his eyes or in the handshake that he extended. Harry did not have large or particularly strong hands, but, even so, he could feel the bones of the major's hand almost squash within his grasp and he regretted concentrating too much on giving a good, old-fashioned, firm handshake: Harry thought that perhaps he should have left that back in the old time movies too.

Harry forced himself to at least reserve his judgement on initially meeting Elizabeth's father.

After Maude's quiet withdrawal the four of them left shared a tasty shepherd's pie, followed by traditional apple crumble with custard. The major expressed his general appreciation of Mrs Frobisher's care and cooking, though she had already slunk away by the time he was commenting on the chronic rise in food prices. The food had been accompanied by a bottle of red wine, which tasted wonderfully smooth and rich to Harry's inexperienced taste. Harry was informed quite pompously upon his enquiry that it was, again, a bottle of 'Chateauneuf du Pape', this time well preserved in the cellar from one of the major's past jaunts to Provence. The host had been very pleased to note both Harry's enjoyment and lack of knowledge.

'At least I can still offer a decent bottle of wine,' their host commented and Harry felt a surge of sympathy towards the old gentleman considering his obvious current financial troubles and his subsequent fall from grace.

The major, likewise, appeared to warm towards Harry when, during the natural enquiry into his background, Harry had related quite openly an outline of the career and domestic break-ups that had led to him suffering depression during the previous year. Perhaps it had been the unaccustomed influence of the wine that had led Harry to such candid exposure of his failings, but, rather than feeling diminished, Harry felt good to be able to state his recent failings in front of their host and to demonstrate that it was no secret to Elizabeth either.

The evening meal passed pleasantly enough with sufficient cordiality between them all, though Maude had only appeared at the table later and in order to take Grace to bed. Elizabeth had asked Grace to kiss her grandfather goodnight and Harry had also been pleasurably surprised to receive a hug around the neck from her too.

Elizabeth also gave each of the men a chaste kiss upon the cheek when retiring quite early to her bedroom, before the major and Harry then took easy chairs beside the fire to savour a generous glass of brandy that the host poured from a waiting decanter. Harry had been a little reluctant to join him in drinking brandy since in his inexperienced drinking past, he had found the spirit to be quite harsh, but again Harry had been impressed by its depth and smoothness. Its pervading warmth allowed him to relax even more and, although they did not drift into further revelations of their pasts or weaknesses, Harry began to believe that there might just be grounds for a decent relationship to develop between the two of them.

A small incident the next day would, however, dispel such belief.

*

Christmas Day had begun well, as it always should.

Thankfully, Harry had put on a tie and his best pair of trousers, since as he entered it was clear that the three females had certainly dressed for the occasion. Grace and her mother wore dresses made from matching material – a quiet tartan of blues and greens – and both wore a string of pearls at the neck. It made Harry smile to see Grace dressed so sophisticatedly yet still appearing so innocent and childlike as she bounced around the room in her excitement.

'You look nice,' he smiled at Elizabeth, who returned the smile with her lips if not with her eyes. She appeared nervous.

There was still something of a chill in the air, despite the fire in the living room having been rekindled. A procession of presents had been lined up along the mantelpiece above the fire, to which Harry hastily added his own. As Harry turned back from the hearth Major Hall was there in full regimental dress including trousers in the same tartan as his daughter and grand-daughter. He took a tray of filled glasses from the hands of Mrs Frobisher, who stood behind him: lemonade for Grace and sherry for the adults. They each raised a glass as the major addressed them all with a hearty 'slainte mhath' then, following his example, they downed the contents. The sherry, rich and smooth though it was, hit the back of Harry's throat like a globule of fire and he spluttered dramatically to his embarrassment and to the sincere amusement of all the others, who had coped easily in emptying their own glasses, even Maude.

Despite the initial shock, the sherry spread warmly down Harry's throat and seemingly across his chest, making him laugh spontaneously, again to the amusement of the others. Harry's inadequacy with drinking sherry had at least broken any ice that may have formed in the room earlier.

Despite their merriment having been induced by alcohol, everyone appeared to enjoy the opening of presents, modest though most of them were. Harry's wish to buy something personal, but not too intimate for each of the females had finally and unimaginatively resulted in slippers for all three: a reserved and traditional pair for Maude; a more contemporary and expensive pair with small red hearts upon them for Elizabeth, which for some reason made him blush slightly as she opened them; and a pair shaped like fluffy rabbits for Grace, who said they were her favourite thing in the whole world. Even Maude smiled, however, as Harry described his clandestine efforts to check out the correct sizes from looking into their existing pairs. For the host he had bought a bottle of what he hoped was really good quality Cava. His wise friend, Howard, epicurean though he was, had often gone on at length about the unnecessary expense of Champagne against other sparkling wines, so Harry had thought it a good choice: though after the previous evening's French wine and brandy, it was one that he now regretted.

There was more amusement as Harry opened his own package, which had been addressed simply 'to Harry from Grace, Elizabeth and Maude'. Harry guessed upon the contents halfway through the opening and joined in the laughter as his present was revealed as … yes, slippers!

The major had presented a gift for Grace alone. It was obvious to all adults there that the wrapping paper contained a small globe, though Grace opened it with relish and did a good job hiding her bewilderment and disappointment when it was fully revealed. She was able to move on quickly to her present from Maude, who had unashamedly bought her a very life-like girl doll and who had guessed correctly how much it would please the innocent teenager.

Grace's present from her mother was quite small. She pulled the paper off quite clumsily to reveal a jewellery case, which she struggled to open. Elizabeth came to her aid, opening the case, placing the enclosed pendant around Grace's neck, and then steering her towards a mirror. Grace goggled at it, not quite knowing how to react. Shyly, she moved into the circle of adults so that they could inspect her present as well. It was a simple pendant with a single stone, but the quality of the gem was so apparent that it dazzled them all.

'Is that real?' her grandfather exclaimed openly.

'Yes,' replied Elizabeth. 'It's a sapphire from Sri Lanka.'

She hesitated and took a deep breath. It was given to her, she told them, while she was on the island, and by a very dear and precious friend, and her voice caught emotionally on the pronunciation of the adjectives. Only just recently, she continued, had she found enough courage to have it set in a pendant of white gold for her precious daughter: and her voice and emotion caught on the words again.

The other three adults also took in a deep and meaningful breath: partly from knowing just a little of her relationship with the dear and precious friend in Sri Lanka; partly from recognising a mother's love for her daughter; and partly in awe of the gemstone's startling beauty. It would have been easy to guess at the reasoning behind the friend's choice of stone, since its sky-blue purity reflected almost exactly the hue of both the mother and daughter's eyes: a blue that was also shared, though in slightly faded shades, by both Grace's grandfather and his remote sister.

It was a moving and gratifying scene, though Harry could not help feeling a tinge of regret that his own growing affection for Elizabeth was somewhat outshone by what he imagined had existed between her and her Sri Lankan partner before. It was almost a relief when Mrs Frobisher entered with another tray of sherry-filled glasses, and both mother and daughter decided that the pendant should be put away for the time being.

Sherry before breakfast on Christmas Day was, Harry had been informed, a tradition within Creake House that even Maude and Elizabeth followed. Naturally, upon empty stomachs, the liquor made quite an impact, to which they reacted for some time in fits of puerile laughter and hilarity as they shared a breakfast of bacon and scrambled eggs on toast.

Their Christmas breakfast had been an unexpected episode of tensionless fun, though, as always with such stimulants, their spirits and emotions inevitably dropped as the effects of the alcohol wore off. Unfortunately this natural reaction of dropping emotions plunged to its unwelcome nadir as the major approached his traditional assault on Grace's academic prowess, or rather her lack of it.

'Come to me, my dear,' he commanded her in near military style, 'let us see how you have been progressing with your studies.'

Grace looked across at both her mother and Harry. She even had the temerity to smile, despite her reluctance to take part in the anticipated test.

'Let me ask you a simple mathematical question … are you ready?'

She smiled. He hesitated and looked around the room.

'What is … tell me … … four times six!?'

Harry felt that Grace had looked at him as if he had betrayed her. The adults looked at the mean old man as if he had betrayed them all.

They all stared at the frozen smile on the major's face. It was as if not only the scene in the room, but time itself had frozen to await the answer.

Their numbed suspension was eventually broken by a tiny tear that began its sorrowful course down the length of one innocent and delicate cheek. An instant later Maude stepped across the room to remove the victim from her unfair and uncalled for ordeal.

'Why didn't you ask her the three times table?' Elizabeth whispered out.

'Well, I knew she had a tutor. And I guessed she just might have been practising,' came the vindictive, almost victorious, reply. He held his frozen smile for a while longer, until, in the face of Elizabeth and Harry's silent, but unmistakeable, abhorrence, it eventually faded.

Harry moved to within a very short distance of the man, fighting to overcome his own bitter animosity and aggression in the face of his old age and obvious frailty.

'You bloody fool!' was all he could say before escaping from the room, grabbing his coat and stomping off outside.

Harry was eventually rescued from his trance of bitterness and disbelief by Elizabeth, who came up from behind to wrap her arms around him. At first he resisted in an attempt to keep out anything that might intrude into his own private anguish, but realisation that it was her and the desire to be close to her prevailed, and Harry allowed himself back into consciousness.

'Do you have to go through that every year?'

She nodded.

'Why does he do it?'

She shook her head. 'Why? Why does he do it?' she considered gently, before realising with some insight, for perhaps the first time. 'I don't know, but I think that, deep down, he hates himself more than we do. And he is so powerless in his own failure that he can't help himself from taking it out on someone else … on Grace.'

She allowed the thought to hang in the air between them.

'It's not fair! It's so juvenile!'

She nodded again.

'You shouldn't have to put up with it!'

She nodded, then shook her head. Harry was beginning to feel slightly juvenile himself.

'You don't have to come here each Christmas!'

She turned her face towards him. There was not a nod or a shake of her head this time.

'But I do have to come here! Come with me, I'll show you!'

Taking Harry's arm, she turned him around to face the length of the garden to the rear of the house. Like the front, it comprised a long expanse of lawn; this time running back to a clump of what appeared to be very old yew trees. As they approached the yews and the end of the garden, Harry could distinguish an arrangement of large stones within the circle of their protective embrace. Elizabeth took him right up to the stones, then dropped to her knees before the largest.

Harry watched intently as she stretched out her forefinger to the letters moulded there on a bronze plaque attached to the stone. Her finger moved along the lines, not like a blind woman reading braille, but, he realised as he followed the letters himself and allowed their significance to sink in, like a mother lovingly caressing the anguished memory of her lost child.

'In Loving Memory of
Samuel Jay Hall
Born and Deceased
29th February, 1984.
Rest in Peace.'

'That's Grace's birth date!' Harry breathed to register his presence next to her.

'Yes ... they were twins.'

Harry knelt beside her and put his arm around Elizabeth's shoulder as huge sobs began to shake through her whole body. After a while she rose to her feet. Harry looked down into her large eyes. Little pearls of tears trickled down to join those around her throat.

'Elizabeth, I ...' he began, but quickly she raised her finger to touch his lips and silence them.

She held Harry's gaze for a while and he tried unsuccessfully to read what lay behind her tearful eyes, but then she turned and he followed her back to the house. Just before entering she looked back towards the circle of yews just one more time, choking back a final, forlorn sob as she did so. The sob and the sorrow etched across her face gave Harry some suggestion to the depth of the desperate sadness that she held inside.

*

Within half an hour they had packed and departed. Elizabeth and the old man had shaken hands at the door, but no words had been exchanged. The rest of them had been quick to seek the refuge of the car, ready for their quiet journey back to Bede House.

The rest of the day passed quietly also. Harry tried to lift their mood by lighting a few of the crystals of myrrh, but this time around the aroma merely felt oppressive. When Grace and Maude had departed to their bedrooms Harry had begun to make his own farewell, but Elizabeth had asked him to stay. So he sat there with her on the settee sipping the hot chocolate that she had brought from the kitchen.

'Did you name the little boy after his father?'

It took a while for Elizabeth to answer.

'Samuel was a name we had shared … for … if one day we were to have a son. And Jay … was the name of … the man … that I loved.' It was clear that it took a good deal of pain for her to speak these words, and even more for the sentence that followed. 'But he was not the father of Samuel and Grace.'

'Do you mean there was someone else?' Harry pursued for reasons that were uncertain to him, even though he could see the distress it was causing.

Again it took a while for her to compose herself.

'There was never anyone else,' she whispered, unable to meet his look.

'But ...'

'I ... I ... was raped ... The very same day that I learned of Jay's death ... I was at ... he ... he was my boss ... ... and he ... I was raped!'

The control that she had forced across her face held for a while against the anguish wrought by the memory and by the simple statement of fact. Harry's own body ached with sympathy and support though he was unable to put it into words. She turned her eyes to him to wrest a small, contrived smile just for Harry's sake. But then the emotion that had been concealed for so long broke: her smile collapsed like sand before a wave. For the second time on that fateful Christmas Day she wept, and again Harry just held her until the sobs finally stopped.

Elizabeth remained quiet for the next couple of days, though Harry did get to see her every day and she did appear content with his presence there. After all the dramatic events and revelations of Christmas it was right that the days should be calmer and more routine.

Grace had lost the sparkle of anticipation that had coloured her cheeks before that day of unmitigated harshness in Norfolk. They still shared stories, but she was reluctant to leave the house or even to join in with anything else. To be fair, the unfortunate girl was still ailing from the illness that she had suffered through December and her mother regularly reminded them that it would take quite a while for her to recover.

To make up for Grace's absence as a walking companion, Elizabeth had agreed to accompany Harry for walks. Though they were generally quiet companions, they did share that powerful sense of intimacy that grows from just walking with someone. She soon took to slipping her arm through Harry's and it was more than pleasant for him to wander the promenade or the town's placid parks and avenues with her.

And, thankfully, there was Moses' birthday to look forward to, which gave them all reason to be more cheerful.

*

The day of Moses' eightieth birthday arrived with a pleasant sense of excitement, though it was cold and grey and not at all in keeping with what any of them would have wished for on such an auspicious event. Harry met Grace and Elizabeth at Bede House so that they could walk to Moses' place together: though she had made a cake with pleasure, Maude had declined the invitation to attend.

Harry thought to himself that the three of them must have made an amusing pageant of colour as they walked along through the greyness of Scarborough Avenue, one behind the other with their brightly wrapped presents in their arms before them.

On arrival they placed their presents proudly upon the table in what Moses called his 'parlour', after being welcomed in by Eadie, whom Harry introduced to Elizabeth. The two women appeared to instantly strike up an open, friendly relationship, which certainly pleased Harry, who was anxious for two of the few people in his life to get on well together.

Moses did not appear for a further five minutes, which was long enough for his arrival to create a minor tremor of drama. Grace immediately leapt to her feet as he came into the room and clapped her hands together, prompting the adults to applaud also.

'Don't know why yer all clappin'' he grumbled quite cheerily. 'Getting' old aren't no cause to clap a person!'

'No, but reaching eighty in such good condition is!'

And then he was able to enjoy the warmth of their attention while pretending that he thought it uncalled for. Grace, of course, was eager for Moses to open the presents, especially her own. Harry thought that she had not had too many opportunities to give them and she was keen to enjoy this one. Moses lived up to the expectation, showing delight in her story and making her read it out loud to him. Grace read beautifully without any sign of inhibition in front of all the adults and Harry could tell that, like him, Moses and Eadie were touched by her innocence and charm. At the end of the story her mother expressed her pride as well so that Grace was almost beside herself with pleasure. Certainly, for her, it seemed like the best party ever, though she must have been just a little perplexed by the mixture of emotions that followed.

Moses had nothing but candid pleasure in opening Elizabeth's box to reveal an immaculately iced birthday cake. Then opening the brown paper around Harry's painting prompted a clearly evident clash of emotions.

'That's Old Bob's place all right!' he let out with an emotive sigh. Then his eyes watered and he was moved to turn away. 'Thank you, lad,' he managed to breathe out eventually.

'My pleasure,' Harry assured him. 'But I think you had better sit down for the next one!'

Moses eyed Harry suspiciously, but did as asked, joining Eadie on the settee. When she handed him a neatly wrapped but unpretentious envelope, his expression not only became more suspicious, but rather anxious too.

'What's all this then, Eadie?' he enquired, but she just nodded her encouragement for him to open it. Moses did so.

Moses took out the contents of the envelope and stared at them for a long time. He stared at Eadie and then back at the envelope. The three other spectators looked at the two of them with increasing anticipation and apprehension. Unlike Harry, Grace and Elizabeth did not know what the contents of the envelope were, but they could tell that Moses was battling with his emotions.

'I can't take these ... I can't do that! ... I can't just go!' he exclaimed to Eadie.

'Course you can!' she replied. 'You're a strong man. And you're a father!'

'What is it?' Grace chipped in, unable to deal with the suspense and drama of not knowing.

'They're tickets,' he told her as if finding relief in a simple explanation of fact. 'They're aeroplane tickets ... to ... to Australia! I can't take these, Eadie ... I can't go all the way to Australia!'

'Yes you can, Moses,' she told him calmly but tenderly. 'You can get on that plane and go to Australia ... and meet your Alec ... and tell him you're sorry ... and tell him how much you love him.'

Moses regarded her with affectionate exasperation and began to shake his head. Eadie engaged him earnestly once more before he could gain any momentum to his denial.

'You can get on that plane and go to Australia ... and ... and see your boy ... before it's too late.' Eadie remained calm but emphatic. 'Because if you don't you'll never forgive yourself ... and neither will I!'

Moses looked like a man trapped. He glanced briefly, perhaps desperately, at the others, but then, realising that there was to be no escape, turned his eyes back to Eadie. She smiled at him.

'And if you look, Moses, you can see there are two sets of tickets ... I'm coming with you!'

After a moment of further, tense stillness while he continued to visually scrutinise the tickets, Moses lifted his eyes to Eadie's encouraging smile.

'OK,' he said simply. 'I aren't sure, but I guess we'd better go!'

The room exhaled in relief and considerable happiness. Harry dragged Grace and her mother out into the kitchen to make tea while the two old would-be-adventurers gently held hands and appraised themselves of the journey and the challenge ahead. By the time they had begun to ferry the sandwiches and golden-brown pastries into the parlour, Eadie had already extricated herself from their collective conjectures to help them arrange the party food that she had so assiduously assembled for them all. Moses continued to sit on the settee and shake his head in wonder.

'Well, well, well,' was all he could utter until Elizabeth sent Grace to bring him to the table. Then Moses managed to bring himself back to some semblance of being a host and they were all able to enjoy a celebration of his birthday, even though the rest of the afternoon paled into mundane normality in comparison to the mildly sensational giving of presents that preceded it.

Greetings in anticipation of the new year were exchanged and all the visitors returned to their homes in a state of awe, which was, nonetheless, milder than that of Moses.

JANUARY

Harry awoke to the new year with the sensation that there was something special in the air. On opening his curtains it was just light enough for him to make out large flakes of snow whirling silently down through the stillness. The snowflakes kissed the ground only to melt so that as soon as the flurry had ceased and passed there was not even enough snow on the ground to show any sign of their falling at all. Harry felt slightly saddened that he had been unable to share the moment. But then he realised that a short walk would soon bring him to those people with whom he would most like to share the snowflakes and simply everything else in his quiet life. And that thought made him feel special again as he dressed for the day and the new year ahead.

Though there was no further snow the skies remained uncertain for the first few days of the new year. On the Saturday Grace had declined the invitation to join him for a walk so Harry took Elizabeth down to the lake. There had not been enough light in the January sky to show up the lustre of the lake, so they went inside together to share tea and scones in the little, old-fashioned café that sat beside the waters and the collection of boats moored there. Even in the dullness and sat amongst the sedate clinking of teaspoons and china, Harry soon felt the stirring of emotions within him that came from his growing affinity for the woman whom he realised he had come to love. Against his better judgement and seemingly involuntarily, he suddenly unburdened these feelings to Elizabeth.

In a spoken revelation that shocked himself, let alone Elizabeth, he told her that, though he enjoyed just being together with her, he was worried that he would never mean more to her than just being a friendly companion.

'Because,' he told her softly, 'I don't just want to be your friend … I want to love you … I mean I do … … … I love you!'

And as Harry spoke those simple, but distinctive, last three words, the other half dozen occupants of the café had, as if with mystical intuition, completely stopped their own conversations, so that Harry's words fell with unintended, but deafening, effect into a pristine vacuum of silence.

The two of them shrank into themselves in embarrassment. It would not have surprised Harry if the aged ensemble had broken into applause, but they did not and after a few seconds the others returned to their conversations as if nothing had happened.

But, there in those unpretentious tea-rooms, something had happened for the two of them. They continued to sit as if in suspended animation, though inside Harry was panicking: it was all so far removed from anything that he might have imagined as being a suitable time or place for such words and meaning.

Elizabeth showed no sign of emotion for some time before looking up to deliberately meet Harry's stare. She still said nothing and he could feel his own heartbeats as he waited for a response. The waiting felt like an eternity.

Then at last, she smiled.

And it felt immediately as if the sun of good fortune had suddenly broken out from behind all those clouds of doubt and misgiving. She still did not speak, but the smile was sincere enough, and good enough for Harry to allow a great surge of happiness to well up inside. She had not spoken to accede to his eccentric outburst, but at least his hope had not been crushed. He looked out to see that the sun had physically as well as metaphorically broken through.

'Come on. Let's walk back before the sun disappears!'

As they made their way out of the café, one of the old ladies there stretched out her hand to lightly touch Elizabeth's wrist. Harry thought she was going to say something wise or congratulatory, but she too just simply smiled serenely and the couple passed by without comment.

Outside the café they looked back at the remaining patrons of the café, who were still staring through the windows, looked at each other and then laughed. A skein of Canadian pink-footed geese landed on the water beside them in a shattering of reflected sunlight, which Harry took as a perfect flypast to mark the moment.

They walked, arm in arm, back to Bede House without further incident and almost without further conversation. Harry felt that they were comfortable in their quietness together and he did not mind that the rest of the world was taking no notice at all. Just a moment before they reached the door of Bede House, however, Elizabeth put her hand on his chest to halt him. She appeared to be searching for the right words, though when they finally came the message was consummately simple.

'You must be patient with me, Harry.'

Inside Bede House it took some restraint on Harry's part not to mention anything to Grace or Maude, who appeared to find it quite natural that the returning couple should sit quietly on the settee, contemplating the intricacies of the Persian rug and smiling contentedly together.

*

The days passed. All too soon Elizabeth had, with naturally some reluctance, returned to working long days. Harry continued to visit Grace in the afternoons. He had been pleased to note a slight but gradual improvement in her health, so that he had felt confident in encouraging her out for a walk.

'Come on, smasher … got to make the most of the new year!'

'What happens in a new year, Harry?' Grace asked without looking up from her customary arrangement of dolls and pebbles set out on her windowsill. She had a way of asking seemingly simple questions that could absolutely stump him.

'Well … it's a chance to do things … differently … or better. That's why we make New Year's resolutions.'

'What are you going to do better, Harry?'

Another simple question that left him floundering.

'Well … I am going to … enjoy each day as much as I can!'

'How are you going to do that, Harry?' she enquired with complete sincerity on her face, though he did have a niggling feeling that she was just winding him up.

'Well … I'm not sure how, but I am sure that you can help.'

'And how can I help, Harry?'

'Well … you can stop asking any more difficult questions …' he prevaricated as realisation of being skilfully led up the garden path sank in, ' … before … I lock you up in a very dark dungeon!' he shouted, while gaining his feet to chase her playfully out onto the landing and down the stairs. Unfortunately, her laughter had quickly turned into a fit of coughing and breathlessness that left him quite worried and realising that he needed to take things more gradually with her.

'The most important thing we have to do is to get you fit again … Let's get you out in the fresh air. How about a visit to Moses?'

On the strength of a nod and a smile they left straight away. They arrived to find Moses rooting around in his garage where he told them that he was sorting things out before his big trip to Australia.

'I found a little present for you, princess!' he told her. 'Close your eyes an' 'old out your 'ands. See if you can guess what it is!'

Grace stood still with eyes closed and hands held out. She loved this sort of game. Moses placed a small object onto her upturned palms. Grace was unsure: she kept her eyes closed, but started to squirm around in embarrassment and uncertainty.

'Go on,' encouraged Moses, 'you've got to guess!'

'I don't know.' Grace was beginning to get a little insecure under the pressure.

'I don't know! And I can even see it!' Harry interrupted.

'You don't know!' Moses admonished him. 'Look ... keep your eyes closed, princess, an' I'll give you a clue.'

Moses took the article from her hands, held it to his lips, and blew. A strange humming and buzzing noise came from the trinket causing them all to laugh.

'I don't know ... it sounds rude!' said Grace, which, in turn, had Moses filled with amusement.

'Open your eyes an' look then!'

It was a remarkably fine object in the shape of a duck's bill made, Moses informed them, in silver and ivory. He then went on to explain to Grace that men hid in the reeds to blow the 'duck caller' so that other ducks flying by would think it was another real duck and land on the water nearby.

'That's nice,' said Grace, '... what do they do then?'

Moses looked at Harry mischievously, but Harry shook his head at him firmly.

'Oh, I expects they jus' gives 'em some bread or the like,' Moses told her at last. 'Any way, if you creeps into the kitchen an' blows it 'ard, you might just wake up Eadie … an' get a slice o' bread yourself! … Go on, gal … see if you can find 'er.'

Grace crept toward the house on tiptoes.

'She's not really asleep in there is she?' Harry asked in concern.

'No, you barmpot! Course she's not … I think she's bakin' or sommut. But she'll be 'appy to see the lass … I reckon she loves 'er like 'er own already. She would o' made a great gran'ma, but never 'ad no kids of 'er own. Reckon that's why she's been so set on findin' our Alec fo' me … She's even got a private detectives on the case in Australia.'

'And what about you? Aren't you keen?'

'Well, I am … I knows I did 'im wrong … an' sayin' sorry to 'im is something I'd like to do more than anythin', but … but I'm just not sure.'

'Well, you should be sure, Moses! If I could meet my dad or my mum again … and I know I can't … but if I could and they said something like "sorry" to me … then it would just be … the best thing!'

As Harry spoke the words there was an ache inside him like a cry trying to escape. He realised that he had never thought about his parents like that before, but the thought of some kind of reconciliation with them made him feel very sad and very happy at the same time.

'You do it, Moses … It might just be the best thing you ever did!'

Harry felt like telling Moses that he loved him too, but two people in one week would have been too much, so they just shared a grin before Eadie appeared at the door. Grace was hanging on to her arm and laughing enthusiastically.

'Quick, Moses! ... We've got a duck in the kitchen!' the old woman cried.

'You never 'ave!' he cried with great gusto so that Grace laughed louder, though Harry imagined that Moses' own surge of passion might have been more to do with his release from the emotion that surrounded the old man's prospective paternal reunion.

'Well, just one little duck!' announced Eadie producing an iced cake from beneath her apron with an iced image of a duck in its centre. Grace clapped her hands wildly and danced around more enthusiastically than Harry had seen her do so for a long time. Predictably, however, Grace's delight was cut short by a further bout of coughing that hushed all the adults into worried silence.

Grace did recover enough for them all to enjoy their tea and cake before Harry took her home. Despite the bout of coughing, he was pleased that some brightness had appeared at last into her complexion and hoped that she was on the way to a full recovery soon. Certainly, on their return, Elizabeth noted that they both looked pleased and happy with themselves even before Grace began to regale her with noises from the silver duck caller.

*

Excepting his concerns over Grace's health, Harry had begun to meet each new day with an increasing sense of wellbeing. A year previously, before meeting Grace, he would not have been able to imagine that life could improve so dramatically, and he felt a wave of gratitude when he met her for an afternoon. Though his relationship with Elizabeth was still platonic in its expression, they were growing closer all the time, and the glimpses that she had allowed him into her troubled past had been more than enough to persuade him towards patience.

Now that Grace had resumed her college attendance, however, and Harry had more time to himself, the feeling of needing to gain more from life had begun to sit a little more uncomfortably upon his shoulders again. Moses was not unsympathetic, but tied up in his own plans. Eadie had persuaded Moses to travel with an open ticket so that they could set their return date depending upon what happened once they were in Australia. Though his trip had been planned to coincide with the quietest time of the year for gardens in England, he was anxious for Harry to register everything that needed to be done in all the various gardens with which he was involved so that everything would be in order on his return. Moses had persuaded him not to worry, though, inside, Harry was a little daunted by the prospect.

'You'll soon 'ave so much to do that you won't 'ave time to worry 'bout nothin'' Moses told him. 'Mother nature don't wait fo' no-one!'

'Nor does Mother Springthorpe!' Harry reminded his old friend and Moses was at least able to share the joke.

The next week Harry found Moses sorting furiously once more through boxes in one of the outhouses. The old man informed him, with a hint of panic in his eyes, that the departure date for the flights to Australia had been set for the first day of February.

'That's only a couple of weeks away!'

'I know that! Tha's why I'm gettin' organised!'

'But, what has sorting out all your old junk got to do with getting organised and prepared?'

The old man sat down in a slightly crumpled and crestfallen manner. 'I suppose … I suppose I don't really know how to get mi'sen prepared,' he admitted. 'An' what about all that gardenin'?'

Harry promised Moses sincerely that he would put his heart and soul into looking after his horticultural obligations, without knowing that subsequent events would conspire to push them completely from his thoughts.

'Life could be so simple,' the old man mused as Harry passed him a cup of tea, 'but we got an incredible 'abit of makin' it so complicated!'

'Come on, old timer. Give yourself a break,' said Harry to distract him. 'Elizabeth has to work this Saturday and I thought I'd take Grace to Brid' on the bus. How about coming with us?'

Despite his protestations at the time about having too much to do and about the chilling winds in January, Moses had gladly joined them for their Saturday excursion. Grace looked after Moses as if he had never been on a bus before, but the old man enjoyed her attention nevertheless.

The sun did its best to brighten the morning, though it was frequently masked by a ragtag procession of cloud that arrived inland on a chilling east wind. It was not long before the trio sought refuge from the chill in a promenade shelter. Unfortunately, the off-sea wind was blowing straight into their shelter, and Harry set off alone to find a café that might be open.

Harry had not been gone long so it was a shock on his return to find Moses holding Grace before him in a state of clear consternation.

'What's wrong?!'

'She said she saw "the Bastard"! ... I dunno ... that's what she said ... she saw "the Bastard" ... I didn't quite make it out at first ... There was a bloke ... but then 'e was gone ... I dunno!'

'She doesn't talk like that ...!' Harry looked at Moses in

confusion. Then he looked at Grace, who was staring with a somewhat glazed expression.

'Grace! What is it? Who was it?'

'It was "the Bastard" … that's what Mummy calls him. We don't like him. He's "the Bastard"!'

Harry looked into Grace's face, but it appeared that he was not going to get anything further. He ran off in the direction that Grace had been staring, but if there had been a man then he had disappeared.

Harry and Moses could hardly believe that their well-intended trip had turned so suddenly into such a calamitous mischance, even though it appeared to be turning into something of a habit for Harry. They did go into a café because Grace appeared so cold, but it was just a soulless interlude before they caught the bus home again.

Back at Bede House Elizabeth had been preparing a special tea to mark Maude's birthday. It was hard and sad for Harry to see her face turn so quickly from expectant pleasure to undeniable horror when he began to explain the morning's woebegone incident to her. The involuntary hand across her mouth and the wide-eyed dismay across her face told him without words that 'the Bastard' was by no means a figment of anyone's imagination.

Elizabeth ran up to Grace in her room. Harry could hear their muffled talking and crying before then hearing Elizabeth's erratic footfall across several of the upstairs rooms. More than an hour passed before Elizabeth was able to return downstairs to sit beside him. At first her talking and breathing had been just as erratic as her stomping around, but gradually she was able to inform him more clearly about the situation.

Her explanation was not far removed from the guess that had entered Harry's mind on the bus journey back. 'The Bastard' was real. And he was, without doubt, the darkest of her mother's living nightmares. He was the man who had been her director in Sri Lanka, the man who had taken cruellest advantage of her vulnerability when Jay had died by callously and brutally raping her. Harry could, through the empty ache in his own gut, just begin to imagine how awfully the revelation presented itself to Elizabeth.

He held her tightly in his arms, but there was no joy between them, only horrific anticipation.

Elizabeth went on to explain that this man had tried to make contact with her on several occasions before. It was the reason why she and Maude and Grace had moved house so many times. It was also, Harry imagined, the reason behind her safe room in the tower of Bede House. And, he imagined further, the reason why she found it so difficult to relax into a relationship with another man.

'He's bound to find us now!'

'Yes ... and when he finds you ... I will find him!'

*

Moses had listened in almost silence while Harry had related all he knew about 'the Bastard'. Like Harry, Moses had been able to understand why Elizabeth had not been able over the years to take her problem to anyone in authority, not even her father. They had both learned enough over their years to understand to some degree how a woman's plight is so often not easily appreciated or even accepted by society.

Moses kept his thoughts to himself, however, even when Harry had explained his own intention to seek retribution with 'the Bastard'. 'It seems he just lives his life like what he has done doesn't matter!' Harry had uttered in quiet anger. 'Well ... he needs to know how much it matters to me!'

The days passed very slowly for Harry. At first both Grace and Elizabeth had stayed home from college and work, but after a week without any sign of the dreaded Mr Samuels, as Harry learned the dreaded person was named, they began to hope that Grace's sighting might have been a mistake after all, and life began to return to some semblance of normality.

Unfortunately, the strain on Grace's emotions had impaired her progress towards better health, even though she had managed three days at college. Harry had taken her around to Moses' place on several occasions, where she chatted to the old man as he continued with his reorganisation of the outhouse collection, or where she was able to enjoy helping Eadie in the kitchen.

At last it was time for her and Harry to say goodbye to the old couple, since on this final day of January they had decided upon 'an early night' before the next day's travel. They planned to leave early the next morning, driving to a friend's house in York, where they would leave Eadie's car before taking the train to London.

There were sincere and hearty hugs all round. Harry was naturally happy for his old pal to be embarking on what he was sure would be an epic trip, but he felt genuinely sorry, and a little anxious, to be losing Moses' company at such a time. He hid it as best he could behind nonchalance and a promise to take care of all the gardening. Grace had noticed the sadness as well as happiness between them, though Harry was sure that she had no concept of 'a month or two'. She was unusually quiet as they left to make their way home.

The onset of evening had brought rain. There had been just a few droplets as they had left Moses and Eadie, but before long they were pushing themselves through a downpour, which had soaked their outer clothes by the time they arrived back to Bede House. At the door and despite the rain, Grace stopped to look back anxiously over her shoulder, but it had been nothing more than the growing storm hammering against the hedges. Harry led her in before hanging his dripping duffle coat on one of the walking sticks of the stand in the hallway. He then took Grace up to her room where they immersed themselves in the comfort of *Shadow the Sheepdog*.

Elizabeth's anxiety when she arrived later, wet and panting inside the hallway, was far more palpable. Grace and Harry had, as usual, rushed down the stairs to meet her.

'I might be imagining things … in this weather … but I am sure … I think … something … someone … was watching me!'

Harry felt the pins and needles of nervous anticipation across his shoulders and neck. He paused to imagine how frightened the three females of the house would be feeling. He felt the need to take hold of their situation.

'Right … now it is probably nothing … and I know no-one is hungry … but we are going to sit down at the table … like we usually do … and we are going to eat and drink something … and … and think about what we are going to do,' he told them with as much calm as he could manage.

Indeed, no-one at the table had appetite for more than the merest portions of food, but the ritual of serving and sitting together did give them enough composure to share their thoughts.

Despite Harry's initial urging they eventually agreed that, even accepting Elizabeth's reluctance to talk to anyone outside about her past mistreatment, there was not enough substantial evidence to involve the police right then. Harry's other natural inclination had been to call Moses, but he knew that the old man and Eadie would have already taken to their beds for their early night, and so he had reluctantly ruled that option out.

'We'll just have to sleep on it and decide what to do in the morning. I can't imagine that anyone is out there in this terrible rain, so we'll lock—'

Harry's forced calm was shattered by a desperate scream from Elizabeth. She ran out frantically from the table shouting 'The doors! … I haven't even checked the doors yet!'

Thankfully, her trepidation on that account proved unwarranted. All the doors and windows were checked and found to be completely secured. But it had been an unwelcome jolt to everyone's nerves.

'God, I could do with a drink!' Harry declared, and it was Maude who found the decanter to pour him a large measure of brandy. The women gathered round Harry as if he would be able to solve their problems.

'Look … I'm going to sleep right here on the settee and make sure … make sure we all have a calm, safe night. Then … in the morning we'll think about … what we can do.'

Harry had delivered his thought with as much confidence and authority as he could gather. For the moment at least it seemed to suffice. The women quietly sorted themselves and said goodnight to him.

'Thank you, Harry.' Grace and Elizabeth both planted tentative kisses on Harry's cheek and he settled down to enjoy the brandy and his own bravado. He felt good to be the man of the house doing what he knew was right.

'Take care,' Elizabeth whispered to him in what Harry took to be a loving way.

'You take care too. And don't worry ... I'm not going to do anything stupid!'

The small sips of brandy had spread warmth and comfort through Harry. It was a pity that he had not lit a fire since the lashing rain outside had brought considerable coldness to the house, but he snuggled down as best he could beneath the blankets that had been provided. His clothes had pretty much dried and he thought that he would be able to sleep without too much bother. There had been no sound from upstairs for a while and he imagined that all the women had already succumbed to sleep. As he tucked the blanket even more securely around himself, he considered that, despite the earlier anxiety, he was pleased to be in such an assured position within the household. Perhaps, he thought to himself, some clouds do have silver linings. He managed a small smile.

Then a sudden burst of electricity exploded in the back of his head. The piercing sound of the front door bell burst with alarming penetration into his consciousness like a drill. It rang for only a few seconds, but its effect was like a bullet into Harry's fragile cocoon of security.

Harry leapt up from his makeshift bed and ran to the door. He put his hand to the handle, but then hesitated: no, worse than hesitated: he froze. His brain seemed to have been shocked out of rational thought, though he would have liked to have blamed the brandy for making him so indecisive. He ran to the foot of the stairs. No sound came from above: there was just the interminable resonance of the bell echoing around Harry's cranium.

Harry forced his brain back into rational action. He padded silently up the stairs so that he could peer through the window above the door. Despite its devastating effect upon his own senses, the ring had seemingly not woken the others: Grace always slept through everything; Maude had, no doubt, detached her hearing-aid; and Elizabeth, he learned later, had taken a sleeping pill. Harry was on his own: apart, of course, from the unknown presence outside.

Harry stood at the top of the stairs with the pulses of his own heartbeats pounding into the silence that had returned to his ears. Somehow the passivity of the bedroom doors, or more likely his love for the women behind them, enabled Harry to steel his determination. What had been initial shock and fear was gradually replaced by an even more powerful sense of anger: burning anger against all the evil that Samuels had done to those women. And not just anger, but a thirst for retribution against the Bastard.

Another look through the landing window revealed nothing other than incessant rain, but Harry was now on a mission. He crept quietly back down the stairs with as much stealth as he could command, then, leaving aside his duffle, but gathering up the heavy, ivory-tipped walking stick beneath it, he moved furtively out through the front door.

The slap of ice-cold rain hit him like a blow, but as the door clicked closed behind him he was able to discern a movement of shadow amongst the laurels near the gate. The frightful lunge of Harry's heavy stick came down with sickening power, but met nothing more substantial than the limp leaves and twigs of the laurel. He looked around wildly in the drenching darkness and, suddenly, there was more movement: someone was running away along the avenue.

Without thought, Harry gave chase. He could just make out the running figure in the meagre streetlight, though, as housing gave way to fields, the fleeing image disappeared from his view. Harry stopped at the bridle path. He had only run a few hundred yards, but his chest was already heaving. The insides of his lungs burned like torrents of magma and running had become pure pain. But he pushed himself on. Sensing rather than seeing, he made his way down the bridle path and on into the drenching blackness, his feet struggling for grip in the sodden ground beneath them. It was dark and wet, but his hunch was rewarded by another blurred glimpse of the running figure ahead.

Pure rage pushed him on further. The rain had frozen his exposed head and hands into bloodless whiteness, but he gripped that heavy stick with grim determination and kept going. Though it was hard going for Harry, it must have been even harder for his quarry, since Harry was edging closer.

By the time they had reached the cliff top path Harry could even hear the gasping breath of his prey just yards ahead. Harry hoped that Samuels was even more drained than he felt himself.

Though Harry did not know it the fugitive certainly was struggling. His exhausted body soon slumped into an inert heap right there on the path in front of his pursuer.

Indeed, Samuels was so breathless, so frozen and so scared, that he could barely hold his hands up in front of him as he cringed before Harry in pathetic submission right there on the cliff's edge. He could retreat no further. Harry staggered forward into striking range and lifted his heavy stick in a menacing arc above his head ready to silence the Bastard forever.

'You evil bastard ... you ruined that woman's life ... and now you're going to pay!' He had barely enough breath to speak, but there was enough strength left in his arms and enough hate in his gut to do the deed.

Samuels, Harry knew it must have been him, whimpered like a child, though Harry was close enough to see by the faint phosphorescent light of the rainwater that ran across the furrowed face that Samuels had become an old man: a pitiable, old man who was now too weak to even cover his head with his hands. He was completely beaten and defenceless.

Harry stood above Samuels with unchallenged power, his face contorted in hate and his body tensed to bring the stick finally crashing down. He hesitated. It was back to the petrified rabbits of his boyhood. He was mighty in victory, he was blind with fury, and he was determined, but he was no killer.

He stood there above Samuels in frozen indecision. And instantly, the old man knew it: the hunted was about to become the hunter. From somewhere Samuels found the strength to raise his head. He had no room for compassion: if his attacker was too squeamish to finish him off, then Samuels would fatally punish the weak fool.

Harry recognised the reversal too. Indecision had changed to fear. He could sense that his former prey was struggling to his feet. And, in that moment of fearful self-preservation, Harry found, at last, the drive and determination to bring down that wicked walking stick with brutal finality.

There was an almighty roar as Harry hauled down his weapon. But rather than feel the sickening thud of the stick upon Samuels unprotected head, his blow fell upon emptiness.

Harry reeled from the deafening assault upon his ears. The huge roar veritably hammered against his brain and shook his whole frame. He gaped forward into the echoing bellow of noise, but there was nothing there to see: nothing at all. He realised with shock that he was standing on what had suddenly become the new edge of the cliff. Whatever had been there before had crashed with a rumbling roar into the raging sea below: tons and tons of disintegrating clay, which had lain so peacefully beneath the quiet pathway of their favourite walks, had suddenly and violently disappeared forever.

Harry remained in petrified numbness on the new edge of the cliff. His powers of reasoning had been, seemingly, swept away by an instance of natural destruction so powerful that it had taken the last ounces of his strength and determination with it. He just stood there in the tumultuous uproar of noise, trembling on the precipice. The crumbling cliff had taken the Bastard and Harry stood waiting for the natural force to take him too. He just stood there.

But then he was moving involuntarily, back from the brink of destruction and back down the bridle path to security. He did not know how he came to find his way back. It was as if some benevolent power outside of himself had wrapped its arm around his shoulders to propel him homeward.

His faltering footsteps finally stopped before the welcome sight of a familiar front door. His last dregs of energy took him up the stairs and onto a familiar bed where he, at last, allowed himself to sink completely into the depths of deep sleep.

FEBRUARY

Harry awoke the next day with a start, like he had fallen from a bad dream. His body ached and he was very thirsty. He sat up onto the edge of the bed to begin moving his arms and legs in slow stretches despite his muscles complaining at the movement. He noticed that he was still wearing his clothes, though his drenched and mud-splattered shoes had been placed neatly together on the rug beside the bed. He could not remember placing them there and thought it strange that he had taken the bother to do so.

He looked around. Though the room was as familiar as ever, Harry's shoulders sagged even more beneath a feeling of strange unknowing and apprehension. His mind was struggling to put the broken jigsaw of his thoughts and senses back into cogent order. Then, as he pulled back the curtains, he noticed that, though it was not raining, the lawn before the ash tree was drenched and full of puddles.

Then he remembered the storm.

Then he remembered everything.

Without pausing for the shower or drink that he desperately needed, Harry dashed downstairs. It took a few seconds to comprehend the absence of his duffle coat before he grabbed the donkey jacket that he usually wore when working with Moses and left. Hesitating momentarily at the gate to further recollect that his old friend must have, by then, already departed on his long flight to the other side of the world, Harry headed up the avenue towards Bede House.

Elizabeth met him at the door with troubled eyes, reflecting the emotional pandemonium into which the household had plunged since awaking to find their protector gone. She waited until he had taken a seat on the settee before beginning her earnest enquiry. 'Where were you, Harry? You said you would stay through the night ... and protect us!'

Harry looked down into the complexities of the Persian rug once more. He put his hands over his head, pulled them down over his face to rub his chin before looking back up into her eyes. He pulled her gently but firmly onto the leather settee to sit beside him.

'You can't imagine,' he began.

It was true that Elizabeth was not able to fully imagine the events of the previous, fateful night. She listened intently, and sometimes open mouthed, but without comment, until Harry had slowly and carefully related all the details that he thought she should know. There were some details, thoughts and feelings that he considered she was better not knowing. She continued to sit still even when he had stopped talking, as if unable to speak herself. Harry began to feel upset at her apparent unconcern for what he had been through, before she put her arms around him and wept as quietly as she could into his aching shoulder. Harry imagined that he could feel a lifetime of hurt and fear pour out from her with those tears.

'What shall we do now?' she managed at last.

'Well ... first I need a drink.'

'Shall I fetch you a brandy?'

'No. No more brandy for me. I could do with a cup of tea ... a nice cup of tea!'

Harry drank the tea as if doing something so normal as that could restore normality back to their situation. Elizabeth simply sat and watched him until he had swallowed the last drop. Harry then noticed her stare.

'What?'

'I'm just pleased that you are OK,' she told him. 'And ... and that ... that evil man has gone ... Do you think he is dead?' she added with a simplicity that stunned him.

'I don't know. He disappeared with the cliff and I suppose ... but I don't ... I suppose it was him ... I don't even ... and I suppose we should call the police!' he concluded at last with a course of action that had occurred to both of them, but which neither of them had really wished to consider fully.

Once it had been stated, Harry had no option but to pick up the phone and do just that.

He might have sat for a period of quiet reflection while waiting for the police to arrive had it not been for urgent talking upstairs. Elizabeth and Maude had presumed that Grace had been simply sleeping late to make up for all the previous evening's tension and excitement, but now it was becoming clear that there was something more serious and urgent about her condition. The two women had managed to partially awaken Grace, but she was hot, her pulse was racing and her speech was incoherent.

'Help me put her into the car, Harry,' her mother ordered with the night's proceedings apparently dismissed from consideration for something more urgent.

'I'm taking her straight back to that hospital!' she cried as if the return of Grace's poorliness had been their fault for some reason.

Harry carried Grace out to the car and was about to plead his case for accompanying them to the hospital when a man and a woman arrived at the gate. The woman was dressed in uniform, and there was no doubt in Harry's mind that the man was a police officer too.

As Elizabeth's car disappeared Harry and his two visitors went inside. It took quite a while for Harry to explain to Detective Inspector Blackwood, as the man had introduced himself, what was happening with the urgent departure of Elizabeth's car and the two of them inside, and why he was there at Bede House altogether, before he was able to even begin to explain what had happened concerning the events of the previous evening. He told them about the events of the previous day and night plainly, but as accurately as he could remember.

'Did you get any of that down ... DC ...?'

'Finch, sir ... DC Finch. Yes, sir. I made some notes, sir. Do you think, sir ...?'

Her superior officer, Blackwood, raised his finger to silence the Detective Constable from her thought or enquiry. 'Never mind thinking, Finch ... just do as you're asked.'

The manner of the concise order that had been made with such uncaring detachment and contempt for his female assistant, was just one of the things that caused Harry to form an initial dislike of the large, shoddily presented policeman. Another thing was the way in which Blackwood, as Harry simply named him in his own mind, constantly picked at his finger nails while thinking or speaking. At odds with the rest of his appearance, Blackwood's nails were surprisingly long and well-manicured. Still, Harry supposed, the man had not reached his position by trying to make himself likeable. It was not for Harry to either like or judge him, leastways, not yet. He supposed further that the judging would, at that time, be more for the police officers rather than himself.

'So, you say that the incident took place on t' cliff tops?' Blackwood asked, giving away a little of his origins at least.

Harry nodded.

'Well, lead on Mr Harry. Show me the way … Sparrow, 'ave a quick look round 'ere an' join us shortly.'

'Yes, sir … Finch, sir!'

Outside the morning was still grey, not just the sky, but the fields also in the dull light, though it remained rainless. Harry fairly dawdled along the way, almost as if in a dream: the ordinariness of the path and its surroundings felt so strange to him in comparison to the pain and tension of this same journey the night before.

The ardent Finch had caught them up by the time they had reached the vacant fields beside the cliffs. She looked young and unruffled beside them in her neat uniform, even though she must have run some of the way to catch them so quickly. Blackwood paid her no attention.

There was no cliff top path to find, of course, since it had disappeared into the sea awaiting the formation of a new one once the walkers and anglers had gained enough confidence to walk there again. The now quiet sea added to the morning's greyness, though the scars of fallen cliffs showed dark and brown against its edge.

'So where did you commit the deadly deed?'

'I did not commit any deadly deed!' Harry quickly corrected Blackwood: his dislike of the man helping him to remain calm and reserved.

'I did chase … follow him here, but then he stopped … we stopped … and suddenly he was gone!'

It was not the complete truth, by way of omission, but for once Harry was not in the mood for candid confession. He remained guarded and even obdurate with his new adversary.

'Well?'

'That's about it! I ... followed him ... we were both tired, exhausted ... and we ... and suddenly the cliff was gone ... and he was gone ... and then ...'

The policeman waited, but Harry was not falling into that trap. He stood silently and still to return the officer's stare. It lasted for some while before their stand-off was interrupted by Finch's excited interjection.

'Sir! Sir! There's a foot, sir! I can see a foot down there ... in the clag ... sir!'

She was joined by her superior, though not Harry, to stare down for a while at the morass of devastated cliffs and an incongruent, shoeless foot sticking out from beneath. They looked, but made no further comment.

Harry followed them back to Bede House. There he gave them details of himself, some details of Grace and Elizabeth, and the little he knew about the now presumed buried Samuels. He was warned not to leave the area without informing them and then the pair of police officers turned to leave. Blackwood remained expressionless, though DC Finch managed a small smile towards Harry, perhaps of encouragement or support, once her superior had already exited the room.

Through the window, Harry watched them depart. He was startled as he did so by movement from behind, but it was only Maude. He had forgotten about her completely. She looked so frail and forlorn that Harry felt compelled to pull her into an ungainly hug. He was surprised that she allowed herself to be held so, but she seemed so much in need of support.

'Don't worry,' he told her, 'everything will be alright!' He had been thinking about his situation with the law, but then he remembered Grace's illness and hoped with a sudden rush of anxiety and affection that his words might prove prophetic for her too. Harry knew he had to get to the hospital right away. He considered cycling once more, as if some grand gesture on his part might even help, but then decided more pragmatically to take the old Volvo that Moses had insisted he should use to 'keep 'er tickin' over'.

It was something of a déjà vu situation at the hospital, meeting a distraught Elizabeth at the reception and receiving grave news, except this time is was a lot more worrying.

'They're doing tests. They don't know what the problem is yet. They've booked me in to sleep here.'

It was a brief and simple synopsis, but enough to send a shiver of alarm and consternation right through Harry's senses. Later when the doctor requested Elizabeth to come into the consultation room, she asked Harry to go with her. The news was stark and painful, and the frantic emotional discussion that followed was difficult as Elizabeth struggled to come to terms with both the news and the prognosis. Harry also struggled to accommodate the intricacies of the medical explanation and the implications for Grace's treatment. Back at Bede House in the evening he tried as best he could to transfer his understanding to Maude.

'It's her heart.' He waited for Maude to compose herself. 'I can't remember everything ... but it seems that she has always had some kind of ... defect.' Harry winced inwardly at his inability to find the most apposite or even most sensitive word that would have fitted instead of 'defect', but with his thoughts and feelings in such turmoil, it was the only one he could produce.

'Her left chamber, it seems, has not developed as it should have done. So it is, and probably has been for a while, difficult for her heart to pump enough oxygenated blood right round her whole body!'

He paused again to overcome his own upset.

'Look … I know you are a lot more medical than me … but my understanding is that the walls of her heart, in that chamber, are not working properly … and they might be able to fix it with surgery … and I'm sure they will … but … but the operation is not without hazard … and … and with the shock of everything that happened, she's got pneumonia again … and she is rather weak and … and I know she's going to be alright in the end … She will, won't she?!'

And this time it was his turn to fall into Maude's arms seeking comfort.

'Go and make us a nice cup of tea,' he told her gently. 'I bet you haven't had anything to eat all day have you … and I'm not hungry either, but … we had better have something. She's going to need us strong for her when she gets home.'

The words felt empty, but it was the best he could manage.

Though nothing much had happened at the hospital during the next few days, Harry still felt drained in the evenings as he drove the old Volvo back to his cottage. He took to leaving it outside and walking up to Bede House so that he could inform Maude of the current situation even when there was nothing to report.

*

One evening he needed to collect some clothes for Elizabeth, so he drove directly to Bede House. There was a police car parked in the space where Elizabeth's car usually sat and Harry's heart sank. For just a while he had forgotten all about 'the incident' and the police investigation.

Maude answered the door with an expectant expression,

hoping to learn of progress for Grace, but Harry could only hold up his hands with an indefinite gesture.

'She hasn't got any worse!' was all he could offer Maude, whose shoulders visibly sank. Then without words she motioned him towards the lounge. DC Finch sat on one of the leather settees, no doubt working through the intricacies of the rug. She began to stand as Harry went into the room, but he waved for her to sit down again.

'No Blackwood?'

'No, sir. The detective sergeant is … otherwise engaged at the moment, sir.'

'Good.' Harry realised he should not have said that, but the policewoman did not seem offended. He even thought that there might have been the slightest hint of a smile as she held his look, but then she averted her eyes back to the rug.

'There's a mistake you know!' Harry informed her.

'A mistake?'

'Yes … in the rug. The makers are Muslim you know.' And he went on to relate how Elizabeth had educated him previously. DC Finch smiled patiently at his explanation and asked about Grace's health, before reminding Harry that there were still many questions for her to ask him. She had taken care and time to gain Harry's confidence before commencing.

'Yes … of course. Fire away!' Harry thought immediately to himself that he should be more assiduous in his choice of words. It suddenly rocked him back into his seat to consider with wonder for a moment how he, as such a peaceable man, could have gotten himself into such a difficult predicament. Then he steeled himself to face his adversary across the Persian rug.

They eyed each other like combatants ready to begin. Harry felt so much more comfortable without the large, scowling presence of the threatening Blackwood, whose unspoken animosity made him feel like a murder suspect and whose style would, Harry imagined without doubt, have been to quietly but brutally bludgeon the truth out of him. But he was also wary of allowing himself to melt into the quiet repose of DC Finch's kind, green eyes to the point where he might say too much.

'I'm not a violent man!' he exclaimed, instantly regretting such guileless disclosure as an opening manoeuvre.

'No. sir. I am sure you are not, sir ... but there are some areas that need ... clarification.'

In response to DC Finch's first feint of enquiry Harry assured her that he had never known Mr Samuels at any point, but only knew of him through what Elizabeth had told him.

'So, how did you feel about this man, Samuels?'

'I don't even ... didn't even know him ... only ... only that he scared the ... high heavens out of Elizabeth and Grace ... and Maude, no doubt, too ...'

'So, when he rang the bell ...' she waited, but now Harry was keeping his emotions more closely under control. He had warmed to DC Finch, but the contest was now on and the game they were playing was far too dangerous for him to relax into too much candour.

'When I opened the door there was no-one to be seen.'

'So ... how did you know ... it was Samuels ... especially since you had never even seen him before?'

'It had to be him. We knew he was around ... and no-one ever rings here ... especially at that time of night ... and ... and it was him, wasn't it?' Finch allowed herself to nod in affirmation. 'Then I saw someone moving out there ... so ...'

'So ... you chased him!'

'Well ... so ... I followed him. He'd just rang the doorbell at bloody midnight ... for Pete's sake ...' Harry realised that so quickly composure had dissipated to leave him already a little agitated and that he had emphasised his 'so' to the point of parodying Finch's overuse of the word. He breathed deeply and slowly. He could not afford to deteriorate into the 'angry man' of his previous self and he could not afford to offend his inquisitor either. He knew it was part of the game for her to encourage his passion, but if he followed that path then he was sure to lose. He sat back and smiled as if he was at a loss to know what else to say.

'So ...' She just could not manage without the word and had now become aware of her overuse of it herself. Harry felt that he might just have just moved ahead in the game for a moment. 'Let me just check ...' she smiled to regain her balance, 'you saw movement in the bushes and you rushed out to investigate ... Mr Harry?'

'Yes.'

'Without your coat ...?'

'Well ... I didn't have time to think about ... I just dashed out to ... investigate.'

'Without your coat ...' she paused, allowing her thought to hang in the air, and, with a half-smile like that of a striker about to score, added, 'But ... with a stick!'

'I ... always take a stick ... it's just habit.' Harry was stumbling.

He quickly moved on to go through again the details of what he could remember from the night of Samuels' death, co-operating as fully as he could with all the questions that he received, and realising that polite co-operation and a show of submissive respect was more likely to win Finch's confidence than any clever juxtaposing of words. Beneath this semblance of openness, however, Harry remained wary. Though he did feel some guilt about it, Harry remained determined not to mention the anger and intent that had raged within him at that final confrontation with Samuels, nor about the heavy weapon that he had wielded above his head before the collapsing cliff had so suddenly taken away his opportunity to take out that intent.

So he was then knocked back in stunned shock as the policewoman asked her next question.

'Do you recognise this stick, sir?'

'Yes I certainly do!'

Harry sat mute in his seat. He was not shocked that the canny policewoman had reached down to the side of her own seat to produce a walking stick, but that she had produced the particular one that she held before him. It was an old wand of hazel with a fork at its end. It was Moses' stick!

He took it gently from her and held it in almost a caress with his own hands. The familiarity of the worn shaft of hazel with its distinctive fork at the top was not something that he could ever forget.

'So you can confirm that this is your stick, sir?'

Harry inspected the stick for a while longer while he gathered his thoughts. Its presence there remained a mystery to him, though at length he was able to compose himself to be able to deliver a deliberate lie.

'Yes, that is my stick! Where did you find it? Was it in the sea … or the mud?'

'No, sir. It was just lying in the grass … not far from where you … from where you had indicated that … that the cliff had collapsed. I found it yesterday when I went back to check the scene of ... of the incident.'

'Oh. Can I keep it now?' Harry asked.

'No, sir ... not at the moment.'

Harry began to feel as if he had lost in his battle to appear innocent. But then, without further prompting, she added quite cheerily, 'I'm sure we will be able to return it to you later.'

And with that Harry suddenly felt room to hope that perhaps she was a supporter rather than an adversary in the game after all.

Though her comment had reassured Harry somewhat, she then proceeded to worry him severely again by asking about an opportunity to speak to Elizabeth.

'No. You don't need to do that! She won't tell you anything about the past ... with Samuels ... and she's got enough to worry about with Grace ... and, besides, she was asleep throughout the whole night when ... when Samuels died. He is dead, isn't he?!'

'Oh yes, sir. He is, sir. Completely dead, sir!'

Soon after the policewoman departed. Harry did his best to put the possibility of police proceedings out of his mind, since matters at the hospital were more important to him.

*

One afternoon later in the week Maude had handed Harry a postcard from Australia that had arrived at Bede House: no doubt, its writer had thought it more likely to reach Harry there than on his own rarely visited doormat. He put it into his pocket to read later at the hospital. The thoughtful Maude had also prompted Harry to take Grace's box of toys and possessions with him to the hospital. He and Elizabeth arranged some of them on the few empty spaces around Grace's bed in the hope that they would comfort her on regaining consciousness.

Entering Grace's hospital room, Harry took the postcard from his inside pocket. He was pleased to read that the card had been addressed to all three of them. The front of the card bore the word 'Perth' in bright, rainbow colours above a picture of three Western Australian king penguins; a chick stood between its parents against an impossibly blue sky.

'That's us!' he commented before realising how childish his comment had sounded amongst the daunting background of Grace's bed and the support machine beside it. Rather puerilely he handed the card to Elizabeth to read and she read it aloud to include the still and silent Grace in its audience.

Eadie had written in the small space:

Dear Grace, Elizabeth and Davey,

We are enjoying wonderful weather in Perth,

though it has been a bit hot for us to move

around too much. Moses is expecting to meet

up with his Alec tomorrow.

Hope this finds you all safe and happy.

Love from Moses and Eadie xx

The two of them stood quietly and watched the now sleeping Grace. Probably each of them had been hoping for more from the letter and they found it difficult to move on with any degree of cheerfulness.

'Well, I suppose that's good then?'

Harry remained silent. He had been hoping, ridiculously he realised, that the news from Australia might have delivered something exceptional that might have moved them in some way out of the painfully serious and difficult situation that they were in themselves. He felt tearful, but did not wish to demonstrate his weakness to Elizabeth, who had already more than enough with which to cope.

'Let's go out for a little walk,' he suggested.

Jenny Finch pushed back her chair to stretch her back and legs. She had completed some fairly punishing gym circuits instead of eating lunch and was feeling just a little stiff. The DC had been pretty much rooted to her desk and computer for the past few days and had felt in need of exercise. She reached out to grasp a mug of tea that one of the lads had dropped at her desk: 'They aren't all pigs,' she had thought to herself.

She managed a wry smile between swigs. It was not that she minded deskwork: in fact, she really enjoyed all the detective and investigation work, and felt that she was good at it too. No, it was more that Blackwood, the arsehole that he was, would unfailingly take all the credit for the report before her that she had so painstakingly researched and put together.

He had, just a few minutes previously, swaggered through with one of his cronies to the sanctuary of his own little cell, where he protected himself behind a wall of secrecy and bullying authority to disguise his own shortcomings. Yes, he could rip out a confession from even the hardest cases, and he worked his network of snouts with insidious skill, but, when it needed reasoned deduction and intelligent police work, he was sadly lacking. Besides which, when it came to computers and IT, he did not know his arse from his elbow.

On his way through just now, he had, with tiresome predictability and pathetic overacting, demonstrated to a colleague how he could never quite remember her name.

'Bring it through to my office later, Sparrow!' he had thrown over his shoulder for the benefit of his accompanying officer.

'Finch, sir!'

'Yes, Finch, Robin, Blackbird ... whatever. Prefer great tits meself. What about you, Danno?' And their conspiratorial laughter disappeared down the corridor.

Jenny Finch, DC Jenny Finch, smiled grimly to herself. She knew that the pompous twat knew her name. She knew all too well that Blackwood *knew the name Finch. Her dad had been his superintendent a generation back when Blackwood was just beginning his grubby way up the ladder. She had a store of well documented secrets hidden away in her locker about Blackwood. And one day she would carefully remind him of it.*

No, she was not worried about Blackwood and his little games. When it came to the sharp end, she had more than enough to match him, with or without her dad's helpful documents. She finished off her tea, put her distaste for Blackwood to the back of her mind, and sat up once more to concentrate on the summing up of her report on the death of Clive Samuels.

Her assiduous research, along with what she was convinced was sound intuition, had, she felt, left her with a pretty accurate picture of what had happened, even though she could only include accurate factual details. She could, she was sure, pretty well imagine how that Harry chap had chased Samuels with enflamed passions and ill intent, but there was no hard evidence to indicate that the Harry chap had actually inflicted any injury upon Samuels. No, the forensics had, in fact, disclosed that the outside of Samuels' body had been remarkably unblemished even though his neck and back had both been broken by the fall, which may or may not have had any consequence upon his subsequent asphyxiation beneath the mud. She had come to think that, probably, Samuels had, indeed, as Mr Harry had told them, simply been taken by the collapsing cliff. She had not turned up any hard evidence to show that Samuels had died through anything other than misadventure.

Of course, any inquest would want to ascertain what Samuels had been doing there on the cliffs in a storm at midnight. So far she had not been able to find anything at all conclusive, though, again, her research had led her to some fairly damning indications that his reasons for him being there were less than honourable.

She looked back with pleasing satisfaction at her decision to travel down to London to speak with people rather than just chase things on the telephone. Though none of his neighbours had been at all interested in the aloof, old fellow who had lived beside them without any real impact, visiting the civil service establishment where he had last worked, and had been in charge, had proved extremely interesting.

His former secretary had been particularly forthcoming. She had clearly despised Samuels and had been extremely pleased to take advantage of her opportunity to offload her antipathy towards him. She had painted a picture of Samuels as a tyrant and a lecher. Though she was too prudish to go into detail, she claimed that there were many females who she claimed 'had been terribly wronged' by him, but who had all been too frightened to come out with any accusations. In the absence of any known family, Samuels' former secretary had even been more than pleased to make an expenses-paid journey up to Humberside to identify his body. She had done so without 'noticeably turning a hair' and had then gone on to visit a sister who lived down on the Holderness at Burton something or other for tea.

Finch knew that she would have to interview the Hall woman some time, but she did not hold out a lot of hope that Mrs Hall would be at all forthcoming about her former employer, and she knew from the hospital that the woman had more than enough problems of her own at the time.

No doubt, there was much about, or surrounding, the incident of Samuels' death that she did not know, but, as far as she could tell, Mr Harry was a decent enough man 'following' a strange midnight caller towards his death by misadventure upon dangerously unstable cliffs. She had no hard evidence of ill intent so she was not going to write any into her report. She had felt uneasy about the stick he had apparently been carrying, but there had been no signs that it had been used to batter anyone and so she had not included it in her report: it would have just complicated matters.

Probably, the inquest would not put too much time or energy into the apparently accidental death of an old man in whom no-one appeared at all interested. And, if there was to be any criticism of lacking evidence then they would have to ask the man who would be claiming all credit for the report.

'Good game, Blackwood,' she smiled to herself, 'good game!'

Somewhat against her better judgement, and almost certainly in spite against her oppressive superior, DC Finch journeyed out to the coast so that she could return the strange fork-tipped walking stick to the man whom she assumed was its owner. In fact, she had been met at the front door of Bede House by the lone old woman, who had regarded her enquiring greeting with a blank as well as mute response.

She was aware enough to realise that she had been looking forward to some kind of grateful reaction from their former suspect and was disappointed not to have met him there. She no longer wished, however, to be in possession herself of the stick and so had left it with the old woman to return it to him.

*

For most of the next few days Grace remained sleeping in a near comatose state as the antibiotics battled to quell the raging pneumonia inside her. There had been brief moments when she had been alert enough to open her eyes, and she had even spoken on occasions, though not in a coherent manner. Even behind the brave and non-committal faces, however, it was looking ever clearer that the hospital staff themselves were becoming increasingly concerned.

It had been difficult for Harry to persuade Elizabeth to take a break from her bedside vigil on the Sunday so that they could take another short walk around the hospital's grounds. Elizabeth had become worried that she might miss a moment when Grace might suddenly wake from her torpor.

Eventually they did walk out without talking into a cold breeze. Even in the weak light the strain of the past days was clear upon

Elizabeth's face and appearance. Though she could never appear less than well-groomed, her hair and skin looked tired and lifeless.

To Harry she still appeared completely beautiful. Despite her undemonstrative demeanour, there was a streak of fortitude that kept her head and shoulders upright to adversity. Though he admired her for it, Harry could not keep from his mind the thought that she was going to need all that fortitude and more over the coming days. He had been thinking to broach with her the possibilities of what might happen if Grace ... if Grace ... but he could not even form them himself, let alone explore them with her distressed mother.

'You won't give up on us, Harry?' Elizabeth asked with piercing directness. He shook his head then looked away to hide the tears that were forming.

'No ... I won't ever do that.'

As Elizabeth returned inside Harry broke off towards the car park so that he could drive over to fetch Maude for an afternoon visit. A man was rummaging in the boot of another Volvo parked next to Moses' old car.

'We Volvo drivers need to stick together!' the other man quipped.

It struck Harry as a somewhat inane comment, but there was something familiar about the tall man smiling there. Then he remembered.

'Oh ... it's not your daughter ... or your sons is it?' the awful thought followed on naturally from Harry's previous line of thinking.

'No, no! The kids are fine ... they're in there now visiting. It's grandma, my mother-in-law. Unfortunately, she fell and broke her hip ... and now, sadly for the old girl, she has developed a touch of pneumonia.'

'Pneumonia? That's funny … no, no, it's not funny at all … but listen … I wouldn't want to intrude, but I was wondering if it might be poss' … No it would be too …' Harry dithered in uncertainty.

'Come on, fella … out with it!' the tall man smiled. So Harry told him.

To Harry's relief, once asked by her father, the 'Ducklings Girl' had taken happily to the idea of visiting Grace in her bed and with, it appeared, complete understanding. Harry had not even thought about the possible complication of access by non-family members, but as it turned out, the ward sister happened to be a mother of one of the girl's school friends and soon she was standing beside Grace in her bed. The adults stood back, while the young visitor held Grace's hand and talked to her gently, even though the patient remained still and sleeping. Harry imagined that she would be dreaming, and if she was then there was no doubt in his mind that she would be wandering dreamily down beside the stream, hand in hand with her new friend and followed by a tinkling line of ducklings.

The tenderness of the scene had smitten Elizabeth and Harry into silence. Somehow it felt as if they should leave the two girls to themselves so they went out into the corridor for a short while where they joined the visiting girl's father. They did not speak much. It seemed as if there was not too much to say, or rather that what there was to say was simply too difficult to express.

As Harry turned to walk back with Elizabeth, the tall man produced an envelope from his own pocket and proffered it to Harry.

'Thought you might like this,' he smiled.

Harry smiled back, but appeared too troubled to take real

notice of the envelope as he followed Elizabeth down the corridor. The 'Ducklings Girl' departed almost as soon as they returned. It was as much as Harry could do to say a simple thank you, but Elizabeth took the girl's hand in both of hers and kissed it. The girl just smiled and walked assuredly out into the corridor and to her waiting father.

Harry did not think to open the envelope until he stood to join Elizabeth at Grace's bedside. Inside there was a photograph. He recognised instantly, of course, where and when the photograph had been taken. In the picture Harry stood with worried frown holding the handlebars of the tandem, while next to him was Grace with what appeared to be a blissfully happy expression upon her face.

He looked down upon her face in the bed before him. She appeared to Harry to be more peaceful in her sleep.

'I think she's smiling,' he whispered to Elizabeth, though soon it became apparent to both of them that the smile was eternally frozen.

A shadow fell across the afternoon. In February the light changes so quickly.

—❦—

LEAVING THE EXHIBITION

The young gallery assistant looked across towards her older colleague, who in turn checked her watch before raising an eyebrow and stretching her head sideways towards the remaining visitors. The young assistant then approached the white-haired old couple who had stood like nodding flowers for more than an hour in front of the giant canvas.

'I'm sorry, sir ... madam ... but the gallery is closing now.'

The two visitors turned and smiled back. Then, without speaking, they made their way towards the exit. The assistants followed, leaving the painted trees on their quiet hillside to stand alone in the stillness of the emptied exhibition room.

Outside, at the top of the steps that led down from the gallery entrance, the old couple stood open mouthed to regard the sudden contrast before them. Snow was falling on a strong wind that hurled the flakes, whirling and twirling all around them, though none had gathered yet on the ground. The man took firm hold of his partner's hand to lead her down the steps, out into the turbulent evening weather, and homeward.

The storm and the holding of hands triggered a sudden cameo of remembrance into the man's mind. The hand he held felt just like the young girl's hand that he had held on a similar evening many years previously as they had ventured out for a walk.

He remembered it so clearly. Despite the weather, they had made their way inexorably down to the seafront where they had clung grimly to the promenade railings as the wind and the snow and the spray had raged all around them. The tide had been fully in so that huge waves had crashed against the wall beneath them. At times it had felt as if the whole seafront had trembled against the sea's onslaught. Even in the darkness, the foaming crests of breaking waves had glowed in phosphorescent fury like the talons of some demented monster too great and powerful to be imagined.

There had been no question of them venturing onto the beach, but it had been thrilling enough just to stand there against all the elements. They had laughed and shouted into each other's faces, their spirits soaring like the spume that had lifted from the waves to be tossed into the night sky.

Two small figures, an older man and a teenage girl, stood against all that power and energy: he had held on tightly to the girl's hand to reassure her: or had it been the other way round?